WHAT IT MEANS TO BE BRAVE

What It Means To Be Brave

WHAT IT MEANS: BOOK 2

Andrea Andersen

Contents

Content Notes

This story has been proofed by sensitivity readers. Meaning, though the author is neither deaf nor hard of hearing, persons who are deaf or hard of hearing have read this story and provided feedback on its authenticity, as well as what verbiage to use regarding D/HH culture. The hope is that the story discusses these topics with the respect and care that they deserve.

Trigger Warning:

This book contains sensitive subjects, such as:

Foul Language
Explicit Sex
Cannabis Use
Car Accident Depictions & Injuries

To those who fear the unknown, sometimes being brave can be as simple as doing things scared.

Prologue

I hated the first week of school.

The first week was always fake. After the first week, the excitement of seeing everyone after a long summer would die down. Everyone would stop dressing in the new clothes they had bought days before school started. Everyone would stop pretending that they were excited to be stuck in this musty building for most of the day. Everyone would accept the fact that school still sucked, and that it was okay to wear sweatpants and crocs to make it through the day. School-work would come in, and social niceties would no longer be expected.

The number of times people would ask me, "How was your summer?" was too much. I knew they didn't actually care how my summer was. I didn't care how their summer was either. It was okay to not care about another person's summer unless you were actually friends with them. It was weird that it was expected of everyone to ask, "How was your summer?" if there was a break in the conversation.

Just say hi and move on.

I was here to pass my classes, graduate, and dip as fast as I could.

Thankfully, this was the last year I would have a first day of high school. Lakeridge High School. It wasn't any place to write home about. It was your average high school, one of two in our suburban town of Lake Oswego, Oregon. It was just small enough that our graduating class would be a few hundred students, and I would probably know most of their names.

I was sitting in Mr. Mittmann's environmental science class; an elective I decided to take to fill up my schedule. I could have taken an early release, but I already had a late arrival and didn't want the colleges I would be applying for to assume I was lazy.

I wasn't the most socially driven kid, I knew that about myself. I had two close friends that I could sit with at lunch and play video games with after school. I didn't feel the need to go to football games—the sport was over hyped anyway—and I was totally happy with having a small friend group.

That is, until her.

I remember the first day I saw Courtney Henderson walk into our class. She wore black leggings and a dark green and red oversized flannel shirt with tan moccasins, and her blonde hair was down but tucked behind her ear to show off her multiple piercings. She was laughing at something one of her friends said as they dropped into the empty seats right beside me.

She had settled in her seat and smiled at me brightly, as if we knew each other, before facing forward and giving our teacher her full attention as he started the class.

I had probably stared at her for longer than I should have, but I wasn't used to sitting so close to someone like her.

Courtney was popular, but unlike most stereotypical popular high schoolers, she was notoriously known for her kindness and empathy. She was never mean to anyone—well, except for the time I'd seen her chew out some of the football team for bullying a Freshman—and her smiles and laughter could fill up the room. Sitting next to someone like her almost felt overwhelming.

We didn't have assigned seats in environmental science but, because humans are creatures of habit, we all ended up sitting in the same seats we sat in on day one. Which meant that Courtney Henderson sat next to me every single day.

She was kind and loud with her friends, but quiet and reserved with the teacher. She never raised her hand to answer a question, but instead would tap her friend sitting in front of her and whisper in encouragement, "You got this."

After a week or two of established seating patterns, Mr. Mittmann announced that we would have lab partners for a project that we would do over the next couple of weeks. We would have to spend time together doing one main study, as well as a handful of mini labs. When he read off the list of pairs, I held my breath. When he read my name along with Courtney's, I thought my heart was going to burst out of my chest.

But fuck me, now I have to talk to her?

I wasn't exactly a social butterfly.

Thankfully, Courtney didn't care.

The first day we worked together she did most of the talking. I said maybe three words to her, but I did my part by nodding my head and making direct eye contact to let her know that I was listening to her ramblings.

"Courtney," Mr. Mittmann interrupted us one day, startling her in her seat, "I think it would be in your best interest to follow Josh's lead here and focus on the task at hand. Instead of talking about…what was it?"

"Oh, um," Courtney's face turned bright red, her deep brown eyes wide as she responded. "The, uh, nothing."

"She was telling me about the systemic patriarchal values our country designed to keep women in their place," I filled in, probably saying more than I had in a week, "…It was interesting."

"I'm sure it was," Mr. Mittmann lifted an eyebrow and glanced between the two of us, "Focus, you have fifteen minutes left."

Courtney's face was still red as the teacher moved on to another pair of students, and she glanced at me once before she started rubbing her thumb over the top of her right hand.

It was then that I noticed her birthmark.

"I'm sorry," Courtney murmured, "I get distracted easily."

"That's okay." I truly didn't mind, because for some reason showing up to class knowing Courtney was going to monologue at me was beginning to be something I looked forward to.

"Don't let those big brown eyes fool you, J!" a student at the table next to us called with a laugh. "Stay strong, don't let her manipulate the book worm into doing all the work for her!"

"Hush," Mr. Mittmann warned, sending a look to the student, and making them duck their head down.

Courtney frowned; her cheeks now pink.

It was humbling to know that someone as beautiful as her was human enough to feel embarrassment. I saw her start to gnaw on her lip, and my heart sank, desperate to comfort her.

"Here, help me with this," I reached a beaker out towards her, which she grabbed enthusiastically. It was probably to prove to the other students that she wasn't an airhead who relied on others to do the work for her. I knew she wasn't an airhead; like she said, she just got distracted.

Turns out, if you just spoke up and reminded Courtney that she was in the middle of doing a project, she was very capable of conducting the experiments. I was in a couple of AP classes as a senior (because I hated myself), but I knew Courtney wasn't. In fact, I believed it was common knowledge that Courtney struggled with math, and that she was a year behind in it.

"Oh!" Courtney gasped when the science project we were doing one day started to work. She bounced on her heels and crossed both of her fingers as she stared wide-eyed at whatever was happening.

I didn't care about the project that much but, after a week of helping her focus on schoolwork, I was excited to see her excitement for her accomplishment.

"We did it!" Courtney jumped and fist-pumped, making me laugh out loud. She met my gaze and reached over to wrap herself around me in a huge bear hug.

I immediately wrapped my arms around her, it was almost as if it was instinct to embrace her just as tight. I generally wasn't a hugger.

"Thanks for taking me seriously," Courtney murmured against my shoulder.

Oh shit.

I was at risk of getting a boner. I didn't remember the last time a cute girl had been this close to me.

"Thanks for taking *me* seriously," I repeated back to her. Girls generally didn't give me any attention. I was tall and lanky, and my shaggy brown hair and thick black frame glasses weren't getting me any prom-posals. To be fair, going to prom sounded like my worst nightmare, so maybe it all worked out for the best.

"You're a great lab partner." Courtney squeezed me once more before she released me, making me feel the loss of her body heat and mourn for it.

"I'm really not," I shook my head once as I started to jot down the results of our project on the worksheet. I had to lean down pretty far due to my height.

"You really are!" Courtney smiled at me brightly, letting me take the lead on documenting the results as she leaned on her elbows and tucked her fists under her chin. It took everything in my body to keep myself from staring at her face as she smiled at me in an endearing way.

Fuck, puberty sucked ass.

Somehow, she convinced me to go get burgers after school. She had a car and I didn't, and obviously eating burgers with Courtney sounded better than driving home in my buddy's Mommy-Missile (what we called his gray minivan) and playing Halo.

Our friendship was born that day.

We would hangout multiple times a week. I would go to her house or she would come to mine. Sometimes we would do homework because she was becoming more comfortable asking me for help, and other times we would watch movies, go on walks at Tryon Creek, or feed the ducks at George Rodgers Park. Other times, more rarely, she would drag me to her friend's parties that usually involved a generous amount of beer and weed.

"Don't smoke it," Courtney grabbed my wrist one time while one of our fellow students held a joint up, offering me to take a hit. "Here, there's some brownies in the kitchen instead. I'll stay sober and be your designated driver." She tugged me towards the house, a motion I was familiar with since becoming friends with her.

She cut off a child's size bite and turned to me to lift the piece towards my face.

"I can eat it myself," I lifted an eyebrow at her.

She rolled her brown eyes and flicked her blonde hair over her shoulder, "Open up, or I'll shove it up your nose."

"Yes ma'am," I stood still and opened wide. She gently placed the bite in my mouth and nudged my chin with her hand to close my mouth.

I chewed a while and swallowed, reaching for a clean plastic cup to fill with water at the sink. "That aftertaste sucks ass."

"A small price to pay for the experience of peace," Courtney quipped, brushing her hands on the thighs of her jeans. I fought to keep my eyes on her face. Her jeans hugged her ass so nicely that I'd had difficulty keeping my eyes off her all night.

"We will see," I hadn't been high before, but Courtney was probably the best person to experience marijuana with first. I would always remember the two of us heading outside and sitting on a picnic blanket, with a wool blanket over both of us to protect us from the chilly Pacific Northwest weather.

Eventually I got a little dizzy, so I laid my head on her lap while she ran her fingers through my hair. I may have been high, but I knew the warmth I felt wasn't just from the weed. Courtney, herself, was warmth.

"How are you feeling?" she asked, catching my eyes. Wow, they felt incredibly dry.

"Wonderful." I gave her a smile to prove it.

"Please smile more." Courtney touched the corner of my mouth with her fingertip, and I turned in an attempt to bite it. She giggled and pinched my earlobe while I settled back on her thighs.

I would probably have preferred to have my face in between her thighs, but I was at the point where I would take what I could get.

"I'm so glad we became friends, J-shua," Courtney reached down to hug me, probably not realizing how wonderful her boobs felt squished against my chest. I wrapped my arms around her back and breathed her in. I may have been horribly friend zoned, but Courtney got me out of my shell. I interacted with more kids at school this year than I had in my previous three years of high school. I was less awkward and shy. I had a small amount of confidence in myself that I definitely hadn't had before.

If it wasn't for her, I would have been in my bedroom playing video games, not laying on a blanket with the prettiest girl in school wrapped around me, soothing me while I experienced the high of marijuana for the first time.

It was impossible not to fall in love with her.

I don't think I knew that's what was happening during the first half of the school year. The second half of the year though, I realized why my heart raced whenever she smiled at me. When she hugged me. When she playfully tugged on my hair that she thought was too long. When she gently removed my glasses and tried them on herself, looking cross-eyed.

I was completely fucked.

I had gotten accepted to the University of Oregon in Eugene. Courtney had bigger dreams than me and had been accepted to a stupid college somewhere in California. I had never been to California, but now I hated the state.

Whenever Courtney would pull out her phone and show

me all the cool sights and beaches she wanted to visit and the food she planned to try, I had to fight not to roll my eyes.

California was taking my girl away from me.

It was inevitable. We had just become friends a few months prior, and even though we seemed to spend most of our time outside of school together, it was unrealistic to think our close friendship would last through college.

"We'll have to get together during holiday breaks," Courtney told me one day. She was trying on her cap and gown in my bedroom, staring at herself in the mirrors on my sliding closet doors.

"Sure." I shrugged, lifting a shoulder as I removed my gaze from her and tried to focus on the textbook I had in my lap. I was sitting on my bed and leaning against the headboard.

"Don't sound too excited," Courtney teased, twirling in her gown once then jumping onto my bed hard enough to make me fumble the book out of my lap.

"I am excited." I shrugged again. A defensive move.

"I guess I'm jumping the gun here." Courtney smiled at me. "You may meet someone at college and have to go spend the holidays with her instead," She teased with a dramatic eyebrow wiggle.

I rolled my eyes.

"Yeah, because I've been so successful with girls. I'll definitely pull my first semester of college." I reached over and pulled her cap down over her face, making her splutter as she leaned away from me to readjust it.

"Have you not? Been successful with girls?" Courtney asked as she threw her hat off and laid flat on her back next to me, her big brown eyes curious.

"Obviously not." I gestured vaguely towards myself, feeling like that said everything I needed to say.

"But you've, like, gone out with girls, right?"

"When have you ever seen me go out with a girl?" I countered, flipping the page in my book. It was odd how comfortable I felt talking to her about this. I was horribly in love with her, I thought about her obsessively almost every day and night (especially at night), and yet I had no issue discussing my lack of a dating life with her. She was a safe space. She was my safe space.

"...Have you kissed a girl?" Courtney asked. My cheeks heated. I was turning eighteen this summer and I hadn't had my first kiss yet. I knew girls obsessed about first kisses and, to an extent, I think boys did too. I never focused on it too hard, figuring it would happen when it happened.

That is, until Courtney elbowed her way into my life.

I had fantasized about kissing Courtney an embarrassing number of times.

"Courtney."

"Yeah?"

"Mind your business."

"So that's a no."

I playfully glared at her, and she smiled brightly back at me, making a smile erupt on my face as well.

"Fuck you." I tossed the book aside and made my way to get up off of the bed, but the feeling of her hand on my thigh holding me in place made me freeze.

"Can I kiss you?" Courtney asked point blank. I swore to whatever deity that my heart stopped. I felt my body heat at her words, and I couldn't stop myself from turning to face her to ensure I heard her correctly.

"You want to kiss me?" I asked, clarifying.

"I do. I think it would be cool to be your first kiss!" Courtney squeezed my thigh and grinned at me, her brown eyes darting between the two of mine. I gulped and looked away.

"Court, it's fine. I don't want a pity first kiss."

"It's not out of pity!" Her jaw dropped as if she was truly shocked that I would assume that. "I'd love to be your first kiss! You are my best friend, c'mon! Let me kiss you!"

"Do best friends kiss?" I lifted an eyebrow at her as I shifted again in an attempt to escape, embarrassed that my pulse was racing simply because we were talking about kissing each other.

"Does it matter?" Courtney lifted a shoulder, "What if you're a shitty kisser and didn't give me this trial run? What if you never let me kiss you and you're at college and you end up kissing some poor girl tongue first?"

I scoffed as I covered my face with my hand and laughed. Of course, that's where her brain went.

"Tongue first? What does that even mean?"

"Have you seen any episode of *The Bachelorette*? That's what I mean." Courtney replied.

"Anyway—"

"J-shua, please!"

"Court, you're being weird."

"Please!"

"Court."

"What if you bite too hard? What if you're a teeth clasher? What if you miss her mouth completely and suck on her chin?"

"Oh my god." I couldn't believe she was pushing this.

"What if—"

I'm pretty sure I had an out of body experience. Here I was, sitting on my bed while Courtney was literally begging me to kiss her (something I had fantasized about regularly) and I was arguing against it. Why? Why was I trying to convince her not to kiss me? Suddenly it was like my brain clicked and thought, *holy shit this is our chance, man,* and my body responded accordingly.

Courtney was in the middle of her sentence when I launched towards her, pushing her shoulders to lay her flat on her back again on my bed. She yelped once and grinned as she reached her hands up to grip my wrists. I shifted so I was lying mostly on top of her while I reached one hand up to grab the side of her face, leaning my head in close to hers.

"You ready?" I asked.

Her brown eyes went wide before she smiled and nodded, "Ready, Freddy."

"Please don't say 'ready Freddy' seconds before I kiss you."

"What else would you like me to say? Lay one on me?"

"Or just…don't say anything? The moment is fading."

"No, it's not, you're just nervous."

"How silly of me. I'm about to kiss my best friend. Why would I be nervous?"

"Ugh, you're so annoying." Courtney rolled her eyes and reached up to grab my face, pulling it down to hers.

The feeling of her soft, warm lips on mine would forever be seared into my brain.

I'm confident it was a shitty kiss for her. There was no way she enjoyed it as much as I did. Though she was the one who touched my lips with her tongue first, and she was the one that taught me in that kiss how much tongue was too much versus just right.

I have no idea how much time passed as we made out on my bed.

I, Joshua Madey, was making out with Courtney Henderson on my bed. She separated our mouths for a second, and I thought she was going to push me off of her and end it (you know, since the deal was a kiss and not me sucking her face off) but instead she leaned up to bite my bottom lip with her teeth and gently tugged.

The groan I made in response was humiliating.

Courtney giggled, finally separating our faces, and gently pushed my shoulders to get me to roll off of her. I did, doing a quick check down myself to make sure my boner wasn't tenting the shit out of my jeans. Thank fucking god for compression boxers.

"Well," Courtney was lying flat on her back next to me, our pinkies barely touching, her chest heaving as if we just went on a run, "For the record, I think you're going to pull just fine in college."

I took a couple of breaths, a poor attempt to calm my racing heart and excited penis, before replying, "Good to hear, could you do me a favor and leave a Yelp review?"

"Of course. J-shua Madey. Great kisser. Won't assume he has permission to grab your boobs."

"I didn't want to risk ruining our friendship permanently." I shrugged, being honest even though it took everything in me not to ask if I could grab her boobs.

"That's very…thoughtful of you." Courtney sighed.

I couldn't tell you how that conversation ended. How we transitioned from making out on my bed, to never talking about it again. I figured Courtney was the experienced one in this department, so if that experience was something she wanted to revisit she would be the one to bring it up.

That never happened.

We graduated; we went to multiple graduation parties. We got high. We got part time jobs during the summer and spent the other half of our time doing what we always did.

Courtney ended up leaving for college first, having to road trip with her parents in their Subaru that was fully loaded with boxes and whatever other shit she packed.

I was pissed.

I was in love with her, and she was just leaving as if our friendship meant nothing.

I knew I was being childish, but I let myself hate the situation every now and then. Now, though, I forced myself to smile and squeeze her in one of my bear hugs that I knew she loved. A part of me knew that this would be the last time I would.

"Call and text me any time," Courtney spoke into my neck, squeezing me back just as tight.

"Of course, you do the same," I mumbled into her hair, breathing in her fruity scent. I knew she was going to thrive in California, no matter what she ended up doing.

"I love you, J-shua."

"I love you, Court." Just not the way you want me to, and I would learn to live without your constant positive energy in my life. Somehow.

1

COURTNEY

It was going to happen.

It had been about six weeks since it last happened, so I was due.

There were two lines for the coffee shop, and the woman in the other line directly next to me was clearly in a state of emotional distress. I had to give her credit; she was doing an excellent job of holding herself together as she finished up her phone call. Her lip quivered, and her eyelids started to turn pink with the tell-tale sign of incoming tears.

I tried to give her privacy, but the coffee shop was small. The space given for waiting in line to order was only so big, so it was difficult to give someone privacy when they were standing less than a foot away from you and on the verge of crying in public. I tried to keep my gaze on the chalkboard menu in front of me. I was still about three customers back from being able to order.

Out of the corner of my eye, I saw her nod as she lowered her cellphone and ended whatever call seemed to ruin her day. I barely turned my head to acknowledge the movement, which ended up being a mistake, because she noticed my interest in her situation.

I knew it.

It was going to happen.

She unleashed a heavy sigh as she pocketed her device and wiped at her tears, giving me a weak quivering smile as she lifted one shoulder in an attempt to make her emotional state casual.

"Mondays, right?" she asked. I gave her a polite smile and shoulder lift in return. Hoping that if I didn't engage too much, she would let me go about my day.

She nodded and blew out a breath that lifted her bangs off of her forehead for a moment, before turning her whole body to face me. I tried not to look too tense. It was too late. I couldn't avoid it anymore. Six weeks had been a good run.

"Do you ever have those days where everything just seems to be falling apart?"

And just like that, another random stranger was unloading their problems onto me. Without any solicitations on my end. This was my curse. Beck made fun of me for it regularly. She said I needed to work on my resting bitch face in order to curb it, and I thought I had worked on it well enough to go six weeks without a stranger randomly confiding in me— apparently not.

I nodded politely at the woman as she told me about how everything at work was falling apart, how her children were seemingly out of control, and how she felt like she was always on the verge of tears with any minor inconvenience. We (mostly she) chatted as the line slowly inched forward. I was able to place my order without her losing her train of thought. She followed me to the pickup side of the coffee house and continued to get whatever she needed off of her chest.

I knew my role here.

I had experienced these odd social encounters enough times in my life to know that all she needed was a polite smile, a couple of head nods, an "Oh wow" or a "That *does* sound hard" and even an "I'm so sorry" just for a little razzle-dazzle.

Then, when we parted, she'd be able to handle whatever else she needed to tackle the rest of the day.

It was still a draining way to start off the week, though.

"Wow, I wasn't planning on unloading on a stranger this morning...but it felt really nice to get that off my chest." The woman smiled as she adjusted the strap of her purse on her shoulder and grabbed her coffee, that somehow was made before mine. I didn't even realize she took a breath to order coffee. I don't know how she was able to both order her coffee and tell me about her "asshole-prick-know-it-all" of a boss.

"Thank you," the woman, whose name I never got and probably never would, smiled again and lifted her coffee in farewell. "Hopefully, you'll have a better day than me!"

"Maybe!" I waved back at her as she left the coffee house, exhaling my own breath of relief as soon as I saw her disappear through the doors. I pulled my phone out to look as unapproachable as possible as I waited the next couple of minutes for my own coffee order to be ready.

That woman needed therapy, not me.

Fifteen minutes later I walked through the back doors

of the early childhood development center I worked at with five coffees secured in a carrier. "Special delivery!" I smiled as I saw my friends poke their heads out of Beck's office to see me.

"Thank f—god," Taylor corrected themselves in case little ears were listening to our hallway conversation.

"I needed this so badly today." Beck barely gave me a smile in thanks before quickly identifying her preferred drink, grabbing it with both hands, and taking a loud slurp.

I frowned at her.

She smiled at me.

The cute little asshole knew I hated loud slurping.

"Sorry for the delay; a random citizen unloaded on me again this morning," I shrugged as I handed Taylor their coffee. Beck and Taylor only nodded in understanding, knowing that this happened to me often enough not to be phased by it. At their silence, I looked around for the newest member of our group. "Where's Adam?"

"One of his clients rescheduled for a last-minute session this morning, so he's already on the floor. I can hold onto his drink for when he's done in about thirty minutes," Beck explained, grabbing her boyfriend's beverage, and disappearing back into her office. Taylor saluted us as they took a quiet sip of their coffee and started back towards the Occupational Therapist wing of the building. Taylor had recently freshened up the undercut on their brown hair, and I admired the mountain-like design shaved into it for a moment then I followed Beck into her office.

I had some time to kill before my favorite client started her session with me later.

"So," I tossed the drink carrier into Beck's recycling bin and clutched my own liquid gold close to my chest, setting the remaining cup of coffee on her desk for now, "She starts today?" I asked, eyeing my roommate to gauge her response.

Beck paused for half a second as she went to sit in her chair, before nodding once and turning towards her laptop. "Yup. I think she will fit in well here."

I nodded in agreement with her. "Parents will definitely enjoy her presence at the front desk, and Pat will appreciate the extra support."

"Yup." Beck paused for a moment then turned her swivel chair towards me the slightest bit. "Adam is a little stressed, though."

"I figured," I leaned a hip against Beck's desk as I took another sip. Adam's ex-girlfriend, Eloise, started working with us today. She would be on the administration side of things, handling the scheduling and billing. I actually liked her, even though all of us were skeptical at first. She and I slowly started to form a friendship a few weeks after the Big Bear work retreat about a year ago. My best friends, Beck and Taylor, hadn't gotten to know her as well as I had, so they were naturally still weirded out by her presence in our workplace.

Adam, I had sympathy for. Their relationship wasn't the healthiest, and he already had a history with Eloise and his mother inserting themselves into his career in a manipulative way. I assured the group that Eloise simply wanted a nine-to-five job and wanted to be involved in the work that we did here, but until she became brave enough to explain her side of things to them directly, they were going to remain suspicious of her intentions.

"He might be a little at ease if..." Beck raised her eyebrows at me, making her large hazel eyes look even larger. I knew what she was getting at, but I took a moment to admire her chocolatey brown hair in her ponytail first before responding.

"It's not my story to tell." I gave her a smirk, knowing she hated being left in the dark.

"Ugh," Beck rolled her eyes and turned back towards her monitor, "It sounds so ominous. I know it probably isn't that interesting, but I'd still like to know what all she told you that night."

Ah, yes, the night Eloise and I bonded at a bar after having too many margaritas. Eloise took advantage of my "people open up to me about their personal problems and fears" curse and spilled her thoughts and feelings all over me that night in a drunken confession. I immediately understood her better after that experience and because she wasn't a rando in a coffee shop, I encouraged her to keep talking and created a space for her to feel comfortable with being so vulnerable in front of me. That was when our friendship truly solidified. But that was months ago. She still hadn't told our friends what she told me, mostly because of her crippling fear of rejection, but until she was ready to do that, I had promised her that I would keep my mouth shut.

Even if that meant keeping her secrets from my best friend and roommate, Beck.

"Yeah, well, you can deal," I shrugged and tapped her once on her pale nose before standing up from her desk and heading out of the room with the remaining cup of coffee.

"Oh—don't forget to keep your last slot on Friday empty!"

Beck called to me right when I was about to shut her office door. I reopened it a little bit and crossed my eyes at her.

"Of course! I wouldn't want to miss a second of our emo concert!" I giggled at her and she rolled her eyes back at me.

"You'll love it, you music snob." Beck shooed me away and I finally closed the door to her office and headed to mine. I preferred Beck's office because she had an exterior one, meaning she had a window to the outside. My office was located near the center of the building, which meant it had no windows. I hated it. But that's where the Infant-Stim wing of the building was, so I had to deal with it. I still decorated the space and changed all the light bulbs out for bulbs with wattages that wouldn't trigger sensory-sensitive kiddos, but still.

It was actually good that Beck reminded me to keep my last session on Friday closed off on the team calendar, because I usually kept that slot open for clients who had to reschedule their regular weekly sessions due to doctor's appointments or unexpected events. I could probably get away with squeezing a client in that time slot, because the concert we were all going to on Friday wasn't until 9:00pm. It also wasn't at a big stadium like SoFi in LA; instead, it was in a small amphitheater about fifteen minutes away from our little townhome in Lake Forest.

I wasn't the biggest fan of the band we were going to see, but Beck had a huge boner for them and I was a supportive friend. So, that was that. Plus, Beck hadn't been to a big-name concert before, thanks to her super religious-but-actually-cult-like upbringing. She had seen live performances of small indie musicians, but no one as well-known as Carbon Cut.

They were *the* pop punk band to listen to this year. Was I excited to support the career of a bunch of mediocre white men who probably did the bare minimum to become as successful as they were? Not really. Though, the fact that their music was feminist-friendly and discussed important topics, such as the environment, helped.

I dropped off the remaining coffee on Eloise's desk, surprised that she wasn't already there, and headed to my own office to follow Beck's instructions by blocking out my last available time slot on Friday. Doing so sent a notification to our team. Moments later, I received a text message from Beck with a GIF of a girl jumping up and down with excitement.

I responded with a *Ted Lasso* GIF, and that was our entire conversation on the subject before we put on our "mature adult" personas and went on with the rest of the workday.

2

"On a scale from one to My Chemical Romance, how emo am I supposed to look for this concert?" I asked, digging through my closet, and not feeling inspired.

"Six point five," Beck responded, laying on my bed and tapping away on her phone. She was probably texting Adam. I smiled at her, happy that my best friend was finally getting boinked on the regular by the introverted red-head. I blinked and refocused my attention back to my brightly colored clothing options.

I let out a loud, dramatic sigh.

"I hear you, one second." A miracle, considering her shitty hearing aids. I had been telling her to go to the audiologist to replace them, since they had been giving her nothing but problems for the last year, but she just hadn't yet. Beck thumbed away on her phone for a few moments before sitting up and pocketing it. "How can I help?"

"If I was going to see Sara Bareilles, I would know exactly what to wear, but for once in my life I'm unsure about my outfit options." I frowned dramatically and widened my dark brown eyes at her, and she rolled her eyes back at me.

"You are overthinking this."

"You are under thinking this. I don't want to stick out in a crowd full of emos who are all dressed in black and studs."

"Do I dress in black and studs?"

She had a point. I looked her over, she was wearing flannel pajamas and one of Adam's oversized t-shirts. It had a hole in the armpit that I poked at regularly just to annoy her.

"What are you wearing?" I asked, lifting a blonde eyebrow. She grinned and jumped off of my bed to run to her bedroom. Within a few moments she came back with a few items of clothing that she dropped on my bed.

"Black skater skirt, red t-shirt tied at the waist to give it a crop top feel, tights and white sneakers for the sake of staying comfortable while standing for a couple of hours." Beck smiled at me, she was so excited for this. Since she hadn't seen any big-name bands in concert before, I was honored to experience this first with her.

I had only seen Taylor Swift in high school when she was slowly transitioning out of her country phase, and I fucking loved it.

Beck had a lot of feelings to process, so I understood her draw towards angry punk music. I supported her appreciation for this band, considering how involved they were with fundraisers and charities.

"That actually helps, thanks." I smiled at her as I pulled out black jeans, a white t-shirt I could tie at the waist to match her, and white sneakers. As I was setting all the clothing on the thrifted chair in the corner of my room, I felt my phone buzz in my boobs. I usually tucked it into my bra when I was wearing yoga pants that didn't have pockets.

"Is that Taylor?" Beck asked, noticing me grab my phone out of my shirt.

I glanced at the screen to see the face of my grumpy gym buddy staring blankly back at me. A picture I took of him against his will so I could have a picture for his contact in my phone.

"No, it's just Logan." I smiled as I thumbed away at his message, reminding him that I'll have partied too hard tonight to make it to the gym tomorrow.

He responded almost immediately with a simple thumbs up. Which pretty much summed up most of my communication with the guy.

"Ah, and is he still yoked?" Beck asked absentmindedly. For a while, Beck was curious about whether Logan and I would have any sort of romantic relationship, and it took a while for her to be convinced that we were truly platonic. I wasn't into him, he wasn't into me, but it was nice having someone to go to the gym with regularly. Plus, I've been in much better physical shape since I befriended him.

I had gone to this new gym in Tustin a couple of times, because it was on the smaller end and it had lots of good reviews from women specifically. Finding a gym to use without worrying about unsolicited advances from men was always difficult. I tried to get Beck to come with me, but she kept telling me that she was allergic to physical exercise, so I ended up going alone. That is, until I saw Logan.

I don't know why I felt the need to approach him that day. Maybe it was because he stuck out from the crowd with his height and size, or maybe I was just tired of feeling lonely at the gym.

Maybe it was both?

I do remember how his large frame physically tensed when I approached him while he was switching out weights at his station. He had Air Pods in his ears that he had to take out to listen to me. I hadn't ever lifted seriously, and Logan clearly looked like he knew what he was doing. I wanted someone to show me the basics without having to pay a fitness instructor who would spend half of the session trying to get me to buy overpriced protein powder from the gym.

I don't remember exactly what I said to Logan as a way of introducing myself, but I do remember the pinch in his dark brows as I spoke to him without warning. I remembered looking at his dark brown curly hair that was on *this* side of being too long, and the unusual scarring that marred his neck and face. Probably a good portion of his chest too, considering how the light pink scarring slipped underneath his gym shirt.

I also remember how he just stared at me and frowned; his dark eyes boring into me as if I was some sort of alien for having the audacity to approach him during his routine. I persisted, figuring that I had no problem supplying conversation as I asked him about the weights he was using and what muscles he was activating.

He blinked, then signed with his hands.

It was quick, a gesture clearly meant to shoo someone off that probably worked flawlessly for him in the past, but I got the gist of his sign, *I don't speak.*

"Oh!" I smiled at him and signed in return, *that's okay, I can talk enough for the both of us.* Logan had closed his eyes once, as if taking a moment to get a handle on his sudden stress, and we have been gym buddies ever since.

He had hardcore resting bitch face according to Beck, but he had since graciously accepted my friendship into his life. I also thought he secretly liked having a gym buddy, too, since it became obvious to me that he was very much introverted.

I actually thought he and Adam would get along well, but that friendship had yet to bloom.

"Yup, still benching twice what I can do. Something I'm hoping to rectify this year." I frowned a little at the reminder. I may be smaller than Logan by height and muscle mass, but having someone like him around was very motivating for me. I wanted to be strong.

"Don't they measure lifting success by like...the size you are versus the weights you lift? Wouldn't it be kind of un-realistic for someone your size and mass to lift the same as Logan?"

"Nope," I responded, popping my lips at the end of the word. "With enough training and motivation, I could prob-ably get there. I'll have absolutely shredded arms." I lifted mine up in the stereotypical strong man pose, grinning at the slightest definition my biceps already had.

"Huh. Cool. Be sure to record that when you reach that point," At that Beck walked over to my mirror to start ap-plying her makeup for the concert, and I continued to get dressed.

***

After Taylor and Adam picked us up in Adam's black Tesla, we carpooled to the venue. Beck was the one who booked tickets for this concert, and she said they were specialized tickets for guests who needed additional accommodations for the concert. After meeting at the guest relations booth and going over options, Beck decided to opt out of the equipment the venue offered for guests with hearing loss. I tried to convince her to take it in case her hearing aids acted up with all the excessive noise of the concert, but she shook her head and insisted that they kept the equipment for other guests who had worse hearing than her.

Her hearing loss was pretty severe without her hearing aids, so her logic baffled me. But she was a grown woman capable of making her own choices, so instead we wandered through the stadium to find our section.

Our section was *awesome.*

We arrived early so that we would get a good spot, but even if we were a few rows of bodies back we still would be in the very front. Because we were one of the first groups to show up for the deaf and hard of hearing section of the standing room, I could reach out with my hand and touch the stage in front of us. We were that close.

Following through with my impulsive thoughts, Beck ended up smacking my hand away as soon as it landed on the polished wood of the stage.

"Stop it, you're being weird." She grinned as she fidgeted with clearly nervous energy.

"Beck, we're *so* close! We will probably get the band's sweat on us."

Her eyes widened at that, "You think we will?" Her grin made me look at her boyfriend with a lifted eyebrow, who just shook his head with the smallest smirk known to man.

"Don't give her ideas," Taylor added, running their hand through their hair to brush it out of their eyes. "She will probably collect it in a jar and take it home."

"I think if one of them just looks at me I'll pass away. I can't fathom having the confidence to collect their sweat, too." Beck shrugged, making me widen my eyes at Taylor in alarm, who then laughed at my horrified expression.

"You're a little obsessed." I leaned my elbows on the edge of the stage and stretched my neck and back out. We had some time before the opening act was about to start.

"Can you blame me?" Beck asked, crossing her arms, and shifting her weight onto one hip. "I'm about to listen to my favorite band live! I can see their pretty faces as they play my favorite songs!" Beck bounced on her heels once, right before Adam wrapped his large arms around her waist, swaying them both side to side.

I found myself staring longingly at Beck and Adam more and more lately.

I would be lying if I said I wasn't a little jealous of them.

Not in a spiteful way. I was glad that they both had found happiness with each other. And I wanted that happiness to last as long as possible. They both deserved it.

Though, I couldn't help but feel lonely at times.

During my college years and early twenties, I had no issue with the casual dating scene. With my school load, and then building my career, I loved the flexibility casual dating brought. I had secured stability in my life by moving in with Beck and her grandmother, Susan, years ago, which made this year officially the longest I had ever lived in one place in my entire life.

My parents moved around a lot, which made things feel a little unstable growing up. They were wonderful people, the best of the best—just not with each other. I understood that usually having divorced parents brought sad or disappointed feelings in their children. At least, that was the gist I got from speaking with other children of divorce in school growing up.

Nope. Not me.

My parents were excellent co-parents. They never spoke poorly about the other in front of me, though I was sure that they were human and had reasons to be annoyed with each other. They were divorced, after all.

No, what brought sad and disappointed feelings towards my parents was whenever they decided to get back together. My parents were experts at dating, depending on how you viewed it. They absolutely sucked at commitment, though. The number of partners my parents each introduced me to during my childhood was alarming. I ended up taking a note out of the movie *John Tucker Must Die* and started referring to their partners as "Skip" as a teenager.

That wasn't the worst part.

My parents were the poster children for on-again-off-again.

Whenever the stars aligned and both of them ended up being single at the same time, they would eventually decide to try things out again. Sometimes my parents would date each other for a few weeks, other times for a few months. I was too young when they got divorced for me to have any memories of them being married, but the longest I remembered them dating each other was probably close to two years.

If there was one word to best describe my parents and their relationship habits, it was "unstable."

Naturally, after unpacking a lot of my childhood in therapy as an adult, I learned that I crave stability. It's why I loved the idea of living with Beck and Susan, knowing that Susan was getting older by the day and would appreciate the extra hands around the home. We all fell into a reliable routine that brought me peace and comfort, especially after underwhelming dates from whatever trending dating app I was using at the time. I could rely on Beck and Susan to always be home in a way I couldn't ever rely on my parents. Sometimes my mom was there, sometimes she was there with whoever she was dating. Sometimes my dad was there, sometimes he was there with whoever he was dating. Sometimes they were both there. When I got older, closer to sixteen years old, that was when they weren't always there. They realized I could take care of myself. There were a number of times that I would come home with a note from one of them (or both of them) saying that they were just "figuring things out" along with some money to order takeout.

But now Beck was dating Adam, and I had no reason to doubt the reality that they were going to stay in each other's lives forever. Whether or not they would tie the knot legally was up for debate, because Beck had mixed feelings about the importance of marriage after being raised the way she was.

I, however, had a huge boner for marriage.

I understood how juvenile it was, but thanks to my therapist, I was able to understand that, because my childhood was such a huge clusterfuck, the idea of a legalized partner with two point five kids and a white picket fence seemed very appealing to me.

I thought living in one home for this many years with Beck and Susan was enough to bring me that comfort, but seeing Beck with Adam was making me realize that…maybe I wanted more.

I wanted a partner. I, too, wanted to be dicked-down on the regular. I, too, wanted to find someone who loved me and was committed to me just as much as Adam was committed to and in love with my best friend. I wanted someone to look at me the way Adam looked at Beck. I wanted that person to always be there, to be a constant in my life.

I simply just hadn't found that person yet, which was a real bummer.

"Excuse me, please don't do that," I heard a man's voice behind me, pulling me out of my longing thoughts and making me turn my head.

"Oh, sorry!" I removed my elbows from the stage and took a step back, following the security guard's instructions and hand waving.

"Please keep your hands off of the stage during the performance," the sweaty security guard, who looked younger than my twenty-eight years, scolded.

I nodded my head and saluted him.

He huffed and sulked off to the side of the stage.

"Court, please control yourself. It's embarrassing," Taylor teased with a tsk of their tongue as the lighting of the concert shifted and the crowd started to get louder. "I think the opener is starting soon!"

Beck made the girliest squeal I had ever heard and clapped her hands together before pulling out her phone, and opening up her hearing aid app.

I frowned as she adjusted the levels on her devices and then pocketed the phone.

"No squealing?" I asked, wondering if the audience screams would affect the aids.

"Nope!" Beck smiled, but I still wasn't convinced as she stepped up next to me to loudly cheer on the opening band as they took the stage. I had never heard of them before, but apparently I was in the minority because Beck, Taylor, and Adam all sang or hummed along to a couple of their songs. There was one that I thought might have sounded familiar, but there was no chance I could pretend to know the words. It wasn't until the opening band was wrapping up their last song that I realized something was missing from the experience.

"Hey!" I shouted towards Beck to grab her attention. Her head whipped around, making her brown ponytail hit her red-headed boyfriend in the face. He took it gracefully, gently brushing her hair over to her other shoulder as he glared at the people standing behind us. Now that the concert was in full swing, everyone was crowding closer to the stage.

"Hey!" Beck smiled back at me.

"Wasn't there supposed to be an interpreter?" I asked, glancing around the stage once more and coming up empty. I swore that Beck had mentioned there being one at most of their concerts.

"Huh," Beck glanced around, "Yeah, there was." She

frowned once, but then when she saw me noticing her frown she quickly smiled again and shrugged. "It's okay."

I shrugged once and glanced at Taylor and Adam, who both looked mildly disappointed in the ASL interpreter's absence. We weren't the only hearing people in the deaf and hard of hearing section of the crowd and, looking around, I could see that there were people who were definitely bummed that there was no interpreter, yet.

Before I could ponder that thought further, the crowd erupted in cheers.

I glanced up to the stage to see the band members of Carbon Cut making their way to the center, waving enthusiastically to the sea of fans in front of them.

3

"Holy shit," Taylor shouted over the squealing fans, draping their long arms over both Beck's and my shoulders, "He's so much hotter in person."

"Isn't he?" Beck agreed with wide eyes and a smile that showed every single tooth she had.

"Who?" I asked, smiling at my horn dog friends, and scanning the band members.

"Josh!" Beck shouted at me. I nodded once.

"Which one is he?" I asked. I noticed that the shortest man of the band, the drummer, had bright purple hair as he took his seat and started twirling drumsticks in his hand. The bassist, the most vanilla-looking one, wore almost the exact same outfit that Adam was wearing—jeans, a plain grey t-shirt, and casual sneakers. I didn't even think he had a tattoo or piercing on him, unlike the rest of the band. There was a guitarist who had dark black hair with the sides of his head shaved and tattoos painting the sides over his ears. He wore a cutoff shirt and made a show of flexing his forearms as he strummed his guitar, eliciting a loud squeal from every woman in the audience.

"The lead singer! The blonde!" Beck clarified, pointing with her finger as if I wouldn't be able to pick out who that was on the stage.

He definitely stuck out from his band mates, that was for sure.

Lead Singer Josh was clearly the tallest of the group, emphasized as he stood forward with a microphone stand placed in front of him. Blonde might have been a generous term, since it was clear that he had bleached his hair. Based on the color of his eyebrows, I guessed that he actually had brown hair like Beck's. He had tattoos everywhere, even up on his neck. They seemed to be a blend of earthy, musical, and...scientific? I swore I saw a chemical equation on the inside of one of his arms. He also rocked both an eyebrow piercing and a lip ring, which I hadn't seen on a guy in a while, but facial piercings were making a comeback.

I hadn't dated a single guy with facial piercings in my lifetime, but Beck and Taylor were right. Lead Singer Josh was attractive. He had high cheekbones and a cut jaw and sharp nose. His lips weren't the fullest I had ever seen, but they were symmetrical and his smile more than made up for it.

I would probably plant one on him even with the lip ring, if given the opportunity.

As he grinned and waved to the screaming fans, I realized I wasn't completely out of touch with this band. "Oh! Okay, yeah. I know him!" I nodded and smiled at Beck, expecting her to be proud of me for recognizing one band member.

"You do?!" Beck screamed, making Taylor flinch away from us and rub their ear. Beck ignored their wince and gazed at me intently.

"Yeah, I've seen pictures of him before." I nodded and lifted an eyebrow at her, thinking that it was a little excessive for her to be *that* excited about me recognizing a member from her favorite band.

Beck's smile faltered, but then she made herself recover as she turned towards the band just as they finally quieted the crowd.

"I love the energy tonight!" Lead Singer Josh spoke in the microphone, lip ring glistening off of the stage lights, "Before we get started, I need to apologize," he glanced towards all of us in the deaf and hard of hearing section, giving us a polite frown, barely tipping the corners of his lips downwards, "The ASL interpreter we had lined up is suddenly sick, and though our team has been working frantically to try to rectify the situation, we haven't been able to find anyone else to fill in so last minute. We know this will impact your experience with us tonight." The crowd awwed, but I cupped my hands and loudly booed. Beck quickly turned to smack her hand against my gut, cutting off my boo and making Taylor and me giggle.

How dare we say or do anything negative towards her favorite band?

I glanced back at the quiet red-head behind us, who just shook his head at our antics.

I swore on my life I saw Lead Singer Josh's eyes narrow towards my direction as I booed, but I doubted that he could pick me out specifically in the crowd as the booing culprit, with how bright those stage lights usually were.

"I know, we will have to do better in the future." Lead Singer Josh nodded once in our direction, silently apologizing again, then turning his attention forward and strumming his guitar once, livening the crowd back up again.

The deaf and hard of hearing section was to the far left of the stage, and because we ended up being in the front row most of us were either turning our necks or bodies to see the band head on.

They were good.

Thankfully, I knew a lot of the songs that they played. Adam had been busting his ass to learn ASL for Beck, and he had picked it up incredibly well. One method we used to help him learn shorthand phrases was listening to Carbon Cut and teaching him how to interpret the songs. Thus, after Beck purchased tickets to this concert, I had heard most of these songs on repeat.

There will never be anything more swoony to women than a man who looked like Lead Singer Josh, and who could *actually* sing well. It was obvious he wasn't lip syncing like other artists have been caught doing, and his range was impressive. I didn't realize how difficult it could be to sing some of their songs live until I noticed the changes in his pitch, or how he would inhale differently in the song than he did on the recording. I was thoroughly impressed with the band's overall skill set.

I had definitely seen him online before. The more I stared at him, the more familiar he looked to me. I was surprised I didn't already know he was the lead singer for the band, because I felt like I had known him for a while.

Odd.

The band was singing the last verse of one of their songs,

the three of us dancing and shouting along with the lyrics while Adam swayed with Beck, grinning at his girlfriend having the time of her life, when I noticed Beck's eyes squint shut and widen again in alarm. Both of her hands quickly went to her ears, and I stopped dancing to see what was happening.

"Shit!" I heard Beck curse over the loud music and screaming audience.

"What? What is it?" I asked, getting Taylor's attention as well.

"My hearing aids just died!" Beck groaned, her deaf accent taking over.

I frowned.

Taylor frowned.

Adam frowned more than he usually did because he already had resting frowny face.

"Do you have spare batteries?" Adam asked, finger spelling B-A-T-T-E-R-I-E-S so Beck could understand what he was asking. She shook her head no and pulled out her case that she kept her devices in, before pocketing them in her bag. She then pulled out ear plugs, because her audiologist had given her grief in the past for not going out of her way to "protect what little hearing she had left," which seemed ridiculous to me because it was my understanding that hearing aids amplified sound. Wearing earplugs at a concert you were previously wearing hearing aids at seemed like a moot point to me.

"It's okay, I'll be fine," Beck reassured the group, the four of us being the only still bodies in the crowd as the band continued to play.

"Are you sure? Can you hear the music at all?" Taylor asked, I quickly signed their question for Beck to understand.

"The base tones I can hear, but I can also feel the music, so I'm still experiencing it. Seriously, don't worry about it!" she shouted at all of us, smiling and trying to de-escalate our concern. Adam looked at Taylor and me before lifting a shoulder and wrapping one of his tatted arms around her shoulders. She responded by gripping his forearm and smiling up at the stage.

Well, this fucking sucked.

My best friend goes to her first concert to see her favorite band in the world, and her shitty hearing aids die. She didn't deserve this. She deserved to experience Carbon Cut at the fullest.

How dare they not do the bare minimum and hire a backup ASL interpreter? *They honestly couldn't find one in the entirety of Orange County?* I thought. *Even I could sign for the crowd if necessary.*

Whoa, that was an idea.

I blinked as I replayed that thought, looking at how close we were to the stage. It was literally inches away from us. It would take absolutely no effort for me to hop up there and run towards the small, lifted platform where the sick ASL interpreter should have been standing tonight.

The band ended their song and someone threw their bra up on stage. Lead Singer Josh had the world's fastest reflexes and caught the bra in his hand, before hanging it from the microphone stand in one smooth motion. As if he had lots of experience handling rogue underwear mid-performance.

"I think you guys are going to like this next song we have lined up…" Josh continued talking, but turned his head mostly away from us, so Beck turned towards us to interpret for her. Taylor's signing was pure horseshit (no matter how hard they tried), and Adam was still learning, so I signed to Beck what the title of the next song was.

"Oh!" Beck looked crushed for a moment, then she caught herself and put her 'Everything Is Fine' mask on for us, "It's just…that's my favorite, is all."

The audacity *that this band has to do this to the* sweetest *woman in the world!*

Adam squeezed his girlfriend, providing comfort to Beck in a way I couldn't. Taylor grabbed Beck's hand, a silent apology for how the night was going.

The drummer tapped his sticks together before starting off Beck's favorite song, and I had one more moment where I acted on my impulsive thoughts that night. *I could sign for her.*

Before I could give my brain time to convince myself that I shouldn't, I slapped my palms on the edge of the stage and lifted my butt onto it, making myself half a body taller than the section we were in. Beck squealed in shock, whereas Taylor audibly asked, "What the *fuck* are you doing?"

I ignored their question as I lifted my hands and intently listened to the lyrics coming from the singer. I wasn't that far away from the crowd, and if I straightened my legs that were hanging on the edge of the stage, I could knock my friends over. It wasn't like I was jumping up onto stage to rush at the band or anything.

I knew my time sitting on the edge of the stage was

limited, especially if that sweaty security guard came to pull me away to concert jail. So, I kept my focus on my task. Interpreting. Thankfully, because this was Beck's favorite song, I knew it well and could anticipate the lyrics as Lead Singer Josh sang them.

Beck started fangirl screaming at me. Taylor just wrapped their arms around Beck and jumped up and down with her while Adam pulled his phone out to start recording the concert experience for us.

The stage lights were hot as hell, but I wouldn't let my sudden back sweat sway me to stop. Especially since Beck had started signing the lyrics along with me. She was able to keep up with the song better now that she knew where the singer was in the verse.

Suddenly, Beck's eyes widened and she stopped signing, just as the singer wrapped up the first verse. Instead, she palmed her hands over her mouth to cover her loud squeals as I felt a presence hovering behind me to my left. I glanced a peek over my shoulder, expecting the sweaty security guard, only to find myself looking straight into the dark eyes of Lead Singer Josh.

I yelped and covered my cheeks with my hands, embarrassed that the singer of the band had finally wandered over to our section of the stage, probably to see why I was sitting on it.

He started singing the second verse of the song and nodded towards me, clearly encouraging me to keep signing, and the crowd erupted with cheers. Who was I to not give the audience what they wanted? I signed *thanks* to Lead Singer

Josh before turning back to my friends and finding my place in his song for me to interpret.

Beck was screaming so loudly, I thought for sure the rest of her hearing would be shot if she wasn't wearing protective ear plugs. I felt him wander away from us toward center stage again, and I felt a little less stressed. Though, somehow, having the band's blessing to sign their concert for them did *not* make me more confident signing, and I found myself more nervous and messing up the occasional phrase.

It was better than no interpreter at all, but still.

I felt the singer's presence beside me again, and when I saw a pair of long legs clad in worn out, black jeans swing over the edge of the stage next to me, I panicked and covered my cheeks in embarrassment again, a nervous giggle escaping my lips. I glanced over to see him situate the microphone stand to adjust to his new height in between the verses. Once he was sitting inches away from me on the edge of the stage, (the only thing keeping him from being tackled by fans being the rope that separated the main audience from our section, who didn't feel the need to ambush him) he turned to me and winked before continuing with the song.

I felt my heart flutter in my chest.

He was so attractive. With him sitting this close to me, it was easy to notice.

He sang, I signed, and I'm pretty sure I ovulated as a result of the experience.

This was officially the coolest moment I would ever have in my lifetime.

The song came to an end and everyone started screaming

and cheering, my best friend included. As he set his guitar on stage to stand back up again, I felt him lean towards me, inches away from my face. I held my breath as he spoke towards my ear so I could hear him over the fans. "Thank you for filling in."

"Thanks for not kicking me out," I responded. He smiled as he pulled back to make eye contact with me, hesitating the slightest bit as he met my gaze and narrowed his eyes a little.

"She's Courtney Henderson!" Beck started screaming. I raised my eyebrows at her, *be cool! He literally didn't ask!*

Josh turned towards Beck screaming at him, and she repeated herself. His eyebrows raised the slightest bit at her words. He turned back to me to scan my face quickly before reaching out and grabbing the wrist of my right hand, making me startle and tug against his grip.

He didn't let go, but he was still gentle as he held my hand up to examine the semi-colon shaped birthmark on top of my right hand, his facial features relaxing the slightest bit as he locked eyes with me again.

At this point, he had been silent for a little too long, and the crowd was screaming at him to figure out what was going on.

I would have liked to know that myself.

"Court?" I barely heard Josh ask, his mouth pulling into a wide smile as he held my wrist captive in his grip. I tugged once, and he released my hand that I tucked safely against my chest.

"Yes?" I asked, feeling the heat from the stage lights filling my cheeks.

"Aye!" Purple Haired Drummer shouted into his mic towards Josh, "Stop flirting with the fans, we're on a tight schedule here!" Laughter erupted from the crowd, and I released a nervous laugh with my friends at his odd behavior. Sure, I sat on stage. That didn't mean I wanted to be manhandled by anyone.

"I'm catching up with an old friend!" Josh called back into his own microphone. I furrowed my brows at him. We weren't old friends. I didn't even know his last name. Based on how he reacted to my expression, he understood my confusion just fine. He looked up towards the sky and laughed at himself once before shaking his head and taking hold of my right hand once more, squeezing three times.

That was a…familiar gesture…

Wait a second.

Did we know each other?

Instinctively I squeezed his hand back three times and he grinned, then hopped back up to a standing position, taking his guitar and microphone back with him to the center of the stage and setting up for the next song.

I was in a daze, and therefore, stumbled over signing the next song the band played. Lead Singer Josh didn't come back over to our section of the audience again after that, but our group still had an excellent time. Others were signing back to me in the crowd, thanking me, and signing along to the lyrics I was displaying for them. It was a humbling experience, knowing that if I hadn't gone out of my way to learn a language for my hard of hearing roommate in college years ago, that I probably wouldn't be living this once in a lifetime experience right now. I did my best to get over the weird interaction with the singer and focus on the moment of it all.

That moment came and went way too quickly, and once the band wrapped up the finale I quickly hopped off of the stage and into my friend's waiting arms.

"Holy fucking shit!" Taylor screeched, squeezing my biceps, and shaking me a little, "I can't believe that just happened!"

"You signed the absolute *shit* out of this concert!" Beck squealed, mumbling her words the slightest bit. I laughed and hugged my friends, startled when I felt a tap on my shoulder. I glanced behind me to see a woman with bright red hair, wearing a headset, crouching down from the stage, a bundle of lanyards in her hands.

"These are for you!" She called, waving us closer to her so she could distribute them to the four of us.

"What are these?" I asked her, forgetting to sign for Beck's benefit.

"Backstage passes! You're going to meet the band!" The fake red-head called back over the noise of everyone getting ready to leave. Her words resulted in another loud squeal from Beck, who must have read her lips just fine.

4

"I can't believe this is happening!" Beck exclaimed, bouncing on the backs of her heels as we all waited in the tiniest makeshift room known to man.

It was filled with thrifted furniture and had random graffiti all over the walls. Adam stood off in the far back corner, giving his energetic girlfriend room to hum with excited energy. Taylor was taking pictures of the random room we were told to wait in, and I pulled my phone out to take a selfie with my backstage pass to send to Logan.

I was rubbing it in his face. I had asked if he wanted to come with us to the concert, texting him before Beck purchased tickets for everyone, but he declined. For whatever reason.

As soon as I sent the picture, a knock sounded at the door and the fake red-headed woman poked her head through to gesture us out. "They're ready for you guys now!"

Beck hummed excitedly as our group was led down a hallway before taking a turn and stopping in front of a black door with random scribbles of writing on it. The woman opened the door and stepped aside to allow us entry, and all of us knew to let Beck go in first.

She panicked at first, freezing in her spot. Beck didn't take a step until Adam gently gripped her shoulders and nudged her forward. Taylor and I laughed at the interaction as we followed them into the room.

"Hey!" a couple of the band members greeted us at the same time, standing up from their spots on the worn-out furniture that was scattered throughout the room.

I stayed back behind my friends, knowing that I should let the super fans say hi first. I figured this meet-and-greet would be way more memorable for a fan like Beck than someone like me.

Though I did catch myself scanning the room until my eyes landed on the lead singer, who was already looking at me intently. As soon as our brown eyes connected, he walked around his band mates to make it over to me as quickly as possible.

Now that we were standing in front of each other, I realized just how tall he was. I was probably around five six, if I was remembering correctly, and this guy felt like he was almost a foot taller than me. I had to crane my neck back the closer he approached.

"How tall are you?" I blurted out without thinking. I didn't realize that he was playing with his lip ring, gnawing on it with his teeth, until he released it and grinned at my random question.

"Six four," he responded, sounding a little cocky about it.

"Well, shit." I made a show of looking him up and down. His Doc Martens were well-used, and tied together his whole punk rock look. He wore a dark grey cutoff top that contrasted with his ink and hair nicely.

"What? No, 'how are you'? No, 'it's been a while'?" he countered, folding his hands across his chest as if he was hurt by my reaction to him, showing off the tattoos on his forearms in the process.

Yup, that was definitely a chemical equation on his arm.

"…Has it been a while?" I asked, confused as I let my glance flick across the room to our friends. They had quickly halted whatever conversation they were all discussing to watch the conversation taking place between Lead Singer Josh and me.

He had dark brown eyes that seemed to be searching for something in mine as he studied me with a grin, and when I continued to stare blankly at him, he let out a laugh as he ran both of his hands through his bleached hair.

"Oh my god, you still don't recognize me," he mumbled to the ceiling.

"Ugh!" I heard Beck groan. I gave her a 'what the fuck' look that she returned to me.

"Courtney Henderson," Josh tsked his tongue at me and raised his finger to shake with obvious mock jest, "I have to say, I'm a little disappointed."

"I'm…sorry? What is happening?" I was starting to feel embarrassed, receiving such direct attention from someone like him. He wasn't intimidating per se, but he gave off this air of confidence I was a little thrown off by. It didn't feel like he was confident because of his celebrity status, but he was confident because of whoever he thought I was.

Wait a minute.

"Do we know each other?" I finally managed to ask.

"Yes! Of course, we—wait, hold on. This might help." Josh raised a finger towards me as if he was afraid I had someplace to run off to, before stepping to the side of the room where a black backpack was tossed. He grabbed the backpack and dug around in the pockets of it for a second, pulling out an eyeglasses case covered in random stickers. He took out a pair of black framed glasses and quickly slid them on, then he made a show of facing me and framing his face with his hands. "Now," he said, "Picture me with my brown hair."

I stared at him.

Then I blinked at him.

After an embarrassing amount of time, his facial features started to piece together a puzzle for me. "Wait…"

"I am. Don't you worry." Josh winked at me, which made a laugh slip out of me because he was so charming, I couldn't help myself. I weirdly had the confidence to step closer to him, momentarily forgetting about our audience in the room, and I saw his smile widen a little more at my approach.

That smile was when it clicked for me.

"…J-shua?"

At my question he released a loud and relieved exhale. "Finally!"

"Oh my *god!*" I don't know where I got the sudden confidence, but it was as if a glass wall shattered in my brain, immediately flooding with images and memories from high school with one of my most favorite people, "J-shua Madey!"

"In the flesh!" he removed his glasses and carelessly tossed them onto the crusty couch before closing the distance between us and wrapping his long arms around my back, lifting me up in one of his classic bear hugs.

You're home.

Whoa, *that* was an intrusive thought if I'd ever had one.

I was closed-mouth squealing as I wrapped my arms around his shoulders and my legs around his waist, just like I used to. It was as if we were good friends who had only gone months without seeing each other instead of friends who hadn't seen each other for about a decade. I tucked my head in his neck as I felt one of his hands come up and cup me behind my neck.

I don't know how long we were like this, Josh supporting the entirety of my weight as I wrapped my limbs around him like a koala bear. I thought I heard low voices of our friends still in the room with us, but I couldn't tell you what they said as my soul reconnected with this person. I didn't realize it missed him so much.

"I can't believe it!" I squealed into his neck, making him release a chuckle at my response.

Joshua Madey.

How the fuck did *that* kid become *this* man?

I pulled back to look at him as he slowly slid me down the front of his body to return my feet to the floor. "What? How? When? *What?*"

"You mean you didn't expect me to become a musician after high school? Damn." Josh chucked my chin with his hand and winked again, and I was startled at the purely visceral reaction my body had from that simple gesture.

My pulse started thrumming in my veins, my heart racing with excitement from the gentle contact.

I was just staring at him wide-eyed, blown away by this sudden revelation.

I was struggling to picture the shaggy, brown-haired bean pole that was my best friend senior year and believe that he grew up to be this bleach blonde, tattooed, pierced, famous musician that filled out his frame as a fully grown adult.

"I didn't expect you at all," I replied in awe, holding my hands to my cheeks similarly to how I did when he sat next to me on stage.

"You guys knew each other in high school?" Purple Haired Drummer asked, pointing between Josh and me.

"Yes! He was my best friend!" I closed the distance between Josh and I again to wrap one arm around his waist, while his other naturally fell across the back of my shoulders. We fit so well together, just like we did in high school.

"And you didn't know it was him when you came to this concert? You didn't hear his name and think, 'Hey, I knew a Josh Madey in high school, I wonder if it's the same guy?'" the bassist asked, taking a seat next to the purple-haired drummer, close enough to make me suspicious about their whole situation.

"I didn't know his last name was Madey until now," I lifted a shoulder, to which Josh pulled back from me and lifted his pierced eyebrow at me in suspicion.

"You didn't know my last name? But you came to see us live?"

"Well, actually…" I blushed and looked over at my best friend, who was beaming at the lead singer and me, "My best friend came to see you all live…and I tagged along…" I felt embarrassed, which was ridiculous because it was completely reasonable to be a moderate fan of someone's music without knowing the full names of the band members.

"Wait…" the dark-haired lead guitarist with the tattoos on the side of his head narrowed his eyes at me, "Are you saying…that you're not into our music?"

"What?" Josh dropped his arm from my shoulders, as shock and hurt colored his expression.

"I'm sorry!" I cried.

"I call cap," Purple Haired Drummer shook his head at me, "You interpreted our songs way too well to not be a fan."

"What is everyone saying? You're all talking too fast for me to keep up." Beck asked everyone in the room. I frowned, disappointed in myself for forgetting that her hearing aids were dead as I lifted my hands to sign for her.

"They're roasting me for not being their number one fan," I explained vocally and with my hands. Beck nodded once in understanding.

"I listen to you guys all the time, and we've interpreted your songs to teach Adam ASL," she reached behind herself to grab her boyfriend's hand, who silently eyeballed everybody in the room as if this many people in the small space made him uncomfortable. "Courtney really is just a good friend."

At Beck's confirmation, Josh gasped and held his hand to his heart. "How could you!" he cried, making warmth fill my heart at how natural this behavior felt from him. It was as if every second we spent in each other's presence, we naturally fell deeper into our old rhythm.

"Oh, please! You guys are doing just fine without me

pinning up all your posters on my bedroom wall." I reached over to pinch Josh's tatted forearm, and he retaliated by reaching out to pinch my side. I was quick and dodged it.

"Will you pin up posters of us now, though? Since you and...wait, what did you call him?" Purple Haired Drummer asked.

"J-shua!" I smiled, thrilled when I saw a slight tinge of pink color his cheeks at the childhood nickname.

"That...is a nickname..." Taylor added, giving Josh a very apologetic look, "Sorry, man."

"For the record," Josh's dark brows lowered as he draped one of his long arms over my shoulders again, tugging me back into his side as if I belonged there, "She is the only one who can call me that. I swear to fuck if any of you—-"

"I already updated my contact for you. It's done." The dark-haired guitarist chuckled as he pocketed his device.

"How do you spell that?" Vanilla-looking Bassist asked, pulling out his phone to follow suit.

"The letter J, dash, S-H-U-A," I responded without hesitation.

All the band mates laughed, either covering their eyes or pinching the arch of their noses.

Josh turned to give me an annoyed look, one that I could immediately see through as he pretended to scold me for sharing his childhood nickname with his buddies.

"Oh, you'll be okay. You can cry yourself to sleep on your massive pile of money." I patted his chest, which definitely was more muscle and less chest bone than when he was a teen.

"Good god. Where have you been keeping her, J-shua?

I think I'm in love." Dark Haired Guitarist chuckled as he sauntered over towards us to reach for my hand, but Josh quickly used his arm wrapped around my shoulders to steer me away from his band mate.

"Nope! No. Absolutely not." Josh wrapped both of his arms around me, making us chest to chest, as he looked over his shoulder and down at the man. "I just found her, hands to yourself." Then he turned back to look down at me, since I had decided it would be less weird if I also wrapped both of my arms around his waist and rested my chin on his firm chest, "Garrett doesn't wash his hands after he pees. You don't want to touch him."

"Fuck you!" Dark Haired Guitarist, who apparently was named Garrett, replied. "Kate wouldn't come within an inch of me if that were true."

"Why Kate comes within an inch of you at all, is a mystery to all of us," Purple Haired Drummer chimed in. I was busy trying not to save the scent of Josh's cologne in my brain permanently when I let my gaze slide over to my friends, and I panicked for a moment.

Nobody had been signing for Beck.

I did see, however, that Adam had pulled out his phone and was recording most of the interaction. Based on how Beck's wide hazel eyes were beaming at Josh and me embracing each other, I figured that the chances of her forgiving me for slacking were high.

"Kate can hear everything you dumbasses are saying in front of the fans." The fake red-haired woman from earlier chimed in as she entered the room, startling all of us and making Garrett breathe a loud "Fuck" in surprise.

"Babe, I promise it's not what it looks like," Garrett lifted his hands as if to tame the little woman, who reminded me of Ariel from *The Little Mermaid*, "I was simply hitting on Josh's high school girlfriend to make him act like a territorial asshole."

Kate lifted an eyebrow at this, "Did it work?"

Everyone turned to look at Josh and me, as we were slowly untangling each other from our embrace. Based on how hot my cheeks felt, I was blushing.

But it was fine, because so was Josh.

He raked his hand through his sweaty bleached hair, the way that men did when they were feeling nervous. It was sweet and reminded me a little of the boy I knew back in the day. Also, I needed to find out what cologne he wore. It was delicious and doing alarming things to my libido (or libby-doo, as Beck would say) in this small room filled with people.

"Wait, are you two?" Taylor asked, pulling attention away from the two of us as they wiggled their index finger between Garrett and Kate.

Kate closed her light blue eyes and exhaled a deep breath, "Yes, but we were trying to keep it on the DL."

At that, Taylor and I both zipped our lips closed. Beck saw what we were doing, and zipped her lips closed a second after us. I laughed at her, and she stuck her tongue out at me.

"What did I just promise to never talk about?" Beck turned to ask her boyfriend, just now realizing that he was recording the experience for her. She smiled at him and lifted up on her tiptoes to kiss his cheek.

"Sorry to wrap the reunion up short, but the guys actually

do need to get going," Kate looked genuinely apologetic at me as she said these words. Maybe it was because after she spoke, I felt my heart sink into my butt, and icy fear flooded my veins at the thought of not being able to see Josh again.

I quickly turned towards him just as he pulled his phone out of his back pocket and handed it to me. "Give me your number."

5

"This feels weird."

"No, it doesn't."

"No, Beck is right. This feels weird."

"You are being dramatic. It's not weird. You're making it weird."

"Yes, because it's weird," Beck repeated herself as she set down the snack tray on the coffee table.

"This just feels…oddly formal," Taylor added, plopping themselves down on the yellow couch and snagging a potato chip off the tray Beck made.

"I guess it's a little formal." I quirked my lips to the side at that, eyeballing the drinks I had mixed together for tonight. Eloise was coming over to our townhome for a 'Girls, Gays, and Theys' night, which really just meant that Adam wasn't invited—not that he wanted to spend more time with his ex-girlfriend now that she was helping Pat run administration at work. I figured once Beck got the gist of what was going on with Eloise, she'd be able to relay that information back to Adam and he could finally pull that massive stick right out of his ass in regard to Eloise.

Then we could all hold hands, sing *Kumbaya,* and move on with our lives.

I was glad Eloise approached me at the end of the workday to request this little meet up. I had been keeping her side of the story locked away in my brain for months, waiting for her to gather the courage to talk to Beck and Taylor about what she's going through. I knew that they would have sympathy for her, but I wouldn't betray her trust by sharing her story for her. Frankly, her behavior last year when she was pursuing Adam (back when Adam was clearly only interested in Beck but trying not to be inappropriate about it at work), made a lot more sense to me. But, due to Eloise's crippling fear of rejection, she had to take her time to work up the courage to open up to my friends. Just like how she opened up to me that one drunken night at the bar.

I was grateful that she spilled her guts, thanks to her lowered inhibitions. I doubted that if she hadn't had a rough day (and too many margaritas) that she would have ever told me anything about her personal life, and we would all still just be awkwardly skirting around her existence.

I thought that she could end up fitting into our friend group reasonably well.

There was a knock at the door and Beck's grandmother, Susan, appeared out of the hallway to answer it. She wrapped her knitted shawl around her shoulders tighter as she opened the door, successfully fitting every Granny stereotype in existence.

"Hello!" Susan gave Eloise a bright smile, and I noticed

Eloise's shoulders drop about half an inch at the comfortable greeting she received.

"You cut your hair!" Taylor accused Eloise with an aggressive point in her direction. Eloise nodded with a nervous giggle and toed off her shoes in the entryway before making her way towards all of us in the living room. Susan followed after her and took her spot in one of her ugly accent chairs.

Eloise was very pretty.

She had bright, almost pale blonde hair that was recently chopped to just above her shoulders, with a smattering of freckles over her nose and cheekbones. Her eyes were a bright, almost clear blue. Her lips were a natural fullness that probably starred in the fantasies of most of the men that she came across.

"It looks cute!" I approached her and gave her a hug, because I was a touchy-feely person and wanted her to feel welcome in our little home.

"Thanks! I was feeling adventurous after work, so..." Eloise's lips quirked to the side and she shrugged her shoulders, taking an empty seat on the yellow couch across from Taylor while Beck sat in the second ugly accent chair. All the furniture was angled towards where the TV stood on the entertainment center, but all our bodies were angled towards Eloise.

I had no intention of starting the movie until after we had this conversation.

"Alright, let's rip the band-aid off," Taylor started, leaning forward, and resting their elbows on their knees. "What's going on, Lo?"

Eloise's bright eyes widened the slightest bit as a nervous smile tilted her lips, "Lo?"

"Yes. Apparently, we are all allergic to using full names. Beck, Court, T, Gram, J-shua, etcetera." Taylor waved their hand in the air as if this was silly to even discuss.

"Why not Elle?" I asked, curious as to why Taylor shortened the middle of her name instead.

"Hmm, no. It's giving *Stranger Things* vibes. She's a Lo." Beck and I nodded in understanding while Gram snickered at Taylor's antics and stood up to head towards the kitchen. Eloise watched her elderly form retreat before exhaling a large breath.

"Before we start, can we all talk about the fact that Court is being pursued by Joshua Madey?"

"Oh my god, yes! Please!" Beck raised her arms in exasperation then slapped them on her legging-clad thighs.

"Oh, right! Fuck! How have we not discussed this?" It was the Monday after the concert, and a busy day at work. Beck and I spent Saturday mostly sleeping and zoning out on our phones because we were recovering from the concert, and Sunday I spent running errands and going to the gym while Beck most likely spent the day at Adam's condo. Beck and I hadn't discussed the events of the concert other than "I can't believe that happened" or when she caught me wandering to the shower in a sleepy daze, she asked, "Are you going to call him first or wait for him to call you?". I had just shrugged at that, because I wasn't awake enough to discuss things. Then she had to run to the audiologist for her early morning appointment to get replacement hearing aids until her new ones she ordered came in.

"Footage that Adam and other audience members recorded keeps popping up all over the bands social media pages, and the comments are *so* chaotic," Eloise pulled her phone out to start scrolling, "But honestly, the way he grabbed your wrist was *so hot.*"

"Agreed." Beck added, giving me a suspicious smile.

I rolled my eyes at my friends.

"That's because we used to be best friends in high school." I smiled at the memory of backstage, "I am actually so glad we reconnected, even if it was in the most unconventional way."

"I bet he fucks great," Taylor claimed around a mouthful of potato chips they were snacking on. "After watching the way he handles the mic stand and guitar, I think Court is going to be a lucky girl." They winked at me as they took a paper towel to wipe their salty fingers off.

"Whoa!" I held my hands up, palms out, wanting my friends to calm down, "There wasn't any fucking in the past, so I doubt there will be fucking now. If that's your hopes from him asking for my number, I would lower your expectations."

Susan reappeared with the tray of drinks that I had made in the kitchen and forgot to bring, and began passing it around to everyone. "Courtney is in denial, obviously."

"How the fuck would you know, Susan? You weren't there."

"When was the last time a straight man asked for your number and didn't want to sleep with you?" Susan countered with a dramatic lift of her eyebrow. She took the last drink off the tray and reclaimed her seat in the living room.

I sat quietly for a moment before shrugging and replying, "Touché. But Josh and I have history. We were joined at the hip in high school, and we never…um…" I realized I was about to lie and stumbled over my thoughts long enough for my friends to pick up on something.

"What? What happened in high school?" Eloise asked, crossing one leg over the other and sipping her cocktail delicately. "Did you two fool around?"

"Oh my god," Beck slapped her hands on her thighs again, dramatically, "Was he your first, you know, *time?*"

I frowned into my drink, "No, but I wouldn't have minded that at all."

Taylor let out a pained gasp and set their drink on the coffee table, adjusting their position to face me head on. "Did you have a little crush on him in high school?"

"No," I shook my head once as I felt myself blush, "I had a massive, huge crush on him in high school." everyone released cute awws at that. "But he had put me clear in the friend zone."

Beck's frown was very noticeable and it made me laugh. "That's not true," she said.

"What do you mean?" I asked, confused by her statement.

"Well, just," Beck closed her eyes once to gather her thoughts before opening them again and explaining, "I have a feeling that every single boy you went to school with probably had some sort of crush on you. So, it would make sense if he did, too."

"Well, the evidence says otherwise." I was remembering my time with him senior year more and more each day; the memories becoming clear as they came out of the fog that time created. "We kissed once, mostly because I begged him to." I looked up to see everyone in the room, even Susan, eagerly waiting for me to continue my story.

"I'm sorry, you had to *beg* that boy to kiss you?" Beck asked, leaning in as if she couldn't believe it.

"I did," I laughed at the memory, it was so juvenile to think about as a grown woman. "He had told me that he hadn't kissed a girl, yet. So, I asked if I could be his first kiss. My reason was something so stupid. It was along the lines of, 'I needed to teach him how to kiss before he went off to college' or something ridiculous like that."

Eloise giggled from her spot on the couch, "That's actually kind of cute."

"Did it work?" Taylor asked, eyeballing the potato chip bowl as if debating whether or not to eat more.

"Yup. He planted one on me, and my teenage heart thought that he would realize he was hopelessly in love with me afterward. But nope. We stuck our tongues in each other's mouths and then we just...moved on as if it never happened." I remembered how embarrassed I felt after. How I wanted to keep kissing him forever, but then he made some sort of comment about ruining our friendship, and I immediately thought that I was being selfish by wanting a relationship with him so badly. I didn't want to ruin our friendship because I wanted to keep him around forever.

That ended up not mattering at all, because once I went

off to college down here in California, he ghosted me. I never saw or heard from him whenever I came back to Oregon to visit. As soon as I drove away, I never received a single message from him again.

Wait, that's right! What the fuck? If he calls me that will be the first thing I ask him about.

"Ugh. Teenagers are so annoying," Taylor shook their head after finally taking a couple more chips and crunching them loudly. "Anyways, keep us posted for when he realizes he fucked up as a kid and wants to make it up to you as adults. Preferably with orgasms."

"Will do!" I laughed and gave a thumbs up as they turned their body towards Eloise, reminding me of why we all gathered here today.

"Alright. Back to the band-aid rip. Are you still trying to get Adam back?" I saw Beck wince at Taylor's blunt words, but I appreciated them. Asking direct questions would help Eloise cut to the chase.

"Oh! No, no," She turned towards Beck to make eye contact, "I do *not* want Adam back. I promise." Beck gave Eloise a nervous smile in return as she sipped her cocktail a tiny bit before giving her a head nod.

"That's...a relief to hear," Beck replied. "It's just kind of felt like that, with you getting a job at the clinic and everything."

"And I totally get why you think that! It's just..." Eloise's bright eyes glanced over to me and I gave her a smile to encourage her to continue, "...I have issues."

"Ma'am, we all have issues," Susan chimed in as she tipped

her cocktail glass back in an attempt to get every last drop of the drink I mixed. She had downed the whole thing.

"It's true. So, what are yours specifically?" Taylor asked, taking the potato chip bowl off of the coffee table and tucking it underneath so temptation wouldn't be so difficult to resist.

"Well..." Eloise's shoulders started to hunch in on herself, and I knew the word vomit was coming, "I think I only ever dated Adam because our moms wanted us to. Not that Adam isn't a great guy. I mean, we've known each other since we were kids, and it was nice dating someone so familiar. Plus, our families are *super* close. So, it made sense to try dating. But, like, I wasn't ever 'in love' with him or anything."

There was a moment of silence before Beck broke it, "So...why did you want to get back together with him so badly?"

"Because his mom kept telling me to," Eloise closed her eyes and sighed, "And *my* mom kept telling me to...I don't know, they kept saying that his 'mood swings' were just a phase. And that if I tried hard enough, that I could get him back. I just never questioned it. It wasn't until after the Big Bear trip I had organized—and after talking with you all, after he turned me down that last time—that I realized that...I wasn't pursuing him because I actually *wanted* him. He was just, familiar, I guess. An expectation I felt pressure to achieve, so that our parents would be proud of me. Of us. I don't know..."

The silence was heavy, and we all gave Eloise a moment to stare blankly at the coffee table as she gathered her thoughts.

Her cheeks were flushed pink, and I saw the rim of her eyelids start to turn pink as well.

"Well, fuck," Beck stood up from her ugly accent chair to wander over to the couch next to Eloise. "I didn't realize—I mean, I understand what it's like receiving that kind of pressure from parents." She threw an arm around Eloise's shoulders and tugged her close.

Eloise sniffed and leaned into Beck's side, taking comfort in the contact, "I realize how shitty it is to refer to that period of his life as 'mood swings', but that's what they kept calling it...for the record, I don't think that his depression is anything less than it is."

"Thank you for clarifying that," Beck snuggled close to Eloise once more. "It sounds like both of your moms are real pieces of work, though."

"Um, yeah," Eloise shrugged with a nervous crooked smile, making me remember why she was so successful as a model some time ago, "I've been going to therapy the last few months. I'm starting to realize some...things...about my relationship with my parents."

"What kinds of things?" Susan asked, taking the potato chip bowl Taylor had hidden under the coffee table and setting it on her lap. Taylor reached over to grab some more chips out of the bowl, but Susan smacked their hand away.

"Well, that I'm a textbook people-pleaser—" Taylor, Beck, and I all nodded in agreement, because this wasn't news to us, "—And that my parents have gone out of their way to, I don't know, raise me that way? I don't know if it was intentional on their part. I think they just raised me the same way they were raised. With expectations. But those expectations eventually became overwhelming to me."

"It sounds like the expectations they set on you would be overwhelming to anyone, Lo," Beck replied, resting her cheek on Eloise's forehead. I smiled at the interaction, glad my friends were so empathetic towards her.

It truly sucked to realize that your parents weren't perfect people, and that maybe they made some mistakes that impacted your development. No matter how mature and well-rounded you thought yourself to be.

"The thing with the job," Eloise continued, gaining confidence in the safe space my little family created for her, "I just...I had never worked a nine-to-five job before. This is embarrassing to say but, I don't know, my parents never said these words to me directly or anything. But it was heavily *implied* that nine-to-five work was for a 'certain class' of people; that I was meant for jobs more along the lines of event planning."

"Or underwear modeling," Taylor nodded with a smile in Eloise's direction, failing yet again to get more chips from Susan's quick reflexes.

"Yeah," Eloise smiled back at Taylor as she wiped a stray tear from her eye, "The modeling thing was temporary. That happened because I was taught to embrace my type of face from an early age." Thank fuck she knew that she was beautiful, I couldn't imagine going through this and also having confidence issues tagged along with it. "I should actually thank Adam at some point. His curveball of changing his career—and finding you, Beck—regardless of Edith's opinion, helped me realize that maybe I don't need to keep doing things simply because my parents expect me to. That maybe I can be happy with myself, even if my parents aren't."

Eloise squeezed the top of Beck's thigh, who smiled at her.

"Shit, I'm so fucking proud of you right now," Taylor scooted over to the couch to wrap up Beck and Eloise into a bear hug, which made my FOMO immediately trigger. I jumped off my spot on the ottoman and lunged at them, completing the bear hug by wrapping my arms around the three of them and successfully squishing Beck's face against my boobs. We almost tipped the yellow couch backwards, but thankfully managed to land it back on its feet without catastrophe.

"Thanks guys," Eloise let one little whimper escape her lips as she leaned into our embraces, and I felt my heart fill.

She would fit in just fine.

"Anytime," Beck squeezed her once more, shrugging Taylor and me off to give everyone their space. "Now, time to watch Mr. Darcy flex his hand and obscenely obsess over it."

6

Elizabeth had just rejected Mr. Collins's proposal in the most fantastic way when I felt my phone vibrate in my pocket. I leaned to the side to slip it out, feeling my heart thump when I saw that I received a text message from Josh. I had saved his number into my phone as soon as we got into the car after the concert, trying not to get my hopes up about reuniting with my old best friend.

Josh: What is your schedule like this week?

Me: Hi. I'm doing well, thanks.

Josh: Still a smartass, I see.

I smiled at myself, feeling like a giddy teenager again. I always got butterflies whenever Josh used to message me. I also got butterflies whenever he simply looked at me with those dorky but loveable black rimmed glasses. Or when he helped me with our science projects.

Me: I work full-time during the week. But I'm free this weekend?

Josh: Damn, we are flying out Saturday morning. What do your evenings look like?

I thought about it for a moment because I was planning

on spending most of my evenings at the gym with Logan to make up for slacking last week. I didn't want to blow him off again, and I also wanted to take my physical health seriously.

Me: I actually am pretty busy in the evenings. What about next week? How long are you gone?

Josh: I should have known you're still popular, are you doing anything in the evenings that I can help you with?

Me: If you don't mind going to a stinky gym and exercising with me, sure.

Josh: Send me the details.

I held my feminine giggle in and rattled off the address to my gym, along with the times Logan and I would be there. I couldn't picture high school Josh lifting weights with me, but I also couldn't picture punk rock Josh lifting with me either. Though, I did notice in the limited time we spent together backstage, that his arms were more toned as an adult than they were when he was a teenager. I wondered if adult Josh tolerated physical exercise better than teen Josh.

Would I ever see Josh and see the two versions of him in one? Or would I always separate him into his past self and current self? Was he doing the same for me? Did he think about me as much as I had thought about him ever since the concert?

When the movie was over, the gang lingered in the living room, casually chatting about work tomorrow in hushed voices since Susan had gone to bed already, even though she always took her hearing aids out to sleep. The cannabis I had taken during the movie had finally kicked in and I was craving a yummy snack, so I set about roasting s'mores over the stove while lost in thought about the punk star.

My phone buzzed in my pocket, and I grinned ear to ear to see that he had texted me again. This time it was a couple pictures of the two of us in high school. His shaggy brown hair was just as I remembered it, and one boney arm wrapped around my shoulders while I held him tight around his waist with both of mine. Another picture showed me open-mouth laughing as he poured a bag of popcorn into his own mouth, obviously spilling half of the contents on his stomach as we lounged on his living room couch.

I wondered if his parents remembered me at all.

I heart-reacted to the picture, saving them both to my phone immediately. I thought about switching his contact image to the one of us as kids but found myself staring longingly at the image we had taken backstage before saying goodbye.

Usually, bleached hair looked horrible, but he must have gotten it done by a professional salon because even though his brown roots were starting to show, it looked good. Because he was covered in tattoos (which were slowly becoming less punk to me and more scientific and nerdier the more I stared at them), he could pull off the oddly colored hair just fine. The more I stared at him with his colored hair, the more I was starting to settle this new image of him into my mind. It was less unnerving.

The picture of us in high school made it obvious how close we were back then, whereas the image of us as adults looked a tiny bit awkward. Like we weren't sure where we stood with each other. Which I guess was true. But if Josh was going to keep texting me and going out of his way to meet up, I was hoping that we would become just as close as we were in high school. If not closer.

Was this the universe giving me an opportunity to make a move with Josh?

Did I want to make a move with Josh as adults?

Or did I just want to check some unchecked box that I had been holding on to since high school?

I shook my head once because I was clearly getting ahead of myself.

I returned to the s'mores before I realized it was unusually quiet in the townhome, and I glanced over my shoulder to see that my friends were all staring at me from their spots in the living room; Beck with her arms dangling over the back of the couch, and Eloise resting her chin in her hands with her elbows on the back of the couch. Taylor was standing over the coffee table finishing off the rest of the cheese and crackers.

"What are you thinking about?" Beck asked, wiggling her eyebrows at me with a smirk.

I let out a dramatic sigh as I threw my head back to stare at the ceiling, "My hot childhood friend." I never felt the need to hide my thoughts from them.

"What about your hot childhood friend?" Taylor pressed around a mouthful of food.

"Just..." I shrugged as I plated the s'mores and brought them over to everyone, "Daydreaming about things that could happen in the future. I don't know. He sent me these photos of us just now." I pulled the photos up on my phone and tossed it to Beck, before sitting down in between her and Eloise on the couch.

Beck eyeballed the pictures greedily and smiled before holding the phone to her chest. "These are so cute. Oh my god." She passed the phone to Taylor who passed it to Eloise, who finally gave it back to me.

"Question," Eloise said, before taking the most delicate bite of a s'more I had ever seen, "If he made a move on you, like, tried to kiss you, would you kiss him back?"

"I wouldn't even question it." I smiled. It was true. I was dying for him to make a move on me in high school. He never did. He obliged when I made a somewhat subtle move on him the one time we kissed in his bedroom, but it clearly didn't mean the same thing to him as it did to me.

My phone buzzed in my hand again, but this time it was message from Adam. He was probably spending his night alone looking up new recipes to cook and was sending me the best ones—we'd been bonding over learning new meals and trying them out on our friends.

Except it wasn't a recipe.

I opened his message and was surprised to see just a couple of links to news articles.

Links to news articles that had *my* face on them.

Specifically, my face that was gawking at Josh for grabbing my wrist so quickly at the concert. Because the images were from the concert we had been to a few days ago. I silently walked around the yellow couch and plopped down right between Eloise and Beck, opening the articles, and reading what they had to say.

I didn't read it thoroughly, because they weren't long articles and it was easy to get the gist of what they were gossiping about.

Josh and me.

Dating? Not dating? Secret lovers? The articles had no idea, but they had no problem theorizing. They even had my name, *Courtney Henderson of Lake Forest, California*. It was only two articles, but that was still two more news articles that had been written about me than before the concert.

"Whoa." Eloise's eyes got large as she peeked over my shoulder to read my phone, just as Beck had been doing.

"What?" Taylor asked, taking over Susan's seat in one of the ugly accent chairs.

"Courtney is on Hollywood's radar," Beck explained, taking the phone from my hand, and scrolling to the next link Adam sent. "Like, these are gossip articles about Courtney and Josh. With pictures of them from the concert." Beck scrolled for a few more moments then tossed my phone to Taylor, who caught it with one hand as they plopped one last cheese cube into their mouth before investigating themself.

I didn't know what to say.

All that my brain kept thinking was, *this is weird.*

"Ooo, I bet there are some jealous ladies reading this," Taylor's blue eyes narrowed as they scrolled to the bottom of the gossip articles to the comment section, "Huh. Only a few jealous ladies...but they can all suck a fart."

I smiled at their words before catching my phone that they tossed back to me.

"Guys, this is super weird," I finally spoke, "I'm not sure

how I feel about random people I've never met knowing my name and city."

"...Do you have your privacy settings on your social medias on?" Taylor asked.

"Huh? Yes. No? I don't think so. Why? Should I?" I quickly pulled up my social media apps to check.

"Well, if you didn't have them on in the past, it's probably because you don't actually care if strangers know your name and location. However, I would make your accounts private now." As soon as Taylor spoke the words, I saw the video clips that Beck posted on her socials (all the ones Adam recorded except the backstage one) and they had over a million views. I made a choked sound and Eloise and Beck leaned over my shoulders to see what I was reading, while I sat there silently gawking at all the comments.

CarbonCutMeOpen: Lucky bitch.

BreedRead69: It's always, 'you up?' And never, 'possessively grabbing my wrist and making prolonged eye contact in a stadium filled with thousands of people.'

Aeum17: Why is this so fucking hot?

Bookslug09: I would simply pass away if I was her.

ASLindsey: Guys. She spontaneously signed the entire concert for everyone. We need to protect her at all costs.

CarbonCutFansOnly: How the fuck does she get to hop on stage and not immediately get kicked out of the concert?

> **MrsMadey69:** If they don't fall in love and get married and have musical signing babies, I will go feral!
>
> **JMadeyFan13:** What I wouldn't give to be in her shoes!
>
> **Yimn23:** Maroon 5 would never.
>
> **TunaMan69:** Reason #876,283,046 why Joshua Madey is the female gaze.
>
> **Ander77828:** Them, how many times have you watched this clip? Me, yes.

"Holy shit," Eloise chimed, making me blink and set my phone down, "They all love *and* hate you."

"This is so weird!" I rubbed my eyes, realizing how late it was getting and not knowing how to process this information. As Beck and Eloise spoke about the funnier comments on the list, I quickly went into my socials and made all my accounts private, rejecting message requests I had already started to receive from people I didn't know.

Yikes.

7

The next day I was walking out of work alone. Beck was going to spend the night at Adam's condo and Taylor had squeezed in a client last minute to accommodate a hectic father's schedule. That's when I had my very first run-in with reporters.

I didn't realize it was happening, because based on all the books I've read and all the movies I've watched, usually paparazzi travel in large mobs to ambush unsuspecting people aggressively and angrily.

That's not what happened to me, thank fuck.

Instead, I was walking through the parking lot intending to make my way to the bus stop, when I saw a young woman with a shoulder bag eyeballing me. She was short, had shoulder length black hair, and was gnawing on her lip to let me know she was debating on approaching me or not.

I stopped in my tracks and stared at her.

She stared at me, turned around as if she was going to run away, and then quickly turned back and started walking towards me intently, her lips in a determined line.

"Hey, is everything alright?" I asked, looking around to see if I could see any sort of person who may be causing problems for this woman.

"Courtney Henderson?" She asked, clearly struggling to gain confidence, and failing miserably. I was a couple inches taller than her, and I barely noticed the small device she pulled out of her pocket as she approached me.

"Um, yes?" I asked, adjusting my bag on my shoulder.

"I—I—Um—I'm here—because—fuck it, never mind." She quickly turned around and made it look like she was going to run off again, paused, mumbled to herself something I couldn't understand, and then turned back to me.

"Ma'am?" I asked, closing the distance between us, and resting a hand on her shoulder. "Is everything alright? Are you safe?" I asked, scanning the perimeter of the parking lot again. At this, she finally looked me in the eye. Her dark eyes widened as she stared at me for a moment before fumbling with the small device in her hands.

"Oh god, you're so nice!" She squeezed her eyes closed and pinched the bridge of her nose with her fingers as she took a deep, steadying breath, "I'm so sorry. My boss sent me here, and this feels so icky—I just—" She shook her head once as I interrupted her.

"Can I help you?" I asked, still not making any sense of what was happening.

"Yes! No. Ugh." She looked at the device in her hand, a recording device, then pocketed it, giving me an apologetic smile. She puffed her chest up as if to gather some sort of courage, "My boss sent me here to corner you, and to ask you about your relationship with Carbon Cut's Joshua Madey." I blinked at her, because for some reason I hadn't been expecting that at all. "But you're just minding your own business, and I know reporters are probably the last people you want to talk to right now—trust me, I get it! I wish I was assigned any other story! But I'm kind of starting at the bottom here, you know? I have to do the shit work to work my way up the ladder. I'd rather write about important issues, not bothering some woman trying to live her life."

I nodded, finally understanding that she was a reporter—just one that had the confidence of a skittish fawn, "I get it."

She stopped her rambling and blinked at me, "You do?"

"You're, like...paparazzi?" I asked, raising an eyebrow at her to clarify my understanding of the situation. She nodded and then looked down at our shoes, clearly embarrassed about the whole interaction thus far. I felt for the woman. She clearly had no desire to bother me, or 'corner' me like her boss instructed her to do. However, I also understood the need for grunt work to be done.

Plus, if there were people out there wanting to know more about me, wouldn't it be better if they heard from me, directly? Instead of some gossip article over-analyzing three minutes of a concert?

"Are you hungry?" I asked her, pulling my phone out to make sure that I remembered directions to the nearest Thai place correctly. She looked up at me, nervous suspicion clear on her face.

"Um, why?"

"I'm hungry, and I was originally going to go home and reheat leftovers, but I figured this was a good opportunity to treat ourselves to a decent meal. Do you have a company credit card?" The woman silently shook her head no. "Damn, it was worth checking, anyway. Guess we will just have to pay for ourselves. Do you like Thai?"

She nodded her head at me, "You want to get dinner together?"

"Sure, that way you can take your time asking me whatever questions you have, and I can use this as an excuse to indulge myself." I looped my arm through hers, careful not to bump her bag too much in case it had equipment in it. "I have never been harassed by paparazzi before. This is fun."

"Fun?" She asked, a giggle escaping her lips as I led her through the parking lot towards the Thai restaurant around the corner. "So, wait, I can interview you?"

"Sure thing." I smiled at her, and she smiled back. Her shoulders dropped significantly, clearly pleased that I wasn't offended or yelling at her for just trying to do her job, "I figured people will learn what they want about me one way or another, so you might be a good opportunity for me to make sure things are told correctly—or better—I can start spreading crazy rumors about myself and see which ones get around the fastest."

"Oh my god, you're amazing! Thank you *so* much, I really appreciate this!"

*∗∗

I was sitting at my desk at the end of the week (officially one week since the concert), bummed that Josh hadn't been able to make it down to go to the gym with Logan and me. I was trying not to throw myself a pity party by focusing on filling out reports for one of my clients, when my phone started buzzing on my desk with an incoming FaceTime call.

It was Josh.

The picture we took together backstage showed up as a thumbnail on my screen, and I took too long to stare at the image because the call ended before I answered. I cursed at myself and double checked to make sure my office door was closed before hitting the redial button, quickly checking my hair in the camera that showed my face until he picked up.

"There she is!" Josh greeted me as soon as he answered, making me blush.

"There he is!" I smiled back, setting my phone against my desktop organizer so I could save and click out of my report.

"Did I catch you at a bad time?" Josh asked, his brown eyes flitting around the screen as he studied where I was.

"I'm just finishing up some reports before I leave work. What's up?" I asked, turning in my chair to face him/my phone directly. I rested my elbows on my desk and placed my chin on top of my fists.

There must have been a brief delay, because Josh's image stared at me for a couple seconds before speaking up, "I'm assuming you've seen the article that you were interviewed for earlier this week?"

"Ah, yes. Honestly, Tammy is a homie. I'd let her interview me every dang day."

Josh chuckled, "She seems like one. Too bad she wouldn't go in on your prank and write those horrible things you suggested she use to 'spice up' the read." Josh closed his eyes, clearly holding in laughter.

"Ugh, yes. I will say that was disappointing. I was giving her gold to work with, and instead of selling the rumor she ratted me out. C'mon!" I rolled my eyes, even though I wasn't actually irritated that she didn't run with the prank. I remembered reading that part of her article, because she sent me a copy the same moment she sent it to her editor, who was going to publish it that day.

> *Throughout the dinner, Courtney kept suggesting that I use made up stories about her to "spice up" the article for my readers. Some of these rumors she suggested that I use were:*
>
> 1. *that she had a third butt cheek*
> 2. *an extended tailbone that made it look like she did, in fact, have a tail*
> 3. *a robotic eye that takes pictures and videos of intel for Mother Russia*
>
> *Though I was tempted, I decided to go against it, because a woman willing to make up silly rumors about herself for the sake of a new writer's career seemed spicy enough.*

It was probably a good call. I wasn't sure how I would feel ten years from now knowing there was an article out there in the world talking about my hypothetical third butt cheek.

It would have been hilarious in the moment, though.

"I am both surprised, and not surprised at all," Josh chuckled again, "It's like you haven't changed at all, Court."

"I'd like to think I've gotten hotter, at least." I winked at him, silently hating myself for being so flirtatious and forward. However, I was plenty forward with him as a teenager and he still never made a move on me. I figured he'd either realize that I think he's sexy as hell, or he would do what he did in high school and just ignore it.

"Alright, cut to the chase, Josh," I heard a familiar woman's voice before his phone turned and Ariel's—I mean Kate's—face showed up on the screen. "First of all, I applaud the way you handled your first run-in with reporters. It's really a wonderful article, and that woman clearly loves you for it."

"Thanks!" I smiled at her, trying to hide the fact that I was mildly embarrassed that I just hit on my childhood bestie in front of his coworker.

"The thing is, though," Kate was tapping away on her iPad with one hand as she took Josh's phone with the other, making me realize that he wasn't calling me to catch up as old friends, "The internet is losing their shit over the two of you."

"They're losing their shit over Courtney, actually," Josh chimed in from out of view.

"I'm not the celebrity here, J-shua," I reminded him. I heard him laugh at that as Kate ignored us and continued talking.

"I'll cut to the chase; I think that it would actually be beneficial for both parties if the two of you started dating."

My heart stopped.

I don't know what my facial expression showed, but whatever it was it made Kate laugh as Josh quickly took the phone from her. I got a view of his sharp jaw as he scolded his employee. "Whoa, are you serious? You didn't tell me that this was your idea!"

"Yeah, I know. I thought it would be fun to surprise you. And I was right. You're blushing." Kate's tone was flat and matter of fact because she clearly wasn't fazed by Josh's anxiety about the bomb that she just suggested to the both of us.

"Kate—" and that's all I got because the call immediately ended. I just sat there in my office, staring at my blank phone screen, processing what just happened.

Kate, who I was assuming was some type of band manager, just suggested that Josh and I date. We had spoken maybe a page's worth of words to each other in person. We hadn't spoken to each other in a decade before that. I hadn't really spoken to him since the concert where we'd exchanged numbers. I reiterated as much in the article that Tammy wrote.

"So," I asked, admiring how Courtney stuffed her face with spring rolls without worrying about me analyzing every movement, "Are you and Josh together? You looked fairly intimate on stage."

"That's because he remembered who I was before I remembered him," Courtney explained, after swallowing dramatically and drinking half of her Dr Pepper in one gulp. "Before that, we hadn't seen each other since high school. Small world, I guess."

Courtney must have had a wonderful poker face, because I genuinely couldn't tell if she was hiding something or if she was telling the truth. I had no reason to disbelieve her at this point, which made me a little disappointed.

Throughout the interview I had the realization hit me, that Joshua Madey would be lucky to be on the arm of someone like Courtney Henderson.

After a few moments, the phone started ringing again, this time from a different number that wasn't saved, and I answered the FaceTime call.

"Alright, now that Josh has his shock and awe out of his system," Kate started, setting the phone down on some large table that she and Josh were sitting at, "Let me fill you both in on a number of details that will, hopefully, make my proposal more logical."

"Logical?" I asked, still not entirely sure I was understanding.

"Court," Josh took Kate's phone and his sharp face filled the screen, and I saw myself staring at his silver eyebrow piercing, "You can say no to any of this at any time, I truly didn't know this was Kate's idea when she suggested I call you."

Wait, she suggested that he call me? He didn't want to call me, himself?

I kept my curious but impartial expression on my face as I felt my heart deflate. Not only did I openly hit on my childhood best friend, but he also wasn't even calling me because he wanted to catch up. His...manager? Agent? Told him to.

"What exactly would I be saying no to, though?" I asked,

finding my gaze lingering on Josh's lip piercing now, until Kate took her phone back from him.

I realized in that moment that I was dying to see him in person. Even though this happened to be a weird business meeting, I didn't get enough time face-to-face with him backstage. I wanted to memorize this new version of Josh. Adult Josh. Most likely sexually experienced, Josh.

"Here's the thing, Courtney: Josh needs to date," Kate started, as if she was making a sales pitch and not talking about romantic relationships. "He has absolutely zero dating history since Carbon Cut's first album was released three years ago, and it would be beneficial for our brand if fans saw him dating."

"...Oh..." This was the absolute weirdest FaceTime call I had ever been on, and I had listened in on a number of FaceTime calls between Beck and her parents who were in a literal religious cult.

"Does this make a little more sense, now?" Kate asked, raising an eyebrow at me. I sucked my lips in between my teeth as I shook my head in the negative.

"I'm sorry, so this is like a...business deal? Like a dating contract situation?" I blinked as Josh laughed on the side of the phone, while Kate just smiled at me.

"Whether or not you and Josh actually date doesn't matter to me either way. I have some paperwork that you'll need to sign, but what you do beyond that is up to you. I'm just saying, based on the viral footage of the two of you at the concert, plus the interview that painted you in the best light possible, it would be beneficial for us to take the opportunity that the fans are shipping."

"People are shipping us?" Did my heart seriously just jump at the sound of that? Did people ship us back in high school, too? Nah, probably not.

"Um. Yes." Kate shook her head once as she looked down at her iPad, not willing to elaborate on that comment further, I guess, "Women love Josh. The internet keeps referring to him as the 'female gaze' but he has yet to be seen with a woman on his arm."

"Which is fine," Josh grumbled from the side of the phone.

"Of course, it's fine." Kate rolled her eyes. "Again, this is just a good opportunity. Being in the public eye for positive reasons is never a bad thing."

I blinked at her for a moment before rubbing the corners of my eyes and clearing my vision, "So, dating me is a positive thing for Josh? For the band?" I reiterated, still not sure I understood why.

"Yes, they're the 'woke' musical group. Josh and the guys are known for being rockstars that openly praise women for all the right reasons. They create rock music *for* women, music to empower them and make them feel like they can do anything they want to do and be anything they want to be. So it makes sense to have Josh be seen with a woman who is confident and kick-ass. It would help complete the image." Kate set her iPad down on whatever conference table they were sitting in front of and leaned into the screen so I could see her full face. "You and Josh have chemistry. The audience loved you two. Social media loves you two. You're an opportunity we should take, but only if you're willing."

I found myself frowning the slightest bit and picking at

my fingernails, then I quirked my lips to the side and thought about the reality of publicly dating Josh, and questions started to come to mind.

"So, what all does dating Josh entail?"

"Court…" Josh turned the phone screen so he took up the frame again, and I couldn't stop the smile that tugged at my lips at the sight of him. He really needed to recolor his hair, though. "…Please don't feel pressure to do this. Seriously, it's just a suggestion. You can say no."

"Do you want me to say no?" I asked, suddenly self-conscious, but I made the question come off as playful and challenging.

Josh stared at me for a moment, his brown eyes boring into mine through the phone screen, "No, I don't."

And just like that, my heart fluttered in my chest at the little spark of hope I suddenly felt. "Alrighty. Let's talk details," I rested my elbows on the table and interlaced my fingers, suddenly all business, "How many dates do I get? Because I'll be honest, I'm a stage five clinger. I think once a week would be doable if Josh's schedule allows for it."

"Excellent, glad to see you're on board." Kate took the phone back from Josh and started tapping away on her iPad again. "Once a week if they aren't jam packed with other events sounds good. Thankfully, they don't go on tour again for another six months or so. Most of their time will be spent stateside."

"Good to know," I smiled at the fake red-head, loving how weirdly professional she was about this. I sat a little taller in my chair and tried to channel some of her vibe. "Let's talk gifts."

"Gifts?" Kate asked.

"Yes. Gifts. Treats. Special things you get partners you're romantically involved with. Josh might not remember this from high school, but I'm not exactly a flowers kind of girl. Instead, I'm more of a—"

"Foodie. You liked savory snacks, like popcorn," Josh spoke up from off camera, making Kate turn to give him a proud smile, "Any kind. Whether it's specialty flavors, or a bulk box from Costco. But popcorn is Courtney's preferred gift. Right?"

Kate lifted an eyebrow at me, waiting for me to confirm, "Yes, he's right." I gave Kate a thumbs up as she smirked at me, writing that down.

"And, if I'm remembering correctly, Josh likes milk duds and cheesecakes."

"It's like time never passed," Josh laughed from off camera. I both agreed and disagreed with him. Sure, memories came flooding back the more we chatted, but I still felt like I didn't know him at all. My body, however, had high desires to get to know his, and I started to feel a little guilty about those feelings.

I only saw glimpses of Josh the rest of the call, which lasted about an hour. Thank goodness nobody came into my office to check on me or ask questions about clients, because I was so absorbed with every word in that meeting that I definitely would have jumped and yelped, just like Beck so often did whenever anybody snuck up on her.

At the end of the call, I sat back in my chair and stretched my back out, staring up at the ceiling as I contemplated what I had just agreed to. An email came through on my phone, letting me know that Kate had already sent over the documents that I needed to sign to make this dating contract official. I tapped open the email and signed them all digitally, without hesitation, because the more I thought about what I had just agreed to, the pieces of an idea started to form in my mind.

8

"It's the fake dating trope!" I announced to our friends in the living room later that evening. We had just finished watching *Sense and Sensibility*, since we learned that Eloise had never seen the film adaptations of the famous Jane Austen books the last time we were all together. Beck had asked me if I had heard anything new from Josh, and I was so excited to tell her about the latest update with that part of my life, that I blurted out the main thing I had been thinking all day.

"The...what?" Taylor asked, crossing their ankles on the edge of the coffee table. Beck turned to give them a disbelieving look.

"T, read a book." She scolded.

"Beck, go outside."

"No."

"Explain what you just said, I'm so confused," Eloise interrupted the two.

"Josh and me. We're officially the fake dating trope," I explained as I tossed a kernel of popcorn into the air to catch it with my mouth. I was reclined on the opposite side of the couch as Taylor, with Beck squeezed into the middle. Eloise was sitting in one of the hideodorous accent chairs.

"Oh my god, are you serious?" Beck's eyes widened as she twisted in her seat to face me directly, giving Taylor her back. Taylor grunted in annoyance and adjusted in their seat to look around Beck's body to me.

"I'm not kidding at all; I can show you the contract I signed and everything." I actually couldn't. Technically, I was supposed to keep this under wraps, because we were supposed to be a convincing couple. Having word get out that Josh and I were only going to date for publicity would negate the whole purpose of the stunt. However, I told Kate that I was absolutely going to tell my friends about it. She shrugged and said it was fine.

"How? What? Why?" Beck asked.

"Wait, trope? Like in literature?" Eloise asked, still stuck on the opener I gave everyone.

"Yup! Josh and I are going to fake date for six months. Long story short, the internet is shipping us because of the concert and article about me, and I guess he is the 'female gaze.' Kate, the band's social media manager, said that letting the world see how Josh is when he is in a romantic relationship with a woman while they're off tour would help the band."

"Help them how?" Taylor asked, their brow furrowing more and more with each sentence I said.

"With like, publicity? Engagement? I don't know, whatever fake social media points the band needs to stay relevant in the public eye. Honestly, I just got super excited about the thought of dating Josh once a week, fake or not."

"So…you're not actually going to date? You're just putting on a show?" Eloise clarified. "And you're excited about that?"

"Yup," I smiled at her confused expression and scrunched up freckled nose, "Because, to nobody's surprise, I like Josh. I loved him as a kid, and I'm super turned on by him as an adult. He's given no indication that he's changed enough as an adult for me to dislike him. So, maybe with enough fake dating, I can convince him to actually date me during these six months. And also sleep with me."

"Wait," Beck held her hands up, halting my explanation, "You *just* want to sleep with him?"

I paused.

Did I *just* want to sleep with him?

I wasn't against monogamous relationships. I had dabbled with going steady many times throughout my twenties, just not in the last year or so. I wanted permanent stability at some point in my life (e.g., white picket fence and two point five kids), so why wouldn't I want to give Josh a shot at being my boyfriend?

Was I just focusing on sleeping with him because I was afraid of being rejected by him again?

…It was very likely.

"No, I guess not," I quirked my lips to the side. "It's just…he wasn't interested in me back then. Sure, I've aged well, but he hasn't given me any hint that he's changed his mind in that area, you know?"

"Besides asking for your number," Taylor chimed in.

"And not being able to keep his hands off of you backstage," Beck added.

"And sending you cute pictures of the two of you from high school," Eloise finished.

"Sure, but I hit on him pretty directly at the beginning of the FaceTime call—before I realized Kate was there and it was more of a business proposal—and he didn't react at all."

"What did you say?" Eloise asked, adjusting her seat so she sat in the ugly accent chair sideways, swinging her feet off of one end.

"He said something about me not changing since high school, I responded with something stupid like, 'I hope I'm hotter at least' or something."

"Yikes." Taylor smiled at me, probably thrilled that I bombed something like that when I'm usually relatively smooth with people I am attracted to.

"Well, maybe he just didn't want to engage with Kate there?" Beck asked, gnawing on her top lip, Troll Face on display, as she thought about all the information I just told her about the lead singer of her favorite band.

"Maybe." I shrugged, shoving more popcorn into my mouth as I thought about it all too. "But I have decided that I'm using this fake dating trope as an opportunity, as one does with fake dating tropes."

"And what's that?" Taylor asked.

"If we get to know each other again and end up hitting it off like we did in the past, I'm going to try to convince him to make it real."

9

―――

Logan was such a fucking show-off and the fact that he didn't even realize it made the showing-off he was doing somehow worse.

I was spotting him, which was ridiculous when you thought about it. The reality was, if Logan's muscles gave out and he suddenly couldn't set the bar he was benching back on the rack, there was definitely no way I could help. He was benching close to what my full weight was. Soaking wet. After hitting up a buffet. And not exercising for a month.

As he laid back on the bench in front of me, with my hands hovering inches underneath the bar he was pushing away from himself, I saw many a gym bro eyeballing him in what was pure envy.

I mean, I was envious too. How kickass would it be if I could bench my own weight? My arms and shoulders would be shredded.

Logan released a sharp exhale as he racked the bar without my help whatsoever, sitting up and grabbing his sweat towel off the floor to wipe at his forehead and neck.

"Hot," I said, as I grabbed my sticker-clad water bottle and took a sip, as if I was the one who had been working hard.

Logan looked at me over his shoulder specifically so that I could see him roll his eyes dramatically at my compliment. I wasn't kidding. Even though he didn't rev my engine in any way, he was still a very attractive person.

I compared the size of his shoulders to my itty-bitty girly shoulders as I watched him bend down on the bench to grab his phone, swiping away the lock screen to check an email.

"Who is that?" I asked, just now realizing he had a picture of a girl on his screen. She looked a little young for him, so I was curious.

She was also blonde, like me.

In fact, we almost had the exact same shade of natural, blonde hair.

Logan's shoulders tensed the slightest bit at my question, taking a moment to finish reading his email as he locked the screen again and tossed the phone back into his open gym bag. He swung one massive leg over the bench so that he was facing me directly.

My sister, Logan signed. I lifted my eyebrows the slightest, because after months and months of working out together, I had no idea he had a sister. Was it normal for siblings to have pictures of each other on their lock screens? Again, she seemed like a teenager. Logan was, I assumed, closer to my age. Maybe in his early thirties even.

"Oh wow, she's so cute! Are you guys close?" I took another sip from my water bottle after my question, eyeballing his facial features to gauge his response.

We used to be, Logan signed back, finally lifting his dark eyes, and meeting mine directly. A challenge. He knew I was nosy, and he was fully prepared for whatever interrogation I was about to give him.

"Used to be? What happened?" I asked. As soon as the question left my mouth, I realized what the most horrible answer could possibly be, seconds before Logan confirmed.

She died when she was fifteen, Logan responded, eyes still on me. I froze with my water bottle in my hand. I tried so hard to make this revelation seem casual, but the reality is, it wasn't. Logan had just randomly told me that he had a dead sister, and all I wanted to do was wrap him up in my arms and console him, even though he had probably mourned for her plenty at this point.

But also, I wanted to take a moment to acknowledge the fact that he was actually talking to me about his personal life. He was a man of few words (obviously, due to his lack of speech), and was very closed off when we first started exercising together. This was a huge step for us, and I wanted to reward him for it without being a complete weirdo.

"I'm so sorry, that's horrible." I frowned at him, annoyed that he was clearly enjoying how his blunt revelation caught me off guard, based on the mischievous glint in his eyes, "Can I ask how she died? I know that's morbid, but my curiosity is killing me here."

Logan glanced down at his feet, resting his elbows on his knees as he thought about it before quickly signing, *car crash.*

"Ah." I nodded. I already apologized once, so I wasn't

quite sure what to do with that additional information I was weirdly curious about.

It was the same night that, Logan gestured vaguely towards his scarring, *this happened.*

Well. That was interesting information.

"You got all that because of a car crash?" I widened my eyes, shocked. I wasn't sure what could have caused so much damage to his skin, but for some reason a car accident didn't come to mind.

Logan nodded once, standing from his bench, and grabbing his bag. We were going to leave the bench for someone else to use while we wandered over to the black mats near the front to stretch.

"Oh my god, this is *so* interesting! Another Logan layer peeled back," I quickly scooped my own gym bag into my arms and followed him, his large legs always walking at a pace faster than mine. "What happened? Did the car roll or something?"

Logan paused in his steps to look at me briefly before pulling his phone out of his bag to thumb away on it.

Well then, it looked like the conversation was over.

I wasn't surprised, it took a lot for Logan to open up to me. No idea why, since he knew every single detail about my life at this point—including my run-in with my old best friend at the concert, who went from the cute-boy-next-door that I remembered to tattooed-talented-sexy-celebrity. As well as the weird internet fame that I was trying my best to ignore even though it felt impossible now, due to our real-life fake dating trope.

Logan's eyes glazed over as soon as I started explaining fake dating tropes to him, but I appreciated how he attempted to act like he was paying attention to how pivotal this was going to be in whatever film adaptation that would obviously be made about Josh and me down the road.

I clearly had big hopes for this whole situation.

My phone buzzed in my bag, and I raised an eyebrow at Logan who wouldn't meet my gaze as he found a suitable spot for us to stop and stretch. I pulled my phone out to see a text from him, containing a link to an old article from a local paper in Anaheim.

> DRUNK DRIVING RESULTS IN FATAL CAR CRASH, LEAVING 3 TEENS DEAD AND 1 IN CRITICAL CONDITION.

I gasped, clapping my hand over my mouth, looking down at Logan as he sat on the mats and started stretching his back out. He gave me a small smirk that on the outside told me he was enjoying my shock and awe, but on the inside, he was feeling nervous about sharing this information with me. I scrolled through the article, gasping again when I stopped on a few pictures of the accident that I had to click on to remove the graphic image warning.

One showed a body bag being loaded up in an ambulance, and I thought I was going to cry.

How the fuck is Logan just casually sharing this trauma with me today?

"Oh my god—oh my *god!*" I scrolled to one other picture, chilling.

It was Logan, but a younger version of him. I would guess late teens based on how young his unconscious face looked.

Unconscious, because he was tangled up in a chain-link fence.

It was horrible, but I also couldn't stop myself from looking at every detail.

He had obviously been ejected from the car, a few feet in front of him, after it ran head on into a pole.

"Logan!" I was so frustrated with him as he just casually shrugged at me, "Oh my god, what happened? How are you alive right now?" My question must have hit a nerve because he frowned and shrugged a little more aggressively this time.

I was a miracle, according to the surgeons who operated on me, Logan signed, rolling his eyes a little at his own words. I glanced at the picture as I finally took my seat next to Logan on the mats, zooming in on the gory image of broken chain-link fence being embedded into his torso and throat. If I wasn't sitting next to Logan right now, I would have assumed I was looking at a kid who clearly died by being skewered by a shitty fence.

"Logan," I glanced up to see that he was looking a little vulnerable, so I leaned into him, "Oh, my sweet, bulky, gym buddy. I'm *so* sorry that you experienced that!" I threw my arms around his shoulders dramatically as he quickly tried to palm my face to remove my body from his. He wasn't big on physical touch like my friends and I were.

Stop it, Logan signed, trying to look annoyed but completely failing. *It's fine. I'm over it.*

"Clearly." I rolled my eyes at him then eyeballed the scarring again. "So, this is why you can't speak?"

Logan raised a large hand to gently rub at the pink flesh on his neck, staring at his feet stretched out in front of him for a moment before signing without meeting my eyes, *I can speak. But it hurts. A lot. And my voice sounds scary and rough, so I decided soon after recovery that I would rather just...not speak.*

"And you learned ASL instead?" I pressed.

Logan nodded once, *I never spoke a lot with a perfect voice box anyway, so I figured this was a good opportunity to avoid unwanted social interactions.*

I dropped my jaw open, shocked.

Tell me you're introverted, I thought, *without telling me you're introverted.*

Anyway, Logan signed, clearly done having the spotlight on him, *are you going to meet up with your rock star soon?*

"Yes, actually, we are all getting together at the townhome to hang out and do a test run of pretending we're a couple in front of other people. Except everyone there will know we're faking it, so they can give us feedback on how we're doing and where to improve. It's going to be super chill. You should come!"

Logan furrowed his dark brows and continued his stretches without a response. I had been inviting Logan to hang out with all of us for a while, and he had always come up with an excuse not to come. Well, that's not true. Sometimes he didn't fake an excuse and just said that he wasn't going to come.

"C'mon! If you're really my friend, you'll come and do your part by suggesting that Josh and I try kissing. Frequently, to make sure that Josh and I get it *just* right. Preferably with tongue. Plus, half of the group signs to some degree, so you won't be stuck in a corner all by yourself—"

"Fancy meeting you here!" I heard Eloise's chipper voice from behind me. I turned around and saw the gorgeous blonde leaning on one hip as she smiled down on us, a gym bag slung over her shoulder. She was wearing turquoise yoga pants with a matching sports bra. Her cropped blonde hair was tucked behind a matching headband, and she was not wearing any makeup but she still looked more like a *Sports Illustrated* model instead of a woman who wanted to exercise.

"Hey!" I greeted as I turned around to continue a back stretch on the other side, "What are you doing here?"

"Straight up? I stalked you," Eloise shrugged, her bright blue eyes flicking over to the introverted man next to me. "I am so tired of going to my mother's yoga class, and this is a small way I can rebel." She plopped her bag down right in front of us and sat cross-legged, looking over at Logan again.

"Hi, I'm Eloise!" she held her hand out, her perfect friendly smile on display. I remembered when Beck told me that she thought butterflies would fly right out of Eloise's ass the first time they met, and held in a giggle. Her analysis made perfect sense. I wondered what Logan's first impression of her would be. Eloise was always perfectly polite, friendly, and upbeat—

partly due to her parents programming her to be agreeable, and partly because she liked to be liked.

Logan nodded once at Eloise, not taking her hand, and continuing to stretch his legs out.

Ugh. Men.

Eloise deflated a little, her smile slipping for a second before pulling her hand back and giving me a nervous look.

"This is Logan," I pointed at the Neanderthal next to me with my thumb, "He's allergic to socializing."

At that, Logan gave me an irritated glare. One that I laughed at, because he was just mad that I was right.

"Nice to meet you, Logan." Eloise smiled at him again. As Logan turned to reach into his gym bag, she noticed the scarring on his neck. I noticed this because her face fell the slightest bit, and I could see her eyes dancing around as she took in his face, neck, and his chest where his shirt hid the rest of the scars.

Scars that I now knew the origin of. What a weird day.

"Oh! You're the guy that Court bullied into working out with her, the one who can't speak!" Eloise grinned a little as she brushed her hair behind her ear, cheeks turning the lightest shade of pink as she kept flicking her glance over to him.

Interesting.

At Eloise's assessment, Logan paused his stretching to lean back on his palms and finally look at Eloise head on. His dark eyes did the quickest scan of her body that I had ever seen, I would have missed it if I blinked. Then he met her gaze, making her cheeks flush even more as he stared at her intently in the silence. I kept looking back and forth between the two as I realized what was happening.

Eloise thought Logan was attractive. Because he was.

Logan hated meeting new people and was trying to scare her off with his tried-and-true silent intimidation.

Eloise was a deer caught in the headlights, clearly not intimidated in the way Logan wanted.

I wished I had some popcorn right now.

Part of me was wondering if I was this obvious when I reconnected with Josh backstage at the concert.

Probably.

"Anyways," I pulled one arm across my chest to stretch my shoulders, as if we all hadn't just sat in silence for the past fifteen seconds, "I'm trying to convince Logan to come hang out with everybody this weekend. I want Josh to meet *every-one*." I lifted an eyebrow at him meaningfully, making him pull his attention away from Eloise long enough to give me an annoyed look.

Did these two have chemistry? I thought, *would I ship these two together?*

"Oh! Yes, you should definitely come!" Eloise nodded once, looking back at me for half a second before turning her full attention towards Logan. "Beck and Susan are so chill, and their home is the coziest I have ever been in. Plus, Courtney clearly wants buffers so she doesn't jump Josh Madey's bones first thing." Eloise finished her persuasion with a wink in my direction.

That's stupid, Logan signed, finally setting his dark eyes on me, *if you want to hook up with him, just hook up with him. I guarantee that he wants to hook up with you.*

"Logan," I gasped, lightly hitting his bicep, "I never hook

up on the first...group gathering?" I laughed, knowing this wasn't an official date and feeling a little embarrassed at Eloise's accurate interpretation of my feelings.

"Is that what Logan said you should do?" Eloise asked, reminding me that she only knew a handful of signs specifically related to babies and their needs, due to her working at the clinic now.

Princess doesn't sign? Logan asked me before I could answer her question.

"No," I lowered my brows at Logan. I was not completely surprised that he seemed this irritated with Eloise simply because of her presence, but I refused to excuse it. "She's a beginner. Just like you were when you first fucked up your vocal cords."

Logan blinked at me, startled.

Eloise's calm façade broke, a small moment of hurt eclipsing her features as she finally picked up on Logan's prickly vibes towards her.

"I'm still learning ASL," Eloise chimed in, wanting to de-escalate the irritation between me and my gym buddy. "But I'm a quick learner, you know what they say! Practice makes perfect. Maybe you could help me out by teaching me some more signs this weekend?" she said, throwing the grump a bone.

How the fuck would I do that? Logan signed back to Eloise, knowing full well she couldn't understand him, *who do I look like, your personal ASL teacher?*

"Logan." My warning was low and firm, and based on both of their reactions towards me I realized that neither of my friends had heard me use my authoritative voice on them before, "What is your problem?"

Logan's dark brow raised the slightest bit and he nervously started rubbing his shoulder, stretching one large bicep across his chest. Eloise didn't understand what he said, but she picked up on the energy of it just fine.

"It's okay," Eloise looked back at me but then down at her crossed feet, not wanting me to read her so well again, "Actually, I just remembered that I have to go." Suddenly she reached for her bag and started to stand up.

"What? Where?" I asked, knowing full well that Eloise was perfectly organized and forgot literally nothing. I vaguely registered Logan's face tilted towards her direction as Eloise got ready to book it.

"I have a thing. An appointment. With my therapist." Eloise squeezed her eyes shut, knowing that I wasn't buying her lie.

"You forgot about an appointment with your therapist?" I clarified. Eloise reopened her eyes to look at me, intently ignoring him.

"Yup. You know me. Super forgetful. Probably why I need to stay in therapy," Eloise squeezed her eyes shut again before rubbing her forehead in obvious embarrassment, "Anyways. Sorry to crash your guys' thing. Bye."

"Lo!" I called after her, but she turned on her heel and walked as fast as she could until she was outside of the gym. I saw her form retreat through the glass doors until she was out of sight, before turning towards my friend and punching him hard in the arm.

The asshole barely flinched, instead he just stared at the ground as one hand came up to gently rub his bicep that I hit.

"God you're the worst," I grumbled, turning to grab my own gym bag.

She doesn't know what I said, Logan signed to me as he watched me stow my water bottle and phone away with, what I was shocked to see was a worried look.

"You're not that incompetent," I rolled my eyes before glaring at him. "Actions speak louder than words, Logan. Your body language said enough, and so did my reaction to your words. Eloise is fragile, and you've successfully made her run away in tears."

She wasn't crying, Logan challenged, picking up his bag and following me out of the gym.

"Why do you think she ran so fast, Logan? She didn't want us to see her cry. God, why are men such insensitive, emotionally numb children?" I grumbled as I kicked the door open to the gym. As soon as we stepped outside, we saw Eloise's shiny Lexus driving past us on her way to exit the parking lot, wiping away at her cheeks without noticing us. When her car disappeared around the corner, I stopped and turned to Logan pointedly, who had clearly seen the same thing I did.

His shoulders deflated a little before his face hardened again, *It's not my fault that—*

I cut him off.

"Nope. It's your fault. She was perfectly polite to you and *you* were the asshole, no matter what you tell yourself to help you sleep tonight," I started marching towards Susan's old

Honda Accord before turning around after a few moments and yelling at him, "And you're coming this weekend!"

Logan was looking after me, his expression worried, until he heard my demand. Then his lips just flattened into a line.

"Don't argue with me!" I challenged, "You're coming this weekend and you're apologizing to that sweet girl. You're also going to be there for me while I fangirl over my childhood crush, because that's what friends do, Logan! I'll pick you up and drag you there myself if I have to!" I left him to stare angrily at my back as I finally made it to Susan's car, opening and slamming the door shut behind me for dramatic effect as I checked my phone and plugged in the aux cord.

J-Shua: Is Susan a wine drinker? Or is she more of a tea drinker? Is tea a normal house guest gift?

J-Shua: Should I just bring her a houseplant instead?

J-Shua: I just passed this bouquet of flowers that reminded me of the one your mom's boyfriend gave her during Spring Break. What did you call the color scheme? "Hideodorous"?

I smiled at my phone, my heart picking up at the random series of text messages from this sweet man. It was comforting to know that these parts of Josh's personality had lasted through the years, because I would have been so, so sad to know that college and adulthood hardened J-shua in any way.

Me: Susan would love a houseplant, even when she tells you that you 'didn't have to.'

J-Shua: Thank fuck because that's the option I went with when you didn't respond right away.

Me: Sorry, I was at the gym yelling at Logan for being an ass.

J-Shua: Whoa. Sounds serious. Want me to beat him up for you?

J-Shua: Is it insensitive for me to beat up a man with no vocalization?

I laughed out loud in my car. Josh had texted me last week apologizing for not being able to come to the gym with me, because of something along the lines of last-minute rewrites for the album they were working on.

I told him that it was fine, and that he would have to meet Logan another time.

He immediately asked me who Logan was, making me a little giddy at the thought of Josh being potentially jealous of another man in my life. Then I remembered that I was supposed to be fake dating him and doubted that he was worried about any romance between Logan and me. I sent him a picture of Logan anyway, though, knowing that Logan was obviously attractive and feeling a little petty in the moment. I wanted to see if I could spark any jealousy from Josh. I didn't.

I then explained that Logan was my ASL buddy at the gym because he didn't speak. Josh was immediately interested in his back story, even though I didn't have it at the time. I made a mental note to get Logan's permission before I told everyone about his car accident.

Me: I'm already punishing him by making him come over this weekend to finally meet everyone. No need to assault him.

J-Shua: You're cruel! That's an introvert's worst nightmare.

J-Shua: He would probably prefer it if I just beat him up.

Probably. I pictured someone as lean as Josh trying to actually get the upper hand on someone the size of Logan. It was best to avoid that if at all possible. Josh's pierced face was too pretty to risk.

Me: Maybe. But I wouldn't.

J-Shua: Then say no more. I can't wait to see you again, Court.

My heart fluttered in my chest. It wasn't out of the realm of our past friendship to say something like that, but I had to be honest with myself. Part of me truly hoped that Josh and I would become something more than friends. The attraction I've felt growing for him over the FaceTime calls and random text messages was something I needed to address—but only if he was giving me signals that the attraction was reciprocated. The fact that he was willing to leave his cozy lifestyle in Hollywood to venture down to my little townhome to "hang out" said a lot.

I texted Josh goodbye before buckling my seatbelt and pulling out of the parking spot. As I exited the lot, I saw Logan sitting in his black truck, with the vehicle running but not moving from its spot. Both of his large hands were on the steering wheel as he gazed directly at the gym building, clearly deep in thought.

10

"What is a tasteful amount of cleavage?"

"How are *you* the one asking *me* this?" Beck responded, laying in her bed texting her boyfriend without glancing at me. I turned away from the mirror that I was standing in front of and eyeballed my best friend. Half of her time and energy was spent with Adam now. Half the time she spent the night at his condo. Half of the time we were together, she was also texting him. It's escalated lately, which was odd because usually once the honeymoon phase was over, people cooled off and they weren't as obsessed with each other, but that hadn't been the case with these two.

Sure, Beck and I still hung out all the time. We lived together, after all. But she was clearly being pulled in two different directions. One being me and her grandmother, the other the love of her life. It would be weird if they didn't discuss things like moving in together soon.

That realization was when I felt myself panic for the first time.

This house was officially the longest place I had ever lived, and now Beck was probably texting Adam about the logistics of living together. Would he move in here? Would I need to move out to make room for them? Four people in the townhome just seemed like too much. Was Beck out growing me? She deserved lifelong happiness, and it was clear that Adam was able to provide that for her in a way that her best friend simply couldn't.

I was both excited for her, and anxious for myself.

Fuck, I should probably talk to my therapist soon.

The lights in the room began flickering on and off. It was a cool system that was installed for Susan and Beck, the two hard of hearing women in the household, since they couldn't always hear the sound of someone knocking on the door, or an actual doorbell. We both looked at each other in silence for a moment before Beck bolted off of the bed and raced out of her bedroom.

"Fuck!" I cried, forgetting to double check my hair and makeup in the mirror one last time as I rushed to follow her. But, let's face it, I looked fantastic.

Eloise and Taylor had already shown up and were chatting with Susan in the living room when Beck and I raced each other down the stairs, all of them looking up at us with alarm at the sudden intrusion.

"Beck! Wait!" I shouted at the deaf brunette, grabbing her arm at the bottom of the stairs, and wrestling her back so that I could get in front of her. For a woman who loathed the idea of physical exertion, she was unusually strong as she fought to beat me to the door.

"I got this!" Beck cried, laughing as I jumped onto her back and wrapped my arms around her neck. She managed to make it to the door and yanked it open with a loud groan as I clung to her back, only for both of us to stop fighting each other at the underwhelming sight of Logan at the doorstep.

Not that Logan was an underwhelming person. In fact, he was large enough to take up a good chunk of the front door frame, generally creating an almost overwhelming presence. He just wasn't a member of the most popular pop punk band in the country. Our disappointment was justified.

"Hey! Come on in!" I immediately hopped off of Beck's back and righted myself as Logan's dark brows furrowed at the sight of us, clearly confused but not willing to communicate more than a slight head nod. I reached around Beck to grab Logan's wrist, feeling his fight or flight response kicking in at the abrupt answering of the door, and pulled him into the entryway. I noticed that he was carrying a box of White Claws, one that Beck immediately took from his hands as she ran to the kitchen with it. I looped my arm through his and introduced him to everyone in the living room.

"Everyone! This is Logan!" I smiled. Susan stood up from her spot and shuffled over to greet him, at the same time Taylor waved, and Eloise wiggled her fingers before looking down at her phone.

Oh, right.

Things with Logan and Eloise were probably going to be super weird. I made a mental note to analyze everything between the two of them tonight.

"Courtney tells me that you're helping her with strength training?" Susan asked Logan, taking his other arm, and tugging him to a seat in the living room. Logan looked over his shoulder at me as the elderly woman led him away, unease in his expression.

Deep breath, you got this, I signed to the anxious man.

Logan's expression didn't change as he turned towards Susan and signed to her, thankfully remembering that she and Beck were the most fluent in ASL in the room.

The lights flickered again, and I raced to the door again only to be disappointed to see Adam standing at the doorway. I shooed him inside as I took one last scan of the street, happy to see a large black Suburban pulling into the driveway behind Adam's Tesla.

Oh god, it's him.

I guess *them* was a more accurate term, since the entirety of the band and Kate all emerged from the Suburban to take in Susan's cute little townhome that they were parked in front of. As cool as the other band members were, I found myself holding my breath until Josh appeared. He was the last one to emerge from the vehicle. The other band members waved hellos to me as they made their way up the driveway, but I couldn't tell you what I said in response to them as I waited for my childhood crush to get out of the car and notice me.

The first thing I noticed was that he had colored his hair, concealing his dark roots with the blonde color he was into at the moment.

The second thing I noticed was that he was wearing his black glasses, the ones that helped me remember who he was backstage the last time that we were face-to-face. I smiled brightly at him, feeling my cheeks pulling as far as they could go as soon as his grin hit me, his lip ring glistening in the California sunlight.

The third thing I noticed was how his dark eyes scanned my body behind his glasses. If I wasn't looking for that movement specifically, I might not have noticed it behind his frames, but I was dying for him to view me as something more than a good friend, so I was naturally analyzing every movement this afternoon.

Per my instructions, Josh and the band dressed casually. Because we were a casual group of people. Everyone wore different types of jeans, and Josh was in a plain white t-shirt that hugged his lean form in his chest and arms. Even though he wasn't as beefy as Logan or Adam, the fit still complimented his toned body. I found myself bouncing on my heels, standing on the front porch as he shoved his hands in his jeans pockets and made his way to greet me. He stood two steps below the porch, which made us eye level.

"Court."

"J-shua."

He smiled at me, making my heart soar just as his smiles did back in high school. Every second I stood in his presence made my body remember just how much I missed the thrill of being near him.

"Are you going to invite me in?" Josh asked, tugging on his lip ring with his teeth. A movement that made me think that maybe it was his new nervous habit.

I wanted to tug on that lip ring with my teeth.

Good god, get a grip, Court.

I forced my gaze away from his lips and made eye contact

with him as I opened my arms wide, demanding my bear hug from him just like I used to. Back in high school, I would demand bear hugs from Josh as payment when he wanted something. I had a specific memory of stealing his strawberry milkshake, taking a huge sip, and opening my arms wide as I demanded a bear hug in exchange for his shake back.

High school Josh would roll his dark eyes before complying and wrapping me in a firm hug that I felt deep in my soul.

Adult, rock star Josh had gained some confidence. His dark gaze clearly made a quick glance at my cleavage (just like I was hoping it would) before he smirked at me and wrapped me up with his arms.

This booby-sundress was a good call on my part.

I enjoyed a moment snuggled in his arms, soaking in the feel of our warm bodies pressed against each other, before he quickly released me and took a step back, nodding towards the direction of the townhome.

He made his way ahead of me, and I had to fight not to frown at how short that hug lasted.

Baby steps, Court.

Inside, everyone was greeting each other.

Beck was beaming, handing out the White Claws that Logan brought to everyone.

Susan was sitting next to Logan on the couch, smiling at all the new people in her home.

Taylor was standing and fist bumping Kyle and Tom (Beck had made sure I knew the names of the drummer and bassist, considering they would be coming to my house, and she would die of humiliation if I didn't remember something as simple as their first names).

Adam was shaking the hands of Kate and Garrett, who had his index finger through the loop of her jeans as she smiled politely and clutched her iPad to her chest.

Eloise was sitting in an ugly accent chair, eyes wide at all the celebrities in the room.

Logan was staring at Eloise, a small pinch in his brow as his lips turned downward the slightest bit.

I snapped my fingers once to catch his eye, lifting my hands to sign, *Apologize to Eloise.*

Logan nodded once, letting me know that he knew what was expected of him today. While Josh's tall back was turned to me as he joined his band mates, I made sure to remind Logan of the other item on his to-do list: *Also, help me show Josh that I am a sexually available woman—not just his friend from high school. And that dating me would be great.*

Logan smirked a little as he eyeballed the lead singer quickly before lifting one large hand and giving me a thumbs up with a shrug of his shoulders that said, *I'll try.* Even though he clearly had no idea how to do that. Susan had seen that last sentence I signed to him and nodded her confirmation at me with a sneaky smile of her own.

I heard Beck snort her laughter as I turned to see that she also saw the last item of Logan's to-do list and saluted me with her support. I signed *thank you* to everyone just as Josh turned around to look at me.

"Are you signing behind my back?" Josh asked, raising his pierced eyebrow.

"Yes." I smiled, walking up to him, and patting his arm. We were always touchy in high school. Touch was one of my love languages. Anyone who was good friends with me knew this, so Josh knew this. We were always touching or hugging or cuddling (platonically, to my chagrin) in high school. Now, I needed to carefully incorporate a few more intentional touches that would maybe convince him to see me in the light that I was hoping for. It would be tricky though, balancing the line between our fake dating arrangement and being blunt enough for him to know that I was thinking outside of our fake dating arrangement.

"I was telling everyone to paint me in the best light possible." Josh's expression became puzzled as I winked at him and walked past him, giving him ample opportunity to admire the low cut in the back of my sundress that also made my ass look perfectly grabbable, "I want to be the best fake girlfriend you've ever had."

"Yeah, because you have a lot of previous fake girlfriends to show up," Josh teased, the sound of his footsteps letting me know that he was following me. I led everyone towards the kitchen, where I had prepared a number of appetizers with Adam earlier in the day before he went back to his condo to shower and change for tonight.

"Alright, first things first, everyone needs to sign NDAs," Kate announced, producing a stack of papers from her shoulder bag, and setting them on the kitchen counter, "If any of you tell anyone outside of this room about the arrangement between Josh and Courtney, it's—what did Court call it? A no-no."

"Literally the only people I talk to are in this room right

now," Beck chimed in, wiggling between the many bodies in her home and taking the top sheet of paper.

We all awkwardly signed the NDAs, Taylor and Beck making quiet comments to each other that I couldn't hear from the other side of the kitchen.

After appetizers were finally served, everyone gathered between the living room and the kitchen to sit and chat. It was wonderful to see that everyone was getting along so well even though half of us didn't truly know the other half. Beck and Adam were chatting with Logan, whereas Eloise and Susan were chatting with Taylor, Tom, and Kyle. Garrett and Kate were off in their own world on the counter as she took pictures of all the NDAs and scanned them into her iPad. All business.

I was noticing how Logan's gaze kept flicking over to Eloise on the other side of the open concept space, when I felt a warm hand grace the back of my arm. I smiled and looked up into the eyes of Josh. He and I were both leaning against the kitchen counter to watch our two circles slowly become joined under the charade we were to put on.

"So," Josh started, standing close enough for our arms to touch each other, both of us had crossed them over our chests, "One date a week, huh?"

"Oh! Yes!" I turned my body to face him fully, letting my breasts lightly brush against his arm. He didn't move out of their way (point one to me), "I was thinking a one-on-one date for our first, yes? That way we can get to know each other again." I smiled brightly at him, my gaze snagging on his lip ring for half a second before I met his eyes. He must have noticed, because I saw his lips twitch as if he were holding back a smirk.

"Right," Josh let his dark gaze flick around the room once before landing back on me, making my pulse race, "I was thinking a hike, if you're still into things like that." I was surprised, because as kids I wouldn't really consider what we did as hiking. Mostly, I would consider it as us just dicking around in the woods. We always wandered off trails, careful to stay away from poison oak (or was it ivy?) and often found a random spot to unload our haul of snacks and drinks we had packed from our houses. We would take edibles, get high in the woods, and be prepared with a plethora of food and water to help us ride it out. Josh was a Boy Scout and had learned the basics of navigating the woods in daylight, meaning that as long as he told his parents exactly where he would be during the day, they gave him their blessing to frolic with me.

My parents made sure I had enough snacks and water, as well as an emergency first aid kit. We never hurt ourselves, minus a few scrapes on our legs from stray twigs and branches, and it was one of the more romantic things we had done as kids. Sometimes, if I was high enough, I would pretend that we were picnicking together as a couple. Like he was some sort of geeky Edward Cullen taking me to his favorite field.

The reality was, I came up with these trips because I had learned that Josh got easily overstimulated. When he was overstimulated, he became cranky. Hiding away in the tall trees and green foliage the Pacific Northwest had to offer, seemed like a great way to help his mind reset so he could handle the other places I dragged him to, like high school parties or dances.

"That sounds great! Where at?"

"I hear there is a place in Newport Beach called Crystal Cove?" Josh asked, his shoulders dropping the slightest bit at my confirmation for our first date activity.

"Oh, excellent choice. I'll bring the edibles." I winked at him, another attempt at flirting. My winking game was pretty strong, I had mastered the exact facial movements needed to make it not creepy and not too forward, so that if he rejected me again, he could easily pass it off as me just having a "flirty personality" like he would tell me in high school.

"I'll bring the savory snacks, for when you get the munchies." Josh winked back at me before looking forward again. I found myself beaming at him, thrilled that he had returned my flirty gesture.

"Quick question," He quickly jutted his chin forward once to the direction of everybody else, "That's Logan, right?" His voice was lower, and he leaned closer to me so that I could hear him clearly. We were gossiping now, and I obliged by scooting closer until our sides were pressing against each other.

"The large man with curly brown hair? Yes. That's him." Josh nodded once as I confirmed his suspicion.

"…Does he have a thing for the girl with the short blonde hair?" Josh's eyes bounced between the two people as I turned to follow his gaze. Logan was still eyeballing Eloise, who would sometimes feel his stare and glance in his direction. When they would make eye contact, they both immediately looked away from each other. As if they were both embarrassed to acknowledge the other.

"No, at least, I don't think so." I furrowed my brows, realizing I had no idea how to tell if Logan thought a woman was attractive or not. I hadn't ever seen him interact with one in a flirtatious way before. "He was rude to Eloise, remember?"

"Oh, right. But you didn't want me to beat him up." Josh nodded as he remembered our text conversation.

"Correct, you're too pretty to risk. I'm sure this face has some sort of insurance coverage." I reached up and pinched one of Josh's cheeks, to which he responded by scoffing and gently grabbing my hand to push it away. He held my hand for about two whole seconds longer than necessary before dropping it and continuing our conversation.

Another point for me.

"Is that why he can't stop staring at her?" Josh asked, leaning the arm closest to me on the back of the counter. His new position made it look like he was resting his arm around my back, so I took advantage of his open side by snaking my arm behind him to rest on the counter as well. He didn't move away, so I added a third point to the tally that I was keeping in my big fat brain.

"I told him he needed to apologize to her, but he sucks at socializing, so I think he is spiraling about having to do that. Otherwise, I'll be a brat to him at the gym."

"You? A brat? Never." Josh chuckled again and I stuck my tongue out at him.

"Are you saying I was a brat in high school?"

"*Never*," Josh repeated, laying the sarcasm on real thick.

"I'll have you know, I am an absolute delight. Until you are an ass to one of my friends for no reason. Then I will respond accordingly." I shrugged against his side once.

"That, I'll agree with. I remember how you used to stick up for me back in the day." Josh's smile dropped the slightest bit. I knew he didn't have the easiest time in high school. I didn't know him the first three years, but what I knew of him senior year made me obsessed with him. He just struggled with first impressions at the time, something he had clearly managed to overcome as an adult. He was so much smoother and more confident now; I could tell just by the way he held himself in the room.

I guess it made sense. Though it would be adorable to have a famous singer be unbearably shy, it probably wouldn't be great in the profession.

"...I don't think he's going to do it," I murmured towards Josh, steering the conversation away from the past for now. "He seems way too on edge to go through with an apology."

"Hmm..." Josh agreed, blinking, and coming back to the moment, "Maybe we can help give him an opportunity?" He stared down at me and winked. This was the third wink in the conversation, and I felt air quietly escape my lungs. Josh was something else. I was obsessed with the idea of seeing him in person again, wanting nothing more than to stare at his face with my own eyes, without a phone screen separating us. Now, as we both leaned against the countertop with our arms wrapped around each other, without our hands touching each other, I realized that I actually wanted much more than that.

Here, in this moment, with our sides touching, I felt

grounded. Not that my life was particularly stressful or over-whelming, in fact, I would argue that I had it very good compared to other women my age. Regardless, standing in this kitchen in Josh Madey's presence as he stared down at me with his dark brown eyes behind his glasses, a smirk on his lips, and showing off his glistening white teeth, I felt stable.

Whoa, interesting thought, Courtney.

Was our situation actually stable? No. Because currently, it was fake. Our friendship might have been real, as real of friends as we could possibly be, after seeing each other twice after a ten-year hiatus. It was clear we still had friendly chemistry, as Kate had mentioned previously over FaceTime. However, I knew that whatever I was pursuing with Josh during our fake dating trope, was only meant to last six months. He was going on tour, and my dream of having a house with two point five children and a white picket fence didn't exactly mesh with that of someone who traveled the world half the year to have women's bras tossed up to him on stage.

Not that his career was a bad choice, clearly, he was successful. And good at it. He should obviously keep it up.

But I wasn't lying when I warned him that I was a stage five clinger during our call.

I knew what I wanted in the long run. And I knew what kind of partner I needed in the long run. Yes, having Josh Madey back in my life was thrilling and igniting some type of flame inside of me. But I knew the end game. I knew the end result was us parting ways at some point.

Even if I managed to convince him to see me as something

more than his childhood bestie, I knew that things would end, no matter what, in six months. In my mind, that didn't mean that I needed to waste this opportunity. Meaningful relationships could absolutely have an expiration date. Just because a relationship didn't end happily ever after, doesn't mean that it was a wasted experience.

My soul craved Joshua Madey, as more than just a fake boyfriend and more than a wham-bam-thank-you-ma'am situation. I wanted something real with him. Even if it had a deadline.

"Court?" Josh asked, his smirk faltering as he scanned my face. I had no idea what expression I was making as I let my brain run wild with the mental gymnastics needed to justify my current goal.

"Yes?" I smiled a little too enthusiastically after the pause that I created, "Let's see if you and I can play puppet master."

<h1 style="text-align:center">11</h1>

We could try—whether or not the puppets complied with the strings we pulled, however, was up for debate.

Susan went into the hall storage closet and pulled out an old karaoke machine Beck had gifted me a couple of years ago. Could any of us in the townhome sing? No. Not at all. Was it hilarious for two hard of hearing women and a woman who couldn't hold a tune to own a karaoke machine? Yes, yes it was.

"I appreciate that on our day off from writing and creating music, we are now singing and playing other people's music," Kyle joked, as we dragged chairs from the kitchen to create more seating in the living room. Kyle and Tom were joined at the hip, always choosing seats next to each other in the room. I only noticed because Kate and Garrett had chosen their seats next to each other, as well as Beck and Adam (who I was dying to hear sing), and Josh and me (because we were supposed to be practicing).

There were other single people in the room, Susan, Taylor, Eloise, and Logan, but Tom and Kyle stuck together. I lifted an eyebrow as Kyle patted Tom's thigh once after taking his seat next to the drummer, and made pointed eye contact with Josh, who went out of his way to break the eye contact with me.

Ah, I see.

Taylor tore up pieces of paper and wrote random song titles on them then threw all the scraps in a bowl, so whoever's turn it was to sing had to pick a song out of the bowl and perform for everyone. After everyone was a few White Claws in, they were loose enough to have fun with the activity and not be absolutely humiliated. It was even more embarrassing because there were actual musical professionals in the room.

After Taylor and Beck made a horrible performance out of Katy Perry's "Firework", Josh and Garrett took their turn by pulling a song title out of the mystery bowl.

"'Jealous' by Nick Jonas?" Garrett's brows furrowed as he read the name of the song. "I don't know this one."

"Yes, you do." Josh took out his phone and pulled up the song for Garrett to listen to, while we all cheered for the two of them to perform for the first time this evening. After a few seconds of the song, Garrett raised his eyebrows and nodded, remembering it.

I had just walked back from the kitchen after grabbing another White Claw, choosing to sit on Logan's other side on the couch, making him scoot closer to Eloise. Eloise's brow furrowed as Logan's large frame encroached on her couch space, but she quickly wiped the expression off her face, and put her everything-is-happy-and-fine Eloise mask back on as Josh and Garret set up their song.

I had already sung with Susan after she picked ABBA's

"Take a Chance On Me" and, contrary to everyone else's opinion, we killed it. Logan was just suffering through all of our performances, due to the injury on his vocal cords.

"Alright, ready?" Josh asked, handing the second mic to Garrett as Logan started the machine for them.

Everyone started clapping and cheering, excited for these two to sing and show us up.

The mood entirely changed when the music started and Josh took the lead.

The song was a sexy song. Maybe if it hadn't been for my big fat crush on the tatted man standing in the front of our humble living room, I might not have had the visceral response I had as Josh started singing.

Garrett crushed it by layering backup vocals, even though it wasn't necessary for this karaoke machine, but Josh was the one who held all my attention.

The two men were dancing as they sang the song, making everyone crack up at their attempt at gyrating their hips in a sexy manner and flexing their chest muscles. I found myself laughing too, except I was also blushing hard as Josh's eyes locked on mine during the first verse and started serenading me in front of our intimate audience.

My body did not understand that this was a joke.

It also didn't understand that there were a dozen other people in the room, and that it wasn't an opening to make a very big move on my fake boyfriend. As Josh sang arousing lyrics regarding hypothetical jealousy if other men looked at his woman, all the tell-tale signs were there. My flushed neck and face, my beating heart, the warmth in my lower belly, as well as my sudden need to cross my legs in an attempt to hide the fact that things were happening down there.

Fuck, am I into rock stars?

No, I was just into Josh.

He danced his way over to me as the second chorus hit, turning around, and swinging his hips in front of my face sensually as if he was giving a lap dance. The problem was that he was a very good singer, and he wasn't pitchy or tone-deaf like the rest of us in the room were. I managed to laugh and cheer Josh on, knowing the rest of the room was cackling and cheering as they watched Josh tease me with his ass inches from my face.

I glanced over and saw Logan pinching the bridge of his nose, his cheeks puffing as if he was struggling to keep from laughing. He cracked one eye open to look at me, communicating everything he needed to with that one glance.

You're a goner. It's so obvious.

I pretended to ignore Logan's knowing look and smacked Josh's ass as he started the third verse, making him plop right down onto my lap. He turned and swung one arm around my shoulders as he sang passionately into the karaoke microphone, making me cackle as I covered my face from embarrassment.

Embarrassment from the attention I was receiving from him in front of everybody.

And embarrassment from how badly I wanted to climb him after what should have been a very cringey performance.

"Bravo! Encore!" Beck clapped as she leaned back into her boyfriend's embrace. She had been perched in Adam's lap for most of the evening, and even he was laughing at Josh and Garrett's sensual performance as he wiped a stray tear from his eye.

"Is it hot in here, or...?" Garrett playfully asked as he tugged at the collar of his shirt and wiggled his eyebrows suggestively at Kate. She gave him a quick smirk before leaning over and nudging Eloise.

"Are we next?" Kate asked her. Eloise was flushed from laughing at Garrett and Josh, wiping at her cheeks as she shrugged and nodded good naturedly. The two of them took the microphones from Garrett and Josh, who hadn't left my lap yet, and walked to the front of the room.

"You two are perfect, by the way." Kate smiled at Josh and me, making me realize I had looped my arms around his waist and was subtly taking a gander at his stomach muscles with my fingers. Damn, Josh must have been pretty cut, based on what I could feel through his t-shirt.

"Court is excellent arm-candy, it's true." Josh wrapped both of his arms around my shoulders, resting his cheek on the top of my head. He was so long that his legs rested over both mine and Logan's lap, making Garrett smack his feet as he claimed the spot Eloise had vacated next to Logan.

"He's an excellent fake boyfriend," I added, squeezing him in my arms once. I felt Josh's arms twitch around my shoulders at the compliment, and part of me panicked that I had been too touchy-feely with him in the moment. Then I reminded myself that he was literally crushing me into the couch with the entirety of his body weight on my lap and realized that I was overthinking.

I caught Beck's gaze as she gave me a suspicious smile

before adjusting her seat on her boyfriend's lap and looking up at Eloise and Kate in the front of the room.

"Oh, I love her so much!" Eloise smiled as she showed Kate the song, who nodded her confirmation, then handed the paper to Logan to adjust the machine accordingly. Logan's large hand reached out to take the paper from Eloise, and his fingers definitely skimmed hers. Eloise quickly snatched her hand back and I thought I saw her brows furrow the slightest bit as she positioned herself front and center next to Kate.

"Trustfall" by P!nk started playing.

Nobody was prepared for what happened next.

I think everyone in the room expected Garrett and Josh to be the stars of the show tonight, but as Kate and Eloise started to sing, we all quickly realized that there was competition.

"Oh my," Susan gasped from her ugly accent chair as Eloise took the lead on the song, Kate harmonizing with her flawlessly. Susan pressed one hand against her chest in shock, while grasping Kyle tightly with her other hand. He and Tom wore matching open-mouthed expressions as he squeezed her hand back.

"Lo! Are you kidding me?" Taylor cried, leaning forward, and holding their face as Kate and Eloise sang at each other, gently wiggling their shoulders and hips with the music in a less dramatic way than the previous performers. Eloise and Kate both took turns flipping their hair dramatically as they had fun singing the song, thrilled they had both managed to shock everybody in the room (as well as each other) with their ability to sing.

"Hey," Josh murmured in my ear as he nudged his chin towards the big guy sitting next to us. I turned my head just enough to eyeball Logan without making it obvious. Logan was staring almost wide-eyed at Eloise (not Kate, I double checked) as she commanded the room with her powerful voice. He rested his hands on top of Josh's legs, both of his hands curled into fists as his lips hardened into a flat-line. He was clearly lost at the sight of Eloise belting her little heart out to P!nk.

"Interesting," I murmured back to Josh, turning back to face him in my lap. His face was incredibly close to mine. All I had to do was lean a little closer to him as he eyeballed Logan with a lifted eyebrow, and I would be able to plant my lips on his easily.

I was dying to know what it would be like to kiss Josh with his lip piercing.

Not now, a little voice inside my head warned me. My conscience was probably right. Our first kiss as adults probably shouldn't be a surprise attack, like what Beck did to Adam at Big Bear about a year ago. Even though it ended up working out for the both of them.

"Interesting," Josh murmured back to me as Eloise started to finish up her song, his eyes making me unable to look away. His lips tipped up on the corners as his head inclined closer to mine.

Oh my god, was he *going to kiss* me?

Nope. Instead, he leaned his head to the side to give me a quick friendly peck on the cheek as he turned back to Eloise and Kate.

As the two of them finished their performance, the room erupted into cheers. Almost everyone stood up to clap and wrap the women up in hugs, as we all processed the fact that these two women just spontaneously blew it out of the water.

Josh never stood up, and therefore neither did I.

Obviously, Logan stayed seated too, never going out of his way to touch another person.

"Holy shit, Lo!" Taylor cried as they cupped Eloise's cheeks in their hands, making her giggle in embarrassment, "How did you pull that huge voice out of your cute little ass?"

Another round of laughter followed Taylor's question, even though I don't think they meant for it to be as funny as it was.

"There was a time where I wanted to be a professional singer, I took lessons for a few years." Eloise shrugged good naturedly. She went to take her seat but halted when she saw Garrett residing. He saw her intention and quickly hopped up.

"Here! I can move—"

"No, it's okay—"

"No, no, it's your spot." Garrett tugged on her arm and practically threw her down in her spot on the couch right next to Logan, who was staring down at his hands as he unclenched them.

The opportunity was there as everyone shuffled about the room to make way for the new singers, and I took it because I was a super annoying person. "Logan, wasn't she amazing?" I asked, releasing one arm that was still holding Josh around the waist to lightly punch him in the bicep.

He turned to glare at me as I lifted my eyebrows knowingly at him, my gaze said, *here is your opening. You better take it.*

Logan turned to face Eloise, whose eyes immediately dropped from his face to focus on Josh's shoes dangling off the end of Logan's lap. Logan waved his hand once to get Eloise's attention, and as soon as her clear blue eyes lifted to watch his hands move, Logan started signing.

I vocalized for him, *that was unexpected.*

Eloise blinked, no hint of a smile as her lips stayed in a line. Her eyes shot up to Logan's. For Eloise, it was the closest to a glare I had ever seen from her.

"Surprised?" Eloise's blonde eyebrows lowered the slightest bit, not enough to create a pinch in her brow, but enough for her snide comment to hit home.

Logan glanced back at me, looking for help. I just stared back at him as Josh pretended that a lock of my hair was very interesting, probably feeling the secondhand embarrassment just as I was. Logan turned back to Eloise and tried again, relying on me translating, *yes, I was surprised that you could sing that well.*

"Believe it or not," Eloise crossed her legs and folded her arms across her chest, leaning back on the couch and refusing to look at his face directly, "I am a capable person. If I want to learn something, I do. I'm sorry that I haven't learned ASL on your preferred timeline yet, but if that means I don't need to bother trying to befriend you, then it's probably for the best."

Whoops. Maybe I shouldn't have told Eloise at work what Logan had specifically said to her at the gym that day.

The room was quieting down as Tom and Kyle took their turns picking a song from the bowl, and a couple of suspicious glances were thrown at Eloise and Logan's quiet conversation as soon as everyone realized Eloise's normally positive body language was quickly shifting to the body language of someone barely tolerating the person she was conversing with.

Logan glanced at me again, this time I was the one pretending that the tattoos on Josh's hand (the one playing with a lock of my hair), were incredibly interesting. To be fair, they were. The top of his hand was covered with an image of an evergreen, along with tribal designs surrounding it. I immediately pictured what that hand would look like in other situations. Josh and I were exploring each other's body type situations.

Another strong blush hit my face and neck, and Josh immediately noticed.

"Are you too hot? Should I move?" he asked, adjusting as if he was going to leave my lap so I could have air. To be fair, I was warm. Josh's large body emitted a ton of heat, but I loved being this close to him again. My soul was craving physical contact from him, just like it did back in high school.

"Nope, just thinking," I replied, tightening my hold on his waist to keep him in place.

"About what?" Josh asked, quirking the eyebrow that had the piercing in it.

"Did that hurt?" I asked, realizing I had left Logan to fend for himself with his conversation with Eloise, but not necessarily caring, since I held the attention of the man in the room I was currently obsessed with.

"Which one?" he asked.

"Both, I guess." My gaze kept bouncing between his two facial piercings, and I immediately noticed the way Josh stuck the tip of his tongue out to wet his bottom lip, the one with the ring.

"These ones weren't so bad." Josh shrugged, ignoring when his band mates started their song. They were singing LMFAO and had the attention of everyone else in the room, so I didn't bother to pretend to listen to their performance.

"You have others?" I asked, disappointed in myself for not realizing that he probably did have other piercings.

"I do," Josh's cheeks turned the slightest shade of pink, which would have made me think he was embarrassed, except for the way his lips tipped up in a devilish smirk. "C'mon, ask me where."

"Let me guess, you have two sparkly nipple piercings." I smirked at him, which made him chuckle.

"Nope, I don't have any nipples pierced, shockingly," Josh's gaze was locked on my face, a challenge.

"Belly button?" I asked.

"Nope," was his quick reply, his eyes dropped to my lips. Another point for me tonight.

"Then where...?" I quickly closed my mouth as I realized what his answers implied. *Did he really...? No, the Josh I knew would never...but would adult Josh...?* He could clearly see my brain spinning with questions, something he obviously took joy in, as his grin widened a bit at my stupefied expression.

"I guess I should keep the mystery alive," Josh murmured as he kissed my forehead once and promptly removed himself from my lap in order to make his way to the kitchen to grab another drink.

I wish I didn't sit there in shock as long as I did, because

Beck noticed my expression and lifted her eyebrow at me in question. I just blinked at her once, not bothering to shake off her concern as I processed the possibility that Josh would have genital piercings. How does one even get that idea? What is the benefit of such a thing? Did he just love sticking needles in his body? The tattoos all over him would suggest that was a yes.

I felt Josh's presence return behind me on the couch as he cheered on the drummer and bassist, laughing when they struggled to do the LMFAO famous shuffle dance. As soon as I felt his large hand rest on one of my shoulders, I instinctively lifted my hand to cover his. He gave my shoulder a comforting squeeze, and I marveled at how quickly we became physically affectionate with each other.

I expected to slowly graduate to affectionate touches to some degree, but even though this was the second time Josh and I had seen each other in person, we were already back at the point where he felt comfortable openly twerking in front of me and making me his personal chair. As I squeezed his hand on my shoulder, I caught Kate's eyes from the other side of the room. She had been holding her phone up and was clearly either taking a picture or recording of Josh and me. As soon as I met her gaze, she lowered her phone and gave me a thumbs up with a secret smirk.

Right.

Because we were supposed to be practicing being a couple tonight. And frankly, we were doing an excellent job.

A cool wave of doubt filled my stomach as I thought about the possibility that Josh was simply fulfilling his role, and that he wasn't as thrilled or excited about the prospect of spending time with me as much as I was with him. If that was the case, I doubt he would have gone out of his way to peck my cheek and forehead, right?

12

"So, tell me how this happened."

"How what happened?"

"This!" I emphasized my words by gesturing vaguely towards Josh's tall presence. As we started at the beginning of our trail for a leisurely hike at Crystal Cove, I again took note of what he was wearing.

High school Josh always wore jeans and blank, solid color t-shirts.

Adult, celebrity, rock star Josh wore designer jeans with intentional holes, as well as designer t-shirts that had more than one color to them. Instead of the Doc Martens boots he wore at the concert, he wore hiking boots. When he had shown up on the doorstep of the townhome to pick me up for our first one-on-one date (something I had been way too excited about since he and the rest of the band left our home last week), I had immediately asked him what kind of sociopath wore jeans for a hike. He rolled his eyes and pointed to himself, and that was that.

He had driven us in the same big black SUV from the week before, and when we arrived at the parking lot (with him wearing a baseball cap and large sunglasses in an attempt to disguise his well-known face), I had realized that another big black SUV was following us.

When I pointed it out, he had shrugged nervously and said that it was his personal security, and that they would keep a distance from us so they wouldn't interfere with our date. I sat dumbfounded in the passenger seat of his vehicle as he set the parking brake, processing the fact that my J-shua was famous enough to require "personal security."

Okay, he wasn't "my" J-shua. But in my heart, I felt some moronic claim on him, since I loved him before the rest of the world knew who he was.

"I need you to be more specific," Josh replied, nudging me forward with his large hand at the small of my back. I had been staring at the two men who exited the second large SUV, who dressed like they were two random people going on a hike. I had been scanning their apparel to search for weapons when I asked Josh my original question.

"How did you go from me dragging you by the hair to any social gathering in high school, to you singing on stage in front of thousands?" I clarified, looking over my shoulder at him. I would have preferred for us to walk side-by-side, but the first part of the trail was very narrow. We could only walk single file during this part.

At least maybe this gave him an opportunity to stare at my backside, maybe ogle it a little bit and create some fantasies that I would be more than willing to fulfill for him.

"Ah," Josh chuckled at my accurate assessment, and when the path widened, I slowed my step so that he could walk beside me, "It's not that interesting of a story."

"I promise you it is," I countered, staring at how his hands were both tucked up and grasping either strap of the backpack he was wearing. It wasn't a long hike, and it was almost impossible to get lost. The landscape wasn't comparable to the Pacific Northwest where we grew up. Crystal Cove had a small smattering of trees, but mostly it was open fields with the occasional ocean view.

"Alright, well," Josh inhaled a deep breath before smirking at me out of the side of his eye. Seeing that the sun wasn't blinding and that we were alone, he began swapping out his sunglasses for his regular black framed ones. I wanted to pinch his grown adult cheeks with the endearment those glasses filled me with, "I had always played around with the guitar. Remember the one I had in my bedroom?"

"Yes, I also remember you plucking on it occasionally. I had no idea you were so serious about the instrument, though."

"That's the thing, I wasn't," Josh shrugged, keeping his eyes up on the trail ahead of us, "I mean, I wasn't terrible at playing. I just didn't care to pursue it. It was mostly something for my hands to do when I was a kid. But then, I went to college. I knew nobody, and I wasn't exactly trying to get in touch with anyone from high school who also happened to go to college in Eugene. So, I forced myself to...expand."

"Expand?" I asked, gently kicking a loose rock out of my way and into the brush.

"Yeah. So, Tom was my roommate my second year," My brain reminded me that Tom was the vanilla-looking bassist.

"He had told me that he and his buddies were trying to start a band and asked if I would be interested in seeing them play. I said sure, and the next day Tom had a fake ID printed for me so I could get into the bar. Anyways, they were good. But their lead singer was kind of…off."

"How so?"

"He was an absolute ass," Josh chuckled at the memory, "You could tell by the way he presented himself onstage, that he thought he was the shit. Which, sure, his voice wasn't terrible. But even I could tell that there was beef between the guys and the singer, whose name completely escapes me at the moment," Josh quickly let go of the straps on his backpack, shaking his hands out as if he had been gripping it too tight, and I let another impulsive thought take hold of my actions. I reached forward and took his hand closest to me, intertwining our fingers and giving him an encouraging smile to continue the story. "So, eventually, the lead singer quit the band. Left the guys high and dry. It was a real dick move; he gave them no warning. Anyways, they ended up having auditions for someone to replace him."

"And you auditioned?" I couldn't believe it because the Josh I knew would never dare.

"Not exactly," Josh's cheeks turned the slightest shade pink, and a nervous smirk tugged at his lips, "Tom heard me singing in the shower one morning."

"Oh my god," I clapped my hand over my mouth, picturing Josh passionately singing into a bottle of shampoo and giving his all for a pretend audience, "That's amazing."

"I guess," Josh shrugged, "After that, Tom brought me to their band practice and made me sing in front of the guys. I was terrible and choked at first. Then they gave me a shot to clear my nerves, and I must have been able to perform better, because here we are."

Josh smiled down at me, his lip ring glistening in the sunset that we were walking along side of.

"But that was just your second year of college," I pressed, swinging our hands forward and backwards as if we were children frolicking, instead of grown adults practicing how to be intimate with each other, "So what all happened between then and now?"

"Oh, well, I graduated college. Got a job doing lab work in Beaverton for a while, but we always kept in touch. We would play at local venues, or even travel to LA once in a while, to perform for potential scouts," My heart sank a little at that. He knew I was in Southern California, and he never reached out to me once, "It wasn't until a few years ago that we actually got a record deal, and that quickly escalated to where we are now." He looked forward, using his top teeth to chew on his lip ring as he pondered his story.

As we walked along the dirt trail hand-in-hand, I wanted to ask him why he dropped all communication with me. Why he didn't bother to return any of my messages. I would go weeks without reaching out, waiting for him to reach out to me first. But none of that happened. As soon as I waved goodbye from the window of the packed full Subaru, he never spoke to me again.

"Your turn," Josh chimed, interrupting my ability to gather courage to ask him my question, "What have you been up to? Are you a teacher?"

I blinked at him. "What? No."

Josh looked a little confused, raising his pierced eyebrow

at me. "Ah, it just looked like you were in a classroom when, uh, Kate and I spoke with you."

Back when she suggested we date for fake social media points, trust me, I remember.

"Oh, well, I do work with kids," I shrugged. "I'm an infant therapist. I work at a clinic with Beck and Adam, who are speech and physical therapists."

"Oh," Josh nodded, eyeballing a bench up ahead that gave us a perfect view of the ocean, and tugged me towards it until we were both seated next to each other, his long legs angled towards mine, "I have to admit, I don't know what an infant therapist is. What does that mean?" He had let go of our hands to stretch his arm along the back of the bench, still leaving plenty of room between the two of us.

"It's pretty much a glorified job title that means I get to play with kids all day," I smiled, loving the way his dark eyes were giving me all his attention, as if he was genuinely interested in my work. "My clinic is an early intervention center, meaning babies and toddlers who are experiencing global delays come to us for help to get them back up to speed."

"Like speech delays?" Josh asked.

"Yes, but not always," I pressed my lips together, wondering how to best explain it to someone unfamiliar with the field. "I incorporate signs and speech into my play, but my main focus is helping kids *learn* how to play. Whether that's matching colors, working on puzzles, or simply learning how to investigate new toys. A lot of times, these skills are interlaced with global delays in fine or gross motor movements. So, a lot of clients I see are also meeting with Beck or

Adam or Taylor. It's like...pre-preschool. A lot of my job also includes helping parents learn how to communicate and understand their kids with these delays. Half the time I feel like I'm picking up on certain behaviors their kids are displaying and explaining to the parent why their kid is doing that. So not only am I helping these kids develop play and communication skills, but I'm also helping parents meet their kids at their level, if that makes sense."

Josh was staring at me intently during my very watered-down explanation of my job, his lips tilted up in a soft smile that made my cheeks flush from the very direct attention I was getting from him.

God, when was the last time I had gotten laid? A few weeks? I usually went out of my way to find a man to hook up with every couple of months, but the number of hormones raging through my body simply from direct eye contact from someone as stunning as Josh made me realize that my needs might be amplified.

"That's, wow..." Josh blinked, as if clearing his head. "That sounds amazing. Is that why you ended up learning sign language?" He adjusted his seat on the bench so that his arm no longer rested on the back, but instead his elbows rested on the tops of his knees, his bleached hair falling towards his forehead a little bit.

"No, I learned sign language for Beck. She was my room-mate all throughout college," I explained, reaching forward to brush his hair off of his brow. If the touch made him uneasy, he didn't show it. He made me his own human chair a week ago, so I assumed we could get away with fixing each other's hair at this point.

"Wow. You're friend of the year. So, is Beck deaf?" Josh asked, running a hand through his hair to continue brushing it out of the way. He then adjusted his glasses by pushing them up on the bridge of his nose, a movement that made me feel nostalgic. I had seen him adjust his glasses like that countless times a teen, and I finally got to witness it again.

"She's hard of hearing, so she can hear lower tones and murmurings without her hearing aids. But she can't exactly make out specific words," I shrugged. "Her hearing aids died during your concert. So, she could only really hear the bass and drums, I think."

At this, Josh frowned a little, "I felt so guilty when the interpreter bailed. It was literally ten minutes before the show, there was no way we could find somebody that quickly."

"It's cool, I took care of it," I flipped my blonde ponytail over my shoulder dramatically, lifting my chin up in a faux display of arrogance. Josh smirked at my dramatics before his dark eyebrows lowered and he leaned towards me, accusingly.

"Wait, were *you* the one that booed us?" Josh asked, placing one tatted hand over his heart.

"I don't know what you're talking about. Anyways, tell me about your tattoos!" I quickly reached out to grab the hand over his heart, tracing the fern and giving myself the opportunity to study the rest of the artwork that took over his entire forearm.

"That's a yes, but that's okay, you're forgiven," Josh chuckled. "What do you want to know about them?" He closed the remaining distance between us, our thighs pressing against each other as I held his hand in my lap, letting my fingers trace all the shapes and colors that took over his skin.

"What is this?" I asked, tracing a chemical equation on the inside of his wrist.

"Dopamine," Josh explained. I caught a loud burst of laughter in my throat. I tried to tamp it down, but I ended up snorting through my nose. I clapped one hand over my mouth as my shoulders started to shake with the restrained laughter. "What? You think my artwork is funny?"

"No," I giggled, then shook my head, "Well, maybe? It's just...I guess I never thought about what tattoos you would get if you wanted one. But the more I stare at them, the more I realize how *you* they are. Plants, beakers, scientific formulas, it's all so *you.*"

I glanced up to see Josh staring down at me, his dark eyebrows wiggled once as he leaned forward and lowered his voice, "Been staring at my arms, have you?" I rolled my eyes playfully and pinched his forearm, because yes, of fucking course I had been staring at his arms. I, like any warm-blooded woman, loved a good forearm.

"I'm allowed to, you're my fake boyfriend," I countered. Josh's devilish grin faltered the slightest bit, before he straightened in his seat and quickly flexed his arms in a strongman pose, much like the one I presented Beck with the night of his concert.

"It's alright, I'm used to being ogled at. It's a burden I must endure." He twisted his wrists to change the way his muscles flexed, and I snorted my laughter again, gently patting his stomach with the back of my hand to get him to drop the act.

"You're also really humble, I've noticed." I grinned up at him, suddenly so grateful that I was here, sitting on this random bench on a trail in Crystal Cove, chatting with one of my favorite people from my childhood who turned out to be just as wonderful as a grown man.

And I wanted to bang him.

A lot.

"More like resigned to my fate. The amount of lingerie I've been sent by women the last two years is actually alarming."

"Can you blame them?" I asked, feeling heat crawl up my cheeks the slightest bit because I had always been a forward person and it had gotten me absolutely nowhere with him thus far. "So, as someone who is interested in toning her own muscle, can I ask what you've been doing? You just look so..." I glanced up to meet his dark eyes again, he was looking at me with a raised eyebrow, "Physically fit," I decided to land on.

"Oh, well, it's easy really," Josh shrugged, leaning back on the bench and crossing his arms over his chest, allowing me more opportunity to admire them, "All you have to do is sign a record deal with a billion-dollar company, have them drop thousands of dollars a year for a personal trainer or nutritionist, and have a career that allows you to exercise and eat prepared meals every day of the week." He shrugged his shoulders as I laughed at his explanation.

"Oh, well if that's all!" I rolled my eyes as I leaned back on the bench too, except I chose to close even more distance between us to lean my head on his shoulder, "I'll be sure to share your secrets with Logan. He'll be happy to know how easy it is."

"Logan is doing fine, based on what I saw last weekend,"

Josh's playful tone died down a little bit and he crossed his ankles in front of him, fidgeting in his seat. "Um, so, you and he never...?"

"Logan?" I asked, turning my head to look up at Josh. He was biting his lip ring again; a sure sign that he was nervous, "No, no. We haven't ever been interested in each other like that. I mean, I call him hot to his face all the time..."

"Who wouldn't?" Josh mumbled, making me pause for a moment to watch the blush creep into his cheeks.

"...but he has made it perfectly clear that he is not interested in me like that. Nor I, him." I finished, keeping my gaze on Josh who suddenly wouldn't meet my eyes. I watched him squirm in his seat, even more fidgety now after he interrupted my sentence. Based on his body language, his "who wouldn't" seemed to have erupted out of him against his will. I stared at Josh, trying to mask my suspicion.

"Um," Josh cleared his throat, sitting forward suddenly and making me remove my head from his shoulder, "Before we, um, keep doing this—I should tell you something."

I lifted an eyebrow at that, because I had literally already signed some type of agreement Kate sent over, and all our friends signed NDAs regarding the "fake" of this relationship between us. I was curious what he was going to possibly say to make me reconsider the whole thing enough to scrap those documents.

"...I, um, am not exactly straight..." Josh looked down at the ground, his elbows on his knees as he fidgeted with his own hands.

"Oh." I blinked. I immediately forced my own thoughts and feelings out of the forefront of my mind, putting them on the back burner. Mentally rearranging myself to be a safe person for Josh to come out to.

"—I still like women." Josh turned to look at me then, his eye contact more determined than before.

I just blinked at him again.

Oh. So, maybe my big fat crush on him isn't entirely inappropriate, then.

"Oh." I repeated, not knowing what else to say.

"I mean, I think I like women more. At least, as far as I know about myself," Josh shrugged again, running his hands through his hair. "But, I mean…during college…I've learned that…I also, sometimes, enjoy the company of…men."

I just blinked at him, my shoulder lifting the slightest bit, "Okay."

Josh sat up straighter, angling his entire body towards me. "I just felt like that was something you should know about me. Before we continue to date publicly. I don't exactly advertise that part of myself because it's no one's business but mine. But, with you, I just…wanted to be honest."

I felt my cheeks tug a little bit, a smile spreading at the honor I just received. Josh felt the need to share a very private and sensitive part of himself with me. "Thank you."

His brow relaxed the slightest bit. "For what?"

"For sharing that with me," I reached forward and wrapped one of his tatted hands in my own, my heart racing with the endearing vulnerability of his expression. "I'm grateful to know every part of you, Josh." I leaned forward and kissed his cheek, wanting to reassure him that this literally changed nothing between us.

"Well, thank you. For letting me," Josh smiled at me, looking significantly more relaxed. "Wow, I didn't realize how scary it was for me to tell you that. Not that you ever gave me a reason to think you wouldn't be accepting."

I shrugged again, "I understand. It's not always easy to reveal who you are capable of loving."

Josh smirked at me. "I mean, I've never been in a relationship with a guy. I've only really been romantically interested in women thus far in my life."

"Romantically interested?" *Would my heart cool it and stop fluttering with any sprinkle of hope Josh gave us?*

"Yeah, after experimenting in college," his cheeks flushed at those words, the cutie, "I realized that while I may enjoy, um, physically being with men on occasion, that doesn't necessarily mean I desire a cis man as a, um…partner."

"Ah," I nodded, understanding that sexuality was a spectrum, "So, what you're saying is…" I lifted an eyebrow, remembering who I was talking about previously, who triggered this confession from Josh in the first place, "That I don't need to worry about Logan swooping in and stealing my childhood best friend from under my nose?"

Josh grinned wide at that, "While I admit that Logan is very nice to look at, no. I'd much rather date you than him."

"HA!" I thrust a fist in the air, "I'm *so* rubbing this in Logan's face—if you ever want to come out to him, that is—" I released the hold on Josh's hand to fist bump the air with both hands. "HA! Suck it, Logan! You may be hot as hell, but I'm still superior in the eyes of J-shua!" Josh started laughing as he leaned forward to cover his eyes with one hand, chuckling at the ground at my dramatics before looking back at me and capturing my hands in his.

"So, that means I don't have any competition with Logan, either?" Josh clarified, pulling me closer to him. Oh god, how could Josh even consider such a thought?

"Absolutely not," I grinned and leaned forward to rub noses with him, "I'm *your* fake girlfriend, for as long as you'll have me." Josh closed his eyes at that, pulling away from our little nose touch to inhale a deep breath before exhaling, though his eyes looked strained after he opened them to meet mine. "Perfect."

13

After that conversation, Josh and I continued our hike, sometimes holding hands, other times not, depending on how narrow the pathway was. I had almost forgotten about the two disguised bodyguards following us a few yards away during the whole date.

Fake date.

But hopefully a stepping-stone that led to real dates.

Because Josh said that he was still romantically into women. That he preferred women as partners, and my silly little libido clutched onto those words way harder than it needed to.

We got home a little late after stopping at In-N-Out for dinner. He and his bodyguards dropped me off at a reasonable hour. Josh even leaned over the center console to give my cheek a quick peck, something I both loved and hated. I wanted more, but I needed to respect the time it would take for us to build the foundation of our friendship again to be able to handle actually dating during the next few months before the band left on tour.

I made it home, listening for any sound of movement to

indicate Beck or Susan were awake. Instead, I heard silence. I sigh, walking up to my bedroom and checking my phone to see that I had a missed call from my mother.

Oh god, I thought to myself, realizing that I hadn't thought to update her on the J-shua aspect of my life. I only missed her call by ten minutes, so I hit redial as I quietly shut my bedroom door behind me. It took a lot for Beck or Susan to wake due to noise, but I still tried to be considerate either way.

My mom answered on the third ring, "Hi honey!"

"Hey, mom!" I greeted, putting the phone on speaker, adjusting the volume so it wasn't too loud for my roommates, and setting it on my dresser as I changed.

"I hope I didn't call at a bad time. I know it's late." I could see my mom, who looked exactly like me if I were twenty years older, wiggling her blonde eyebrows suggestively.

"Unfortunately, you didn't interrupt anything," I giggled. "How are you? What's up?"

"Oh, nothing. I just wanted to call my daughter and catch up," my mother sighed, clearly getting comfy, "I just got back from work and I am packing a bag, I'm going out of town tomorrow." My mother's excitement made me suspicious.

"Where to?" I asked. My mother rarely stayed in one place longer than a few months. Even if it was just a weekend getaway to the Oregon coast, she struggled with feeling trapped in her life.

"Cannon Beach, nothing fancy," she replied. "Your father is coming, too." I could hear her smile on the phone, which made mine falter as I pulled pajamas out of my dresser.

"Oh, you're doing that again?" I asked. My mother laughed,

even though I was only partially asking her that as a joke. She knew my opinions on the subject whenever she decided to reconnect with my dad in that way, so I didn't feel the need to elaborate my concern.

"Yes, yes, your parents are still hot messes. Sorry to say," she laughed, "He's just so handsome, and we have this perfect understanding that neither of us really wants more from the other—"

"As much as I love hearing my mom talk about her friends-with-benefits situation with my dad, I don't. Please, dear god, change the subject." I checked my phone to look at the date, mentally guessing how long their little relationship would last this time. Just the weekend? A week? A month? Who was to say, really?

"Fine, fine. You have boundaries, I get it," she laughed, "So is anything going on with you?"

I hesitated, only for a second. My mother and I have always had a very open relationship with each other, and she never made me feel like I had to keep secrets from her. However, that didn't mean that I wasn't prone to feeling uneasy talking with her about my dating life. We had very different goals as grown women. My mom had absolutely no plans to be tied down, yet insisted she wanted a partner by her side at the same time. It was why she was bouncing around from guy to guy (sometimes, landing on my dad when it was convenient for her), whereas she knew my dream of eventually being tied down and never worrying about the dating game ever again.

Maybe that was why I was hesitant to bring up Josh to her. She would obviously remember him from high school, and probably how I would silently cry in my room during the holiday breaks from college when I was reminded that he wanted nothing to do with me.

Fuck, I really needed to ask Josh about that. I was clearly holding grudges there.

"I am seeing someone, actually," I started. At my mom's suspicious but clearly dying to know every detail tone, I eventually caved and told her everything. Starting with Beck buying tickets to the concert and me being a supportive friend to Adam and using the band's music to teach him ASL. By the time I was done retelling the most interesting aspect of my life at the moment, forty-five minutes had passed by. My mom chimed in occasionally with "huh" and "oh wow" and a few "no ways" as I unloaded the latest onto her.

After I finished my ramblings, it was oddly silent on the other end of the phone.

"...Mom? You there?"

"Oh yes, I'm just thinking. One moment." My mom breathed into the microphone for a few seconds more before putting me out of my misery and asking, "So, what do you get out of this?"

"What do you mean?" I said, blushing. I may have glossed over the part where I was dying to date him for real, even though I knew our relationship had an end date to it.

"Josh gets to sharpen his image by having a gorgeous woman from his childhood on his arm, but what do you get out of the deal? Money?" My mom clarified, thankfully without judgement in her tone.

"Oh, right," I smiled, "They're donating a pretty large sum of money to local organizations like my work. To help fund therapies for infants and toddlers with additional needs." I smiled. Kate originally offered me a fat paycheck, but I just felt too icky accepting a paycheck when really, I would have agreed to fake date Josh without any sort of incentive.

"I'm glad to hear Josh is still a sweetheart," my mom said, her smile evident in her voice.

"Honestly, I'm glad too," I agreed, finally dressed in my pajamas as I picked up the phone to turn off speaker. I laid on my bed and pressed it against my ear.

"So, what was his excuse? For dropping his friendship with you all those years ago?" my mother asked. Beck always teased Taylor and me for asking blunt questions, even though it sometimes made her squirm. I had no idea where Taylor got that personality trait from, but I knew for a fact that I became a blunt and forward person because of my mother.

"I haven't asked him that yet," I rubbed my temple, the one without the phone pressed against my ear, "I was about to on our hike, but the conversation got away from me."

"Hmm, I'd be curious to see what he says. I always thought that boy was in love with you, it surprised me to see him cut you off so harshly," her voice was clearly disappointed now, and I realized that it would take a lot for Josh to make amends enough for my mother to believe him.

Whoa there, Court. Who said anything about Josh making amends with your mother? What relationship with an expiration date ever needed to involve parents?

"I just don't understand why he disappeared," I said quietly, as a wave of sadness and exhaustion hit me. "I think I'm going to go to sleep now, Monday is coming."

"Alright, I'll let you go. Please keep me posted on all of this. I love you!"

"I love you, too." After reminding her that the fake of our relationship was supposed to stay a secret, I hung up the phone and flopped onto my bed, quickly glancing over to the opposite wall my bed was on and admired my small library. Bookshelves covered almost the entirety of the wall, except for the small space my dresser took up. I had a variety of books on it: thrillers, sci-fi, fantasy, but mostly romance novels.

Beck would tell you otherwise, but she got me completely hooked on them back in college. I found her "secret stash" under her bed and flipped through them. I weirdly kept going back to her secret stash and starting the books from the beginning. Eventually, I treated her secret stash like my own personal library. Now, years later, I have my own personal library.

I decided to start up a comfort read of mine again. I had a huge boner for enemies to lovers, or star-crossed-lovers, or anything that paid tribute to *Pride and Prejudice*. I also loved rereading my favorites as many times as I wanted. It was why I went out of my way to stock my room with all the bookshelves to accommodate the printed copies of my favorite books. I loved having each book I read on display, even though Beck constantly teased me about having similar habits to a serial killer who liked their trophies.

I always thought her comparison was a little out of left field, but then again, Beck was always a little out of left field.

I grabbed my well-used paperback and snuggled back

underneath my covers, using a small reading light to see the pages until I finally started to feel sleep overcome me. I dreamt of a tall man with colorful tattoos and the voice of an angel, who was glued to my side.

14

"Can you say, 'open'?" I spoke to my favorite little client a few days later at work. I signed for her as well, holding my hands together flat and opening them up to show her how to communicate. The two-year-old furrowed her brow and glared at me, her dark brown eyes pouring into my soul, communicating her irritation with me far better than any signs or words would.

"C'mon, Maddy, you can do this one." Her mother, Ava smirked at her daughter's attitude but still managed to provide an authoritative voice. Maddy did know this sign, she had done it with me many times. She was just excited for me to open up her favorite sensory bin. In amongst the various marbles and rocks and things from the craft store's clearance section, it had the tiniest figurine of Ariel from *The Little Mermaid* in it. Maddy was obsessed.

"Can you say, 'open'? Ready? Three, two, one. Open!" I signed for the little girl again, making her huff a breath of annoyance before wiggling her legs in anxious anticipation for me to just get on with it and open her toy.

"Maddy," Ava playfully scolded her toddler, leaning

forward and gently placing her hands on Maddy's elbows to encourage her to sign. Without looking at me and instead choosing to glare at a picture on the wall over my shoulder, Maddy finally signed the word "open".

"You did it! You said, open! So now, I'm going to open!" I signed it a couple more times for her before finally clicking open the plastic lid on the sensory bin and gently setting it down between us, smiling as Maddy's eyes went wide and her grin took over her face. She immediately searched through the mess of the bin and pulled out Ariel.

"She knows what to do, she just doesn't like to do it," Ava shrugged as we watched her daughter play independently with her favorite toy, her reward for communicating with me.

"Yup, it's just all about consistency with her," I smiled at the mother. I had been seeing Ava and Maddy since Maddy was thirteen months old, and I was her favorite therapist at the facility. She always stopped to wave her little hand at me in the halls, and sometimes Beck would call me in to regain Maddy's attention when she became too overwhelmed during speech.

Maddy was turning three soon, meaning she would age out of our early intervention program and would start receiving her therapies and care through the school district they lived in. It broke my heart a little to know another one of my clients was graduating from our program all too quickly.

As I watched Maddy lay down on her back to properly admire the little Ariel in her hands, a knock sounded at my door.

"Come in!" I called, knowing Ava was a chill parent and

never cared when other therapists stopped by to ask me a question during her child's sessions. Eloise's blonde head poked through my door, grinning brightly at me as she held out a gift basket.

"Delivery!" Eloise chimed, smiling at Maddy and greeting Ava. "I'm just dropping this off for Court."

"Ooo, what is all that?" Ava asked as she eyeballed the gift basket that Eloise set on my desk.

"I don't know," I shrugged, standing up from the floor out of my crisscrossed position to take a better look. "Want to open it up?"

"Yes," Ava nodded as she stood up from her chair to join Eloise and me at my desk. I inspected the gift basket through the plastic wrapping and saw a small, green house-plant, as well as a little popcorn bucket that might barely be big enough to hold one bag of popcorn, and a variety pack of different popcorn seasonings and kernels.

"Here's the note." Eloise plucked it off of the top of the basket as I pulled the ribbon to remove the plastic packaging. "It's from your boyfriend."

"Boyfriend?" Ava's blonde eyebrows wiggled at me play-fully. She was a young mom, younger than me even, which I sometimes forgot. I generally thought that anyone who had a child was more mature and therefore older than me, but Ava was playful enough to remind me that I was, in fact, older than her. We got along well. I smiled at her as I opened the little note to see Josh's message.

The first of many "treats" for my official girlfriend.
Enjoy, J-Shua

I laughed as I gave the note to Ava to read, before combing through the contents of the basket. I was definitely excited about trying out all the different flavors.

"This is so precious," Eloise grinned, taking an envelope of kernels to read the packaging.

"Aw, he knows your obsession with popcorn!" Ava smiled as she looked over Eloise's shoulder to read with her. My phone started buzzing in front of all of us on the desk, a FaceTime call from Josh coming through.

I silenced the call.

"Did you just ignore his call?" Eloise asked me, clear blue eyes wide.

"I'm working," I explained, vaguely gesturing towards the center of the room where Maddy sat happily alone with her sensory bin.

"She's fine, in fact, I think she'd love it if you took a call and didn't make her work a little bit longer." Ava picked up my phone off the desk and held it out to me. I quirked my lips to the side. It really wasn't professional to take personal calls during a session with my clients, but if I was ever going to, Ava and Maddy were the ones to do it with.

I hit redial and Josh picked up within the first ring.

"I got your package!" I smiled, holding the phone up so that he could see all three of us happily going through it.

"Great! I was hoping you would. Is it okay that I sent it to your work?" Josh chewed on his lip ring as he asked me this question.

"Of course! I love getting surprise treats at work." As I spoke, Maddy had stood up and wobbled over to the desk to take a random package of popcorn for herself, staring at it with seriousness as she plopped herself down to flip the package over. "And apparently, so do my clients."

"Oh my god, that is the cutest little person I have ever seen," Josh cooed at his small view of Maddy as she brushed her brown ringlets out of her face so she could better appreciate the popcorn's packaging. "I'm sorry, are you in a session right now? Should I call back?"

"No, the client's mom gave me permission." I smiled and turned the screen so that Ava and Josh could see each other, and Ava waved happily after taking a moment to blink at Josh. I guess she wasn't expecting to see me date a guy with neck tattoos and facial piercings. To be honest, I wasn't expecting it either.

"Hi." Ava smiled.

"Hi, momma," Josh greeted, making Ava blush. I didn't blame her. He dropped his tone a little with his greeting, which made his voice very flirty. "So, Court, I did have another reason to call and talk to you really quick."

"Oh?" I asked, setting the phone down so he could still see me but allowed me both hands to look at all the yummy popcorn in the basket.

"Yes, the band and I were gifted tickets to a Duck's game, and I have exactly one extra ticket with your name on it." I smiled at him on my phone screen.

"Sure, when is it?" I asked. Josh gave me the date and time, but then I realized another question that might prove to be important. "What are the Ducks again?"

"...Did you just ask, 'what are the Ducks'?" Ava asked me with a teasing tone.

"Yes, like, is that football?" Because I knew that Josh went to the University of Oregon, where they had a well-known college football team known as the Ducks. But I doubted that they would care to have him attend one of their games.

"I think the Ducks are basketball, or maybe baseball?" Eloise added, clearly not knowing much about sports either.

"Oh my god, never mind. You're uninvited," Josh scolded me through the phone, making all of us laugh.

"No! Wait! I want to go!" I spoke in between giggles, "Just tell me what sport we're seeing!"

"Guys, it's hockey!" Ava laughed, shaking her head at me. "Courtney's boyfriend, if she doesn't go, I'll happily go. Just find me a babysitter and I'll be there!" Josh laughed at Ava's teasing.

"No!" I cried, grabbing my phone, and holding it away from my client's mother as if she was going to steal my fake boyfriend. "I'm going! I love hockey! I have read many hockey romances, thank you very much!" At that, everyone else laughed even more, making Maddy glare at all of us for causing a ruckus during her precious independent play time.

"Hockey romances?" Josh asked. I waved my hand at him, because I wasn't in a place to elaborate more on that subject.

"Yes, so I know all about goalies and puck bunnies and hat tricks. That's basically the whole sport."

"Well, I'll be glad to have a real hockey expert during the game." Josh winked at me, and my heart fluttered in my chest. I was pretty sure I blushed a little bit too, which was ridiculous because it wasn't even that flirty of a wink.

"Just send me the details, I'll be there. Not Ava. Me." I gave a pretend glare to both of them, just to make myself clear.

"Excellent. Another thing," Josh cleared his throat one last time, his laughter gone and a hint of nerves teasing his voice, "Just be prepared for some, um, cameras. Everyone will know that the band will be there, and we have pretty visible seats. So."

"Oh, okay, I'll look sharp." I gave Josh a finger-gun, making his lips pull back in another smile.

"Great, I'll let you get back to work." Josh tugged on his lip ring once with his teeth as I waved and said goodbye, before ending the call.

I looked up to see Ava staring at both Eloise and me, her gaze bouncing back and forth. Eloise quickly waved goodbye and excused herself from my office, shutting the door behind her. Ava then turned to me and lifted one of her blonde eyebrows.

"Cameras? Are you guys famous or something?"

I exhaled a breath through my mouth, gently tucked my hair behind my ear as I explained the best way I could. "Have you heard of the band Carbon Cut?"

"Oh, yeah. My husband and I listen to them all the time—*oh my god!*" Ava's face slackened and blood drained from her cheeks. "Was I just on a call with *the* Josh Madey? The singer?"

I laughed at her as I checked the time on my phone and resumed my position on the ground next to her daughter. As

I played with Maddy and made her explore her sensory bin by matching colors together, I explained the whole situation to Ava the best way I could. It didn't take nearly as long as it took for me to explain to my mother, because I was just summarizing our reconnection to Ava since we weren't friends outside of work.

I didn't even tell Ava that it was actually fake dating, just like Kate and the contract I signed told me to do.

"...I still can't believe you didn't prepare me to speak to an actual celebrity, my god." Ava leaned back in her chair and scrubbed her hands down her cheeks in embarrassment, making me giggle. The rest of Maddy's session ran smoothly, because she had a lot of preferred independent play, which made her more willing to focus on more difficult work like color matching or stacking toys.

I kept eyeballing the gift basket on my desk throughout the rest of the workday, and all my friends had made stops by my office after hearing from Eloise that Josh was officially sending me shit to my workplace.

Everyone made some sort of comment about how he already knew me so well, considering instead of flowers and fruits, he sent me a simple green houseplant with a shit ton of popcorn.

It was perfect.

After Taylor finally came in and inspected the delivery, I felt myself become exhausted with the, "he knows you so well" comments. I wasn't confident that he did truly know me so well. Sure, I didn't think I'd changed a dramatic amount since high school, but I have changed a little bit since. We all have. It would be concerning if I was truly the same exact person that I was over a decade ago. And yet, when Kate and Josh were talking to me on the phone a couple weeks ago when they first dropped this fake dating contract in my lap, Josh immediately remembered my love of overheated, salted buttery corn.

So, maybe he did already know me well enough.

Maybe he and I were already getting to know each other again, which would really work in my favor. I still had intentions to make our fake dating contract not a thing, instead replacing it with an actual relationship. Even if there was an expiration date on it. I would be grateful for whatever time I could spend with Josh. Back in high school I was thoroughly convinced that he and I were soulmates. Until we kissed and never talked about it again, that is.

As I spun around in my office chair pondering the last few weeks, I was finding comfort in the knowledge at how, well, comfortable Josh and I were together already. I loved that we didn't shy away from touching each other, even though the touches could still be considered platonic.

I wanted to tread lightly either way, because I didn't want to scare him off by begging him to kiss me like I did in high school. Maybe if I had been able to control my hormones better in high school, Josh wouldn't have ghosted me after graduation. Maybe we would have still been long distance friends during college, and maybe he would have realized that we were, in fact, perfect for each other.

Knowing that dwelling on the past wasn't going to answer the questions that plagued my mind today, I released a heavy breath with determination in my current plan.

Maybe I wouldn't beg Josh to kiss me again, but instead, I could give him ample opportunity to make the first move.

Step one, I wanted to look kissable.

15

I looked hot.

Maybe that was a vain thing to think about myself, but it was true, nonetheless.

As we walked towards our seats in the cool arena, I made sure to remind myself to give Josh ample opportunity to check out my body. Getting up and stepping over him to get food. Getting up and stepping over him to go to the bathroom. With how narrow the seats were, I figured it wouldn't be that hard to pull off. I just needed to make sure not to sit on the aisle.

"Is this your first NHL game?" Kyle asked, his light eyes shining as he took in the sight of Josh and me holding hands. As soon as we got dropped off at the front, the band's bodyguard was always nearby. I forgot his name, but he also seemed like someone who didn't want to be addressed at all, so I let him act as a shadow for the band and me. I didn't want to distract him if there was an actual chance of Josh or his friends getting harmed.

"Yup! Who are the Ducks playing again?" I asked, tugging

on Josh's hand as he found the row of seats our tickets were in, and stepped to the side to let me in first.

"The Black Hawks," Josh replied, placing a hand on my lower back to guide me.

I smirked, that move was classic. Did I need his support on my lower back to walk to my seat? Nope. Did he feel the need to touch me in a public space as some weird way to claim me as his for everyone to see? Yes. I felt a flicker of feminism leave my body at the touch.

We settled into our seats, and I glanced up only just now to realize that we were in the front row. Damn, not bad.

"Which one of you is into hockey?" I leaned forward and addressed the rest of the band. They weren't dressed like your average pop punk band. Instead, they wore Ducks jerseys and baseball caps. They had all the swag.

"This is our first game, too," Garrett replied, stealing some of Kate's popcorn. She and I were the only ones not wearing swag. I immediately felt underdressed in my leggings, tight sweater, and hat.

"So why did you all get tickets?" I asked, lifting an eyebrow. Kate swatted at Garrett's hand, which was making another grab at her snack, before leaning forward and explaining.

"The Ducks aren't doing that well this season, people aren't coming to their games as a result. But if people knew that a popular band would be here..." she let the sentence trail off.

"So, it's just a publicity thing?" I asked, resting my chin on my fist. I saw Josh's gaze peek down my low-cut sweater for half a second before his eyes immediately went back to the ice.

Ha, dance for me, puppet.

"Kind of. It's a break from recording, we needed something to do together as a band in public, and we needed you two to be seen together. It's like, a win-win-win." Kate shrugged and threw a piece of her popcorn at Garrett who had started slurping from her soda cup.

"Cool," I replied, sitting back in my seat and patting Josh's leg. The way his body stiffened for half a second let me know I was a little too close to something resting on the inside of his thigh. Cheers started throughout the mostly crowded arena, but Kate was right, there were a lot of empty seats. The teams started flooding out of the tunnel that we happened to be sitting right next to, black and orange jerseys taking to the ice and starting drills.

"Look up," Josh leaned in close to my ear, and because of the cool arena keeping the rink frozen, his hot breath sent immediate chills down my neck. I followed his instructions, glancing up at the jumbotron above the rink to see that the cameras had spotted us. I waved before crossing my eyes and sticking my tongue out.

"Excellent." Josh chuckled, reaching over and resting his hand on my thigh.

And that was it for me.

I wasn't paying attention to the game at all as it started. Instead, I focused on how high up Josh had decided to rest his hand on my thigh. I clasped my hand over his, keeping it there—not that he had ever made a move to lift his hand off of me, but still, why risk it? We were both just casually resting our hands on my leg, just a couple inches lower than where I would have loved to have his hand rest.

Maybe not in public, though.

My blood started running, my body both rushing and stressing about the simple contact that Josh provided as he gently squeezed my leg throughout the first period of the game. He would go out of his way to use his other hand to sip from his soda, which meant that he liked resting his hand on my leg, right? It was a nice leg. Working out with Logan kept my muscles toned, but grabbable. Heat from Josh's hand seeped through the material of my leggings, making my leg feel ice-cold when he finally lifted his hand.

I resisted him for a second, clutching his hand a little more as he made to raise it off of my body. Josh smiled at me as I did, the side of his mouth that had the lip ring was tugging up as he leaned forward to talk in my ear again, "You alright?"

"Yup, it's just that my leg is cold now that you've been touching it for so long. I'm afraid you're going to have to keep it there the rest of the game." I shrugged, as if I wasn't trying to flirt with him while also acting nonchalant about the way my body hummed with our close contact, our arms resting against each other.

"Ah, are you too cold? Want my jacket?" Josh was wearing a jacket over a hoodie, completely bundled. I thought my sweater would be thick enough for the game, and frankly it was just the spot on my leg he had been holding that was cold, but I wasn't going to pass on the opportunity to snuggle in a jacket that smelled entirely like Josh. I nodded and smiled at him. He smirked and shrugged out of it, holding it out to me and letting me slip my arms through.

I glanced up at the jumbotron to see that the cameras were now showing Kate and Garrett, smiling and waving politely in between plays.

I also noticed the stats and players on the bottom of the large screen, as I sat back in my chair and grabbed Josh's hand to place it where it belonged. My body. I was truly hoping that him grabbing my leg wouldn't be everything I would experience tonight. Then the camera panned to Josh and me, and Garrett started fist-pumping and chanting "Kiss! Kiss! Kiss!"

I needed to remember to send a gift basket to Garrett at some point.

It wasn't even a kiss cam, but everyone sitting around us also started chanting, "Kiss! Kiss! Kiss!" I smiled and turned to Josh, more than ready for this moment.

Josh laughed at the camera then turned towards me, his tattooed hand coming up to cup my face as he leaned his head down to mine.

Oh my god.

It was happening.

Josh and I were finally going to kiss. On the mouth.

My body was ready.

As soon as I felt his warm, firm lips on mine my heart soared. It wasn't even a deep kiss, just a gentle quick brush of lips.

And then they were immediately gone.

I blinked at him, keeping my smile in place as he leaned forward to kiss my forehead and sit back in his chair.

What the fuck was that? My mind screamed. I played it cool, keeping a calm friendly mask on my face as if I wasn't wildly disappointed in the first kiss we had as adults. I glanced back at the jumbotron to make sure my mask hadn't slipped and felt my shoulders sag with relief when the image of the two of us looking happy and cuddly filled the screen. The camera panned to other members of the audience, and I glanced back at the players and stats again.

I squinted at the small headshot of one of the players, taking way too long to realize that I recognized that face.

And that name.

"What the *fuck?*" I quickly grabbed both arm rests, scooting to the edge of my seat to gape at the jumbotron and then scan the players on the ice.

"What? What's wrong?" Josh asked, reaching forward, and grabbing my hand over the armrest in between us.

"Logan!" I called, vaguely gesturing my free hand towards the rink right in front of us. A couple of players had slammed themselves into the side of the rink off to the side of us, but I didn't jump at the loud noise. Instead, I was scanning the names of the jerseys.

Sure enough, on his way to get involved with the little scuffle as the players fought over the puck, was Logan St. James. His helmet concealed most of his face and scarring, but the number on his jersey, the "St. James" stamped on his back, gave him away.

"Logan? From the gym?" Josh asked, leaning forward, and following my gaze. I pointed at the large man as he slammed his entire body into one of the Black Hawks players and successfully stole the puck from him, fans screaming as he raced across the ice and passed it to a teammate.

"Wait. Logan plays in the NHL? Since when?" Josh asked, wide-eyed and smirking at this new revelation.

"I don't know! He never told me!" I rubbed my hands with my cheeks, mind officially blown as we watched my grumpy buddy glide across the ice with the grace of a figure skater, but the expression of someone who hated everyone and everything.

"What in the world?" Josh chuckled as he reached for my hand again, making my heart thump at the contact we made. "This is amazing. You look like you've just been bamboozled."

"I feel bamboozled." I blinked up at Josh, his dark eyes scanning my facial features as his smirk stayed in place.

"I'm sorry, but I can't wait to see how he's going to react when you roast him about this." Josh wiggled his eyebrows with anticipation and I snickered, before squeezing his forearm through his hoodie.

"I don't think I can wait until we go to the gym again. I think I need to get his attention." I blinked, looking around and wanting to stand up. We were in the front row, so I really just needed to wait until he skated close enough to us again to start banging on the plexiglass.

"Court," Josh's low voice murmured in my ear as his hand slowly slid across my upper thigh and gently gripped, an attempt to hold me in my seat, "There is a reason he hasn't told you this yet. Maybe getting his attention in the middle of his game might throw him off his performance?" Josh knew that I was going to stand up and bang on the plexiglass based on my eager expression. He knew me.

I blinked, partly processing Josh's words but mostly focusing on his warm hand on my upper thigh. The warmth that pooled in my lower belly from that touch was downright embarrassing.

"Ugh," I rolled my eyes and leaned back in my seat, glaring at Logan as he shoved a Black Hawks player off him and took off towards the opposite end of the rink, "I can't believe I'm just going to have to sit here and watch him play without doing anything."

"You'll get through it; I believe in you." Josh chuckled as he squeezed my thigh once more, leaning forward and gently pressing his lips on my temple. I found myself turning towards him as he leaned away from me to settle in his own seat, keeping his hand on my thigh as we watched the game.

As it turned out, there was more to hockey than romance novels seemed to illustrate. Putting my own bitter feelings about Logan's secret aside, Josh managed to distract me with his touch on my leg. Enough for me to focus on both the rockstar beside me and the action taking place on the ice.

Hockey players were straight up mean.

Large bodies were constantly slamming and elbowing each other. At one point, someone threw an actual punch at another player, and they only got a couple of minutes in what looked like a time-out box because of it.

What kind of sport required a time-out box because of the constant physical aggression from all the players?

Hockey. That's what.

It was fast paced, players from both teams only getting a couple minutes on the ice before they took their seats on the bench. Kate had leaned forward and explained that this was normal for hockey because players tend to give one hundred and ten percent during their time on the ice, so it was beneficial to have a constant turnover to reduce the risk of injury.

One player's picture popped up on the jumbotron for some reason, stats and numbers that meant absolutely nothing to me showing up below his image as his half toothless smile filled the screen.

No sport could be worth multiple missing teeth, but what did I know?

As pictures on the jumbotron started to pan across the audience once again, showing all the fans wearing Ducks jerseys in the audience, my revenge on Logan came to me. I grinned, channeling my inner cartoon Grinch smile as I thought about how brilliant my revenge would be. So, I sat back, watching the game as goals were scored and saves were made. When the audience would stand up and cheer, so would I, jumping up and down as if I truly cared about this sport more than just a few minutes ago.

Josh matched my enthusiasm, cupping his hands to yell and cheer in the crowd. The camera panned to us once more, and I scanned the players to see if Logan noticed that the jumbotron was showing Josh and me. The man never looked up. He kept his gaze on the players, ignoring fans cheering his last name in the audience. It was as if he and the teams were the only ones in the room to him.

Well then.

I grinned up at the screen before turning to Josh, who was clapping and grinning at the latest goal the Ducks scored. I turned to look at my oldest friend right as he bent down and wrapped his arms around my waist, picking me up so we were chest to chest and cheering. I matched his enthusiasm and held onto his shoulder as I held one fist in the air. My skin was buzzing simply because my breasts were pressed against Josh's chest, even through layers of clothing.

***

I was feeling a little desperate after the *nothing* that happened between us at the Ducks game. Sure, we were in public, as well as with the rest of the band, but I was throwing myself at him.

I was constantly holding his hand or arm, and he would reassure my touch with gentle squeezes. When we stood up after the game ended, he squeezed my hand three times before leading us out of the arena only to be stopped by fans who had recognized Carbon Cut. I intended to step away to allow him to mingle with the fans, and he responded to my one single step away by tugging my arm back to his side. I obliged, even though I felt very out of place. Josh was charming as he interacted with his fans, who were mostly women.

He posed for selfies and signed whatever item the fans had on them, and Kate made sure to record moments of the experience for social media. All of the band members were great with the unexpected rush of fans, and none of them looked upset or irritated by it. It was expected, something I could tell by their relaxed body language and robotic, trained responses to fan compliments.

Carbon Cut acted like the most easygoing celebrities, even afterward when the crowd died down and we finally made it back to the car, thanks to the band's bodyguard leading the way.

I squished myself up against Josh's thigh to make room, but as soon as we were in the car, he didn't feel the need to hold my hand. Or hold my leg. He lifted his arm to rest on the seat behind me to accommodate how many bodies were squished into the SUV so we could all ride together, but nothing else happened.

When he walked me up to the townhome door, I paused and wrapped him up in a bear hug. I lingered, letting the warmth of his body settle into mine. I lifted my head and rested my chin on his chest, thanking him for the date. He grinned and leaned his head down.

This is it, I thought, *a real kiss. Not that stupid peck he did at the game.*

Nope, I was wrong. He planted a peck on my forehead. Not even daring to go towards my mouth. And I was devastated. My heart sank into my butt. Embarrassment washed over me, but I smiled and played it off as I watched him walk back into the SUV everyone else was packed in and drive off. I let out the longest sigh before finally accepting the failure the date was and let myself inside.

***

"I'm so excited."

"Can you record his reaction?" Josh asked, matching my grin with one of his own. I shouldered the door to the gym open and adjusted my bag on my shoulder as I scanned my pass and eyeballed the weights in the back. I narrowed my eyes as my gaze fell onto the large man, starting his exercise as if he wasn't going out of his way to keep his super cool job a secret from me.

Perhaps this was on me for never asking him what he did for work, but that was beside the point.

"I'll try, but I feel like once he sees my phone, he would be suspicious," I shrugged as I approached him, "Just try to stay on the FaceTime call."

"You got it," Josh saluted me and winked, making me smile involuntarily at him. Josh was truly so handsome. It was becoming an obsession in my mind. The more we texted and FaceTimed each other, the more I felt myself making a habit out of us. I could send him a random picture of a funny meme that clearly was meant for environmental science nerds like Josh, and I knew he would respond within the hour. I felt just as connected with him as I did back in high school, which was both comforting and terrifying. Comforting, because I had missed him so damn much and my soul was starving for his presence in my life. Terrifying, because the past proved that no matter how close we were, we were still capable of not speaking to each other for almost ten years.

Blinking my spiraling thoughts and insecurities away, I squared my shoulders as I approached Logan, who had his large, muscled back to me.

"Say hi to Josh," I called, turning my phone around right as Logan turned his head towards me. He nodded once at my fake boyfriend as he set up the weights we were starting with today.

"What's up, Logan?" Josh asked, the excitement for my reveal evident in his tone. Logan didn't catch on though. He just gave Josh a thumbs up in response as he sat down on the weight bench to start. I set my phone down against my gym bag, careful to angle it so that Josh could see Logan perfectly in the screen. Logan lifted a questioning eyebrow as he saw me do this.

"Josh wants to compare what we do for weights with what his trainer tells him to do," I shrugged, the lie naturally falling from my mouth.

"It'll just be for a couple minutes, I got to go soon," Josh added, going along with my lie that I had just pulled out of my ass. Logan shrugged, not caring at all as he grabbed one of the lighter weights to hand to me. I paused and held a finger up to him.

"Oh, one sec, I'm kind of cold so I'm going to put on an extra layer," I turned around and started digging around in my bag, careful not to knock my phone over. Logan's expression stayed flat as he set my lighter weights down next to him on the bench while he started curling his heavier weights.

Fucking show-off.

I pulled the extra layer out of my duffle, a smile spreading across my cheeks as I quickly threw it on over myself. The jersey was long and fell almost mid-thigh. The sleeves were long too, but it was the only size left because apparently Logan St. James wasn't the most popular hockey player on his team and nobody felt the need to stock extra sizes of his jersey.

I straightened the jersey so his name was visible and turned around to face my gym buddy, hands on my hips as I proudly announced that I knew his secret.

He didn't look at me at first, he kept his gaze on his hand as he curled the dumbbell, but after a moment or two of silence from me he must have felt my gaze. His dark eyes glanced up at me, quickly flicking down to the weight again before doing a double take. Pausing his exercise mid-curl, his dark brows furrowed as his lips turned downward. Logan glared at my jersey before glaring at me, and then glaring at Josh on my phone.

"Want to know what Josh and I did for our weekly date a couple days ago?" I crossed my arms over my chest, tapping my foot repeatedly like I was Logan's mother and he had lied to me about finishing his homework.

Logan closed his eyes before inhaling and exhaling the loudest breath I had ever heard from him.

"What Courtney is trying to say," Josh chimed in from my phone, "Is that we loved watching you kick ass at your hockey game. Seriously, you guys were great." At the sight of light pink touching Logan's tanned cheeks and ears, I couldn't stop myself from snickering at his embarrassment.

Aww, the NHL player didn't like attention.

Guess he should have thought about that before joining the fucking NHL.

"Seriously, what the hell, Logan?" I cried. Josh laughed, then announced that he had to go, so I picked up my phone and blew the singer a kiss before tossing the device in my bag. I removed the jersey and tossed it angrily at Logan, who caught it effortlessly and rolled his eyes at the sight of his name on the back.

I dug around in my bag again, pulling out a Sharpie and tossing it to Logan as well. He caught it smoothly but raised a questioning eyebrow at me again.

"You're going to sign it, and I'm not going to tell all our friends that they hang out with not one, but two celebrities regularly." I nodded towards the jersey in his hands, encouraging him to get a move on. Logan's shoulders relaxed slightly as he uncapped the Sharpie with his teeth and quickly got to work on signing his own jersey.

Ugh. Men.

16

"Romance, huh?" Josh asked, swinging our intertwined hands back and forth as we strolled through the small indie bookshop. The shop was relatively new, and only stocked romances. Needless to say, it was my favorite type of bookshop. After doing something with a lot of bro energy, like going to a hockey game, I suggested we do something on the opposite end of the spectrum for our next weekly date.

Of course, Josh was down. He didn't question it or look disgusted when I had suggested going to my favorite romance bookstore an hour south from us, in the north part of San Diego. We drove together, his bodyguard tailing us in a separate vehicle like always. I played Carbon Cut's music, asking Josh about his inspiration for a lot of his songs.

Apparently, my feminist ramblings had a lot of influence on him in high school. A number of Carbon Cut's songs were feminist anthems, even if the lyrics weren't obvious about it. I felt a warmth fill my heart as Josh admitted that certain phrases and words I had used when I was distracted in science class (ignoring the experiment in front of us to, instead, process everything I was learning about the patriarchy) had stuck with him.

"Have you read this one?" Josh asked, pulling me from my memory of the car ride over. We both had coffees in our hands, and it was early enough in the morning that the marine layer created a nice grey overcast outside. It reminded me of growing up in the Pacific Northwest. Josh was wearing sunglasses and an NHL beanie he had bought at our last date, a dark hoodie completed his stealthy appearance in an attempt not to be easily recognized.

"I have," I nodded, taking the book from his hands, "I even have a signed copy at home. The author is local." I smiled as I admired the cover art before putting the book back on the shelf. Josh was a very fun person to take to the bookstore. He wasn't turned off by all the pinks and purples and feminine designs the bookstore had. He didn't laugh or make fun of me for reading romance novels, or *only* reading romance novels. He had been asking questions the entire time, genuinely interested in this niche hobby of mine.

"Oh, I love this one!" We had wandered over to the fantasy section of the bookstore, and I had pulled down a book I had only read on my e-reader. "I love a good enemies to lovers." I grinned as I held the book in my hands, loving the feel of this story.

"Enemies to lovers?" Josh asked, taking the book from my hands so that he could skim the back synopsis.

"Yes, it's my favorite trope," I explained, eyeballing the book in his hands. I was debating on buying a copy for me to reread. I had already read the story, but I knew I would enjoy reading it again. And having a hard copy of books I loved was a guilty pleasure of mine, as my overflowing bookshelves in my room could prove.

Josh blinked at the cover before looking around the bookstore and leaning towards me, whispering, "What's a trope?"

"Oh, it's like a plot device that occurs throughout stories. The plot device can be enemies to lovers, forced proximity, only one bed. Things like that."

Josh nodded twice at my explanation, smiling as if he understood my definition perfectly. I thought I'd explained it well enough, until he lifted his hand to press a button on his smart watch, asking the device, "…What's a trope?"

I smacked his arm as he chuckled, "It's like, I don't know, a subtopic in a genre! So, like, let's say you like reading about when couples are forced to share one bed together, you can literally search books by tropes. Like enemies to lovers."

"Ah, yes, yes." Josh nodded again before lifting his watch and whispering, "What is enemies to lovers?" I groaned as his watch pulled up the definition of a trope.

"A trope is a common or overused theme or device," his watch said, making a couple of heads turn in our direction at the sound of a robotic woman speaking.

"That's literally what I said." I rolled my eyes before taking the book out of Josh's hands and flipping through the pages. For no other reason than to feel my hands flip through all the pages.

"What you said made no sense." Josh chuckled as he reached behind me, momentarily pressing our bodies together as he pulled a book down from the top shelf, "What trope is in this book?" Josh asked, holding up a black book with red and grey fantastical designs on it.

I felt my cheeks heat at his question.

"I don't know." I turned around and started skimming the pages of the fantasy book I held in my hands.

"Well, that's clearly not true," Josh spoke low, his front pressing into my back as he gently pinned me against the shelf so that he could wrap his arms around me. The smutty fantasy was trapped in my line of sight in front of us. "What's this story about?" It took me a moment to process his question, because all I could focus on was the fact that Josh was pressed behind me. As if we made this sort of physical contact regularly. As if it was natural for him to gently pin me against a bookshelf with his hips, the filthiest books I had ever read stocked in front of us. I allowed myself to gently melt into him, subtly letting him know that I wasn't nervous receiving this contact from him.

"It's...got very little plot." I shrugged, feeling his bicep against my shoulder with the movement.

"Really? It's a thick book, almost four hundred pages." Josh started flipping through as I just nodded.

"Yup." He wasn't wrong. It was a lot. Throughout the four-hundred-page book, the characters did things to each other that I would never consider doing in reality. That didn't keep me from reading every damn page, though.

"...This is erotica, isn't it?" Josh rested his chin on top of my head as he paused on a page in the middle of the book, the words displayed in front of me making my cheeks heat as I realized he had opened to the reverse-harem part of the story.

I cleared my throat before nodding, making his chin on my head nod with me.

"Oh, wow," his voice stayed low, and I felt my pulse race as I realized that Josh was actually reading the scene in front of us, "You've read this?"

"Mm-hmm," I hummed, my heart racing as I also studied the words in front of us. I was blinking a lot. I felt overstimulated by Josh's tall, warm body hovering behind me while the main character in the story that Josh held was being dicked-down in the most descriptive possible way.

"What were your thoughts?" Having finished the page, Josh turned to the next one.

"It was fun," I replied without thinking, making Josh's laughter rumble behind me. His chest vibrated, and I felt my body shiver from the sensation of feeling his laughter so close.

"Fun." Josh closed the book and shelved it, seemingly satisfied once the main character reached her climax from two of the four men present. I wasn't pinned to the bookshelf anymore, but he clearly enjoyed the closeness as much as I did as he wrapped his arms around my shoulders. I leaned back and grinned at him, glad I seemed to have won that game of chicken he initiated.

"Are you going to get that one?" Josh asked, eyes glancing at the cleaner fantasy book I held in my hands.

"I think so, I already read it but I love it." I grinned, holding it up so we could both admire the cover art.

"Because of the thrope," Josh nodded. I rolled my eyes.

"Yes, the *trope*. But also, it caught me off guard," I

explained, holding it to my chest as I browsed the spines of the other books, taking a tentative step out of Josh's embrace. It was dangerous for me to stay wrapped up in him too long. I kept imagining ways to turn around and stick my tongue in his mouth, but I didn't want to do that until I was one hundred percent certain he wanted my tongue in his mouth.

"How did it catch you off guard?" Josh asked, standing next to me, and pulling some other book off of the shelf to flip through.

"This story isn't about the main character," I smiled, "It's about the side character."

Josh blinked, "Oh, that sounds boring."

"You'd think," I shrugged, "But fantasy romances all have very similar story structure; it's somewhat difficult to write one that isn't a little predictable. This book embraces that, letting the hero of the fantasy have their story while the side character, usually known for being humorous and carrying the plot, can have their time in the light."

Josh stared at the book in my hands, weighing something in his mind, before his dark gaze met mine. A smirk tugged at his lips, making his lip ring glint in the light. "I'm curious, out of all the products in this store, which five books would you recommend for me to read?"

My eyes widened, a grin spreading across my cheeks as I clutched my fantasy book to my chest. "Oh my god, you want to read romance novels?"

"I'd like to know more about my girlfriend's hobby." Josh tugged on his lip ring with his teeth once.

An older woman, probably in her forties, overheard our

conversation and walked past Josh to pat me on the shoulder before murmuring, "You better keep him forever."

Josh heard her, a devilish smirk on his lips as he mouthed her words to me, "You better keep him forever." I giggled and nodded my head in agreement with the woman.

I grabbed Josh's wrist and tugged him from section to section, telling him quick details about many different books I thought he would enjoy reading the most. I was an easy-to-please romance enthusiast, meaning I could read anything from closed door/fade-to-black PG love stories, to dark, twisted monster orgies. However, I wanted Josh to read what I enjoyed reading, and those included at least one intimate scene between the lovers.

We ended up leaving the bookstore with almost a dozen books. Josh had his stack, and I had mine. His bodyguard was sitting at the small coffee shop across the street and nodded at us as he saw us approach our car, immediately abandoning his own coffee to get into his separate vehicle.

Josh asked me to start reading one of his books, and the entire drive home was spent with me reading one of my favorite comfort reads to him. Throughout the drive I would catch him smiling at the words I read aloud, and other times I saw him chewing on his lip ring in contemplation. The couple of times our eyes met, his gaze was fleeting, as he quickly scanned my body curled up in the passenger seat. I smiled as I realized that I felt a little bit of a deeper connection with him. The fact that he proudly bought romance novels simply because his fake girlfriend was interested in them was enough to make my little heart swoon. As well as the other hearts of fellow uterus owners in the bookstore.

He wasn't intimidated to be the only guy in the store and he wasn't worried about what everyone else's opinions of him were. He was there for me. He wanted to learn more about me and what I enjoyed. I held all his attention, and yet, my soul wanted more. Craved more.

Later that night, after dropping me off with another stupid peck on my forehead, as if I was his little sister instead of a sexually available woman, I found myself rereading my fantasy novel. The complex emotions of the different characters struggling with which side of morality they needed to stand on were a good distraction for my longing.

Then my phone buzzed next to me on my bed.

I unlocked my phone to see that Josh had tagged me in a photo on social media. It was a picture we had taken before we had bought our book haul. We were holding all the copies we intended to buy while Josh held his phone up to take a selfie. The caption said, "I learned all about thropes today, and how she's a huge enemies to lovers fan."

I cackled before liking the picture, pleased to see that comments had already started to flood the image, explaining to him that it's *trope* not *thrope*.

***

The next few weeks flew by.

We had our weekly dates, as well as many FaceTime calls. Sometimes Josh and I would go out on our own, other times the rest of the band or my friends would join us on whatever random outing we could come up with. It was comforting to know that both of our groups mingled so well together.

I had also attended events specifically designed to publicly announce our courtship, similar to the Ducks game. The events were as simple as sightings at famous restaurants in LA, where photographers had plenty of opportunities to photograph us, or attending movie premieres and art show galleries. I ended up meeting a couple of other celebrities in the pop punk music genre, but was disappointed when Josh had to remind me multiple times that he did not personally know Taylor Swift or Harry Styles and thus, the likelihood of me meeting them was almost nonexistent.

At that point I started wondering if fake dating my celebrity childhood crush was even worth it.

Because the reality was, I was getting frustrated. Also, sexually frustrated.

I hadn't ever had to struggle with men. Meaning that I had mastered the art of displaying physical touch in subtle ways that made it obvious to men that I wanted to sleep with them. Perhaps I had taken this for granted, because I hadn't ever had to go out of my way to bluntly make the first move or ask the first question. Perhaps it was the benefit of having a pretty face and pretty blonde hair. Who knew? Whatever it was, it was getting me absolutely nowhere with Josh.

Perhaps I had been going about this all wrong?

Though I had completely gotten used to the tall, filled out, tatted, charming, confident Joshua Madey, I would still see glimpses of the scrawny, teenage, glasses wearing J-shua. I found myself emotionally clinging to him in those moments, as if I was trying to grab on to the boy I was infatuated with in my youth, before all pieces of him disappeared from me forever. It was ridiculous, and I tried my best to not fixate on that unhealthy behavior too much, because the reality was that I was simply grateful to have adult J-shua in my life now. It was unconventional, but I had felt like I was on cloud nine after every interaction with him. Even if it was just a simple FaceTime call or text message, I felt better with his constant presence in my life.

That being said, it was still frustrating that we hadn't been able to take the next step past platonic friendly touches. That moment in the bookstore where he pinned me against a bookshelf filled with erotica almost felt like a dream at this point, because nothing ever happened like that again. If we were in public, and cameras were present, he would give me quick closed-mouth pecks on the lips, or the temple of my head. I had half a mind to just open my mouth on him one time, but the thought of embarrassing him in front of the cameras made me hold back and take whatever he was willing to give me.

I hated those stupid pecks.

It felt worse every time, as if he somehow made it possible for our lips to have less contact with each other after every peck. Or maybe I was just sexually frustrated?

The number of times I had to go through my stash of sex toys after a date with Josh was embarrassing. I had never been this desperate for release. I wasn't exactly a needy woman and didn't feel the need to take care of things myself more than once every two weeks. Maybe once a week if I was truly feeling it.

I won't even bother sharing how often I was Womansplaining myself, just know that it was ridiculous, and I was genuinely fearful that my clit would build some sort of callus. Needless to say, fantasizing about Josh simply wasn't enough for my raging hormones.

I was walking to the bus stop with Beck after work one day, lost in my spiraling thoughts about my very inappropriate feelings for my childhood friend, when she threw a curveball at me. "Adam and I have been talking about the next step for us."

I stumbled my step a little bit, not expecting that direct of a statement from her. She was the more subtle one between us. "Oh? What is the next step?" I asked, my stomach sinking.

"Well, we want to live together. Under one roof," she shrugged, keeping her eyes forward at the bus stop in front of us. "At first, I thought it would freak me out, living in sin with a man. But the more we've talked about it, the more excited I am about the idea of always being around him."

I blinked at her, my grin wavering enough for me to feel it but hopefully not enough for her to see it. "That's so exciting!" She smiled back at me, pleased with my reaction. "Do you know where? Like, do I need to start packing boxes?"

"Don't you dare," Beck's eyes widened at me with disbelief, "We haven't decided the details yet, because we aren't exactly rushing into this. Though, Adam has said repeatedly how his condo feels lifeless."

"Yes, but if you move in, it probably wouldn't," I shrugged, doing my best to be the encouraging friend, and putting my feelings of abandonment on the back burner, "I mean, you'd come with all your junk."

"True, but there's also Gram, and I don't know if I want to leave her..." Beck quirked her lips to the side, her head lifting up to catch the sight of the bus approaching. I hadn't even heard the vehicle, because I was so focused on every detail of our conversation. Of course, Beck wouldn't want to leave her only blood relative she was on speaking terms with. The most logical solution would be for me to move out so Beck and Adam could take over upstairs. Me living with the three of them just wasn't realistic, and I was confident that Susan would prefer that her granddaughter's boyfriend move in, instead of her granddaughter's best friend staying put while Beck moved out. I needed to start looking around. Maybe Eloise needed a roommate? There was no way in hell I could afford much on my own, not with how inflated housing was in Orange County.

We rode the bus home, Beck letting me know that Adam was coming over with a bunch of groceries we needed to make our curry that Beck and Susan loved. I smiled, glad I was still getting some bit of routine and familiarity after the news I knew was coming. Beck was growing up, moving forward with her relationship with Adam. I wasn't, I was stagnant, something I loved and grew fond of. The stability and safety that came with routine was grounding, even if it seemed illogical.

I knew it was illogical. Beck moving out didn't mean that she was ditching our friendship. Beck would never do that. She had proven time and time again that no matter how involved or dedicated to Adam she was, that there was still room for me in her life. But things changed when people moved. It's a reality we cannot escape. Without the familiarity of seeing each other every day, the routine of our friendship would become unpredictable. Unstable. It would be the equivalent of me wondering which of my parents would be living with me during my youth. Whenever mom moved out, I saw her sporadically, and whenever she swapped places with dad, he ended up being the one showing up randomly and without preparation.

Yes, my parents and I have had long talks about their spontaneous behaviors as I was growing up. Thank you, therapy. However, I still had scars from the experience. My body immediately created anxiety with any sort of threat from the life I was familiar and happy with. Logically, I knew that Beck needed to take this step with her boyfriend if she felt it was right. Logically, I knew that it made the most sense for me to move out so Beck and Susan could stay together. Logically, I knew that with the tiniest amount of effort that my friendship with Beck would stay strong no matter where I ended up living.

Emotionally, my body remembered the hurt and longing that came from constantly being thrust into new situations with the new romantic partners my parents would introduce me to. I hated growing a bond with someone, whether it was over playing video games or cooking together, only for one of my parents to sit me down and explain that sometimes adults don't stay together forever, and that sometimes it was for the best if they went their separate ways.

Even as a teenager I understood that not all relationships ended in happily ever after, but would it have killed my parents to be a little more intentional with whomever they decided to bring home and introduce me to?

I was spiraling about all of this when I felt Beck rest a hand on my leg, a concerned pinch in her brow as she leaned forward to catch my gaze. "Are you alright?"

"Yeah, sorry," I blinked and shook my head once, "I think I had a long day. I just completely disassociated the last few minutes. My bad." I blinked again and rubbed the corners of my eyes.

"Oh, I get it, Maddy was giving me grief today, too. The little stinker." Beck smiled at the thought of our favorite client and let me sit in comfortable silence on the way home. I eyeballed her texting Adam next to me, not reading their messages but simply allowing myself to be a little bitter about the fact that not only was she making plans to move in with her boyfriend, but that there was also a hundred and ten percent chance that she was going to get successfully laid tonight.

Whereas I was expecting a package to arrive in the mail today, because the motor on my favorite vibrator was starting to sound concerning (probably due to the overuse the last few sexually frustrating weeks). I didn't want it to officially die during the worst possible moment, so I decided to be responsible and order a new one so that I wouldn't have to bother waiting any longer than I wanted to…take care of things.

17

This weekend we were all meeting up at the Josh's fancy condo in Hollywood, and Eloise was excited about a new pie recipe she had mastered and wanted to share. The plan was literally for all of us to hang out, eat pie, and maybe play a party game or two. Something I had learned about Kate and Garrett was that they were both very competitive and enjoyed party games more than expected. Watching the two of them play silly games like charades against each other was top tier entertainment. It was going to be fun.

Though at this point I was both thrilled and nervous about being in Josh's presence again. At some point I needed to figure out if pursuing him was worth it or not, but the thought of not being as physically affectionate made my gut sink. Almost like the reaction I had when Beck announced that she and Adam wanted to live together.

I couldn't handle both realities at the moment, so when the day finally came and we all carpooled in multiple vehicles to Josh's bougie Hollywood Hills condo, I decided I would wrap Josh up in as many bear hugs as I was capable of until further notice.

Josh was in one of those apartment buildings that had security, and you weren't allowed past the lobby unless your name was on the list. Our group was large enough to travel in two separate vehicles, even without Logan who had to arrive a few minutes late because he was busy with his whole "secretly a professional hockey player" thing, so it took a while before everyone showed their IDs and we were finally allowed in the elevator. We made it to one of the highest floors, which made me suspect that he had one of those penthouse units that took up the entirety of the top floor of condominiums.

I was right. As soon as Josh opened the door and accepted my wide armed demand for another bear hug as the others filed in behind me, I saw that his condo had stairs to a second level inside. Wild. He had a large open concept space, where the living room rested a step below the entryway and kitchen and dining area. His décor was very male, all neutrals and sharp lines and modern art. The only piece of color in the condo was a colorful red rug in the middle of the living room floor.

The rest of the band was already inside, and Kate and Garrett were setting up some type of party game that involved the TV, Garrett tugging on one of Kate's belt loops and pulling her closer to his body.

I internally sighed at the cuteness.

Sure, Josh and I held each other and hugged, but there was a wall between us that always let me know that that's all it would be. I longed for something different, but I felt the divide all at the same time.

Eloise put the pie in the oven to warm up, and ten

minutes later Josh buzzed Logan up the elevator. As everyone settled into Josh's living space, I noticed every single time Josh reached out for my hand, or rested his arm across my shoulders, or went out of his way to sit by me. I soaked it up, unable to stop myself from hoping for more.

I was doomed.

A little bit later, Josh and I were pretending to be looking at something on my phone, but the reality was we were both watching Eloise and Logan. We were obsessed with these two lately. Logan was off to the side, glaring at whatever he was typing on his phone, as Eloise eyeballed him after she served Beck and Adam some pie. Once those two retreated to the living room, she quirked her lips to the side, then stared at the pie in front of her. She picked up the last plate and took a couple of steps towards where our friends went, before exhaling and stepping back in front of the pie.

"Logan," Eloise spoke, her voice flatter than when she spoke with anyone else in the condo. Josh inhaled a shocked gasp as she spoke his name, and I tried my best to hold in my giggle at his emotional investment in my two friends. Logan's eyes glanced up towards Eloise as she stood in front of the pie, clearly surprised to be addressed directly by her. "Do you want some?"

Logan glanced at the pie then stared back at Eloise. The poor man was clearly dumbfounded that she was not only talking to him, but checking to make sure he participated with a slice of her treat. But her patience with him was wearing thin.

"Logan?" she tried again, "Do you want a slice?" Then she attempted to sign to him, another white flag thrown his direction. Except she didn't sign to him correctly. Nope. Eloise did the thing every single person who was learning ASL did when attempting to guess signs. She took both of her hands, placed her thumbs and index fingers together to create a type of triangle, attempting to sign the word "slice."

Except that was not what the sign meant.

Logan's eyes bulged before he clapped a hand over his mouth to try to smother his choked laughter, his face and ears going red. Eloise's brows furrowed at his reaction, and she glanced over to Josh and me for some sort of explanation.

"What?" she asked, not giving me a chance to explain before she turned a very obvious glare towards Logan, who was eyeballing her hands that still held the sign up. He smirked and set his phone down on the counter to sign back to her, my mouth vocalizing on its own accord, *at least buy me dinner first.*

Eloise frowned at my translation, her bright blue eyes staring wide at me and actually waiting for an explanation this time. "That's...not the sign you think it is," I explained, trying to smother my own laugh.

"Why is Eloise signing vagina?" Taylor asked as they entered the room, helping themselves to another slice of Eloise's pie. Eloise gasped as her face turned bright red. Logan smirked at her embarrassment as her mouth opened and closed, and she immediately dropped her hands and spluttered for a moment.

"I wasn't! I mean, I didn't mean to! I was asking Logan if he wanted a *slice* of pie!"

"Oh, I'm sure he'd love a slice of what you just offered

him." Taylor winked at Eloise as they scooped up some goop of berry filling and sucking it off of their finger with a loud pop.

"Wait, how do you know that sign? You suck at ASL!" Eloise accused Taylor as they took their plate and made their way back towards the living room.

"That is true, but I made sure to learn all the curse words and body parts first thing, specifically so I wouldn't do what you just did." At that, Taylor saluted Eloise and winked at Logan before they skirted out of there.

"Oh my god," Josh muttered as he turned to hide his laughter into my shoulder. I reveled in the way his breath tickled my skin, naturally leaning into his body as his shoulders shook with laughter at the situation.

Eloise gave me an embarrassed smile, before hardening her expression and shooting Logan with a look that I was sure would melt his face off. At her glare, he immediately stopped smiling and looked to me in a panic.

I couldn't have helped him even if I tried.

Eloise had already taken the plate with her slice of pie on it, marched right up to Logan, and smooshed the slice right into his dark grey t-shirt. His arms came up, as if he was about to shove her away, but I think the shock of the situation made his entire body freeze as she twisted the plate against his wide chest. She did her absolute best to ensure the pie stain was never coming out.

Without a word she took the plate, set it on the countertop next to him, and marched right out of the kitchen. If I knew Eloise, I would guess that she was going to run into the bathroom and compose herself before returning to the group again.

Logan stood there in the kitchen, shellshocked that she had so easily assaulted him with the dessert. He quickly caught pieces of pie in his hands that were falling off of his chest. Once he held his shirt away from his body and contained the mess, he looked up at me with an expression of shock and confusion.

I giggled into Josh's shoulder as I spoke to Logan. "I don't think she liked being teased for her slip up, from you specifically."

Logan walked over to the sink to clean up and held his hands out like, *Really?* Or maybe, *How was that my fault?* I just shrugged, because frankly I saw no scenario where Eloise would happily take any ribbing from Logan at this point.

Logan glared at his spoiled shirt after attempting to rinse it off in the sink and dabbing away at it with paper towels. He exhaled roughly as he stomped out of the kitchen, probably on his way to find a laundry room or bathroom to clean up.

"Those two are such a mess," Josh snickered, pulling his face out of my shoulder now that we were in the kitchen alone.

"They're hopeless," I giggled with my friend, rubbing his side since my arm had somehow found its way looped around his waist.

"I'm so invested in their love story." Josh chuckled as he leaned away from me to wipe a tear away from his eye. I grinned at him, glad that my friends brought him so much joy. Even if a snarky part of my brain was screaming at him, *why can't you be invested in* our *love story? I could not be more obvious!*

Josh patted my shoulder once before following our friends to the living room where Kate had an itinerary of party games waiting for us.

I barely noticed when Eloise and Logan both emerged from down the hall, Eloise stepping out first and Logan following a few moments later. They sat on opposite sides of the room and played the trivia game on the TV without ever acknowledging each other for the rest of the night.

It was probably for the best.

I was squished on the couch with Adam and Beck, going as far as to swing one of my legs over onto Josh's so that we were sitting as close as possible.

Josh would poke my side, gently pinch my arm, or cover my eyes in an attempt to get me to lose since he was doing terribly. It was all very playful and affectionate, and I couldn't stop myself from staring at his profile throughout the night.

His sharp jaw.

His pointed nose.

His dark eyes behind his black rimmed glasses he wore on casual occasions.

His lip ring.

I wanted him so badly, but I wasn't getting any direct signals from him. I never had. How could I possibly move past this? How could I either accept this was all we would be, or show him that I simply wanted more?

Even our text conversations and FaceTime calls were starting to become disappointing. As weeks passed, every single time he would bring up a date idea he would somehow add some odd idea on how to get Eloise and Logan to talk to each other. He was convinced that they were meant to be, and my heart would hurt every time he would change the topic from us to them.

Our weekly dates still stood, but I found myself less enthusiastic about including our friends on them. I had a limited amount of time with Josh during this agreement, and whenever he brought up potentially making it a group hangout so that we could try to get Logan and Eloise to do something ridiculous, like play chicken together in a pool (I wish I was making that suggestion up, but nope, Josh's condo had a rooftop pool he thought would be perfect for them) my stomach felt heavy with disappointment.

Did he ever suggest things like playing chicken with me? Nope.

Thankfully, whenever I smoothly suggested trying out a new restaurant or food venue with just the two of us, Josh never pushed. He was more than willing to go on one-on-one dates with me. I just wished he was more enthusiastic about them.

Pictures of us were popping up all over social media, and while I had done a good job of keeping my social medias private and keeping a low profile, I ended up just ignoring my accounts for the time being. I didn't like seeing all the comments about how people loved how cute of a couple Josh and I were, or how they were jealous and wished I had the plague so that another woman could take my place.

Both types of comments simply reminded me that Josh and I were only fake dating.

Tammy had reached out to me via email, asking if she could meet up with me at the Thai restaurant again, and I agreed. She was the only reporter who I knew was genuine, and I respected the fact that she asked for my permission this time instead of ambushing me while out and about like a couple of other reporters had done.

My answers to Tammy's questions were scripted, lines that Kate had suggested I use when reporters got wind of Josh and me being a couple. How we fell in love after getting to know each other after the concert. How wonderful of a partner Josh was (which was true, when he wasn't focused on hanging out with Logan and Eloise specifically). How much fun hanging out with the band was, etc.

It was scripted, and yet not all lies either.

I did love hanging out with the band. Kyle, Tom, Garrett, and Kate were wonderful people who shared Josh's beliefs about the environment and feminism. I had gone with Josh a time or two to fundraisers specifically where the end goal was to provide funds in order for certain organizations to reduce carbon emissions and waste.

He was a wonderful person, and I was lucky to experience being his partner for those pieces of his life.

However, I still wanted to suck his tongue into my mouth.

But I also wanted to respect his boundaries.

Ugh, what was a girl to do?

18

I knew what I was walking into based on the silence I heard from inside of Beck's bedroom, but I didn't care. I knocked a couple of times before testing the knob and allowing myself to enter her space.

Adam was on top of Beck in her bed. They were clearly in the middle of groping each other and had been making out for some time based on their swollen lips as they quickly separated their faces from each other to see me.

"Sorry, you guys can continue in a moment." I had to fight not to roll my eyes at the way Adam blushed under his freckles, as if I didn't know that they were two grown adults who banged on the regular. "I just need a few moments to vent to my best friend, if you could manage to let her breathe for that time."

"I'll try," was Adam's dry reply as he rolled off Beck and tucked his hands behind his head. Beck was flushed and sat up quickly, scanning my face to try to get a read on me. Reading people was something that she was actually terrible at, considering how long it took her to realize that Adam had a raging boner for her since she coughed all over him in her office.

"I'm frustrated and need a sounding board," I groaned as I flopped onto the bed on the other side of Beck.

"Probably not as frustrated as me at the moment," Beck replied.

"What?" I asked, surprised to see her eyeballing Adam still, the smirk on his face almost made me want to vomit.

"Nothing, proceed. Why are you frustrated, best friend who couldn't wait until after I was happily railed to talk to me about her problems?" Beck leaned on her side and rested her chin on her palm, her back to Adam.

"I'm glad you asked," I sighed, ignoring her jab, "How do I get Josh to care about me as much as he cares about Logan and Eloise?"

They both gave me nothing but silence for a few moments after that sentence.

"…What?" Beck asked.

"Ugh, Josh is *so* obsessed with manipulating Logan and Eloise into situations where they have to spend time together or address the other, even though they absolutely hate each other. Which, don't get me wrong, I agree is hilarious. But lately that seems to be the *only* thing he cares about. Like, every time we all hang out as a group, he is entirely focused on Eloise and Logan. When it's just me and him, he finds a way to bring them up. I swear he's going to try to find a way to play spin the bottle with them simply so that he could see the two of them get locked in a closet together for seven minutes in heaven. I'm sure he would love something like that."

"First of all, I'm pretty sure you just mixed up two different teenage party games. Second, why are you so annoyed by this?" Beck asked.

"Why can't he focus on *us*!" I carried on, ignoring her. "I mean sure, we're fake dating so I can understand why he doesn't feel the need to put in a ton of effort, but I am practically *throwing* myself at the guy. I am constantly looking for excuses to touch him and wrap myself around him, and he doesn't feel the need to take advantage of that opportunity at all!" I groaned and scrubbed my hands down my face roughly, waiting for any sort of feedback.

"...Wait, Josh is trying to get Logan and Eloise to hook up?" Adam asked on the other side of Beck.

"Yes. He's playing matchmaker. Which is fine, I love that, but also, I'm dying for him to see that I'm standing right in front of him." I only removed my hands from my face when I heard the sound of Beck laughing, and I eyeballed her from my prone position on her bed to see her covering her eyes as she continued to laugh.

"What's so funny?" I asked, frowning at her. I just interrupted a spicy session between her and her quiet, athletic boyfriend to complain about how untouched I am, and she's laughing?

"Courtney," Beck rubbed a hand down her face before pointing at me accusingly, "He's *you!*"

I kept my frown in place, not understanding.

"How?" I asked.

"Oh, come on!" Beck cried, sitting up fully on her bed, and

turning to face me, "You don't remember trying to manipulate me to be attracted to random men for years?"

"I'm pretty sure that was different—" Beck threw her head back to laugh again.

"It wasn't! You would literally set me up on blind dates constantly. You would hype up men of any stereotype simply because you were obsessed with the idea of me finally finding companionship. You even told me to pursue a coworker!"

"To be fair, that was a good call," Adam added, pulling his phone out of his pocket to check the time. It was fairly late. "Also, I support Josh on his current fixation."

Beck and I both turned to look over at Adam with confusion. He just stared at us blankly until we pressed, per usual.

"You think Logan and Eloise would be a good idea?" Beck asked.

"I do." Adam lifted a shoulder, his facial features softening the slightest bit as he looked at his rumpled girlfriend. "Eloise is always so poised, perfectly put together, and composed. We dated for a whole year and she kept that charade up. Whereas Logan is the only one I have ever known to make her let her guard down enough to drop her act immediately. Whether she verbally tells him off or shoves pie at him, they clearly have some type of passion between them that neither probably realizes. They just need to find the opportunity to explore that without one offending or insulting the other."

Beck's eyes darkened a little at Adam's assessment, reminding me that it took very little effort on Adam's part for her to be aroused by his views on things.

"This is what happens when you read too many of my

romance novels." She blinked at him before turning back to me, lifting a shoulder to let me know she agreed with him.

"Cool. Great. Wonderful. Can we get back to *me* now? God, you two are just as frustrating as Josh!" I reached my hands into my hair and tugged at my roots once before sitting up in Beck's bed.

"Have you ever considered just telling Josh that you want him in a not fake-dating-trope kind of way?" Beck asked. I thought that was a rich question coming from her, who spiraled about letting her own little crush on Adam be known for an absurd amount of time.

"I actually have. I just might have to at this point. However, the fact that I have koala bear hugged him almost every single time we have been together, and the fact that he immediately pulls away as soon as our lips touch, makes me think he has already gently let me down." I frowned again, glaring at Adam's hand as it came up to rest on Beck's thigh.

I may have been feeling a bit petty watching Adam and Beck affectionately touch each other lately.

"Maybe Josh is just nervous because he can't wrap his head around the fact that you are actually interested in him, and not just for some social media charade." Adam shrugged again, squeezing Beck's thigh once.

"I agree," Beck nodded her head, brushing her dark waves behind hear ears. "Here's the thing, you two have been dancing around each other for weeks. You guys jumped into physical touch almost immediately after reconnecting. Weren't you two physically affectionate in high school, too?"

I nodded, my frown loosening until my face was probably a neutral expression.

"So, why would Josh have any reason to believe that how you two touch each other now, would be any different from the way things were in high school?" Beck raised an eyebrow at me, and I blinked at her in surprise. She had a good point. Except I was confident Josh had friend zoned me hard in high school.

"...I guess that gives me my answer," I replied, my shoulders physically deflating as reality started to set in. "It's not different from high school. We hugged and cuddled a ton back then, and he never made a move on me. Now, the only difference is that we have a fake dating contract to uphold, which justifies the stupid little pecks he calls kisses..." I exhaled an annoyed breath as I eyeballed my two friends, who were looking at me with varying looks of pity.

"Maybe he's just unbearably shy and waiting for you to make the first real, unmistakable move?" Beck leaned forward and rested her hand on my calf.

"Or maybe he's just still not interested." I shrugged, feeling my gut sink at the realization but knowing that if that was true, I couldn't do anything about it. If he truly didn't see me through any sort of romantic lens, then I didn't want to bend over backwards to try to change his mind. I had been operating the whole time under the assumption that he might have never considered me a romantic partner and was giving him opportunities to do so. However, if he had already decided that he wasn't interested in me as a girlfriend, then it would be inappropriate of me to push the issue further.

Boundaries.

"Alright, well, I guess that's that." I smiled up at Beck and patted her hand on top of my thigh, "I'll let you guys get back to whatever gross canoodling you two were in the middle of."

"Thank fuck," Adam groaned as I hopped off the bed and made my way towards the door. Beck was about to say something, so I turned to look at her, but she was interrupted by Adam's hands wrapping themselves around her waist and pulling her down on the bed so that he could crawl on top of her.

Cute. But also, gross.

I pretended to gag as I left the room and shut the door behind me, making my way downstairs to get some water before I hid away in my bedroom for the rest of the night. I stopped halfway to the kitchen when I saw Susan sitting in one of her ugly accent chairs, watching *Bridgerton* as she sipped her tea. I checked my phone; it was almost eleven o'clock. Normally she would have been fast asleep hours ago.

"What are you doing up?" I asked as I plopped myself down on the couch next to her. She turned to smile mischievously as she held her mug towards the TV in explanation.

Anthony Bridgerton was pulling himself out of the lake he had just fallen into, his thin white shirt was transparent as it clung to every inch of his skin.

Oh, sure. Susan never missed an opportunity to be a horn dog.

"Smash," Susan chimed. Clearly, she was learning more internet slang from Taylor.

"Hundy P," I replied, grabbing a throw blanket off the back of the couch, and thoroughly wrapping myself up tight. I was nothing but a blanket blob, the fabric concealing my body everywhere from the chin down. Beck's grandmother and I watched the show in silence for thirty solid seconds.

"Spit it out, Henderson," Susan murmured as she sipped from her tea. I lifted a blonde eyebrow at the elderly woman, annoyed at how clear my frustration was taking up residence on my face.

"...I'm feeling petty," I started.

"Why?" Susan asked, shifting in her chair a little so her body was angled more towards me while her eyes stayed glued to the TV.

"...Because I want someone who clearly doesn't want me back." I snuggled further into my blanket blob out of embarrassment.

"You mean Joshua? Because that boy is head over heels for you. Are you blind?" Susan finally turned her head to face me, and I rolled my eyes at her, the blanket now covering me from the nose down.

"If he was head over heels, I wouldn't be sitting here bummed out, Susan," I mumbled into the covers. She blinked at me and held a hand up to her ear, reminding me that her hearing aids only did so much. I wiggled my face free of the blanket before continuing, "We act like we did in high school. But I want more. He hasn't given me any real indication that he wants more, otherwise I would be upstairs getting my freak on just like your granddaughter is doing with her red-head."

Susan nodded, not phased at all at the topic of Beck getting laid. Susan was Beck's number one fan for finding a romantic connection that also brought physical satisfaction.

...I bet Susan absolutely fucked back in the day.

"So, tell him," Susan replied, setting her mug down on the coffee table.

"For some reason, I have been naïve enough to think that my body language said enough about my desires from him." I leaned my head back on the couch, staring at the texture on the ceiling. I had been analyzing the experiences of every interaction Josh and I had since signing the fake dating trope into reality. The more I studied his mannerisms and expressions, the more I saw the playful side of Josh that he had showed to me in high school. A time where he was a good enough friend to humor me with one kiss in his bedroom and absolutely nothing more, out of fear of ruining our friendship.

"Back in the seventies, after Beck's grandfather and I signed divorce papers, I met someone." I lifted my head off the back of the couch to look at Susan, who had raised the remote to pause the TV. "She was beautiful." Susan didn't look at me, instead she kept her gaze forward as if the TV was still on.

Was Susan telling me about a past partner?

"She was the first woman I had been so obviously, overwhelmingly enthralled with. But this was the seventies. It was a difficult time to be a divorced single mother, let alone a divorced single mother who had the ability to love…well…her." Susan released a heavy sigh and closed her eyes, "She was my best friend."

I had never heard Susan talk about another person in this way. I had hardly ever heard her speak about personal matters regarding her past relationships, other than how disappointing her dead ex-husband was. I sat in silence, waiting for Susan to finish her story.

"...Anyways, I never did anything about it. Sure, we hugged, we held hands, but it was clear it was platonic between us. She worked at the library, and eventually met a nice young man and within a few months, they were happily married and expecting their first child. I was even a bridesmaid in the wedding." Susan smiled at the memory, and my heart was seizing at the thought of Beck's grandmother watching a woman she loved walking down the aisle into the arms of a man, so soon after her own failed marriage to one. "Over time, our friendship thinned and we didn't engage with each other more than a few postcards that we sent. That is, until a year or so before Beck moved in with me, just after her college graduation." Susan silently stood up and shuffled across the living room, down the hallway into the primary bedroom she occupied.

She was old as fuck, so it took her a longer amount of time to make the journey than normal, but I stayed rooted in my spot on the couch until she returned to the living room and took a seat right next to me. "She died." Susan sighed as she held an old, wrinkled envelope in her hands.

"Susan, this story is sad as shit. Why are you telling me this?"

"Pipe down and listen." Susan smacked my leg under my blanket lump and held up the wrinkled envelope for me to see. Her name and address were scrawled on the back of it in neat calligraphy-like script. "She wrote me, a couple of days before she passed. Cancer. She knew it was coming. Anyways, at this point her husband had already passed and her children made sure to give me this letter, personally inviting me to her memorial service in Laguna Hills."

I stared at the envelope, waiting for Susan to do something with it. She seemed to change her mind with a silent shake of her head and set the envelope in her lap. "I'm keeping the bulk of her words for myself, but the overall message you can know about her letter is that...she loved me too."

"No way!" I gasped, feeling like I was living in a real-life soap opera.

"Way," Susan giggled, "She loved me, just as I loved her. Don't get me wrong, she loved her husband, too. They had a happy life together, and her children are wonderful people. But...she managed to love me. Back then. Do you know why I'm sharing this with you now?"

I stared at Susan as her hazel eyes, the eyes that matched Beck's eyes perfectly, met mine. I shook my head in the negative. She rolled her eyes and smacked my leg again, hard enough to make me wince.

"Hey! What was that for?"

"You're not that dense, Courtney. I'm sharing a story of when I was too chicken-shit to share my true feelings with a person I loved, and now I have to live with the knowledge that if I had just opened my mouth, I could have found great happiness for the remainder of my life. Don't make the same mistake I did." At that, Susan clutched the envelope to her chest as she stood from the couch, giving up on her late-night viewing and shuffling back towards her bedroom, grumbling something about "kids these days" and that she can't "spell everything out" for me.

I found myself smiling at the surrogate parent in my life,

grateful that she shared something so vulnerable with me in order for me to compare my situation to hers. I wasn't entirely sure our situations were comparable, but I appreciated her effort. It wasn't like I could dive deep with my own mom about this subject. Her advice would probably be along the lines of, "Bang him now, ask questions about his true feelings later." It had failed her many times before, so unlike her I wasn't interested in throwing a handful of spaghetti at the wall to see what happened to stick.

My mom currently was busy camping out in the woods in Washington, probably banging anyone available as her way of coping with yet another breakup with my dad she informed me about a couple of days ago.

My dad was probably now hyper-fixating on his latest career as he attempted to cope with yet another breakup with my mom.

No, my parents weren't exactly people I would take relationship advice from. Anything else, maybe regarding politics or human rights, I would listen with open ears.

My phone buzzed in my pocket as I sat in the silent living room, so I shuffled the blankets off of me just enough to pull my phone out of my pocket and see that I had received another message from Josh.

J-shua: I'm buying you this t-shirt and you are expected to wear it every time we are seen together in public. No further questions.

I smiled brightly at the atrocious white t-shirt Josh was holding up for his latest selfie he sent me. The shirt had a picture of his face, passionately singing into a microphone.

Except the image was ruined with horrible hearts and words surrounding the image. This was clearly a t-shirt designed by an obsessed fan who had daydreamed about her future wedding to Josh many times over. He held it up proudly with raised eyebrows and a cheesy grin. I found myself giggling at my phone screen as I responded.

Me: If you thought I would fight you on that, you're wrong. I'm sure the designer would be thrilled to see Joshua Madey's girlfriend wear such a work of art.

J-shua: *laughing crying emoji* I'm sure Joshua Madey would be thrilled to see his girlfriend so entirely committed to the relationship.

Me: Only if Joshua Madey commits just as hard with a t-shirt of his own.

J-shua: I'll get in touch with the designer for a commissioned piece.

See? See how easy it would be for us? I thought to myself as I sent him back a kissy-face emoji and pocketed my device. In a couple days we would all be driving up to Hollywood Hills again to have another get together, and I would probably lay on the physical affection really thick while Josh reacted nonchalantly to my bold affection. I could picture us now. Me, wrapping my arms around his, and tugging frantically simply to get him to look down at me. All the while, Josh would be rubbing his hands together devilishly as he eyeballed Logan and Eloise, and brainstormed a way for them to rip each other's clothes off.

It was a dramatic, cartoonish image I pictured of the two

of us. Still, the message my brain was telling me was clear. I released a dramatic sigh before removing the throw blanket and making my way up to my bedroom.

Well, vibrators have gotten me this far, I thought to myself as I locked my bedroom door behind me.

***

The weekend came and all of us loaded into Logan's large truck to head to Josh's Hollywood Hills condo. Apparently, Logan's truck was electric, which was something that he and Adam chatted about since Adam was also a nerd about electric vehicles. Anyways, it seated all six of us and it was significantly cheaper to pitch in for fuel than it would have been to use two cars, one of them being Susan's old gas Honda Accord I took to the gym sometimes.

I noticed how there wasn't a single trace of Logan's job in his car. No NHL or Anaheim Ducks decor or stickers. Not even a stray hockey stick or skate in the bed of his truck. It was so clean that, if he told me he bought the truck day of, I would have believed him.

I noted everyone's seating arrangements. I sat directly next to Logan in the middle, Taylor at my right. Adam, Beck, and Eloise all took up the back, with Eloise sitting directly behind Logan. She kept her eyes down the entirety of the drive while Adam, Taylor, and (sometimes, when his hands were available) Logan would chat about electric vehicles and how he was liking the truck so far.

An hour and a half later, we pulled up to the condominium. The exterior was bougie and Spanish style, like most of the homes in the area. Josh greeted me in a bear hug as soon as the door opened, and we all filed into the massive living space. Everyone had gathered around the large island to start snacking on the fruits and vegetables that were set out. It was another laid-back date, but I could tell Kate was feeling competitive and wanted to get started with whatever party games she had lined up for everyone.

I wasn't paying attention to any particular conversation that was happening, instead I was watching Tom and Kyle comfortably snuggle into each other. No one had formally announced if they were dating or not, though I suspected that they were at least friendly with each other when I first met the band backstage a few months ago. I had also noticed a couple of romantic touches when everyone gathered at the townhome, and no one seemed to blink an eye when Tom wrapped one large arm around the purple-haired drummer's shoulders, trying to help him conceal how absolutely blasted the guy already was. We had only been at the apartment for maybe less than half an hour, but Kyle had clearly pregamed before we showed up and Tom was chuckling at his partner's not so subtle behavior.

I met Kyle's drunken gaze and smiled, sipping my wine and saying, "You two are cute."

Kyle and Tom both blushed, but it was Tom who tugged Kyle closer into his body and quietly responded, "Thank you."

I felt a pang of empathy for them. I knew the world was progressing, but bigoted voices always screamed the loudest. These two men were in the public eye, and the details of their personal lives would absolutely influence who would be will-ing to support them or not. While Josh and I were specifically supposed to flaunt our relationship to the public, playing the part of second-chance lovers, Tom and Kyle clearly intended to keep their romance quiet.

My heart squeezed for those two.

I wandered over to them when Kyle almost tipped over and Tom struggled to support the drummer while holding his own beer. "How much did you have to drink?" I asked, standing on Kyle's other side to give Tom some help, since everyone else was distracted with their own conversations. Josh was standing with Beck, Adam, and Logan. I noticed that when Beck vocalized Logan's signing for Josh, he made sure to make eye contact with Logan the whole time. It was easy for people to look at the face of the translator, instead of the person who communicated the words. It was a small gesture, but I felt a little piece of me melt at the sight of Josh continuing to show how wonderful of a human he was.

"He had two margaritas before you guys came over." Tom rolled his eyes, "Believe it or not, this guy is a lightweight."

"Oh, I believe it," I replied when Kyle got embarrassed and started giggling uncontrollably. "Can I ask how long you two have been together?"

I was a forward person, but part of me internally cringed as I realized that maybe these two weren't people to be so blunt with. Thankfully, Tom just smiled at me as he stared down at Kyle with adoration in his eyes, "Officially? Just a few weeks before the FivePoint show we met you all at."

"Oh, so you're still in the honeymoon phase?" I asked as Kyle grinned and smiled at me with his glassy eyes.

"Oh yes, there was *so much* pining on my end," Kyle explained, "I have wanted him for *so long*. He was so blind."

"I was." Tom nodded, holding his beer out and away from us when Kyle went to casually take it from his hands, because this man didn't need more alcohol, "It was hard for me to tell when Kyle was flirting with me, or just, being Kyle."

"Ah," I nodded, "I get it."

"Of course, *you* get it!" Kyle agreed, "Just like you and Josh!" I furrowed my brow at this, barely noticing the color drain from Tom's face as he tried to laugh loudly and distract Kyle, but it didn't work. "Right? Like when Josh was telling us how badly he wanted to fuck Courtney in high school but wasn't sure if you just had a flirty personality or not. And now look at you two! Dating and standing in the spotlight so that Tommy and I can have time to ourselves without reporters poking around our business—" Kyle's drunken words slurred out of his mouth effortlessly until Tom clapped one of his hands over Kyle's lips, an apologetic look on his face as he glanced at me, and then at the lead singer off to the side.

I glanced around the room, noticing how everyone else's conversations had stopped as they all stared wide-eyed at the three of us.

What the fuck did Kyle just say?

19

You could hear a pin drop a mile away with the sudden silence as I absorbed Kyle's ramblings, and my heart rate started to increase. Josh and I publicly dating to take the spotlight off of Tom and Kyle's romance made perfect sense to me. Josh and I were never going to be at risk of being hate-crimed for dating, and they were. It was a shitty reality we lived in, but that wasn't what made my blood pick up the pace in my veins.

"…What did you say?" I asked, leaning towards the drummer with a much more monotone voice than I was intending to use throughout the night.

"When Josh told us how badly he wanted to fu—"

"Shut up!" Garrett interrupted Kyle by reaching over and smacking Kyle on the back of his head, making him groan in shock as he stared wide-eyed at the lead guitarist.

"No—wait." I shook my head and eyeballed Kyle, who turned his head to look back at me. By the way his eyes widened, I figured he had just realized what he was saying. The way Kyle's mouth snapped shut and how the beer bottle in

Tom's hands suddenly held his interest let me know I didn't mistake his words.

I then turned to face the man in question.

Josh's body language was perfectly casual. If I hadn't noticed how white his knuckles were as he clutched his own beer bottle, and how his cheeks turned red as soon as my gaze met his, I wouldn't have suspected his guilt.

"You..." I cleared my throat, because it had suddenly become clogged with my own embarrassment, "You wanted to...and I quote, 'fuck me' in high school?"

Josh's dark eyes never left mine as he lifted his beer bottle to drain the rest of its contents before setting it on the counter that he was leaning against.

"Not exactly," Josh explained. Another wave of embarrassment washed over me. I couldn't deny the spark of excitement and hope that lit up within me at Kyle's drunken confession, so to hear Josh quickly deny it was disappointing.

"Not exactly?" I inquired, setting my own glass down on the kitchen island and taking a few steps towards him.

"Well, yes and no."

"Yes, and no? What the fuck does that even mean, Joshua?" That's right, I full first-named him. His dark brows lowered at that.

"Well, first—if I was lucky—I wanted to have sex with you—"

"Oh, well, *pardon* me! You wanted to 'have sex' with me, not 'fuck' me. My bad for the misunderstanding!" I pinched the bridge of my nose and let out an annoyed growl, blood was starting to rush in my ears. How did I not pick up on these kinds of vibes from him in high school? I would have taken him up on that opportunity in a heartbeat.

"Is there a difference between having sex, and fucking?" I heard Taylor ask from the side, too annoyed at Josh to be irritated at how loudly they slurped through their straw.

"Yes, do tell, Joshua!" He frowned at my second use of his full first name. "What exactly *is* the difference between wanting to 'have sex' with me and wanting to 'fuck' me?"

"The difference, Courtney," Josh pushed off of the counter that he was leaning against, taking a step towards me so that I had to crane my neck to look up at him, "Is that I was inexperienced in high school, to no one's surprise. There was no way in hell that the first time we had sex it would be good for you. The first time would be just that for us, sex. The act itself. Nothing special about it besides the scientific definition of it. Two bodies fumbling around until the end goal is technically met." I inhaled a deep breath through my nose as I did my very best to glare a hole in Josh's forehead, his words making absolutely no sense and only filling me with more irritation. "Once we got those first steps out of the way, however," he took another step as his voice dropped lower, "We would learn, assess, evaluate." I took a step back as he advanced to keep the same amount of small distance between us. "With enough frequent practice, we would learn what works. I would learn every inch of you, every sound you made, every touch that you responded to." A new wave of heat flooded my face, neck and chest at his words, my head was starting to feel light. "You, obviously, would learn what I like. It wouldn't just be sex anymore. It would be you and me craving that intimacy that only we had with each other. Knowing exactly what we both needed. *That* is fucking. *That* is what I wanted."

Silence filled the space.

I knew that the others were in the room, watching this whole thing. But I couldn't be bothered to care.

The only sound I could hear was sand rushing in my ears, as I felt my heartbeat thudding in my skull. I stared up at this man that I had embarrassed myself in front of so many times, thinking that I had been throwing myself at him the past couple of months without reason, because he had never given me any sign or indication that he wanted me the same ways I had wanted him.

Humiliation washed over me.

If he was so into me back then, why wasn't I obviously picking up those same signals now? Did he honestly not know how badly I craved him then *and* now?

He was looking at me with intent, his cheeks flushed. He was towering over me in some weird act of dominance, as if I was the ridiculous one for not understanding him until now. I couldn't tell you how long we stood there in that kitchen, me glaring at him and Josh staring at me, looking like he was waiting for puzzle pieces to click in my teeny-tiny brain.

I closed my eyes and released the breath I had been holding before opening them again.

I turned on my heel to walk back over to where Kyle and Tom were leaning against the countertops, reaching between the two of them to grab the hand towel that was hanging over the oven handle. I then calmly started walking back towards Josh. He stood tall and confident, but his expression was curious. It wasn't until I rolled the towel tight in both of my hands and his eyes widened that he realized what my intention was.

"Court—"

Thwack!

"Oh my god, Courtney!" Beck cried as I whipped the towel at Josh again, becoming determined as he tried to block my attack with his hands. I wished I was satisfied when the towel snapped at the top of his hand and he rubbed the sting, but I wasn't. Adrenaline was pumping in my veins. I had too many pent-up emotions and feelings to think rationally. All I knew was that I wanted to hit him with this kitchen towel.

"Court!" Josh growled at me as he retreated towards the living room. I gave up on whipping specifically and instead just started hitting him aimlessly with the cloth.

"Holy shit, is anyone recording this?" I vaguely heard Taylor ask the room.

"Courtney!" Josh called at me again, attempting to grab the towel from my hands. I was too quick for him, and as I advanced, his legs hit the back of the dark leather couch and he went tumbling over it. I didn't care. I leaned over the furniture and raised the towel again, aiming for his gut, when suddenly it was yanked out of my hands.

I turned around, wide-eyed and seeing red, to see that Logan had stepped up and removed my weapon of choice.

"Give it back!" I yelled at him, as if I was a child whose toy was taken away.

I reached forward to take my towel, and Logan responded

by pushing one large palm out flat against my chest, making me tumble over the back of the leather couch right into Josh's arms.

"Courtney!" Josh grumbled in my ear as he pinned my arms to my sides, holding me so that my back was pressed against his chest. I grumbled back and tried to squirm out of his hold, which just made us tumble off of the couch and onto the colorful rug.

"Oh my god, someone help them!" Beck cried from somewhere in the room.

"Nah, we're good," Kate replied, as if Josh and I wrestling on the floor of his living room wasn't a new thing that had just happened for the first time.

Josh rolled our bodies so that we lay on our sides. His legs wrapped around mine while his arms did an excellent job of keeping mine pinned, my back flat against his chest. Even though I tried with all my strength to escape his grip, simply to start attacking him again.

Why didn't he tell me?

Why did he tell me now?

What does any of this mean?

"Courtney," Josh spoke low near my ear, attempting to calm me down, "I know you're mad, but—"

"Is that why you left me?" I cried, feeling all the energy immediately drain out of my body after I spoke the sentence that made me realize how much hurt I felt over all of this.

As I went limp, exhausted, Josh's limbs tightened around me.

"What?" He asked.

"After graduation. After the summer where we spent almost every fucking day together, you left me." I felt my voice getting smaller and smaller by the end of the sentence, my eyes starting to sting with the threat of tears.

"Oh, shit." I heard Beck mumble somewhere behind us.

"Courtney, you went off to college." Josh sighed, releasing me just enough to roll me onto my back so that he could see my face, his dark eyes scanning my flushed cheeks, ratted hair, and red eyes that I was doing my best to keep from letting a tear escape.

"And you *never* called me back!" I squeezed my eyes closed, unable to look into his eyes as I let the dam of emotions break through with my words. "We said we would stay in touch! That we would meet up during the holidays! The last time I heard from you, was when we said goodbye before I drove away. You *never* returned my calls; you *never* returned my texts. I wrote you emails, Josh. Fucking *emails*. Like a *Boomer*! And you never responded! I came back for the holidays, and you kept ghosting me!"

I was crying now. Not sobbing, because I was able to breathe through my breakdown just fine, but I couldn't stop the tears from streaking down my cheeks.

I finally opened my eyes and found Josh's face staring down at me, his body halfway hovering over mine as his hands kept my arms pinned to my sides. He was clearly fearful that I would start swinging again, but I was too drained now. Exhausted. I had no energy left in me to fight with him.

"Wait...so, Josh is the asshole?" I heard Garrett ask before a loud slap sounded in the room. He grunted in pain and grumbled, "Fuck!"

"Shush." Kate ordered him.

"Was it because you thought I wouldn't sleep with you? Because I would have! I could not have been more obvious! Because I thought you liked me for *more* than that!" After a few more tears fell, I inhaled a deep breath and lowered my eyebrows at him, glaring again.

"Should…we maybe give them privacy?" I heard Tom ask.

"Absolutely not."

"Quiet, nerd." Beck and Taylor spoke at the same time. Later, I would realize I wouldn't blame them, because I would have wanted to stay and watch the tea be spilled, too.

"Court, I didn't *just* want to sleep with you. God, how could you think—" I growled and shoved Josh off of me, rolling to my side and pulling myself off of the ground. I angrily swiped away any sort of dust or dirt from the floor off of myself, as I turned around to face Josh, seeing that he finally stood up off of the floor as well.

I glared at him and flipped him off with both of my hands.

"Fuck you, Joshua!" I yelled at him. "*Fuck* you, for making me beg you to kiss me in high school. *Fuck* you for ghosting me. *Fuck* you for weaseling your way back in my life—only to gaslight me some more! And *fuck* you for not knowing that I have been *desperately* trying to get you to see me as something more for the past few months. Fuck! You!"

"Yes, queen!" Taylor started snapping their fingers as if they were at a poetry reading.

Beck grabbed their snapping fingers and lowered their

hand down, her face looking crumbled as she stared between Josh and me.

"Courtney, I—"

"Nope! I think you've said enough! I'm out!" I lifted up a peace sign as I turned my back to everyone and started marching towards the front door, aggressively tugging my purse off of the floor and stomping heavily just in case my anger wasn't obvious enough to everyone. I realized that we carpooled, and that I would probably have to take an Uber home, but it was worth it to get out of there.

"NO!" I heard Josh shout.

"Oh, my," I heard Kyle murmur as I turned around to see Josh running after me. I barely had a moment to blink before he crouched to football-tackle me and throw me over his shoulder. One of his arms pinned my legs tight against his chest as I started swinging my purse in an attempt to beat his backside with it.

"Josh! I swear to god—"

"Fuck! Stop talking!" Josh growled as he started marching up the stairs, facing me towards everybody else in the room who was watching this whole fight with mixed expressions. Adam, Beck, Eloise, Garrett, and Tom all looked nervous and shocked. Taylor, Kate, Kyle, and Logan were waving good-bye or saluting me as if it was normal for me to be carried off to the second story like a sack of potatoes.

"Fuck you all for letting him kidnap me!"

"Have fun, you two!" Kate wiggled her fingers at us as she clapped her hands once to regain everyone else's attention. "Alright everyone! Let's play charades!"

20

I growled as I gave up my purse swinging and started pinching various muscles on Josh's back.

He responded by roughly smacking my ass.

It really indicated how long this dry spell I had been in was because my body didn't exactly hate it.

"Josh, put me down," I grumbled as he reached his bedroom, kicking the door open only to kick it shut immediately after we entered.

"Gladly." Josh marched over to his bed and dropped me, making me squeak as I bounced on the king-sized mattress. I was tired, so I stayed seated and glared up at my old friend. God, I was so mad at him. How dare he be so attractive and yet so stupid? How dare he handle me rough enough to let me know that he was irritated, but not rough enough to let my body know that this wasn't sexy time?

"So, now what—" at my words, Josh lunged forward and cupped one hand behind my neck while the other one covered my lips, interrupting me once again.

"Courtney, I need you to shut your beautiful mouth and stop talking. Only for a few moments. Can you do that? Can you let me get a word in?" Josh begged, his face unbearably close to mine. His hand was warm and rough against my mouth, so I narrowed my eyes at him as I stuck my tongue out and licked his hand.

He responded by laughing in my face.

"I don't think you realize how often I've fantasized about you licking me, so I'd try a different tactic." Josh winked, and I growled as I kicked his shin, making him release my face.

"You haven't, though!" I growled, "How is that even possible? Do you just not find me attractive now, as a grown woman?"

Josh was squinting his eyes closed as he rubbed his leg. "What? Are you serious? Courtney, look at yourself."

"That's the thing!" I cried, flopping back on the bed, covering my eyes with my hands, "I *know* I'm attractive. I even knew I was attractive back in high school! I thought I was *so* obvious back then, but that you just didn't see me like that. I begged you to kiss me, you clearly tolerated it, and then ghosted me! Now, you waltz back into my life, have me sign some asinine fake dating contract—"

"In *what world* would *you* want *me*, Court?" Josh yelled, leaning over my body on his bed, I could feel his hands press into the mattress on either side of my shoulders, the dark grey walls of the room and the black bed sheets contrasting against his bleached hair and pale tattooed skin nicely. "In what reality was I, looking and acting like I did in high school, even on the radar of someone like you? It was more logical in my small adolescent brain that you only wanted me to kiss you to save me from embarrassing myself at college. There was no chance that you actually liked me like that."

"There was!" I cried, removing my hands from my eyes, meeting his gaze as he hovered over me, "There was, and there is…is that why you haven't responded to me throwing myself at you the past few weeks?"

Josh's dark eyes blinked at me, his brow loosening from of its scrunched expression.

"…I thought you were simply fulfilling your end of the 'asinine fake dating contract'. You kept saying that you were my 'fake' girlfriend, so I figured that was what you wanted."

"I just want *you!*" I growled, noticing his face flush and his expression slacken as he took me in. "I wanted you then, and I want you now. Desperately." I was breathing heavily as if we had just run a marathon. I decided not to be self-conscious about it, because so was he. His gaze grew darker as he cleared his throat, slowly dropping to his elbows and pressing his body against mine.

My breath caught at the contact, and I could feel my anger and irritation slipping away as I watched him studying me. I honed in on his eyes, ignoring how his eyebrow and lip piercings glistened in the light filtering in through the windows. His dark pupils started to expand.

He wanted me.

Joshua Madey, my high school crush, actually wanted me.

How was his self-confidence so off when it came to me?

"Okay." Josh nodded once, his gaze dropping to my lips.

We had kissed before, stupid little pecks on the lips for the public's sake, but this moment felt like we were balanced on the edge of a precipice. I was taking shallow breaths, my body anticipating the thrill of feeling his lip ring again. For real this time.

"Okay," I repeated, my mind spinning with the sudden turn the energy of the room seemed to take. I still didn't understand why he ghosted me all those years ago. It was on the tip of my tongue to ask, but the more I stared at his lips, the question quickly fled my mind.

"I just..." Josh used one of the hands he was leaning on to rest it against my face, his thumb brushing against the bone of my jaw, making my lips part at the touch. His pupils expanded some more.

"If you don't kiss me right now, I am going to scream," I murmured, gentle not to speak so aggressively that he might remove his hand. He smirked at my threat as he leaned closer, his hot breath fanning over my neck as he tilted my head back with his hand.

"I need you to do me a favor," Josh whispered, his lips barely ghosting over my own.

"Anything, literally anything," I breathed, needing him to know how desperate I was.

"...Don't ever stop telling me *exactly* what you want from me," Josh finished before firmly pressing his lips against mine.

I lost control.

I threw my hands around his neck, dragging my nails up into his scalp until my fingers tangled in his hair. I arched my back so that my chest was fully pressed against his, wiggling one of my legs out from under his, and wrapping it around his waist.

"Fuck." Josh groaned into my mouth, taking a moment to regain his senses before matching my energy with our kiss. I plunged my tongue into his mouth, something he immediately opened up for. The feel of our tongues sliding against each other made me dizzy. Our kiss wasn't hurried, but it was heavy. We were inhaling each other's oxygen. We couldn't be close enough, and the feel of his hot hands on my neck and face made my heartbeat take off at a concerning pace in my chest.

"Fuck. Yes. Good idea. Let's do that," I murmured in response to his exclamation, capturing his lips with mine again. He kissed me back before chuckling low in his chest, something I felt against mine.

"Good idea." He smiled against my lips as I released his hair and slipped my hands underneath his shirt, feeling his hot skin.

"Cool. Great." I gasped as he turned my head so that his lips could start nipping at my jaw, creating a path to my ear that made an embarrassing noise escape the back of my throat. "God," I breathed.

"Nope, not God. It's me, I'm doing this to you." Josh breathed on my neck as his hips pressed into my thigh. The feel of the very noticeable erection in his pants pressing against my leg made my lips spread into a large smile.

"I don't know, this feels pretty spiritual," I teased as I reached one hand down and slipped it underneath the waistband of his pants, grabbing his butt over his boxers. Josh groaned and quickly leaned away from me just enough to get me to look at him.

"If you're going to praise anyone for making you feel this way, it's me." He smirked as he leaned down to capture my bottom lip with his teeth, gently tugging and making me whine.

"Praise kink. Good to know."

"Only if it's with you," Josh breathed. I didn't get a chance to process those words, because he quickly pushed off of me to start tugging his shirt off, looking sloppy in his movements as he stood at the foot of the bed, showing off his gloriously tatted chest. He was heaving his breath. I followed suit and quickly crossed my arms over myself to tug off my t-shirt and bra in one swift motion. I was laying on his bed completely topless as he reached for the button of his jeans and he froze, his eyes wide and glazed as they zeroed in on my chest.

"Are you stuck?" I asked with a smile, feeling his gaze burning into my skin as I slid my thumbs under the waist-band of my leggings and underwear.

Josh swallowed once as his gaze bounced between my chest and where my hands were. "Yup. I think I am."

"Huh," I started to pull the waistband of my bottoms down, painfully slow as his gaze scorched me with his attentive eyes, "Well, I'm okay getting started myself, but I'd rather you be an active participant." Josh blinked and his legs shook, as if they were on the verge of buckling beneath him. I finally slid my bottoms down past my hips, taking my time as I folded my knees up and tugged the leggings the rest of the way off. I tossed them away and leaned back on my hands, fully bare and on display for him.

Josh was stuck, his face and neck flushed as his dark eyes struggled to find a place on my body to focus on. His hands still held the button of his jeans. If it was anyone else, I would have been self-conscious by the lack of words or movement from him as he silently catalogued me.

"Actually, maybe I could start on you first," I adjusted my position on his bed until I was on my knees and reached out to tug on one of his belt loops, trying not to acknowledge how wet I already was in between my legs. "It looks like you might need help."

Josh gulped again, his voice dry as I swatted his hands away and took over his button and zipper. "You're just…more beautiful than I could have imagined."

I paused as my fingers curled into the hem of his jeans, looking up to meet his face directly. His expression was slack, eyes hooded as he stared at my lips.

"Josh?" I asked, voice low so I wouldn't startle him.

"Hmm?" He responded, leaning forward to gently brush his lips against my jaw.

"I need you to touch me," I calmly whispered, releasing his pants, and grabbing his wrists to put them on my body, guiding one around to my backside until his hand completely engulfed my bare cheek. "You can touch me. Kiss me. Bite me, whatever…As long as it leads to more."

"More," Josh breathed as his hands started to gain a life of their own again, his hand kneading my backside and pulling me flush against himself.

"Yes…like you talked about downstairs," I reminded him as I returned to my task of removing his pants.

Holy shit, did his tattoos go down to his pelvis?

"I'm sorry, I'm just processing all of this. Courtney Henderson just stripped naked and presented herself to me on my bed. My brain is struggling not to short-circuit at this new reality."

"Courtney Henderson is currently sticking her hand in your pants," I played along, taking no effort to find the rod I was feeling against my thigh earlier. My eyes widened as I wrapped my hand around it, but he didn't see my expression because he was busy making out with my neck and shoulder.

My ass might have a hand shaped bruise by the time Josh was done with it. Both of his hands were now kneading the muscles on each side, and I wasn't complaining.

At the contact my hand made, Josh groaned low and deep. It sparked my confidence as I started slowly stroking him.

"You're really touching me." Josh gasped as I twisted my wrist and snuck my hand in through the hole of his boxers.

A thought occurred to me. "Is there anything else you want me to do?"

"Um," Josh groaned again as I made another pass over him, pausing for a second when my hand came into contact with something hard and metal at the base of his shaft, *did I feel...? No way.* "Meaning?"

"You said you fantasized about this, right?" I reached forward and licked at the column of his neck, loving the way his breath shuddered. "What did you picture?"

"What have you pictured?" Josh countered as I sucked on his collar bone.

"What *haven't* I pictured you doing to me?" I replied, using my free hand to start pushing his pants and boxers down past his ass. A quick glance let me know that, yes, his tattoos almost made it to his genitals. Those must have hurt like a mother.

Holy fucking shit, not as bad as that silver piercing at the base of his dick, though.

"Tell me," Josh breathed against my shoulder, "Every detail. Leave nothing out."

"Well, I pictured you a little less controlled—" He didn't need to be told twice. He quickly gripped my hips and pushed me back down on his bed, pulling his pants the rest of the way down and kicking them off so smoothly I found myself giggling at his sudden eagerness. He crawled over my body, dragging me up until my head rested on the pillows at the head of the bed.

"Less control, got it," He breathed before pressing his lips against mine in a melting kiss and pulling back, "Anything else?"

"I—I don't know," I smiled as I ran my hands all over his body, tracing over all the colorful tattoos he felt the need to cover himself with. "I pictured everything. Me against the wall, me face-down on the bed—"

"I want to look at you—for the first time, at least," Josh interrupted, an almost desperate look on his face as he tugged on his lip ring with his teeth. "Anything else?" I smiled at him, bright and open and holding nothing back. Of course, Josh made our first time have meaning to some degree. I was ridiculous for being surprised by it.

"Alright. I also pictured us licking various desserts off of each other," I shrugged as I reached down in between us and grabbed him again, loving the heavy twitch in my hand, "Every stereotypical thing…You serenading me—"

"*Let's! Get! Physical!*" Josh bellowed in a comically high voice, so loud that I was sure that our friends downstairs could hear it. I burst into laughter at the unexpected tribute to Olivia Newton-John, covering my mouth in an attempt to smother my laughter as he smiled down at me.

His dick was in my hand and he started singing eighties songs to me. How did I picture our first time being anything different?

"I mention serenading, and *that's* the first song you think of?"

"I'm dying to be inside of you, Court. That lyric seemed fitting." Josh shrugged as he nudged himself towards my opening. I was still laughing, but I felt my body relax at the contact, spreading my legs wider so he could fit in between them. Then I remembered something important.

"Condom! Condom, then I'm all yours," I smiled. Josh's face faltered for a moment as he reached a hand up to brush his calloused thumb against my bottom lip. His expression and gentle touch made emotion rise in my chest. He blinked once, and then reached over to his nightstand drawer to pull a long strip of condoms out.

"I don't think you have enough, we might need more," I deadpanned as he leaned on his elbows to rip one off and tear it open.

"You're right. We'll go through this in a couple days, easy,"

Josh replied as he covered himself and leaned over me to kiss my lips again, "I'm addicted."

I smiled, canting my hips so that we lined up again as I looped my arms around his neck and shoulders, "I'm glad you're finally catching up."

Josh scoffed as he nudged my center, "I think you're the one who might need to catch up still, Court." I was just about to ask him to clarify what that meant when he finally shoved his hips forward and seated himself fully inside me.

I gasped because even though I was more than ready for him, the intrusion was still shocking. The reality of it all hit as we took a moment for me to get used to him, *Joshua Madey is inside me right now.*

"You okay?" Josh asked, his forehead scrunched as he held himself still for my benefit.

"Yup," I exhaled through my nose, "Just give me a minute." I exhaled again and reached up to kiss him. Tracing his lip ring with my tongue made him groan in my mouth, and the sound of it sent another wave of heat towards my belly, making me clench around him.

He still held perfectly still until I told him otherwise.

"Alright," I breathed, "Let's get physical." I didn't sing it because I'm not weird. I just smiled and lifted my hips towards him to encourage movement, feeling his piercing brush against me in a surprisingly delicious way. Josh dropped his forehead against mine as he open-mouthed hummed the rest of the lyrics in beat with his thrusts.

"I wan-na get, phy-si-cal, phy-si-cal." I started laughing again, feeling his lips pull into a smile as his head turned and he

rested our temples against each other. I gripped his shoulders tighter until our bodies were flush, our heartbeats rapidly racing against each other.

"I don't think that's the tempo we're going for," I gasped, because he decided to stop humming eighties songs and was now moving in a steadier beat.

"If I don't distract myself with something ridiculous, I'm going to embarrass myself." Josh gasped as sweat started to coat his brow. I lifted an eyebrow as I reached up to lick his jawline, loving how I felt his body shudder again at the contact.

"You're close?"

"So. Embarrassingly. Close." Josh grunted as he hit something wonderful inside of me and I clenched around him again, a gasp escaping my lips, "I can hold off, though." His hot breath kept grazing my neck as he focused the entirety of his movements solely to benefit me, and frankly, it was working.

It generally wasn't difficult for me to orgasm; however, I usually needed some sort of foreplay to take place before penetration did anything. That wasn't the case here. I had been buzzing for Josh for so long, melting at the slightest touch from him, that I was also embarrassingly close to letting go.

However, the thought of him going first seemed like a fun game of chicken, so I made a breathy moan that I knew would make things more difficult for him, "You feel so good." It wasn't a lie, but I was also trying to think of things to set him off.

"Oh my god, don't tell me that right now," Josh groaned as

his thrust faltered once before regaining his tempo. I wrapped both of my legs around his hips and tugged him close, making him sink deeper. It felt euphoric, having his body over mine as I felt his movement inside me in the best possible way.

"You're big," I gasped in his ear, feeling him pulse inside of me and grinning, "I feel you everywhere." Also, not a lie. He was invading all of my senses. Josh was all I could see, hear, smell, and feel. I never wanted this to stop. I felt myself quiver around him once and knew that I was risking losing this game as my eyes rolled, his thrusts harder. He leaned back and quickly took hold of both of my wrists, holding them hostage above my head as his dark hooded gaze met mine, a satisfied smirk on his lips.

"You're not going to come first, are you?" Josh murmured, leaning down to lick my top lip once as he continued thrusting inside me.

"Nope, because you're the one right on the edge—" I gasped as he trapped both of my wrists in one hand and used his free one to start gently brushing his thumb over my nipple. I couldn't take a full breath of air; warmth was pooling in my lower belly at an alarming rate. I hadn't actually experimented with bondage before, not that I was positive that is what this was, but for some reason being pinned underneath him and being unable to move my hands was escalating things at a surprising rate.

"I am, but so are you. So, tell me, how do I make you feel?" Josh murmured the words into my neck as he lightly pinched my nipple, making my back arch up into him.

"I can't—I just feel you," I gasped, thrusting my hips into his because the contact our pelvises made, thanks to his genital piercing, was glorious. "Only you." Josh's eyes flared at my words, as if he wasn't expecting them. He squeezed his eyes closed as he took the time to focus again, opening them to see his hand gently massaging my breast.

"How do I feel, Josh?" I gasped, trying to get my head back in the game. "Is this what you pictured?" He groaned once as he continued to study me, and when I felt the string inside me starting to be pulled taut, I realized I was hopeless to fight it. It was game over for me, "I can't believe—you—" I gasped as I felt myself starting to quiver around him again, a smug smile tugging at his lips letting me know that he knew I was about to lose.

"You can't believe what, Court? Tell me." Josh demanded, gripping my wrists tighter as he captured my gaze again, challenging.

"This literally *never* happens!" I almost yelled, squeezing my eyes closed, throwing the game out the window as I tried to wrap my head around all of this. "How is this happening? How are you already making me co—" It hit me like a bulldozer, completely catching me off guard. I widened my eyes for a moment in alarm as I realized how hard I was feeling waves of ecstasy pulse from my core and throughout my limbs that he still held hostage. My teeth were clenched together as a low groan escaped my throat, both trying to escape the overwhelming sensation but grateful that Josh was pinning me in place as he continued to ride out my orgasm.

I had no idea how much time passed, how long Josh kept his pace up while wave after wave crashed into and consumed me, my mind going numb except for feeling everything Josh gave me. And gave me. And gave me.

He held my eyes through it all, his face looking both shocked and awed as he watched me come undone underneath him. When my vision finally cleared and he knew I was done, he let me tug my wrists free from his grasp as I rewrapped them around his neck and pulled him close, encouraging him to let go.

He did.

Within seconds. He stilled inside of me on one last unsteady thrust and groaned into my neck, holding my body snug against his. We sat like that for a while, catching our breath and gently stroking each other's back and arms with our hands, unable to move.

"...I won." Josh breathed into the pillows we were lying on after an unknown amount of silence.

"How did you immediately know I was trying to win?" I laughed as I squeezed him tighter against me, finally untangling my legs from around his waist.

"Your competitive tone as soon as I revealed my weakness, for one," Josh brushed his lips on the side of my neck, making me shiver.

"Well, there's always next time." At the end of my sentence I felt him twitch inside of me. "You're kidding!" I gasped, disbelief coloring my tone at the thought of actually going for round two so soon.

"I wish I was," Josh chuckled against my skin, reverently brushing his lips against the shell of my ear.

21

Instead of engaging in round two, we decided to take a breather and compose ourselves. Josh got up first, padding to his massive ensuite bathroom and coming back with a warm washcloth to help me clean up. I eyeballed the floor to look for something to cover myself with, thinking that naked activities needed to take a pause until we discussed some things, and reached for Josh's shirt to pull over myself.

Josh tossed the washcloth in the hamper before turning around, still completely nude, pausing to look at me wearing his shirt. I smiled proudly, posing with my fists on my hips. His shirt fell just to the tops of my thighs, barely covering the important parts of me.

"So many fantasies being checked off today," Josh murmured, his eyes dark as he prowled towards me. The possessive glint in his eyes made my pulse pick up with a thrill, but I stopped him with my hand against his chest.

"Put on some shorts or something, I won't be able to focus with you naked like that." I let my gaze linger on his pierced anatomy, wondering what in the hell inspired him to do something like that. Then I remembered how it felt to rub against it while he was inside of me and realized that he actually made a very good call.

"Fine, but after we talk, you're keeping this shirt on for the next round." I widened my eyes as I laughed, I hadn't actually had back-to-back sex in a very long time. Not since my college days, probably. The fact that Josh was suggesting going at it again like rabbits made my skin heat with pride. He really liked me. He already saw everything there was to see, experienced the most intimate part of me, and was clearly dying to do it all again.

His enthusiasm was a big turn on for me.

Noted.

"Deal." I smirked, bending down to grab his boxers and throwing them at him. He trapped my wrists against his chest as he leaned down to capture my lips with his, his tongue making a languid sweep in my mouth and making my head feel light again.

"Alright," Josh breathed as he separated our mouths to pull his boxers on, barely concealing the tent in them, "But I want to hold you while we talk."

"I'd love that." I grinned, wrapping my arms around his shoulders as he bent to wrap his arms around my waist and drop us onto his bed. He tucked me against his chest, reached down for the covers to pull on top of us, and thrust one of his legs in between mine.

I sighed contentedly as I traced the shapes of his tattoos on his pecs, happy that while he used his body to display beautiful works of art, that there was an inch or two here and there of untouched skin. It was like little pieces of the old

J-shua showing through, letting me know that while he was no longer the boy I had known as a teen, that pieces of that part of him were still around here and there.

As I realized how weird it was to get sentimental about his bare skin, I blinked those thoughts away and lifted my head to lock eyes with him. "So, here we are."

"Here we are," Josh agreed, leaning down to press his lips against my forehead. My grin stretched across my face, loving how physically affectionate he was with me.

"We just had sex, while all our friends were downstairs," I mumbled, tucking my lips in between my teeth as I wondered if anyone heard us.

"We did, was that okay with you?" Josh asked, a light trace of worry ghosting over his features.

"Absolutely," I smiled, then dropped my eyes to his chest, my finger still tracing shapes, "You?"

"Of course," Josh's arms flexed around me, squishing me against him one more time as one of his hands came up to cup my jaw. "Court, this wasn't a one-time thing, right?" I blinked, startled, before meeting his eyes and making my face relax its muscles to show how serious I was.

"Absolutely not. Fuck. I've been dying to get you to notice me in this way." At this, Josh pinched the skin on my bicep once, making me yelp and pinch his arm back. He trapped my arms between both of our chests as his chuckle rumbled against me.

"As if I never noticed you this way," he murmured against the crown of my head, "I was just too scared to consider the fact that you might also see me, too."

"...I guess I can understand that." I rested my forehead on

his shoulder, taking a moment to silently enjoy the feeling of being intimately wrapped around each other like this. If only high school me could see me now.

We did it, I'd tell her, *it wasn't all in our head. He likes us, too.*

"...So, at the risk of sounding juvenile," Josh cleared his throat as he asked his question into my hair, "You're my girlfriend now, right?"

"Haven't I technically been your girlfriend this whole time?" I replied with a giggle.

"You brat." Josh laughed again as he rolled us over so that I was flat on my back. He rested on his elbows as he hovered over my body, "Regardless of our contract, I mean."

I couldn't stop the smile from pulling my cheeks back, showing off almost all of my teeth. How did he know exactly what I wanted to confirm with such few words? This was probably going to be the shortest "Define the Relationship" discussion in the history of DTRs.

"Absolutely," I smiled, "This is real. I have loved getting to know you again, J-shua."

"I loved getting to know you again, too, Court," Josh replied as he pressed a firm kiss against my lips, rolling his hips against mine once. "Now that that's settled..."

"Oh my god, everyone is still waiting for us downstairs." I could faintly hear the sounds of yelling and bickering as they continued to play whatever party game they landed on in our absence.

"They can wait a little longer," Josh murmured, sliding down my body, "I need more time." ...Well, who was I to convince him otherwise?

22

Every video clip showing Harry Styles dancing and singing at his concert proves the well-known fact that watching your favorite celebrity sing live is hot. Maybe not always sexually, but the talent to sing and perform in front of thousands without choking, and hitting all the right notes in the song, is an impressive feat that is attractive to anyone. Being able to witness a talented artist sing live, up close, and personal, at their concert, is hot.

This is why Taylor and Beck had huge hard-ons at the Carbon Cut concert we attended a couple of months ago. It's why, while I had never felt physical attraction in this capacity towards someone of Josh's genre of man (i.e., tattooed, pierced musicians), I was able to feel a flutter in my heart and warmth in my belly as I watched him belt high notes, and casually throw around low notes.

What I wasn't expecting, however, was the visceral reaction my body would create after watching Josh in a recording booth.

It was only two months out from Carbon Cut's next tour, a gig that would put them on the road for close to six months.

Because of this, the band was on a time crunch to release their new album. Most of the songs were already recorded and done according to Josh, but there were a couple of songs that the band had changed their mind about, and wanted to re-record, to ensure the music was exactly what they wanted it to be before it got released to their fans.

There was a rapper in the booth with Josh, each of them wearing headphones and standing on opposite sides of the little soundproof room. A clear divider separating the booth in two. The track was just starting as Kate and I entered the recording space—she had to let me into the building due to security, because Josh had been busy setting up.

While getting ready to start the rest of the band was either standing or lounging around the studio, eagerly watching Josh and the rapper, who looked familiar, but his name escaped me. A piano sounded in the room as the rapper took off starting the first verse. At first, I was thrown off by the rapping since Carbon Cut's genre was clearly pop punk and more emo than what this guy looked like. His dark skin was covered in just as many tattoos as Josh, and his curly black hair was braided in rows along his scalp. He had a septum piercing as well as multiple eyebrow piercings.

His rap was nice, the lyrics clearly painting a picture of a woman who had confidence to spare and took up the entire space in a room. I was confused as to how Josh's voice would tie into the music, but as soon as the rapper finished his set, Josh immediately stepped in as deep base started to thud with the piano. Josh and the rapper were grinning at each other, clearly playing off of the other's energy.

Josh wasn't rapping. Instead, his voice was higher and

strained. More on brand for the band's sound. The smile on his face contradicted the emotion given by the lyrics he sang. Watching the muscles in his neck flex as he belted his own verse made a warm flutter take place in my lower belly. The beat dropped at the end of Josh's verse, and the rapper joined in with him on the chorus.

Maybe it was the sound of two grown men harmonizing.

Maybe it was the sound of two genres colliding to create something beautiful.

Maybe it was the lyrics they sang, telling us how the woman they sang about made them feel stuck, immovable.

Paralyzing.

Maybe it was the look on Josh's face as he and the other artist thoroughly enjoyed this part of their job. Whatever it was, goosebumps flushed across my skin at the sight and sound of Josh recording this song I hadn't heard before.

Josh was looser in the booth, smoother. Maybe he had taken an edible before this, but his body language was relaxed as if *this* was where he thrived. While he looked casual and easygoing on stage, he looked at peace in the booth.

Josh and the other artist had clearly practiced this song together before, and I must have walked in during one of their final takes on this set, because I couldn't find a single flaw or error as he and the rapper sang through the entirety of the three-minute song. I giggled as Josh mimed hitting the drums completely in sync with the track that played for them, letting his goofy side take hold as the rapper stepped in for his solo.

Josh nodded his head to the beat before clutching both ears

of his headphones and yelling the lyrics into his microphone for his part next. Yelling was the only way I could describe it, even though his voice was very controlled and intentional. Watching the way he tilted his head back, showing off his sharp jaw and the artwork that coated the skin of his neck, did concerning things to my body.

I swore the temperature rose in the room by at least ten degrees.

His voice was beautiful.

It was strained, raspy, and had depth. Throughout this song, I could easily see how talented Josh truly was by his ability to belt higher notes on command, and then immediately drop down to a strained deep note within seconds.

The bridge of the song came, and at the end of the bridge, Josh placed his lips almost directly onto the microphone as he closed his eyes and murmured a sentence, reminding me that, at the end of the day, he truly was a punk singer.

The beat dropped one last time while he and the rapper harmonized again, repeating the chorus that made chills run throughout my body.

At the end of the song, Josh and the rapper stepped back from their mics to gently remove each of their earphones, chuckling at each other and fist bumping against the clear divider in celebration over their obvious successful take.

"Excellent. Great job, guys." Kate clapped her hands with a smile on her face, her blue eyes glowing with pride for her friend's work.

"I don't know, I think Courtney hated it." Garrett had leaned forward to sarcastically speak into a microphone placed on the soundboard in the room we stood in, which must have spoken into the booth that Josh and the rapper were in, because at the sound of my name leaving Garrett's lips, Josh's head quickly snapped up and locked eyes with me.

I blushed.

Like a fangirl.

Because I was officially a huge fangirl of Josh, and his voice.

"You didn't like it?" Josh smiled knowingly as he spoke into his microphone for me to hear. I rolled my eyes as he and the rapper laughed and left the booth. I was frozen in my spot. As Josh entered the studio that the rest of us all waited in, I couldn't do anything more than just stare at him. *Is this what being starstruck felt like?*

"Are you stuck?" Josh asked, a knowing smirk on his lips as he repeated the question that I had asked him the last time we were with each other. Another blush hit my neck and face at the memory.

"No, I'm just trying to control the raging boner that's clearly tenting my jeans." I widened my stance and gestured vaguely towards my groin, making the rapper throw his head back and cackle as Josh shook his head and pinched the bridge of his nose at my immaturity. The rest of the band all laughed at my crude comment, making Josh shake his head before approaching me and wrapping one large hand around my neck. I rose on my tiptoes to help him out as he tipped his head down to mine, our lips pressing against each other in a firm, real kiss.

A part of my heart soared as I realized I wouldn't have to suffer through those pretend pecks anymore. Every kiss between us was real now.

I grinned against his lip, clutching his shirt to halt his retreat and gently nipping at his lip ring, tugging the slightest bit before the sounds of Kyle gagging broke through our moment.

"God, she really does have a hard-on." Kyle leaned over the couch that he and Tom were cuddled on to grab an empty waste bin and pretended to dramatically hurl in it.

"I'm only about half-mast right now," I playfully glared at the purple-haired drummer, "Grow up." Tom laughed, reaching out to squeeze Kyle's thigh with adoration shining in his eyes. I loved that they were getting more and more comfortable being physically affectionate in front of me. I understood why they were keeping their relationship a secret, but I also longed for the day that they could be public about their love without risking their safety.

The world needed to step it up.

"Hey man, are you going to introduce me?" the rapper asked, his dark eyes shining brightly as he took in Josh and me.

"Oh, right," Josh was staring at me, his gaze on my lips, before he blinked and snapped out of whatever thoughts he was in. He smiled at the artist and placed a hand on my hip, tugging me into his side where I belonged, "Court, this is Felix."

"Hi, Felix," I smiled and held my hand out, happy that he wasn't weird about handshakes and didn't try to crush my fingers in his grip like other men who have shaken my hand in the past, "You sounded wonderful."

"Does that mean I get a kiss too?" Felix wiggled his dark brows, his eyes on Josh. Whatever facial expression Josh gave him made him laugh and shake his head, his dark braids swishing with the movement. "I'm just fucking with Josh. I'm sorry if that was rude."

"No worries." I smiled. A joke like that truly depended on the man making it. Felix gave off a laid-back, positive, nonconfrontational energy. I wasn't offended by his joke in the slightest because my asshole radar wasn't going off. If someone like Daddy James (a single dad at our clinic who kept weirdly flirting with Beck until she had to harshly turn him down) had made that joke to me, I would have frowned and let him know that there was no way in hell that was happening.

"Should we take a break?" someone sitting in a rolling chair at the sound bar asked. I assumed it was a producer of some kind because he had one headphone placed to his ear as he tweaked with the sound board. None of us could hear what he was doing.

"Actually, yeah. I could use a break, and some water." Josh rubbed the column of his throat, making my eyes study his neck and collar bones. I was such a mess for this man. Josh's other hand squeezed my waist as he led me out of the recording studio, down a hall, and into a room that reminded me a lot of the break room at work.

"How was your day?" Josh asked as he kissed the crown of my head before heading to the fridge to get us both bottled water.

"It was good, one client is making huge progress which always makes me feel good," I smiled, remembering the victory we had at the very end of the session. "It started off rocky, the child clearly wasn't in the mood to work today. Even the mother was pretty stressed out about it." I quirked my lips to the side, remembering the bags that were so evident under the parent's eyes. The panicked look on her face as soon as her child started crying and thrashing, desperate to avoid any interaction with me or the new toy I introduced them to.

"That sounds difficult." Josh leaned against the wall and reached a hand towards me, his index finger sneaking into one of my belt loops and tugging me closer to him. As he lifted the water bottle to his lips and took a few deep gulps, his free arm snaked around my back and held me flush against his hard chest. I grinned, wrapping my arms around his waist, and resting my chin on his chest.

How many times had we stood just like this, and yet, this felt way better than before we decided to make things real?

"It can be, but then I remember that while I have to spend forty-five minutes at a time with a cranky child, that the parent goes home and spends the entire rest of their day and night with a cranky child." I shrugged my shoulders, relishing the fact that his fingers flexed against my hip at the movement as if he was worried about me shrugging out of his embrace. "Given that perspective, it makes me appreciate my time with each client a little more. While I have a set time I spend with a child, parents don't get the luxury of seeing the light at the end of a tunnel. Parents are truly stuck with however long the child decides to throw a tantrum."

Josh drained the entirety of the water bottle, licking his lips as he gently tossed the empty plastic in the recycle bin.

I reached up and licked his collar bone.

"Oh god," Josh groaned as he held me tighter, his head bending down so that his lips could kiss at my temple and ear, "Don't tell me how empathetic you are at your job, and then casually lick me like that. It's cruel."

"Cruel?" I asked, smirking as I gently ran my teeth along the bone. My tongue snuck out to lick the dip at the base of his throat, making his breath hitch.

"Yes," Josh breathed, "It's cruel of you to make me this hard for you in the middle of my workday." I flexed my hips, seeing if he was right. Based on the hard ridge my hip felt in his pants, I realized he wasn't bluffing.

"Good god!" We heard Kyle groan, making both of our heads turn to see him covering both of his eyes with his hands as he stood in the doorway of the break room, "Is nowhere safe from your lust?"

"No," Josh and I replied in unison, making us smile at the other.

"I'm just going to be quick," Kyle kept one hand over his eyes as he used the other to find his way to the fridge, grabbing two waters for himself before kicking the door closed with his foot. He finally dropped his hand from his eyes to frown at us, then stomped out of the break room, mumbling something about, "horny-hetero-audacity."

"He's just being a dick," Josh murmured against the top of my head.

"I know." I grinned, resting my cheek in between his pecs. His warmth loosened every muscle in my body, the longer we stayed wrapped around each other the more I felt any sort of hidden stress in my body melt away.

After we became official last weekend, we eventually pulled ourselves out of Josh's bed and got dressed to return to our friends downstairs. Beck was literally holding her breath as she eyeballed me, waiting to see if the night was over and we were all going home, or if Josh and I were finally a real couple.

The cheers and whistles from everyone after we told them we were official was heartwarming, and even Logan smiled at the both of us in celebration. Eloise bounced up to Josh and me and wrapped us up in a tight hug, her girly squeals making us flinch and wince. I loved having everyone's support.

What my friends didn't appreciate was how long they had to wait in Logan's truck while Josh and I made out outside the passenger side door for an alarming amount of time. It took Logan hitting the horn on the truck and Taylor tugging me into the car for us to finally pull apart, but Josh and I didn't care. We had a limited amount of time that we could spend together, and we were going to make the most out of every single minute available.

The same thing happened at the end of this little date, my Uber waited patiently while Josh and I made out on the curb outside of his condo. He had taken us back for takeout. Chatting with him while he was casually tugging me closer to his body while Tom tugged Kyle into his body made my heart burst with warmth. Garrett and Kate weren't as into PDA as the rest of us were, but the flirty little glances they kept giving each other when they thought no one was looking made me smile.

I loved this. It felt like my friend group had doubled in such a short amount of time, and I felt like part of Josh's group as everyone joked around and laughed with each other. I couldn't stay late, since I had to wake up early for work the next morning, which is why Josh and I were making out as much as we were because—clearly, we were both desperate for some sort of release from each other.

"Think that maybe we could sneak up into my room for half an hour?" Josh broke apart just enough to ask me that question, before fusing his lips to mine again. I giggled and broke away to reply.

"I really should get going, it's a long way home." I frowned, then grabbed his collar and kissed him again. Josh sighed his disappointment into my mouth, which made me melt into his embrace even more.

It was in that moment that I suddenly loathed the fact that we lived an hour and a half away from each other.

"I miss you so much when we're apart," Josh murmured, cupping my jaw with both of his hands, and kissing my nose. An attempt to gently slow down our aggressive kisses.

"I miss you too," I admitted, closing my eyes as his lips gently pressed kisses on my cheek bones. It was the truth. I missed him terribly. Every moment I wasn't with Josh, I spent daydreaming about the next time I would be with Josh. I was obsessed, and I knew in the back of my mind that even though we were real, we were still temporary. As soon as that reality crept up to make itself known, I mentally shoved the thoughts into a box and threw it in the back of a random mental closet, knowing I didn't need to worry about those things right now.

Now, all I was interested in was soaking up every moment we had together. We had already wasted so much time apart, that I wasn't going to poison the present with worrying thoughts about the future.

23

"Now, place your thumb in between your index and middle finger—there you go." Beck was sitting in the living room with Taylor and Eloise, Susan must have gone to bed a while ago.

"Perfect," Eloise nodded encouragement at Taylor, who held up the letter T in ASL as they made a perfect cross over their face and shoulders.

"Excellent, now with your hand in a fist tuck your thumb over your fingers. It's easy to mistake this one for the letter A, so the thumb over the knuckles is important," Beck explained, holding up her own fist so that Eloise and Taylor could copy her sign.

"Are you doing what I think you're doing?" I let false shock color my expression as I kicked the front door shut with my foot, dropping my purse on the floor as I made my way to sit next to Eloise on the couch.

"I am," Beck smiled brightly at me. "Now, all together."

At Beck's instruction, the three of them made a T with their hands and used that hand to trace a T over their chest much like the Catholic prayer and followed the motion by making a letter S in their hands while tracing a letter S over face and chest.

"Don't forget the ending," I chimed in, when Eloise dropped her hand, making her snatch it back up to repeat my instruction of kissing my fist and holding a peace sign in front of me, as if I was sending our prayer to our Lord and Savior Taylor Swift to the heavens above.

"This is brilliant," Taylor laughed as we finished our secret handshake. I had shown it to Beck a couple of years back, and she cackled. I told her it was *our* handshake. The fact that she felt it was time to share it with Taylor and Eloise filled my heart with joy, while also cracking it open at the reality that it isn't just Beck and me anymore.

I smiled, hiding my insecurities, and clapping at the juvenile initiation our friends just went through.

"How was the recording studio?" Beck asked, snuggling up in one of Susan's ugly accent chairs as the three of them settled into their seats.

"Very sexual," I replied, making Eloise giggle. It was easy to make her giggle.

"How so? Leave no detail out," Taylor instructed as they retreated to the kitchen to grab a couple of hard seltzers to distribute to all of us. They returned to their spot on the second ugly accent chair with a dramatic flop into the seat.

"Well, watching Josh sing live is probably one of the most erotic things I have witnessed him do." I snagged the throw blanket off of the couch and flopped it open, letting Eloise scoot closer to me so that she could also tuck her feet under the blanket.

"Huh," Beck's brow furrowed a little bit, "You would think getting railed by him would be the most erotic thing you've witnessed from him."

"What is up with you and the phrase 'railed'? Did you just discover this term?" Taylor asked, letting the conversation get sidetracked for a moment. They had point. Beck threw her head back and laughed a little bit before answering.

"I just really love it," Beck shrugged, "It's dirty, but subtle. Railed is so much better than, like, porked. Or dicked-down."

"I beg to differ—"

Taylor quickly spoke over me, "I don't know. Dicked-down is just so straightforward. It's tried-and-true."

"Speaking of, have any of you actually sixty-nined with someone?" Eloise chimed in, making all of us stop whatever we were about to continue saying to stare at her with shocked and confused expressions.

"Were we...speaking of sixty-nine?" Taylor asked with a raise of their dark eyebrows as they leaned towards Eloise, "Or does someone have sixty-nine on the mind?"

Eloise blushed hard, even though she was doing her best to control her grin as she realized her comment was a little out of left field. "I haven't sixty-nined with anyone yet. I don't really know if I want to."

"Then, don't?" Beck both answered and asked.

"But what if I'm missing out on something, you know?" Eloise asked, reaching forward to grab a potato chip out of the bowl resting on the coffee table. "I'm single, I'm dating, I feel like now is the time to try some new things."

"You and I are opposites," Beck giggled, "I would prefer to experiment with someone I am comfortably dating. I didn't sixty-nine with anyone before I met Adam, and even then, we waited months into our relationship to try it." And then Beck snapped her mouth shut, her face and neck turning red as her wide hazel eyes met mine then Eloise's, when an embarrassed choking sound erupted from her and suddenly, she was gasping for air.

Ignoring her inability to breathe, Taylor leaned over to me to whisper loud enough for everyone to hear, "You see, it's weird now. Because Eloise also used to date Adam."

"Oh, is that what's happening?" I asked, playing along. "I thought it was because now we all know that Beck sixty-nines. I'll never be able to look at her without knowing that."

"Guys!" Eloise laughed, standing up to rub Beck's back as she struggled to clear her throat, "It's fine! It's not weird!" Eloise leaned down to catch Beck's eye, who was still tomato-red from embarrassment, "It's not weird. I'm not weirded out that you're sexually active with your boyfriend."

"For the record," I held a finger up, "I'm weirded out. What grown adult sixty-nines anymore? It's a little over-rated."

"Hey, wait—"

Karma was here for Taylor because Eloise interrupted them next, "That's kind of what I suspect, but I also want to try it at least once."

"Sure, but is it worth it?" I asked, raising an eyebrow. I was a fan of oral, like any warm-blooded woman, but sixty-nine was always intimidating to me. I preferred to focus on one thing at a time. The two birds, one stone approach to sixty-nining didn't seem great.

"Is it worth it?" Taylor's wide blue eyes stared at me in obvious shock as they repeated my question.

"I mean, it's okay," Beck shrugged, "I think you really have to be in the right mood for it. It's not something that will be completely enjoyable every single time. What's better is—"

"—Stop dragging my favorite number through the mud!" Taylor cried, irritated.

That did it. All of us lost it in fits of laughter at Taylor's genuine frustration that three out of the four people in the room were underwhelmed with sixty-nining. Taylor rolled their eyes and rubbed their forehead, still in disbelief that this was our honest opinion on the sexual act. I couldn't help it; I leaned over to Eloise who had returned to the couch and rested my head on her shoulder as I laughed so hard that tears were starting to stream down my cheeks. Her body shook with laughter too, rubbing a soothing arm on mine in an attempt to try to calm me down.

"Anyways!" Taylor asked, attempting to calm all of us down, "Back on track, how was your date with Josh, now that you're actually dating?"

"Amazing," I smiled, rubbing my cheeks to ease the sore muscles there from laughing, "Though we discovered that he has the worst superpower of all time." Then I thought about it a second longer, "Or the best superpower, however you want to look at it."

"What is it?" Beck asked before taking large gulps of water—probably having to rehydrate after her embarrassing coughing and laughing fit.

"Whenever Josh picks up a book, any book, he finds the page that will, without a doubt, be at the spiciest part of the story."

"What?" Taylor laughed now. "How did you discover this?"

"It first happened when we went to the bookshop in San Diego. Then it happened again today in between breaks of his recording session. He is in the middle of one of the books that I recommended to him, and when he plopped it open onto my lap, he took one glance at the pages before he started blushing."

"Oh, my heart. He blushed." Beck held her palms up to her cheeks, delighted by the fact, apparently.

"He did," I smirked, "I made him go back to where he actually was in the story, to his chagrin."

"To his chagrin," Eloise repeated, a giggle on her lips, "Speaking of, I've wanted to ask you if I could borrow a copy or two from your mini library up in your bedroom?"

I threw the blanket off of myself as I jumped to my feet, not caring that it had covered Eloise. She spluttered through a face full of cotton and stared wide-eyed at me. "Lo." My voice was quiet, serious, as if she needed to listen very carefully because she had no idea how important these next words were. "You have no idea how much I love recommending smutty books to my friends."

Eloise grinned, her clear blue eyes bright. Then an embarrassed smile touched her lips, making her nose and freckles scrunch, before she rolled her eyes and threw the blanket back at me, "Well, lead the way!" She stood and gestured for me to head up the stairs. Taylor and Beck followed, and we spent the rest of the evening curled up in my bedroom as I rambled about why I liked specific books that they pulled off the shelf.

I loved educating people about the romance genre whenever they showed genuine interest.

I wondered if this was what all those white hetero couples who went on mission trips to foreign countries felt when they monologued about the Bible.

"That's a sapphic novel," I offered when Eloise picked up a cover that featured two women.

"What's sapphic mean?" Eloise asked.

"Woman on woman," I explained. Eloise grinned and handed the book over to Taylor, who eyeballed the cover with interest. They were holding another book from my shelf that was a why-choose romance. I was glad I decided to be more mindful of what romances I read a few years ago, so that I had queer recommendations for friends like Taylor.

"Oh," Beck picked up a book, "I remember reading this one." A sly grin pulled at Beck's lips, and I leaned over to see which book she pulled from the random stack that was scattered on the floor.

"What? Let me see!" Eloise tugged the book down so that she could see what Beck and I were ogling at. "Oh…"

The cover was a picture of a hockey player pulling his jersey up to wipe away at nonexistent sweat on his face, which just *happened* to show off the eight pack abs and Adonis V he was sporting.

Ah, marketing.

I then thought of Logan's weirdly deep dark secret. I blinked again and noticed the obvious look of interest on Eloise's face as she tugged the book out of Beck's grasp to turn it over and read the synopsis.

Maybe Josh was onto something.

I knew that we were in reality, where men grunting and

being rude was simply just men grunting and being rude. Romance novels had done a good job of romanticizing bare-minimum behavior and body language from men. However, I also knew that Logan's lack of social skills and continuous failure to be on good terms with Eloise had a lot more to do with, well, whatever he was dealing with. Whether it was his dead sister (which I really felt like he just glossed over, he'd never brought it up again since), his desire to keep his NHL career on the down low, or the fact that he was horribly introverted.

He could have blown me off any time in the last year we had been exercising together, but he hadn't. Instead, he went out of his way to hang out with us and to try to get on Eloise's good side, even though it was a guaranteed failure every single time.

So maybe now that Josh and I were officially dating, no falsehood about it, I could lean into Josh's fixation on the potential couple with him.

Or Eloise would continue to find different desserts to smush on Logan's clothing. Both outcomes brought me joy.

24

Ladies—if he wanted to, he would.

A few days later Josh had a day off from recording and Carbon Cut duties, so he showed up at the townhome. I was too drained from my own job to make another public appearance with him for fake social media points. Also, now that our relationship was legit, I wanted to keep little pieces of our lives just for us. Not that I was against ever going out again, but the reality was, only seeing him once a week was a little difficult, and the time I did get to spend with him, I wanted to bottle up and keep for myself.

It was childish. We were both grown adults with full-time jobs and responsibilities, but I knew for a fact that if we didn't live almost an hour and thirty four minutes away from each other that we would be spending multiple days a week together, instead of one. Texting and FaceTiming helped, but it wasn't the same as being able to bear hug him in person.

The lights in the house started flashing, alerting me to someone ringing the doorbell.

"I got it!" I called, wondering if either of them had their hearing aids in. I raced down the stairs, seeing nobody. I tripped over my own feet as I rushed to the front door, pulling it open and smiling brightly at the man in front of me. Josh was wearing a grey t-shirt with a nice black jacket layered on top. His dark jeans were worn but still form fitting on his waist and thighs, and as always, his Doc Martens were there to round out the look.

"You dyed your hair!" I noticed immediately. Josh stood tall in the doorway, the tips of his ears turning pink as he brushed his hand through his now brown locks.

"Yeah," he tugged on his lip ring once, "My roots were showing pretty badly, and I didn't want to keep up the maintenance." I kept staring at him as he pushed his black rimmed glasses up his nose with his finger, because even though this grown man was tatted and pierced all over, he looked much more like the boy that stole my heart in high school.

"I love it," I admitted, stepping back to let him in. He smiled at my compliment, releasing the lip ring from his teeth as he entered the quiet townhome.

"Is anyone else here?" Josh asked, his dark gaze flicking around the space before landing on me. His eyes did a quick once-over, which I appreciated since I wasn't exactly dressed to impress. I wore baggy grey sweatpants and a peach-colored tank top, though I guess the thin straps and low square cut did an excellent job showing off my shoulders and breasts.

"I don't think so." I smiled, grabbing his hand and lacing our fingers together to tug him up the stairs. As we passed by Beck's room, I noticed that her door was left open, the lights all turned off. Guess she was spending yet another day with her boyfriend.

Josh cleared his throat as we made it to my bedroom

door. "I wanted to try something, for science." I looked over my shoulder at him when I felt my arm get yanked back, because he had stopped in the doorway of my bedroom when I attempted to haul him inside.

"What is it?" I asked as he released his hand, my frown obvious and evident at the lack of contact.

"You'll see." Josh smirked as he reached up and rested both of his hands on the top of the door frame, his black jacket open and hanging off of his torso as he stared at me intently.

"…Are you going to do something?" I asked, my eyes trailing his tall lean body. The things I wanted to do to him before Susan and Beck returned home…

Josh licked his bottom lip once as he reached one arm out to wrap around my bicep, tugging me towards him as he positioned me to lean against the side of the doorframe he was holding. Damn, he smelled so good.

"I have been doing some research," Josh murmured as he crowded my space, removing the hand on the top of the door frame to place it just above my head. His hand on my bicep slowly traveled up my arm to my shoulder, his fingertips feathering over my skin and creating goosebumps.

"Oh?" I asked, my heartbeat taking off at the touch, paired with the hungry look in his eyes. I kept my gaze on his mouth, specifically the lip ring I now knew the feel of intimately.

"Mhmm," Josh replied. He gently rested his forehead against mine as his hand ghosted over my collarbone, before rising and wrapping itself around my neck. His fingertips applying the gentlest of pressure on the sides.

Oh, my fuck.

Warmth pooled in my lower belly and I gulped, my lips parting as I felt his hot breath along my face. He stepped forward to press his chest against mine, and my hips flexed forward to mold against him.

"What kind of research?" I asked, my voice breathier than I intended for it to be.

"Take a guess," was his response.

He leaned down to brush his lips along my jaw, his lip ring cool as it followed the path. I reached forward to fist both of my hands in his shirt, pulling him against me even more.

"Was this seduction research, by chance?" I asked, snaking my hands under his shirt to tease the skin of his stomach. His muscles flexed under my touch, and I found myself going for the button of his jeans.

"Yes," he breathed, making goosebumps rise on my neck and shoulders. I felt his lips smile against my skin as his hand released my neck, and suddenly I was being guided backward towards my bed with his hands gripping my hips. I giggled as I almost stumbled, but he held me up until my legs hit the bed frame. He pushed me to sit down, then dropped to his knees and slid his palms up my thighs.

Holy shit.

"Thank fuck we have the house to ourselves," Josh murmured, curling his fingers into the waistband of my sweats, and tugging. I laughed as I lifted my hips to help them slide off. Underneath I was wearing comfy, but lacy, black boxer shorts that made Josh rest his forehead on my knee and groan.

"Problem?" I asked, wrapping my other leg around him as I admired the view I had of him on his knees in front of me.

"Give me a second," Josh grumbled, making me giggle and rub my fingers through his now dark hair. It warmed my heart to see him back in his natural color. Though, I realized I didn't exactly hate the bleached look either, as long as the roots were done.

"Take all the time you need," I tugged one hand out of his hair, slid it down his shoulder and arm, then up my thigh. I was about to tuck it in the waistband of my own panties when one of his large hands came up and captured my wrist. My movement halted. He lifted his head enough so that his dark eyes rested above the sight of his forearm before he released his hold on my wrist to quickly shrug out of his jacket and pull his shirt off.

"One fucking look at your panties and I lose focus," Josh mumbled to himself, just barely loud enough for me to hear, as he slid his belt out of its loops and undid the button and zipper of his jeans in record time. I squealed as he launched towards me, making us bounce on the bed as he caged me in and left suctioning kisses on my neck and collar bone.

Oh god, I would never roast Beck about the light hickies Adam left on her neck and shoulders again. I pulled him towards me with one arm around his neck while my other hand tried to snake itself into his pants, but he stopped my progress again by swatting it away.

"Do you not want—" he cut me off with a kiss, and I let him. His tongue immediately plunged into my mouth, and though I wouldn't consider myself much of a tongue woman,

I loved the feel of him like this. I easily became distracted as I felt the dizziness of arousal flood through my body.

"I want to focus on you," Josh mumbled against my lips, his tongue tracing my bottom one lightly before he nipped at it.

"Oh. Okay. I'll allow it." I smirked as I tugged on his lip ring with my teeth. He chuckled at my response, separating our faces and slowly crawling down my body. I propped my-self up on my elbows to see him position himself with his knees on the floor, right in between my thighs.

"Are you alright with this?" Josh asked as he gently lifted my knees to rest my legs over his shoulders. *Was he serious?*

"I mean," I shrugged one shoulder, "I guess it's cool." He tugged at the waistband of my panties and snapped them against my skin in reprimand as he shook his head.

"'I guess it's cool', you brat." Josh mocked me with a play-ful smirk of his lips. I felt myself inhale a deep breath as he gently pulled my underwear down, lifting my legs off of his shoulders only long enough to rid the underwear completely, before settling back in.

"Was this part of your research?" I asked, lifting an eye-brow as he stared at the most intimate part of me.

"No," Josh licked his lips then he brushed them just above where I wanted him, a gentle kiss being left on the line of my hip before he locked eyes with me, "Believe it or not, this is for me." And then he lowered his mouth.

"Oh fuck!" I cried, throwing my head back at the sen-sation I was suddenly feeling. I must have moved, because Josh's hands wrapped around my thighs as he tugged my body closer to him. I both wanted to escape everything I was feeling while also wanting to press myself against him more. The conflict was overwhelming, and I ended up reaching down to grip onto his hair as I felt myself start to gently pulse my hips against him.

"Yes," He encouraged, his demanding voice making heat flood my body, "Give it to me." *Holy shit.* Josh was a dirty talker, and I was here for it. I made an embarrassing whimpering sound in the back of my throat and grabbed his wrists as he held my thighs in place.

It didn't take long. I couldn't even think clearly about what his mouth and tongue were doing to me. All I knew was that one moment I was holding his wrists in a death grip as I struggled to make it last, the next moment I was groaning at an embarrassing volume. All the muscles in my body locked as release pulsed through me in waves.

Once I was spent, Josh lifted his head and kissed the inside of each thigh as he lifted them off of his shoulders.

"...I'm confused," I breathed, my heart was still racing as he used my legs to push himself to a standing position. His hungry gaze took me in, even though I was still wearing my tank.

"About?" Josh asked, though he looked distracted as he shucked his jeans from his body.

"What was your research?" I asked, rubbing my hand over my racing heart.

"Oh," Josh blinked for a moment before a light blush tinted his cheeks, "If me leaning on the door frame and holding your neck would actually turn you on." He shrugged once. "I guess those romance novels can be educational."

I blinked at him as he hovered over my body, kissing his way up my stomach, chest, and neck. After realizing that he was testing out seduction techniques from the fictional men in the romance novels I recommended to him, laughter erupted out of me.

Josh started laughing too, still kissing me in between his laughter enough to make me calm down and focus on the very heavy erection that was resting against my lower stomach.

***

"Your phone is buzzing." Josh nodded towards the device on the nightstand. He looked so good like this. The only light on in my room was the warm glow of my nightstand lamp. Josh didn't bother putting a shirt back on, and I was in my tank and underwear again. We were both sitting up in my bed, our legs under the covers, while we read on my e-reader. Josh sitting there in all his tatted, shirtless glory—complete with his black frame glasses—within an hour of making me cum three times was a sight I wanted to sear into my brain forever.

I sighed happily, making him lift a dark eyebrow at me and smile at me. He pushed the bridge of his glasses up his nose once before pointedly looking at my phone buzzing away, "You gonna get that?"

I finally broke my eyes away from him to see who was calling.

Mom.

"It's my mom, but I don't need to answer it if you don't want me to." I tugged at my own bottom lip with my teeth, holding the phone in my lap as her phone call finally ended. The missed call notification popped up on the screen.

"I don't mind, feel free to call her back."

"…Okay." I guess it was time to reintroduce Josh to one of my parents, at least.

"Hello sweetheart!" My mom's smiling face filled the screen. I had scooted closer to Josh to rest our arms together and make him part of my image that she would see, too. She widened her eyes at the sight of a bare-chested man with me, but blinked twice and rubbed her eyes as she took in the sight of him.

"Joshua? Is that you?" Mom squinted into the camera dramatically.

"In the flesh!" I pointed the camera a little towards Josh so that he could smile and wave hi at my mom. They hadn't seen each other since the day I left for college.

You know, the day Josh ghosted me.

Unease settled into my stomach.

"Oh, so you're talking to Courtney again?" My mom didn't even hesitate. There was no warning. I should have known better. I developed my forward personality because of my mother. Of course that would be the first thing she brought up when seeing Josh after a decade of silence. No, "How are you?" or, "What have you been up to?" She just immediately came to the defense of her only child. I blushed furiously at her antics and turned the phone back towards me so that she could see my embarrassed glare.

"Mom, c'mon!" I groaned. My mother shrugged. Shrugged. She had no shame.

"I feel like it's a valid question." She flipped her hair over her shoulder giving off a false sense of confidence I found myself doing every now and then.

"No, she's right," Josh spoke, grabbing the phone from my hands and facing my mother, "It's a valid question."

I stared at Josh, noticing how his cheeks were tinted a little pink too. The tips of his ears were red as he cleared his throat behind his closed fist and kept his gaze directly on my mom's image.

"So, what was that about?" My mom asked, not swayed in the slightest by my embarrassment.

"Long story short," Josh's dark eyes flicked over to me as he continued, "I was an ass. I didn't think our friendship would last long distance, and I didn't even bother to try. I...I think my ego had a lot to do with it."

"Ego?" I asked, brows furrowing a little at his wording. Josh nodded once before returning his gaze to my mom on the phone.

"Yeah...you see, I was kind of obsessed with Courtney in high school—"

"I know, which is why it was so weird when you cut her off," my mom interrupted, making me tug on the covers to slowly turtle myself into them out of embarrassment.

"I know, I'm sorry." I kept my eyes above the covers enough to see him direct his apology to me, before repeating his apology to my mom, "I'm sorry. I thought about what it would be like to be at two different schools, hearing about all her new friends and potential boyfriends, and it made me sick to my stomach. I didn't think I could deal with that. So...I didn't." One of his hands came up to rub the back of his neck, he was clearly embarrassed too. "It was shitty. And I completely regret it. I should have done better. I *will* do better." Josh's tone on his last sentence was a little louder, and firmer, like he was making a vow. His eyes stayed on my phone screen while my mother sat with that for a couple moments.

I stayed tucked under the covers while I also sat with that for a couple moments.

"Alright," my mom said, "So I take it you're no longer 'fake dating'." At the smirk that teased Josh's lips I knew that my mother had just used air quotes, and I snorted my laughter into the covers.

"No ma'am," Josh's dark eyes landed on me, smiling up at him, "There is nothing fake about it."

I sat there, turtled under my covers for a moment more as my mom asked him follow up questions, like what kinds of dates we had gone on or plan to go on. Josh answered her questions happily, knowing that my mom was just as nosy of a person as I was. I ended up not speaking a lot myself by the end of the FaceTime call, because suddenly Josh and my mother were BFFs. I vaguely remembered a few weeks ago when I had a thought that Josh would need to do a lot to get my mother on his good side after ghosting me so badly all those years ago.

Turns out, my mother was a very forgiving person.

That was probably why she was such an on-again-off-again person with my dad, and other random men that she dated during my childhood.

As Josh handed the phone back to me, I asked him about his parents, weirdly knowing the answer before he even replied.

"You know, same old," he shrugged as he adjusted the

covers around my body, tucking me in tighter so that only my head poked out, "Still in the same house where they raised me, back in Lake Oswego."

"Wow," I sighed, staring off at the ceiling, "That sounds so nice."

"I mean, I guess." Josh smiled as he tucked a strand of my hair away from my forehead. "I'm assuming your parents are still kind of all over the place?"

"Yeah," I smiled, even though it made me sad, "They dated again recently, and the fact that my mom never mentioned my dad on this call, is a good indicator that they broke up yet again."

"Yikes," Josh's eyes widened, but I could tell he tried to conceal his surprise, "I always thought your parents felt chaotic in high school."

"They were," I agreed. "I mean, they're wonderful people. They taught me a lot and I grew up feeling very loved by both of them. But, I mean, I didn't love the revolving door that was their love life...Thankfully, I have gone to therapy since then."

"Thank fuck!" Josh released a dramatic exhale as he scrubbed a hand down his face, making me pinch his thigh under the covers. He yelped and planted a kiss on my forehead in return. "I'm serious. I'm glad you got help, and now you probably have a better way to process how your parents affected you...I also went to therapy."

"Oh yeah? And you liked it?" I smiled, snuggling closer to him. Josh's lips twitched a little as he focused back on the book we had tossed aside for my mom's call.

"Yeah, I was crazy nervous to tell my parents about

singing. Being in a band. And quitting my job at the lab when we got that record deal…All of it." I widened my eyes, but stayed silent for him to continue. "I guess where your life seemed to be all over the place, mine almost felt suffocatingly cookie-cutter. Everything my parents expected of me perfectly laid out in a map for life. I felt nervous to rock the boat, which I can laugh about now, because obviously they were supportive of me no matter what."

I frowned a little, disappointed in myself for not being able to empathize with the stress of a cookie-cutter lifestyle.

"I was so jealous of your home life as a teenager," I admitted.

"Yeah?" Josh's face softened as he glanced down at me, still perfectly snuggled under my covers.

"Yeah." I gave him an encouraging smile, "But I'm better now. I know that my parents' choices don't need to affect me as much as they used to."

Josh smiled at that, leaning down to press his lips against mine in a quick brush, before leaning back and settling in.

"I'm glad to hear it," Josh said, reaching for the e-reader again.

I snuggled in as we continued the story, though in the back of my mind I wondered how compatible we truly were. We both loved our parents, but we clearly had different experiences and therefore, expectations for relationships. Josh mentioned how suffocating a cookie-cutter lifestyle could be, and that sounded exactly like the kind of lifestyle I wanted. What I strived for.

Get married.

Buy a house.

Maybe raise a child or two in that house.

Put down roots.

Live a reliable lifestyle.

Perhaps that was what was going to make our temporary relationship work, in the end. Not that we had spoken about what happens when Josh and the band go on tour, but I felt like it was obvious that we had to end things once we reached that point.

We would each get what we wanted in the end.

Josh got to comfortably go steady with me because we got along crazy well and had wonderful chemistry. But he could still run off and be a rock star at the end of it. The end date was literally written and signed into a legal document.

And I...simply didn't want to think about what I would do once he left.

25

"Oh my god, hide me please," Eloise shouted to Beck and me. A new club had just opened in LA, and Carbon Cut was personally invited, along with a number of other celebrities, to help hype opening night. Obviously, I dragged my friends along with.

We had been here for about an hour, hanging out in the VIP section and testing all the overpriced (but free to us) appetizers. The noise level was so loud, though, that Beck had decided to forgo her hearing aids in exchange for ear plugs, because she could still feel the beat of the music just fine in her body.

A number of things had happened since we arrived. A lot of people recognized the band, and they spent the first forty-five minutes answering questions from fans and signing random things that were thrust over the VIP rope. Josh introduced me as his girlfriend to almost every single fan we met, which earned me an equal number of smiles and glares.

Sorry, not sorry, ladies.

Literally no one recognized Adam from his Olympic days, which I think he preferred anyway.

One single woman recognized Eloise from her short modeling career, and the two girls chatted animatedly about how important it was to make inclusive sizes in clothing. It was at that point in the night that I realized I hung out with a lot of people who were big in the public eye at one point in their lives.

Taylor was chatting the most with Tom and Kyle, the three of them huddled in deep conversation after the rush of fans died down.

Logan was MIA, because he was away in Chicago for a hockey game this weekend, and Josh and I were the only ones who knew why he was gone.

The weirdest thing to happen, I thought, was shielding her face while quickly ducking behind Beck and me.

"Who are you hiding from?" Beck asked as she glanced around. Adam was standing off to the side, right on the outskirts of the VIP section, doing his best to keep a protective eye on his girlfriend as we separated from the group to dance.

"The blonde guy in the white dress shirt. Twelve o'clock." I quickly signed the gist of Eloise's sentence to Beck, turning towards where she directed. Beck followed my gaze to see a familiar face making his way through the crowd.

"Whoa! What are you two doing here?" Daddy James approached us, covered in sweat from dancing too hard for his age, probably. I forgot what his real first name was, but a year or so ago he was a parent of one of the clients at our clinic. His daughter, Stella, was a sweetheart and had Down Syndrome. She was a favorite of ours. Her father, who weirdly stood before us at this random club in LA, was not. He did an excellent job of giving off strange, uncomfortable vibes. He had his sights set on Beck at the time, and even had the audacity to ask her out in the middle of her workday.

She turned him down. It's unethical to date the parents of our clients, but more importantly, he gave us all the ick.

The sight of him clearly startled us, but I quickly put on my fake friendly smile and greeted him as I felt Eloise retreat back to the VIP section.

"Mr. James!" I widened my eyes in surprise, "It's been forever!"

"It has!" He smiled, his light blue eyes shining in the colorful lights of the club.

"How is Stella?" Beck asked and signed, letting him know that she couldn't hear. The dumbass turned to face me as he answered her question, weirdly going out of his way to not address Beck directly.

He was probably a little butthurt about her rejection.

"Stella is kicking ass at preschool!" He fist-pumped the air, showing off a massive sweat stain under the pit of his dress shirt. "I'm so proud of her."

"That's wonderful!" A glance to my side let me know that Beck had followed after Eloise, so I took that as my cue to retreat as well. "It was nice seeing you, but I need to get back to my friends."

"Oh, who are your friends?" Daddy James stood a little taller as he eyeballed where Beck ducked under the VIP rope, Adam's arm already lifted and waiting to tuck her safely into his side as he gave Daddy James a cold glare.

"Just my friends." *Good job, Court.* I waved towards the group as if I hung out with complete nobodies.

"Oh, okay." Daddy James' blonde eyebrows furrowed the slightest bit at my ridiculous response before a young blonde woman, who looked much younger than me, ran up and tugged on his arm.

"Connooooor," she whined, her bottom lip sticking out.

Without her, I never would have remembered that his first name was Connor.

"Oh, hey babe, I was just catching up with—" I used that woman's interruption as an opportunity to leave. I ran back to the VIP section and ducked under the rope to see Eloise sitting in between Garrett and Taylor on the couch.

"How do you know him?" I asked, thumbing over my shoulder as I approached. Josh's arms snaked around my waist and pulled me back up against him.

"Who was that guy?" He asked in my ear over the noise of the club.

"He's friends with my dad at the country club," Eloise explained as she rubbed her cheeks, her eyes glancing out to the dancing crowd as Taylor rubbed at her back in encouragement. "...I might have slept with him."

If Beck had been drinking water, she would have done a spit take.

"What? Why? How?" Beck spluttered, staring wide-eyed at Eloise after reading her lips. She glanced over her shoulder at where we left Daddy James dancing, then turned back to Eloise, who winced under her stare. I tapped the back of my hand on Beck's stomach to encourage her to get it together.

"I don't know," Eloise groaned and covered her face in embarrassment before dropping her hands in her lap. "I was pissed at my dad. He was there. I don't know. It was an emotional decision I immediately regretted."

"You don't have to justify who you choose to sleep with, Lo," Taylor encouraged, squeezing her shoulder.

"It's true, one time I slept with a woman who was stalking me," Garrett added with a casual shrug. We all stared at him in silence. Half of us weren't able to relate to that situation. Half of us haven't been famous enough to be stalked. Kate rolled her eyes and then closed them in annoyance.

"Anyways," Taylor reeled the conversation back in, "You're also allowed to be embarrassed to see him again. It's fine, you're safe." Eloise grinned up at Taylor's encouraging words before a nervous laugh erupted out of her lips.

"He texted me a few times, but I never responded. I left without a word after he passed out in his bed. And I haven't been back to the county club since." Eloise shrugged.

"We are more than happy to play defense for Daddy James. We got sketchy vibes from him at work, too." I leaned forward out of Josh's arms to squeeze her other shoulder, and she rested her hand on top of mine in thanks.

"…Daddy James?" Kyle asked, his eyes dancing around my friends.

"Yeah, that's what they call him," Adam explained, a smile tugging at his lips.

"…That is the most perfect, disgusting nickname," Eloise replied with a giggle that quickly turned into laughter, "Oh god, I slept with someone called 'Daddy James'!"

We all started laughing with her, Beck shoving me out of the way to wrap Eloise up in a tight hug as her own shoulders shook with laughter at the situation. For how populated

Southern California was, sometimes it ended up feeling like such a small world. First Logan at the Ducks game, now Daddy James at a club I couldn't even remember the name of.

I laughed and wandered back to Josh, tugging him onto the dance floor with me. Thankfully the space was more packed, and people were easily distracted by their own dancing (or were just intoxicated enough) and did not immediately recognize a rock star in their midst.

A thought that would immediately be proven wrong the next day as Beck and I nursed our hangovers. We both sprawled out on the couch while Susan made us suffer through another rewatch of *Bridgerton* while we waited for our greasy hangover food to arrive. Beck was scrolling around on her phone and started laughing at something.

"What is it?" I asked her, wincing a little at the sound of her laugh.

"Someone took pictures of you and Josh last night." Beck giggled, sliding over to me to hand me her phone. I took it and immediately turned the brightness down before focusing on the images. The first couple of images brought a smile to my face. They were of Josh and me dancing together. Josh was crouching down, hands on his knees, as he ground his butt against my pelvis. His head tipped back in laughter as I snuck my hand in the back pocket of his pants to cop a feel.

The next couple of pictures were similar. Josh had panicked that he didn't know how to dance, and I told him to wing it, so that's what he did. I played along, leaning into the role-reversal by rubbing my hands all over his chest as if I was feeling him up. One image of me grabbing his pecks as if they were boobs, while he grabbed my wrists and leaned his head back to let a loud laugh escape his mouth, made me smile big. Our faces were flushed, I clearly had a light sheen of sweat on my face, but we were having fun.

By now, I had deactivated almost all of my social media accounts now. It took a while for me to realize, but the experience during girls' night when my accounts started blowing up after someone posted the picture of Josh and me at the FivePoint concert was enough for me to know I really didn't need the internet in my life at all times.

Plus, clearly the world would do a good enough job of capturing happy memories for me.

What there were no pictures of, however, were the couple of discreet romantic touches that Tom and Kyle indulged in throughout the night while we were all out in public together.

26

"Yes! Good matching!" Little Maddy had just successfully matched the red plastic strawberries in the red cup, when Eloise knocked on my office door.

"You have a boy here to see you." She wiggled her blonde eyebrows at me and winked, waving hi to Ava sitting in the chair.

"A boy?" I made a surprised face and placed my palms flat on my cheeks, simply to see how a kid like Maddy would react to such a dramatic facial expression.

She glared at me and dumped the strawberries out of the red cup.

Well, then.

"Wait—" Ava leaned forward in her chair to catch my eye, "You mean—is he—" she thumbed over her shoulder, unable to finish any of her sentences apparently. I smiled at her and nodded as a blush rose to her cheeks.

"Do you want to meet him?" I asked Ava as I cleaned up the color matching game Maddy and I were playing.

"I know I should say no to be polite, but I won't. Yes, I'd love to meet your famous boyfriend." Ava scooped Maddy up in her arms and tugged her purse on over her shoulder, making me laugh at how enthusiastic she was. She usually looked like a tired, run-down parent, but she always became animated when the topic of Josh came up. Eloise giggled at her antics before leaving the door open a crack and making her way to the waiting room, Ava and I not too far behind. For some reason, seeing Josh sitting in one of the black waiting room chairs with a full-on man spread, a dark hoodie with a baseball cap underneath (attempting to look discreet despite how tall he was), thumbing away on his phone made my heart pickup its pace.

Was I ever going to get over this?

Would my organs and pulse ever not be excited every time I simply looked at the man?

"Ahem, you have a fan," I announced as Ava and I entered the waiting room. The closed-mouth squeal she made right behind me helped Josh's eyes pull away from his phone to see us. He smiled, his white teeth on display as his lip ring pulled with his grin. His eyes immediately fell on Ava behind me, and he stood up to approach us with his hand extended.

"Hi, momma," Josh greeted her, making her eyes go wide as a dark red blush coated her cheeks and neck. I laughed at her, and she covered her face in embarrassment after shaking his hand.

"Oh god, you remember me?" Ava spoke into her hand. Maddy hung out on her mother's hip, her dark brows furrowed at Josh. Her classic Maddy glare on full display as Josh crouched and waved hi to her.

"Are those pink hearing aids she's wearing?" Josh asked, looking at both Ava and me when he noticed Maddy's gear.

"Yup, they are." Ava smiled, snuggling into her daughter a little as her eyes blatantly raked over Josh's appearance. I was definitely going to give her shit later for undressing my boyfriend with her eyes while I was present.

"That's the cutest fu—flipping thing I've ever seen." Josh smiled again at Maddy, who quickly turned her head away and hid her face in Ava's shoulder. Josh grinned good naturedly at her dismissal. Because of course he did. He wouldn't be that adult that got weirdly offended that a child didn't like them from the first greeting. Instead, Josh clearly remembered that I worked with kids with unique behaviors and knew not to be offended by a two-and-a-half-year-old giving him the cold shoulder.

"She'll appreciate this moment when she's older. Trust me." Ava smiled as she tightened her hold on her daughter.

"What brings you down this way?" I asked, crossing my arms, and resting on one hip. It was a Thursday, and Josh and I didn't have plans until Saturday morning where we were going to Santa Monica Pier for another outing that would result in our pictures being taken by fans.

"I wanted to surprise you." Josh straightened as Ava stepped around us to approach Eloise's desk to pay for her session with me. "I missed you." He shrugged his shoulders while he stuffed his hands in his hoodie.

"Oh." It was my turn to blush at him, as I tucked my hair behind my ears and grinned. "Well, I missed you too. I'm glad you're here." I stepped forward to tip my chin up, encouraging him to tilt his head down just enough for us to press our lips together.

"Ahem, there are children present," Eloise reminded us as

Ava waved goodbye, then grabbed Maddy's tight fist to wave goodbye as well. Josh chuckled as he waved goodbye to my clients, before leaning to the side and knocking his knuckles on Eloise's desk.

"Wasn't she your last client for the day?" Josh asked, exchanging a knowing look with Eloise who nodded in confirmation.

"Yes, so I guess I'm free to go," I smiled. "Though, I had plans to meet up with Logan at the gym after work. Want to come with?" Josh shrugged, looking down at himself in jeans and a hoodie.

"Sure, can I buy shorts or sweats at the gym?" Josh asked, knowing that exercising in jeans was a no-no.

I blinked at him. "You'd buy the overpriced workout clothes?"

"Yes," Josh blinked back at me, "It's nothing." He shrugged.

Right. He was famous. Thus, wealthy. I shook my head once and lifted a finger up at him while I ran to get my bag from my office.

***

"I really lucked out," Josh mumbled in my ear as we approached Logan. He was sitting on the weight bench, hunched over his phone, and hadn't noticed our arrival yet.

"How so?" I asked Josh, bumping him with my elbow.

"That guy is so hot," Josh explained, holding his hand out towards Logan to show how obvious that statement was. "The fact that you're with me and not him right now, means I'm incredibly lucky." I rolled my eyes and pinched his side, resulting in him laughing and lightly tapping my ass.

"Logan doesn't hold a candle to you," I reassured the literal celebrity. "Who else is going to serenade me with eighties songs while he's literally inside of me?"

Josh halted our approach to grab my bicep and raise his eyebrows at me. "Are there *more* eighties songs you'd like me to sing while I'm inside of you?"

I started cackling at Josh's question, unable to conceal it.

"Shh, we're in public. You're making a scene." Josh laughed as he wrapped me in his arms, an attempt to smother my loud and obnoxious laughter. I broke out of his arms and ran towards my gym buddy, who finally noticed our approach.

"You'll never believe what Josh just said!" I cried, bending over, and holding my gut.

"Courtney! No!" Josh came up behind me and cupped both of his hands over my mouth, straightening me against his chest.

Logan lifted an eyebrow at Josh smothering me, then tossed his phone into his bag and tilted his head towards the weights he had already claimed for us to use today—he clearly didn't care to hear what Josh said as he handed us our equipment. A frown pulled at my lips when I took the weights from Logan, and saw that I was still lifting less than him.

"What's that look for?" Josh asked as he took his weights out of Logan's hands.

"I'm feeling weak in comparison to you both." Both Josh and Logan stopped their movements to look at me directly.

What? Logan signed.

"You're not weak, look at what you're holding in your hands," Josh instructed with a tilt of his chin, and I followed his gaze to the two thirty-pound kettle bells I was holding.

"Now look at the other women." Josh pointed across the room to see a woman doing squats with what looked like a ten-pound kettle bell.

"I mean, I know I'm strong. But it's hard to not compare myself to Logan." I frowned up at the quiet guy, who looked shocked at the words that came out of my mouth.

Don't compare, Logan signed, *it will get you nowhere.*

I shrugged my shoulders as we started our exercises, knowing that he was right and I shouldn't compare myself, but struggling with the need to. Because I was competitive.

Distracting me from my competitive spirit, Josh and I flirted with each other the whole time. We would make silly faces at each other, or I would find Josh staring at my ass during squats and call him out on it. Logan dealt with being a third wheel like a champ. He would just roll his eyes, shake his head, or smile at how Josh and I were with each other as we made it through the set Logan showed us how to do.

Near the end of gym session, though, I noticed Logan staring at Josh and me a little more. Especially when Josh would wrap me up in his arms, or when I would pull Josh's head down to press my lips against his. Josh would take his index finger and brush it along my jaw as he walked past me. I would smack his ass if he bent down too close to me. These casual and loving touches between us were catalogued more and more by Logan as the minutes ticked by.

Josh had just pressed a kiss to my head as he walked off towards the restrooms, and I sat down on the yoga mats we were gathered around as Logan and I started our cool-down stretches.

You seem happy, Logan signed to me when Josh had his back turned. He scrubbed one of his hands down over his mouth, tugging at the pink scarring on his cheek after he signed that to me.

"I think that's because I am," I replied, admiring Josh's stride as he disappeared around the corner, before turning back to the big guy. "I don't think I realized how lonely I was before him."

Logan nodded at my words and signed, *I think I understand that.*

I blinked at him. There were so many questions flooding my brain, but I was struggling to pick one to ask first. "Are you dating anyone?"

Logan gave me a disbelieving look and shook his head, *No, not for a while.*

"Really? I thought hockey players were constantly fucking," I replied. Logan grinned at me and shook his head good naturedly.

You read too many hockey romance books. Logan signed. I needed to remember to give Josh shit for bringing up hockey romance novels in front of Logan tonight.

"That isn't a thing," I countered, quirking my lips to the side. "Do you want to date someone? Like, are you interested in anyone?"

Logan froze for half a second, staring at me as he clearly contemplated his response, before he turned away with pink staining his cheeks.

"Oh, no, no," I shook my head, crossing my arms over

my chest a few times. "Logan, I'm so sorry. I don't like you like that."

Logan's head turned to face me directly, his dark curls swooshing as his confused expression quickly morphed into horror, *No! That's not—No. You look too much like my sister.* And then he scrunched his nose with clear disgust.

I stared at him as I processed his words. "That's why you've never hit on me? Not that I'm upset by that, it's just that I'm used to guys hitting on me." I blinked. Logan nodded, *You remind me so much of her. It really freaked me out at first, but now I'm used to it. So, no, I'm not attracted to you like that.*

"Oh, thank fuck," I laughed with an exhale of relief, "Josh will be glad to know there's no chance of a competition happening with you two." Logan grinned and shook his head, small bits of broken choppy laughter erupting out of his chest as he learned that the celebrity punk singer was mildly self-conscious about mine and Logan's friendship.

"So," I started again, "What was that hesitation about then?" Logan frowned a little at his feet, clearly still debating on keeping his thoughts to himself. I stared at him, making him squirm a little as he tried his best to avoid my gaze before he exhaled in annoyance and finally started signing again.

I don't know, Logan signed, *I never pictured myself as someone with a girlfriend.*

"Ah," I nodded, "But are you starting to consider that now?" Logan shrugged, then nodded once. I squealed with girlish joy before gently tapping his bicep with my fists a few times, making him swat my hands away. Yeah, he needed to get over his aversion with physical contact if he ever wanted a partner.

Josh strolled back, watching Logan swat my hands away with a smile and lifted brow, "Did I miss anything interesting?"

"Yup," I replied, "You'll be happy to know that Logan thinks I look and act like his dead sister, and that's why there will never be any romantic feelings between us."

Josh gaped at Logan then turned to stare wide-eyed at me, "Jesus Christ, Court."

It's fine, Logan signed, elbowing me to vocalize for him, *She has been dead for years. It's not a taboo subject.*

Josh scoffed as he covered his eyes with both of his hands. "How is this a casual conversation?" he mumbled to himself. I laughed as Logan smirked at me, both of us loving that we successfully made Josh uncomfortable. I never had any siblings of my own, but if you asked me, Logan was a great brother to have around.

27

"That guy has the personality of a boiled potato," Josh proclaimed as he shut my bedroom door, locking us in our own little world. A few weeks had passed, and this weekend Josh had come down to hang out at the townhome. Adam and Beck were just getting back from a dinner date, and we had all lingered in the living room with Susan for a while before going our separate ways. Josh asked Adam a lot of questions about himself, realizing that he knew very little about Beck's boyfriend, and Adam responded with short curt answers. Because that's how Adam was.

"He does not!" I defended the introverted red-head. "It just takes time to get to know him!"

"Sure, whatever you say." Josh smiled as he wrapped me up in his arms and tipped us over on top of my bed. Feeling his long lean body against mine was the closest to euphoria I had ever experienced. I couldn't believe I was lucky enough to find him again, and I felt myself gripping tighter as his lips nuzzled the top of my head.

"Are you just agreeing with me to get me naked as fast

as possible?" I murmured against his collar bone, inhaling his scent.

"I'd love to get you naked as fast as possible, but first I want to discuss something," Josh leaned away to roll over and pull me snug against his side, tangling his fingers in the roots of my hair. "I need to leave soon."

I felt my entire body tense at his words. I didn't want to talk about this at all. The Carbon Cut tour started in a little over a week. The closer it came for the tour to start, the more desperate I was to forget all about it. Even though we were real, there was a timeline. An end date. I knew this. That didn't mean I wanted to focus on it, though.

"I know."

"I'm going to miss you," Josh murmured as he rubbed the back of my neck with his rough fingers. I felt the frown take over my face before I could stop it, keeping my gaze on his Adam's apple so he wouldn't see me as well.

"I'll miss you too...this has been fun," I replied, feeling the sensation of nausea return in my gut.

"Yeah, fun is a good way to describe it." Josh rolled his body towards me so that I wasn't tucked into his side any-more, but instead we were facing each other. I'd miss how easily he maneuvered our bodies to his liking. "But how else would you describe it?"

"What do you mean?" I asked, barely glancing up to meet his gaze before focusing on the dip in his collar bone again. I let my finger trace the shape as I waited for his response.

"Well..." Josh shrugged one shoulder then leaned forward to kiss my nose, and then my lips, before pulling back to answer, "If I had to put the last few weeks into words…I would say amazing…wonderful…one-of-a-kind…etcetera, etcetera."

"I would agree," I smiled, "The reviews I'd leave would be along those lines, for sure."

"I'm glad you think so." He pulled his hand from the back of my hair to take my hand that was still tracing his collar bone, and he held it close to his chest, "I just…I want to be honest with you."

I finally lifted my eyes to meet his, which looked a little nervous, "Alright."

"I don't want you to date anybody else while I'm on tour," Josh proclaimed, taking a note from my book, it seemed, with how bluntly he delivered that information.

"What?" I furrowed my brow at him the slightest bit; I wasn't expecting him to say that.

"I want you to wait for me," Josh explained, his eyes pouring into mine, "I have no intention of seeing anyone else now that you're here, Courtney. With me."

I blinked at him, trying to process his words.

"So…you don't want to break up?"

"I never want to break up, if we can help it," Josh blurted out, giving me a nervous smile before tugging on his lip ring with his teeth once. I lifted my hand from his grip to release his poor lip with my thumb.

"…But you'll be gone…" I felt a hole starting to drill in my heart, and I couldn't make sense of why. I knew the logistics of our relationship. I knew we would have to end it eventually, because of how his career was.

"Not forever, just…for a little while. Then I'll be back." Josh's eyes searched mine for what felt like an eternity, which was completely my fault, because I laid there in silence while I tried to make sense of what he was suggesting.

"But…you'll be gone." I frowned the slightest bit, wondering how I could make him understand where I was coming from.

Josh frowned in return. "Right, but like I said, I'll be back."

"…But then you'll just be gone again." I shook my head once. "That won't work."

Josh blinked at me, surprise taking over his features as his dark eyes searched mine, "What do you mean?"

"I mean…" I inhaled a breath that felt incredibly shaky before squeezing my eyes shut, trying to make sense of my feelings, "I don't know if I could do that…you being gone that often." I peeked my eyes open to take in my oldest friend and saw hurt. I leaned towards him instinctively, but he quickly sat up and away from my reach.

"Court, it's my job, it's not like I love the idea of being away from you while I'm on tour, either. But it's my job."

"I know, and I'd never ask you to change your job. You're phenomenal at it, and you do so much good with it as well." I reached out to squeeze his hand three times, which made him squeeze mine three times back. A small bit of relief during this icky conversation.

"So, what? Because I won't be here twenty-four seven, we can't keep seeing each other?" The hurt in Josh's low voice made a crack take place in my chest, and I found myself rubbing the spot in an attempt to make the pain retreat.

"It's not just that…" I inhaled deep before gently releasing my breath on these next words, "It's just that…I want to get married."

The way Josh's head swung in my direction made me realize that my words were probably a poor choice. "Married? Like, right now? …I don't know if I could swing that, but could you wait until after the tour maybe?"

"What? No. I don't need to get married right now. That's not what I meant." I pinched the bridge between my nose as I finally sat up next to him, knowing I was failing at this but not entirely sure why. "What I meant was, I've realized that I *crave* stability. I want to eventually get married to someone. I want to be tied down. I want roots in my life. I want to come home to the same place every night, with the same people. I…" I shook my head and opened my hands, attempting to grasp more words to explain myself, but coming up short. I closed my mouth and let my gaze wander over to my oldest best friend.

"…And because of my job, you don't think you could find that with me." Josh's tone made his sentence a statement, not a question. I shrugged in response because he had pretty much hit the nail on the head.

"Well, it would be hard to, if you're gone on tour for six months out of the year," I explained.

"So, because I won't be physically present in your life for X amount of time, a relationship with me would be 'unstable'." I opened my mouth to respond but he quickly cut me off, "I'm sorry, Court, but that's bullshit."

I glared at him. "It is not."

"It is, and you know it," Josh stood up from my bed and ran his hands through his now naturally dark hair, pacing the room as he spoke. "You know for a fact that just because

I'm going to be in whatever country performing, that as soon as you and I decide, I am *never* leaving you. You'll *always* have me."

I felt my lip quiver once at his words, wanting to believe them and hold onto them so badly, but letting the nausea in my gut take over instead, "I don't know that, actually. That kind of physical space does things to couples."

"But it wouldn't do that to us."

"You can't know that."

"I do!" Josh yelled, making me jump. His guilty expression suggested he regretted his increased volume and he scraped a hand down his face once before trying again. "I do know that Court. How could you not? How do you still not know for a fact that I am completely, *painfully* in love with you? That if you asked me to marry you tomorrow, that I wouldn't sleep tonight until I found us a license and a minister," he snapped his fingers with emphasis, as if it was all that easy, "because whether or not we get married, I'm yours. Fully, completely yours. I'll be the most stable thing you've ever had. Whether or not I'm on tour couldn't possibly change that, because we already know that almost a decade of separation didn't."

I felt a tear start to slide down my cheek, feeling my heart burst and shatter at the same time. Why was he doing this? Why couldn't he just let us be?

"Josh, that's not fair. You've already left me once."

He released an aggravated sigh as he came to sit next to me on the bed again, taking my hand in his. "You're right. I fucked up when you went off to college. That was a shitty thing for teenage me to do. The difference is, I'm not going to make the same mistake again." His eyes bore into mine, watching them fill with tears I desperately tried to hold back.

"I...I..." I shook my head because he wasn't making sense. We weren't second-chance lovers destined to have a happily ever after. We were just...Josh and Courtney. Josh saw me struggling and wrapped his arms around me, tugging me close to his chest.

"Shhh." He was comforting me—somehow, he had just poured his heart out to me and I was the one needing to be consoled.

How fucked up was that?

"I don't think I can do that, Josh..." I murmured against his shoulders, embarrassed that my silent tears were starting to soak his t-shirt already. He squeezed me tighter in response, pressing his cheek to the top of my head as we sat in silence in my little bedroom. I hated that I was the one driving the wedge between us, but I genuinely couldn't do the mental gymnastics to get on the same page he was.

Josh wasn't raised like me. His parents were still together. They never moved or introduced new partners to him. Relationships probably seemed effortless to someone like him.

Finally, after hugging me back tighter for a long moment, he exhaled. "Okay," he said, letting me go and making his way to stand up.

"Okay?" I asked, wiping away at my cheeks as panic started to rise in my chest.

"Yeah, I'm not going to push you on this," Josh lifted a shoulder as he ran his hands through his hair again and looked down at where I was sitting on the bed. "I should go."

"Wait, no." I gripped his wrist with desperation, "Please, stay. We still have time before you leave."

"Court," Josh gave me a sad smile as he shook his head once and crouched down on his heels to look up at me, "You still don't understand, we actually have *all* the time. The rest of time to be together…but I get where you're coming from." He reached one of his inked hands up to my face, his calloused thumb brushing away another stray tear I didn't realize was falling. "I know this terrifies you. I understand. But if you're set on us ending things when I go on tour, I'm not going to torture myself by squeezing in every last second that I have with you this week. If you're saying that when I leave, you'll be done with us, then I need to be able to move on, too."

A broken sob escaped my lips, so I slapped my hand over my mouth once to attempt to cover it up. My eyes were burning with tears that were falling uncontrollably, but I didn't want him to feel pressured to stay simply to comfort me.

The darkest feeling settled in my chest as soon as the thought that this was the last time I would see Josh, hit me. Panic started seeping into my soul, making itself evident as my shoulders started to shake.

Don't leave me.

"…I don't think you want to be done with us, though," Josh tipped the corner of his mouth up in a small smile. "It's okay to be scared, Courtney. But if you need time to realize that you love me too, that you can find stability with someone like me, then I can give that to you…" I shook my head once, squeezing my jaw in an attempt to smother more sobs that were begging to come out of me. "But I can't wait for-ever. I'm already leaving in a week."

I squeezed my eyes closed, desperately trying to prevent more tears from escaping. It was a fruitless effort as I reopened them and saw Josh staring at me with a myriad of emotions in his expression. Pain, love, desperation, defeat, hope. All conflicting feelings that were probably mirroring mine.

I nodded my head once, not confident in any way. I clearly had a lot of baggage to work out.

He nodded once as well before standing up from his crouch and kissing me gently on the forehead, a lingering kiss that brought warmth to my suddenly cold skin. "We can make this work, Courtney. I know we can…I just need you to be brave, love."

I blinked, and Josh was gone.

28

I was depressed.

I don't think I had ever truly experienced real depression until that point, but knowing that Josh was out there, living his life, and not knowing if I could ever be part of it again, crushed me. Not knowing if Josh would, in turn, ever be part of my life again, crushed me even more. I sobbed off and on the rest of the night after he left me in my room. Beck and Susan had both checked on me after he left, giving me tissues, popping popcorn, and quietly leaving me to my mourning.

Because that's what I was doing.

I was mourning the loss of Josh from my life. Again.

Except this time, it was so much worse than before.

I knew I could be dramatic, but I never realized how truthful my thoughts had been when I would tell myself that my soul craved him. Every part of him. Every smile, every laugh, every eye roll, every touch, and every sound. I craved his presence, and I craved his friendship.

I knew it was all my fault.

I recalled Susan's weird pep talk a few nights before Josh and I had realized that we couldn't pretend with each other anymore, how she referred to herself as chicken-shit for not speaking up when it clearly would have benefitted her to do so.

That's what I was right now. Chicken-shit.

Josh told me he loved me, that he wanted me, and that I was it for him.

And I responded as a chicken-shit does, by basically saying, "Nah, that sounds pretty scary. Let's pretend we don't have massive feelings for the sake of my irrational fears."

A week had passed since then.

I was able to put on my Miss Courtney mask at work, letting the little kids believe that everything was fine in my world. However, as soon as I came home from work I dressed in my grubbiest clothes and locked myself in my room, devouring my romance novels to help me feel something other than pain and loss and numbness.

My mother had called and texted me.

I never told her about the conversation Josh and I had, but she knew that the deadline to our deal was coming up and was obviously curious about how it was going. I couldn't talk to her. I had hardly wanted to talk to her when things were going well with Josh—before he had dropped the L-word and enthusiastically agreed with me when I randomly threw marriage around in the middle of the conversation. I definitely couldn't handle talking to her now.

The night before Josh left on tour, the second to last night of his LA shows, Beck gently knocked on my bedroom door and snuck into my bedroom.

By the wrinkle in her nose, I had a feeling it probably smelled.

I was surprised to see Taylor and Eloise follow her in, each of them gently smiling at me and tiptoeing towards me on my bed as if I was some kind of trapped animal.

I smiled back at them, not wanting to scare them off. They had let me wallow in self-pity for a week or so now. It was only a matter of time before they stepped back into my life again.

"What are you reading?" Eloise asked, eyeballing the cover of the novel I was holding. I bookmarked my spot and quietly handed her the novel. She studied the front cover of The Duke and Duchess before turning it over and scanning the back synopsis.

"How are you feeling?" Beck asked, patting my legs until I curled them towards myself to make room for my friends to take a seat on my bed. I sat up, surprised at the feeling of crumbs on my chest. I frowned at my dirty shirt and gently brushed the crumbs off of myself, letting them fall into the sheets.

"Gross." Taylor frowned, reaching forward to brush the crumbs from my bed to the floor.

"I'm okay." I shrugged, not sure how to express the nothing I was feeling.

"Well, that's just not true," Eloise shook her head once before setting the romance novel on the covers. "We're here to talk. Also, to gently encourage you to take a shower."

"And to wash your hair," Taylor added, gently tugging on a greasy lock of mine.

"I know," I sighed, leaning against my headboard, "It's just...hard right now."

"Because you and Josh broke up?" Beck asked, setting a delicate hand on my foot still tucked under my comforter.

"Well, yes, but..." I felt my lip quiver, "We won't actually be broken up until he leaves LA. That will be when it hits me, I think."

At this, all three of them stared at me, mixed expressions that mostly led me to believe that they were confused.

"Wait," Taylor held a hand up, "You're just talking about your stupid little fake dating contract, right? That expires the last night he's in town. But like, emotionally you and he broke up last weekend?"

"Well," I sniffed, hating how sensitive I was talking about this with them, "No, not exactly."

Beck's dark brows furrowed. "Wait, I thought you two broke up last weekend. I mean, he left looking like someone had run over his puppy, and then you—well—have been like this," she gestured vaguely to my slob-like appearance. "But, you're still together?"

"Well. No." I shrugged, rubbing the heels of my palms into my eye sockets. I pulled them back to see that black smudges had been smeared on my hands. Huh, the last time I put on mascara was definitely three days ago. Gross.

"Hold up," Taylor pinched the bridge of their nose and squeezed their eyes closed, "Explain your relationship status to me like I'm five. I'm so confused."

I groaned, feeling a rock burrow itself into my chest as I forced myself to put it all into words. "Well, he gave me until he left on tour to make a decision, about us."

"And what decision was that, exactly?" Eloise asked, laying on her side and supporting herself with her elbow.

"...He told me he loved me," I murmured, wincing a little at Beck's gasp that she quickly tried to smother and tone down, "And that he didn't want me to date anyone else while he was on tour. That he wanted us to continue to *not* fake date." I shrugged, looking at Beck and intentionally chewing on my top lip, like she did.

She ignored the subtle roast I made towards her and just blinked at me. "And what did you say?"

"I told him that I wanted to get married, and he asked if I could wait until after the tour."

"Oh, my fuck!" Taylor gasped, standing from the bed, and running their hands through their short dark locks, "So, you guys are engaged? Are you serious?"

"No, no," I shook my head, leaning forward and resting my forehead on my knees, "I told him that I wanted stability. That I crave consistency in my relationships. That I couldn't continue dating him, because he would be gone for large chunks of time due to his job, and that we would never work out with all the long distance his career demanded."

Silence filled my bedroom, and after an unbearable amount of it I finally lifted my head to see Eloise frowning at the comforter, playing with the fabric in her fingers. Taylor stood a foot away from my bed, arms crossed over their chest with a frown of their own. Beck's wide hazel eyes just stared at me, the tiniest downturn of her lips.

"Did you tell him that you crave stability, because of your parents? Your childhood?" I nodded in response. "...And how did he respond?" Beck finally asked.

I found myself release a short, bitter laugh at the memory, "Not well."

"Honestly, I wouldn't either. So, because of his wildly successful career he wouldn't be a stable enough partner for you? Do you hear yourself?" Taylor asked with a shake of their head as they groaned and paced the room.

"What Taylor is trying to say," Beck shot them a look before turning back to me, "Is that we don't blame Josh for being upset by your reasoning."

"I don't either," I admitted, "But what else are we supposed to do? I...I'm just not good at this. Any of this." I frowned rubbing the temples of my head with my fingertips as my friends continued to study me.

We sat in comfortable silence for a while, all of them either looking at me or looking around my room. Taylor took a special interest in some titles on my bookshelf while Eloise adjusted her position to lay flat on her back, opening up the romance novel to page one. Beck kept her hand on my foot, and after a long bout of silence, squeezed it once before piping up.

"...I wish I had your foot," Beck mumbled, a playful smile tugging at her lips. I felt my cheek pull on one side as I looked at my best friend.

"...I wish I had your knuckles," I mumbled back, eyeballing her hand on my foot. She finally let go and crisscrossed her legs to face me fully.

"I wish I had your old-man foot bunions." I rolled my eyes, a snort escaping my mouth that made Beck grin.

"I wish I had your weirdly sharp canine teeth."

"I wish I had your romance novel collection."

At that, my lips started quivering. I couldn't hold it back. I was an emotional wreck, and as I stared at my best friend, who was doing her best to make me come back to myself, I realized how scared I was for the future.

"I wish I had your perfect house, perfect grandma, and your perfect partner. I wish I knew where I was going to be ten, twenty, fifty years from now after I move out to make room for Adam to move in. I wish—" I couldn't say anymore because sobs were erupting out of my chest. Beck's hazel eyes widened in a panic at my confession, making her launch towards me to wrap her arms around my shoulders as I sobbed uncontrollably. I squeezed my eyes closed, refusing to look at the pitying faces of Eloise and Taylor as Beck wrapped me in her arms and rocked me side to side, just like I had seen her do for many upset children at work.

I don't know how much time passed as I cried into the shoulder of my friend. Beck rubbed her hands up and down my arms as I struggled to compose myself, taking deep breaths through my mouth since my nostrils were clogged from my crying fit.

I finally opened my eyes, my gaze bouncing between the three closest friends in my life. Eloise reached around Beck and squeezed my shoulder. Taylor kept their arms crossed over their chest as they gave me an encouraging grin.

After finally regaining control of my emotions, I exhaled one last dramatic sigh as I smirked at them.

"Sorry about that," I sniffed.

"Don't be sorry. You're allowed to cry." Beck made one more pass over my arms before sitting back and patting my foot underneath the covers again. I smiled my thanks at her as I rubbed my nose again with the back of my hand, noticing how the action made Eloise's nose scrunch as she removed her hand away from my shoulder.

I would be embarrassed about myself later.

"So," Taylor asked, "Are you done?" Their voice was calm and soothing. I shrugged, then nodded, rubbing the leftover tears from my cheeks.

"Yes, I think I'm all cried out." I smiled shyly at them. They nodded their head once before stepping forward and ripping the pillow I was leaning on out from behind my back.

"Hey, what the—"

Thwack!

Taylor started swatting at me with the pillow, catching me completely off guard and making me curl into myself to try to defend the attack.

"You!"

Thwack!

"Ridiculous!"

Thwack!

"Woman!"

Thwack!

"Taylor! What the fuck?" I cried, lifting my arm to deflect another hit from my pillow.

"You!" Taylor held the pillow to their side and pointed an accusing finger at me, "I should be asking you, what the fuck? What the fuck, Courtney?"

I stared at them, slack jawed, "What?"

At this, Taylor grumbled and started hitting me repeatedly with the pillow again. Beck and Eloise had jumped off the bed at this point and seemed to have no problem letting them beat me with the softest thing in the room.

"Taylor!" I grumbled, grabbing onto their weapon, and trying to tug it out of their hands. Taylor was stronger than me, so they yanked it free of my grip with no problem and whacked me against the head with it, making me topple over on my bed.

"Courtney, you are a beautiful, stupid woman," Taylor sighed, tossing the pillow to the farthest end of the bed, and taking a seat in front of me. "You want what Beck has? Her form of stability? Her commitment from her partner? Then you run as fast as you possibly can back to Joshua Madey and pray that he is still smitten enough to overlook your childish attempt at self-sabotage."

I glared at Taylor, because *how dare they?*

"It's not childish! I'm serious! I can't handle the idea of someone leaving me—" Instead of throwing a pillow at me, they settled for reaching forward and tugging on a lock of my hair aggressively. "Hey! Stop it!"

"You stop it!" Taylor palmed my forehead to make me fall backwards on my bed. I grumbled and sat up again, rubbing my head in annoyance as they continued, "You know for a damn fact that Josh will never leave you—in the way that matters!" They quickly reached forward to cup a hand over my mouth when they saw I had intended to interrupt them. I glared at them, before shooting Beck and Eloise annoyed looks as they stood at the foot of my bed, not interfering with Taylor and me at all.

After dropping their hand, I spoke up, "Long distance

never works! Half of our relationship would be long distance while he is on tour!"

"And after?" Taylor asked, raising their dark eyebrows at me in a challenge, "After a tour, where do you think Josh's first stop will be? Tokyo? Zimbabwe? No, he'll run right back to you. Every single time. And you know that."

I felt a wave of embarrassment wash over me; part of my brain definitely understood what Taylor was telling me. I didn't say anything, instead I just focused on Taylor's shoulder as their words hit me like a ton of bricks.

They took this as a sign to keep talking, each word crushing me with their reality. "From the little I have heard about them over the years, your hippy parents sound like the most emotionally immature people I have ever heard of. So what? Because of their shitty choices, you now know exactly what you want for your own life, yeah? Guess who is happily willing to tie himself down with you? Josh. Whether or not he's galivanting throughout Europe, singing for the masses, doesn't change the fact that he is more than willing to be a permanent fixture in your life. You want stability? Consistency? Dare I say, safety? You have us for that. You always will, whether Beck and Adam move out and have tons of ginger babies, or they move in here and you all live like some weird version of *Full House*. You want a partner who has no desire to pursue romantic relationships with anyone else besides you? You better fucking *run* back to Josh. You run right into his beautifully tatted arms, and don't you dare second guess yourself. You deserve to be happy, Court. But you also need to put in the goddamn emotional work to let that happen."

After Taylor's lecture, I felt my lip quiver again. I was struggling to keep my breathing even, and Beck waited a few moments to let me process all of that before speaking up.

"Taylor is right, Court…" She gently sat herself down on the bed, pulling me into a hug as she wrapped her arms around me. "It's scary, finding the person that checks all those boxes you need." I kept my eyes down and sniffled, like a teenager receiving a scolding from her gentle parents. "I agree that you need to find some courage, but also…I have been a shitty friend."

I gave her the most confused look in the world, "What? How?"

Beck gnawed on her bottom lip as she considered me, her hazel eyes wide with uncertainty before she pulled her cell phone out of her pocket and started typing away. "I want to show you something, hopefully it'll help you feel more confident about your relationship with him."

I glanced over at Taylor and Eloise, who both shrugged and looked curious to see what Beck was pulling up.

Beck scooted closer to me and held her phone up for me to see, a picture of Josh paused on the video that took over her screen. "I found this interview of the band minutes before I bought us tickets for the FivePoint concert, the concert you and Josh reconnected at. I never expected you to jump on stage or anything, but I did hope that he would at least recognize you in the crowd. I think I got a little carried away, because I wanted you two to come together naturally and not because of an interview he gave before you knew who he truly was." I sat there, confused as to what Beck was saying, but eyeballed the screen on her phone with morbid curiosity. "I blocked this link from your socials and browser. I grabbed your phone while you were in the shower the day after the concert. Which was silly of me to do since you ended up deactivating your socials. I don't know, maybe I read too many romance novels. I kept wanting to tell you about it, but I also kept panicking and just...didn't. I'm sorry."

Beck struggled with some type of anxiety disorder, which often affected her decision-making skills. I felt empathy for her.

"Okay." I nodded, not sure what else to say. Beck seemed to inhale a breath before pressing play on the screen. The video playing was an interview, the band all sitting on stools where an interviewer sat opposite of them in a wrap dress. Clearly this interviewer was trying to get some gossip, based on her line of questioning and body language. Eventually, the interviewer asked about the guys' dating lives.

"There was this one girl I was friends with my senior year...She kind of took me under her wing, invited me out to parties and stuff like that. She didn't care that I was shy and had the social skills of a hermit. She was truly the most genuine person I had ever met. It was impossible not to form a huge crush on her."

"Where is she now?" the interviewer pressed.

"I'm not sure. We didn't keep in touch after graduation. But I still think about her sometimes." Josh brushed his thumb over the top of his hand. "She had this unique birthmark on her right hand, in the shape of a semi-colon."

I stared wide-eyed at the footage playing in front of me.

I had never seen this interview before.

Josh had never mentioned this interview before.

Beck saw this before the concert.

I blinked at the footage, and then stared at my best friend.

"Is…is this why you bought the tickets?" I asked. Beck shrugged.

"I think I would have bought tickets either way, you asked me if they were touring so I was already looking them up." Beck smiled a little bit, "But maybe this interview was why I specifically got us all tickets in the hard of hearing section…that was at the very front of the stage. I mean, it took less than five minutes of searching Josh on the internet to see that he was from the same town as you and went to the same high school as you. Plus, who else is known for taking people under her wing *and* has a semi-colon shaped birthmark on her hand?"

A memory of Beck shouting my name at Josh while he held my wrist hostage on stage came to mind, as well as her excitement at seeing us embrace backstage.

That sneaky little shit.

She was setting us up from the very beginning.

It was a long shot from the beginning, but she tried anyway.

"Regardless," Beck shook her head and pocketed her device, "Do you love Josh?"

I nodded my head, obviously I loved Josh. I loved him more than any other human on the planet, and that was saying a lot considering who was sitting in my bedroom with me at the moment.

"Are you *in* love with him?" Taylor specified, leaning down to catch my eyes with their own. I sucked in a sharp breath through my teeth before meeting their gaze and nodding my head again.

"Then, that settles it," Eloise chimed in, making us all turn to look at her as she rested her fists on her hips. "You love him. He loves you. You just need to reach out to him and make it right." My brain was spinning, knowing that what they were saying made sense but struggling to reconcile that within myself. I had already been doing so much mental gymnastics to justify the end date of our relationship, that I hadn't even given myself the opportunity to consider otherwise. What life could be like *with* Josh. Whether or not he was on tour, having him always come home to me or, when he's not on tour, having me come home to him. Watching TV together, going on hikes, me massaging his scalp in my lap as he wrote music, or him rubbing my feet as I filled out reports on my clients after a long day at work.

Me flying out to surprise him on tour.

Him surprising me with an overnight visit here in California while he was on tour.

Him proposing to me. Properly.

Us buying a house—but nothing fancy like where he lives now in Hollywood Hills. Something more reasonable, preferably in Orange County. Close to Susan and Beck, and Taylor and Eloise, and even Logan and Adam. These people that have proven their commitment to me time and time again, who I could easily rely on for that stability I was unintentionally starved of as a child.

Maybe Josh and I would have kids, or maybe we wouldn't. Either way, Josh would be there with me.

Actually, I definitely wanted at least one kid. I had always pictured having a child. That would be a conversation I'd have to run by him at some point. Hopefully he would be on board, because a kid that shared DNA from both Josh and me was bound to be awesome.

"Okay," I sniffled, feeling the rocks in my chest start to lift.

"Okay!" Taylor smiled and threw their arms up in the air, jazz hands on display. "Call him up. Right now."

"No!" Beck cried, letting go of me to shake her head at Taylor. "She can't just talk to him on the phone, she has to speak to him in person."

"Beck is right, you don't have an 'I fucked up please take me back' conversation over the phone. It means more face-to-face." Eloise shrugged as she wandered over to my book-shelf, her eyes scanning the spines.

"I'll call him and see if he'd be willing to meet up before he leaves," I decided, reaching over to my nightstand, and unplugging my phone from its charging cord.

"And after, I'm dragging you into the bath. You smell like ass." Taylor said with a gentle pat on my head. I swatted their hand away as I quickly found J-shua's contact in my phone and pressed dial.

29

"I am still confused," Adam grumbled as we all patiently waited for him to unfold himself from the Uber. We had to take two for all of us to make it to SoFi Stadium, and I was bouncing on my heels waiting for Beck's grump to catch up.

"I've already explained, you're just annoyed." Beck grinned as he finally straightened and she clasped her hand over his. I couldn't wait anymore, so I started booking it to the front entrance where Kate had instructed us to meet her.

I had tried calling Josh multiple times the night before, but my calls kept going to voicemail. I doubted he blocked my number, since he said he would wait until tonight to talk.

But I was an impatient person, so I called Kate, knowing she would never let her phone die and would probably make time to take my call. She did. Not surprisingly, she wasn't thrilled to talk to me because apparently, Josh had been a "sad, annoying man-child" (her words, not mine) to work with this last week.

I felt my heart melt at that knowledge, because, same.

After I explained that I needed to talk to Josh, to make things right between us, she was less tight-lipped and let me know that Kyle had dropped Josh's phone in a glass of beer the night before and it had sat there for way too long before Josh even noticed his phone was gone, and he was getting a new phone the next day before his last concert.

I let her know I couldn't wait for his phone situation to clear before I talked to him, since I was on a time crunch. I asked if I could possibly meet up with him before the concert or meet up with him backstage after the concert.

She said she couldn't get me backstage (to Adam's annoyance), but said she'd be willing to supply me with free VIP section tickets to the concert. I was too desperate for a win to question why that was all she could do, so I took her up on her offer.

After Taylor, Beck, and Eloise let me hang up the call, they demanded that I text Kate the number of VIP section tickets I would need. Beck explained that they were all going with me the next day for support—but also because they had an opportunity to see Carbon Cut live again, for free, and that if I was a good friend, I would make that happen for them regardless of my relationship status.

Kate happily supplied us all with tickets. Enough for me to text Logan to cancel any plans he had the following evening because I needed all the emotional support I could get. Thankfully, he had no games to travel for.

We had all decided to meet up at the townhome and call Ubers for us to carpool to LA together. We had no idea what parking would be like at the stadium, and the Ubers sounded like an efficient way to get dropped off at the front and avoid the hell that is parking in LA. The Ubers had arrived and we were all piling in as Logan arrived late in his big truck. He jumped out and walked over to the SUV that Eloise and I were about to climb into.

Eloise eyeballed Logan stepping out of his truck, her gaze direct as her lips pressed into a firm line. Logan was brushing his dark curls out of his eyes as he tapped a text message on his phone, his dark eyes only glancing up at us when he was a foot away. He made eye contact with Eloise, and she blushed.

I then poked Eloise in the ribs because we needed to get a move on. She gave Logan a very obvious once-over, making his dark brows lower in confusion, before letting her eyes noticeably land on his large truck behind him.

"...Sorry about your penis..." she smirked as she disappeared into the SUV. If I hadn't been in such a panicked rush to get everyone loaded and on the road so that I could confess my undying love to the man of my dreams, I would have taken a moment to laugh at Logan's frown at Eloise's hilarious insult.

Well, no better time than the present.

I elbowed Logan as the group followed behind us to gather at the front entrance of the stadium, my neck craning in hopes of seeing Kate somewhere. "Hey, remember that time Eloise made fun of your truck?"

Logan rolled his eyes as he scanned the crowd.

"Actually, she made fun of the size of his truck...and penis," Taylor corrected with a pat on Logan's large shoulder. "My condolences."

Logan immediately shrugged out of Taylor's pat before lifting his hands to sign to me, *is this why I'm here? You need someone to bully?*

"No. You're here because if this doesn't go well, I need every single one of you to hold me while I cry and you try to convince me that there are other fish in the sea," I punched him in the arm, still annoyed that he didn't flinch at the motion. "Get your head in the game! Look for a woman around my height with hair that reminds you of Princess Ariel."

Logan tore his gaze from me and lifted his chin to something over my shoulder. I quickly turned to see Kate calmly walking towards us, an easygoing smile on her face, as if my entire world wasn't on the verge of crumbling.

"You made it!" She greeted everyone, already distributing the badges we were all supposed to wear around our wrists.

"Yes, yes, the drive was great." I was bouncing on my heels again, I only noticed because Beck's hands had come up behind me to rest on my shoulders in an attempt to still my movements as I snatched my pass out of Kate's hands.

"Remind me why we couldn't just get backstage? Why does Court have to get his attention in the audience?" Adam asked, raising a skeptical eyebrow at the band manager.

"Because of security and stuff," Kate rolled her eyes as she handed out the last pass to him and pointed behind her. "Down that way, you'll see a pair of doors with your section number above it. A security guard will check your passes before he lets you in. Once you're inside, you'll need to elbow your way to the front of the audience. Or find another way for Josh to notice you. If he decides to let you all backstage, that's fine. But it needs to be his call." Kate shrugged and then blew us all kisses before turning on her heel and leaving.

"...This seems sus. I'm officially as skeptical as Adam," Taylor declared. I had already started marching in the direction Kate had told us, hearing their heavy footsteps behind me. The concert had already started, so there weren't a ton of people outside the stadium ordering food or making last-minute bathroom stops. That made it easy for us to find our correct door. I quickly held up my badge to the security guard who barely gave it a glance before checking everybody else's badges.

"You're good," the guard nodded to us as he reached behind himself to open the door. A screaming audience followed by Josh's voice immediately filled the space, echoing from all the speakers. My heart fluttered at the comforting sound.

Oh my god, it's him.

Of fucking course it's him, I chastised myself, *it's his fucking concert.*

Thankfully, Beck was finally filled with as much adrenaline as I was because I felt her little hands pushing at my shoulders to make our way through all the bodies in the VIP section of the crowd.

"Go! Go! Go!" Beck cheered, pushing me until the bodies in the crowd simply wouldn't move out of my way anymore. Annoyed glances from men and women in front of me let me know that they couldn't move out of my way even if they wanted to. The closer we got to the stage, the more packed in the audience was. It wasn't like our first concert, where we had a spacious roped-off section at the very front all to ourselves.

"Fuck!" I cried, gripping the roots of my hair with my hands. I turned around to see that, thankfully, all my friends had kept up with me and we were all smooshed together in the crowd. Adam and Logan were both glaring at people who weren't in our friend group for touching them, and I made another mental note to get them to go on a man-date sometime.

"What do I do?" I asked, flapping my hands and accidentally smacking Eloise in the face at the motion. She waved off my apology as we all started brainstorming. The next song started playing, and Beck was stretching up on her tiptoes to see her favorite band perform live.

"Have you tried shouting his name?" I barely heard Taylor shout that question at me a couple of inches away, so I stuck my finger up their nostril in irritation to let them know that was a no. They snorted and swatted my hand away, bouncing on their feet with the loud music that was playing around us.

Logan tapped my shoulder to get me to look at him, *wait until this song is over, then shout his name. It'll be quieter in between songs.*

I blinked at Logan, then grabbed his massive head and made him bend down to my level so I could give him two loud kisses on both of his cheeks. He palmed my face to push me away from him, redness coloring his face as he glared ahead at the band. I smiled over at my friends just in time to see Eloise roll her eyes as Taylor asked, "What? What did he say?"

"That I should call his name when its quieter, in between songs," I explained and signed, in case Beck preferred ASL over trying to single out my voice from the crowd.

"How the fuck is that any different from my suggestion?" Taylor gasped as they tried to stick their finger into my nostril, except the song had finally come to an end and I turned away from them quick enough to cup my hands to my mouth and start shouting.

"Joshua!" I cried; except we were still in an audience where thousands of women were also calling out his name. As well as the rest of the band member's names. This was a fucking noisy crowd.

"Louder!" Beck shouted, shoving me forward when there was a gap in the audience. Our group managed to move a few feet closer, but we were still a few rows back from the stage. I glanced up to see Josh looking down at his guitar that he was tuning, giving the audience fleeting glances as he and the rest of the band adjusted their instruments for their next song.

Fuck.

"Josh!" I cried, making the woman standing in front of me glare in annoyance. I had accidentally shouted right into her ear.

"You—The Hound from *Game of Thrones*," I heard Eloise yell behind me, I turned around to see her smacking the bicep of Logan, who almost jumped at the contact from her, "Let Courtney sit on your shoulders. Her voice isn't enough." I nodded enthusiastically and waved my hands until Logan glared at me and lowered himself, allowing me the opportunity to turn around and sit myself on his weirdly hard shoulders.

"Good idea!" I squeezed Eloise's shoulder before Logan stood to his full height. He was already a few inches taller than the average person in the audience, so the height difference felt dramatic to me as everyone's heads were mostly at my thighs.

"Josh!" I cupped my hands and shouted again, trying to ignore the race my heart was doing in my chest at the sight of him. He was clearly tired from doing the show. He strummed and closed his eyes as he sang his music with nothing less than perfection, and I felt my eyes start to tear up again.

Not the fucking time, eyeballs.

"JOSH!" I shouted louder, adrenaline filling my lungs with a little more power.

"Josh! Joshua!" I heard my friends start to shout behind me. People in front of us kept giving us looks of annoyance and confusion, as we all started timing our shouts together in some poor attempt to make his name louder.

"Wait! It's almost over!" Taylor shouted at us. I took a moment as Josh finished the last chorus of this song to admire the sight of him. He had some light circles under his eyes, and even though he kept his smile on his face and the rest of the band provided enough energy for the whole stadium, I could see that he was worn.

Holy shit, did I do this to him?

Josh sang the last note, lowering his gaze to the floor as he stepped away from the microphone to adjust his instrument while the audience cheered for the latest performance.

"Holy shit, it's her!" a woman in front of us gasped as she pointed at me, still perched on Logan's shoulders. His large hands kept me in place as they gripped my ankles. Her friends all turned around to stare wide-eyed at the sight of me.

Oh, right. I'm mildly famous now.

"I need to get to Josh!" I yelled at them; desperation clearly displayed on my face. They all looked up at the stage because we were a few yards away.

If Josh would have just lifted his fucking gaze and saw that there was a person twice the height as everyone else in the audience, I wouldn't have had to resort to this.

"We'll try to help!" the first woman cried, she and her friends immediately shoving themselves in between the bodies of people in front of us. I couldn't hear exactly what they were yelling at everyone they elbowed, but I caught phrases like "girlfriend" and "interpreter" and "emergency."

I made a mental note to get the names of these women so that I could get them gift baskets. Even though some of them got distracted once they took in the sight of a grumpy Logan underneath me, they managed to make way more progress in the crowd than the rest of us did.

"I think you all will be familiar with this next song," Josh smirked as he grabbed the microphone and spoke into it, his gaze barely glancing at the audience members right in front of him, "Feel free to sing along if you know the words."

"Fuck! Fuck! Fuck!" I cried as we wormed our way through the crowd,

"JOSHUA FUCKING MADEY!" We all heard a scream from behind us, and I turned around quickly to see that Beck had just screeched loud enough to get everyone's attention within a few yards of us. She smiled brightly, making me turn around to see Josh naturally incline his head towards the direction the sudden screech of his name came from, only to do a double take when he met my gaze.

"Josh!" I cried, waving my arms over my head, as if me

sitting on Logan's shoulders wouldn't be enough for him to pick me out from the crowd.

Josh narrowed his gaze and put a hand over his eyes, attempting to see better without the blinding stage lights obstructing his view. I waved my hands some more, even after he removed his hand from his brow. He took a few steps towards the center stage and rested both of his wrists over the top of the microphone stand, casually crossing one ankle over the other as he smirked at me.

"Yes, Court. I can see you. You can stop waving your arms," he chuckled into the microphone. A few other bursts of laughter rippled through the crowd, which was starting to die down a little as gazes from everyone started to bounce between Josh and me.

"What up, C-Dawg!" Kyle spoke into his microphone, waving a hand that held a drumstick at me over his set. He had never called me that once the entire time we had known each other.

"Hi!" I smiled and waved at the purple-haired man, before lowering my hands and nervously looking back at Josh, "I need to talk to you!" I yelled. Josh lifted his pierced brow and removed an earpiece, leaning forward to cup his ear with his hand.

"I said, I need to talk to you!" Other women in the crowd started shouting up at him on stage, relaying my message, "She needs to talk to you!"

"...I don't know if you know this, but I'm kind of in the middle of a concert right now." He let his gaze travel up into the vast stadium seats before he looked at me again, laughter erupting from the audience.

A playful smirk tugged at his lips, and I wanted to kiss it off.

"It's important!" I shouted back, "Can we talk after?" The women did their best to relay my shout back to Josh, whose smile wavered a little bit as he drummed his fingers on top of the microphone, clearly contemplating. I felt my heart sink into my butt, finally feeling actual nerves reside in my body instead of anxious adrenaline like every moment leading up to this.

Josh scratched at his jaw then turned around to look at his band mates, who all gave him encouraging shrugs and smiles.

"Hmm…" Josh hummed as he turned back to glance at a few audience members in the front row, "What do you say, should I talk to her afterwards? I'll have you know; she's put me through a lot of emotional turmoil this last week."

Outrages, gasps, and mixtures of "No!" and "Yes!" echoed back to him in the stadium. He laughed at the audience's re-action as he swung his guitar around till it rested against his back, taking the microphone off of the stand but still leaning on it with one hand as he addressed me.

"Is that Logan?" Josh asked, squinting his eyes as he took in the man I was sitting on, "Wow, I'm honored. This guy doesn't even care for our music." Josh placed a hand over his heart as Logan let go of my ankles, lifting his hands to sign.

If you don't talk to her, I'll never listen to your music again.

"What did he say?" Josh asked, the rest of the audience finally quieting down enough for my voice to be enough to respond. I glanced up to see that cameras had homed in on

Logan and me, letting everyone see his fingers work as he signed his message to Josh.

"He said you should talk to me after the show!" I called back, my voice finally having the ability to reach him on stage. Josh quirked his lips to the side as he thought about my request. I was resting my hands on top of Logan's head in anticipation as I waited for Josh's response. I didn't realize I was clutching fistfuls of Logan's curly brown hair until his large hands came up and removed my hands from his head.

"Nah," Josh shook his head as he smirked at the shocked gasps from the audience, making my heart sink even lower. "Let's talk now. C'mere."

And just like that, my heart was racing again.

Sweat started to drip down my spine at the thought of being on stage with him again, this time for a much more vulnerable reason.

My friends hollered and cheered as the crowd adjusted themselves to make room for Logan and me to finish our journey to the front. My heart rising into my throat at the sight of Josh's face smirking down at me from on stage as we got closer. When we were as close as possible, Logan bent down to let me off of his shoulders. Josh squatted down from his place on stage and reached his hand out for me.

Logan also bent down to grip my hips and help me over the barrier that kept the audience a foot away from the stage, making it easier for me to clasp my hand in Josh's. I was shaking, and Josh squeezing my hands as he lifted me up onto the stage with him, didn't help with that. What did help, however, was that after we were both standing, he squeezed my hand three times before dropping it and leading us back to the microphone.

He wiggled his eyebrows while his back was turned to the audience before facing forward and speaking for thousands of fans to hear. "Alright, what's so important that you had to interrupt the show?"

I was frozen in the spot, paralyzed. My hands were shaking as I attempted to fidget with them enough to stop the movements. I inhaled deep through my nose and stared wide-eyed at him until I heard Beck call to us from the audience.

Damn, it really was hard to hear up here.

"You got this, Court!" I heard her call. Even though I turned my head towards the direction of her voice, there was no way in hell I was picking her out from the crowd with the massive stage lights blinding my vision and making me sweat profusely.

"Um, I—" Josh quickly handed me the microphone, smiling in a way that let me know he knew how scary this was for me, before stepping back and crossing his arms almost defensively.

His dark eyes never left mine, even though we had thousands of eyes on us. I glanced up and could see my terrified expression on the massive TV screens that hung parallel to the stage, as well as the massive hanging jumbotron in the center of the stadium. I glanced back to Josh, who still only had eyes for me in this room. I heard Susan's elderly voice ringing in my head for a few moments before I finally managed to make sound come out of my mouth, *chicken-shit*.

"I'm not done," I winced, knowing that that literally made

no sense. But those were the words that my brain was able to put together at the moment. "I mean. I don't want to be done. With us." I exhaled and rubbed at my cheeks, embarrassment making them heat.

Josh's teasing facial features softened at my words, his lips in a line as the audience made sounds my brain couldn't process at the moment.

Keep going.

"I love you," I blurted, wincing at the abrupt declaration. "I love you. I want you. I want to be brave with you. I—I—" I closed my eyes and took another deep breath, forcing the stress and adrenaline to leave my body enough to allow me to make coherent sentences in front of this man who deserved way more than this. "There is no other way—no other way for me to feel even the slightest bit of the happiness I have felt while being with you the past six months. I don't want us to move on, and I want us to stay together. Exclusively. I want to be waiting for you to come home when you're back from tour." I opened my eyes and stared at him; so much taller than me. He was so much better than me in every way, and I knew I didn't deserve him. But I was more than willing to try. "You give me stability, and I was too scared to realize it. I'm sorry. I was such an insensitive ass-wipe to you last weekend—you didn't deserve my reaction—" Josh stepped forward and clasped one of his hands over my mouth, silencing me. I was startled at first until I noticed the red lining his eyes as he stared at me.

The stadium was almost silent, except for some buzzing

from the audience as they whispered about what I had just said.

It was as if everyone was holding their breath waiting for him to respond, just as I was. Josh gently took the microphone from my hands as he raised it to his own lips to speak.

"…It's okay. You were scared. I understand. I forgive you," Josh replied as he dropped his hand from my mouth, making me suck my lips in between my teeth in an attempt to keep myself from saying something else as his dark brown eyes bore into mine. "I already know what life is like without you, and frankly, I'm not interested in revisiting that again." Squeals erupted from the audience as Josh ignored them and took my hand, tugging my body closer to his, "I love you, Court."

The amount of weight that was lifted from my shoulders as each word left Josh's mouth was alarming. The immediate relief I felt as I smiled brightly with all my teeth on display, moments before I launched towards him to pull his head down to me for a deep kiss, was euphoric. I wanted nothing more than to wrap myself around him, but I settled for kissing him deeply in front of thousands of screaming fans, cheering us on, as I whispered against his lips, "I love you. I love you. I love you."

Josh gasped a little at each declaration, kissing me back just as fervently with one of his hands holding the back of my head. The grip of his fingertips on my scalp let me know that he was just as desperate for us to be in a private space as I was, but I had already embarrassed him enough, so I pulled away from him and kissed his neck once more before landing back on the flats of my feet.

"Well, isn't that the cutest fucking thing?" I heard Kyle ask from his microphone.

"So…can we keep playing? I mean it's great that you guys are in love or whatever," Garrett spoke into his mic, making the audience laugh again, "But these people paid to see us play, not to see you two make it all about yourselves."

"Yeah, my bad, man," Josh leaned over my shoulder to speak into the mic, taking my hand and leading me towards the back. Once we were just behind the curtain, he cupped my jaw with both of his hands to kiss me, his tongue making a languid sweep in my mouth before gently pulling away and pressing his forehead to mine. "Stay here, I'll be done soon."

"Okay," I sighed. Josh's eyes flickered all over my face, a sparkle in them that definitely wasn't there at the beginning of this night, before kissing my forehead and jogging back to the stage where the audience was screaming in encouragement.

…I did it.

I did the thing.

Josh was mine. I wasn't letting him go.

Whether he was here, kissing me on stage.

Whether he was in Europe, touring for his adoring fans.

Whether he was in our townhome, sitting on my lap and serenading me with Nick Jonas songs, he was mine. All mine. I wasn't losing him again.

This was the first time I had really stood on the other side of brave, and nothing in the world could make me feel more kickass than this new reality of mine.

30

"Honey, I'm home!" I called, kicking the front door of the townhome shut behind me. I had just gotten back from Portland, Oregon where Carbon Cut had their most recent performance. I stayed backstage with Kate and the crew, doing my best to stay out of the band's way this time as they played their music for another set of screaming fans. I had texted my mom and dad letting them know that I was suddenly in town for an overnight visit, and they had happily accepted the invitation to hang out backstage at a Carbon Cut concert. My dad didn't bring his new girlfriend, thank fuck. And my mom seemed nothing but supportive and encouraging when I filled her in on the last week of drama.

"I never would have guessed that this is how quiet, sweet Joshua would have turned out," my mother spoke as we stood off stage admiring one of the world's most famous vocalists. She had wrapped her arms around one of mine, resting her head on my shoulder, "I'm proud of you, Court." I smiled and leaned my cheek on her head.

"Thank you, mom," I smiled, hugging her close. My dad stood on my other side, his hand patting my opposite shoulder once before crossing his arms over his chest as he gave Josh a quizzical look.

"He treats you right?" My dad asked, his eyes on the literal love of my life.

"I cannot put into words how well he treats me," I replied, smiling at the approving nod my dad gave. As if his opinion meant anything regarding my romantic life.

My parents were a mess most of the time, and it would be ridiculous to believe that their actions didn't have as big of a negative impact on my romantic relationships as they did. But I was officially taking the steps to overcome that, and I had their full support in doing so. Not a lot of children could say that about their relationships with their parents.

"Oh, you're back!" Beck squealed as she jumped off of the couch to run at me. "How was Oregon?"

"Green," I replied, wrapping her up in a big hug. "Also, we still need to talk about the fact that you hacked into my social media to stop me seeing Josh's interview. Seriously, what the fuck?"

Beck rolled her eyes and pinched my arm, making me yelp and jump out of her way, "Oh please. You still have big I'm-in-love-puppy-dog-eyes, so don't pretend like you care."

"But…what was the point?" I asked, setting my backpack down and joining Susan on the couch. "I mean, you didn't want me to know that he had a crush on me in high school? Like, that would have solved so many problems between us."

Beck smiled and lifted a shoulder. "I thought it would be best if any sort of romantic relationship evolved between the two of you naturally, instead of you randomly seeing that some celebrity was your childhood sweetheart."

I paused as I contemplated her words. Would that have had a negative effect on our relationship, if I knew that from the beginning? It certainly might have saved Josh an ass whooping via a kitchen dish towel…

I shrugged. It didn't matter.

Josh and I were together, and that was all I cared about.

My phone buzzed in my pocket, so as Beck and Susan settled back on the couch to continue watching TV, I checked it.

J-shua: I miss you. I love you.

Me: I love you too. Let me know when a good time would be for me to fly out to you again.

J-shua: I'll have Kate send you some dates, but we are getting on the plane. I'll text you when I land.

Me: Fly safe.

I smiled as I pocketed my phone. I glanced over at my best friend and her grandmother, so grateful that these two women were part of my life and annoying enough to go out of their way to ensure that their friends and family were truly happy. Beck would be moving out soon, and we would deal with those details when the time came. It would be okay. I didn't need to have the exact same living situation in order to have these people be here for me.

They had proven their friendship and trust a thousand times over at this point.

I took some of Susan's blanket and covered my toes with it, snuggling into my usual corner of the couch to rest my head on her shoulder. I would be with Josh again. He would come back to me every single time he left, and that was something I was absolutely sure of. Knowing that my greatest love was out there, belting his heart out and living his best life, all while knowing that he and I were it for each other, was all I needed.

That feeling, itself, was home.

31

I was sweating.

Courtney and I were sitting on a bench, overlooking the views from Ecola State Park on the Oregon Coast. The wind was making our hair fly everywhere, and she cuddled up to my side against the chill. But I was still sweating.

If only the little dweeb I was in high school could see me now, moments before I do one of the scariest things I have ever done in my life.

"So…" Courtney started, giving me a suspicious glance as she squinted her eyes against the strong ocean breeze, "While this is totally beautiful, what if we got back in the warm car?" I could see her cheeks and nose flushed pink, her eyes watering a little as she struggled to keep her eyelids open against the harsh air. Even though it was from the cold, wet wind, it made me think of other ways I had been able to make her cheeks flush.

Like how they flushed for me early this morning in our hotel room.

I adjusted my pants, still blown away at how hard this woman made me after having sex no more than a few hours ago, and stood up with my hand held out for her to grab.

My window was closing, but I wasn't going to make her freeze to death.

"Sure thing," I smiled, pulling her up from the bench seat and tucking her close to my body to shield her. I loved how she fit against me, how the top of her head was the perfect spot for the bottom of my chin to rest. How she clung to me as if I felt just as good to her. How I have had specific permission to hold her to me for almost a year now, and I still couldn't get enough of her.

Clearly, both of our love languages were physical touch.

Something that was very inconvenient while I was on tour for the last six months or so.

We had made it work. Like I knew we would. Sometimes she flew to me, sometimes I flew to her. But she mostly flew to me, because Courtney was amazing like that.

Not going to lie, though, she scared the shit out of me the week before I left on tour. I genuinely thought that she was going to be done with us, and that I would have to stand up almost every night and sing my best for thousands of fans, while also struggling to nurse a broken heart.

But then she showed up.

In the audience, weirdly.

Turns out, instead of just sending her backstage, Kate had told Courtney and her friends that they had to get my attention from the audience. Apparently, the cameras had caught the whole exchange between Courtney and me, and Kate had used all that footage to the band's advantage. I wasn't sure if I should be mad at our sneaky Social Media Manager or if I should send her a fruit basket. Courtney professing her love for me on stage had gone viral, even more so than the first viral video of us where I had grabbed her wrist in shock, like a caveman.

Carbon Cut's views, likes, comments, and whatever other shit, had all gone up.

Once again, thanks to Courtney.

I felt an ice-cold hand slip under my shirt and jacket, making my abs tense at the touch as we walked up the gravel pathway back to the parking lot of the viewpoint.

"You okay?" Courtney asked, hunching against the wind.

"I'm fine," I smiled down at her. *I must look as nervous as I feel.*

"You sure?" She scrunched her nose at me a little, "I feel bad scheduling this trip so soon after your tour. I should have waited longer for you to recover."

I shook my head at her, "No, I'm glad to be here with you. Don't worry. I'm just...distracted." It wasn't a total lie. Having Courtney all to myself without my band around or her friends lingering has been wonderful. It's crazy how a couple of days in a hotel room really rejuvenated a relationship. It was still weird to me to visit Courtney at the townhome, and I usually tried to avoid any physical intimacy unless Beck and Susan were out of the house or dead asleep. I knew that they were both hard of hearing, and that hearing us or walking in on us unannounced was unlikely, but still.

Would I have preferred to take her somewhere warmer, like Mexico or the Bahamas? Yes. I didn't hate the idea of seeing Courtney lounge around in a bikini for a week straight. But we had plenty of time to do that. Hopefully, *all* the time.

I was willing to indulge her in this little Oregon trip she had planned for us.

Courtney's cold hand was warming against my skin, a confused look covering her features. Fuck, she was onto me. I had to do this soon so she didn't figure it out.

"What's on your mind?"

I smiled and kissed the crown of her head, inhaling her fruity scent through my nose. Our SUV with Rick, our security and driver, at the wheel coming into view. "You."

"Well, obviously," Courtney smirked, "What else?"

I gulped, glancing around. Nobody else was here, except for an older couple getting ready to start their hike on the other end of the parking lot.

I had to do it before we got to the parking lot.

"Hold up," I glanced around and tugged us to a stop, making Courtney respond by slipping both of her hands under my shirt now. *Fuck, her hands are freezing.*

"Alright." Courtney hid from the wind by tucking her face against my chest, the lapels of my jacket helping shield her head.

How the fuck am I supposed to get on one knee with her plastered to me like this?

"God, you're so warm," Courtney murmured against my chest. I wrapped my arms around her, deciding that getting on one knee wasn't exactly mandatory for our moment here.

Wrapped around each other like this, this was the most natural for us. We were like magnets, always seeking the other out with our hands and bodies.

Yeah, I was the luckiest man in the world.

"Court?" I asked, my lips warming themselves in her hair.

"Yeah?" She asked, I was barely able to hear her over a sudden gust of wind that I tried to shield us both from.

"I love you."

"I love you too, J-shua."

I smirked, loving that she still called me that on occasion. If only little adolescent, socially awkward J-shua knew where we would end up. Courtney's hands were snaking around my torso, her hands finding the waist of my jeans. My cock tried to free itself from my boxers at the touch, but I tried to focus anyway.

"I want you forever, Court." I spoke. Courtney stiffened a little in my arms, letting me know that my words hit her and that she was onto me.

I quickly slid one hand from behind her back and started to reach into the front of my pockets, before her hand came out from under my shirt and immediately grabbed the bulge in my pants.

Not from my dick, just so we're clear.

She grabbed the bulge in my pants created from the little box I stuffed in there. The many layers I wore to protect myself from the chilly Pacific Northwest weather concealed it just fine.

That is, until Courtney decided to plaster herself to the front of me.

"Josh?" Courtney asked, lifting her head just enough to

squint up at me with those chocolatey brown eyes I had quickly fallen in love with during Mr. Mittmann's environmental science class.

"Yes?" I asked, resting my hand over hers, which was still gripping the ring box through my jeans.

"My answer is yes—"

"I haven't even—"

"Josh, it's *so fucking cold!*" Courtney laughed against my chest, grabbing my hands to tug me up the gravel path towards the parking lot. "I promise I'm going to say yes. You could propose to me in a fast food drive-thru and I would still say yes."

My heart hammered in my chest as laughter erupted out of me. "Seriously? You couldn't even let me ask the question?"

She halted our steps, carefully tugging my head down with her icy hands and pressing a firm, hard kiss to my lips before she spoke against my lip ring.

"Do you have something to ask me, Joshua Madey?"

"Will you marry me already, Courtney Henderson?"

"Depends, did you ask my dad for permission first?"

I felt my heart stop at her question.

Fuck.

I didn't even think to do that.

I had thought she was more modern than that. It wasn't like her dad was a great example for what steps needed to happen here, anyway. At my silence, Courtney's eyes widened as she laughed and continued to tug me towards the car, walking backwards to face me.

"Good, you shouldn't need to. I'm not property that you need to ask my parents for."

Oh thank god.

I exhaled a relieved breath and shook my head at her once, before charging her and making her yelp as I picked her up in my arms. I spun us in a circle twice while she squealed, then set her right again and took her hand.

"How many kids do you want?" I asked as I pulled the box out of my jeans, popped the ring out, and slipped it onto her left hand. Courtney didn't look at it yet, her teeth clattering against another hard blast of wind from the ocean.

"Why don't we try to just have one, and then we go from there? But I want a few years with you to myself, first."

"Deal."

We finally made it to the car, Rick nodding his head at us with a smile as he eyeballed Courtney's left hand after she climbed into the back of the SUV. I followed her, shutting the door behind us as we both physically relaxed into the heat that Rick had been blasting in the vehicle.

As Rick pulled us out of the parking lot, Courtney held her hand up with her lip tucked between her teeth. Her smile was erupting on her face, and she widened her eyes at the ring.

It wasn't big or gaudy, and I definitely would have preferred to spend more on it if she hadn't insisted for something simple and reasonable the few times we talked about engagement rings, but it brought her joy.

That was all that mattered.

"Where to?" Rick asked as he flipped the blinker on.

"Back to the hotel," Courtney told him, making me raise my eyebrow at her.

Courtney smiled before tugging my head down to her and capturing my lips with hers, the feel of her tongue sneaking into my mouth was pure ecstasy.

"Why the hotel?" I asked, my voice quiet so Rick couldn't hear as he tinkered with the radio.

"I want some one-on-one time with you."

"We've spent the last two days at the hotel, you've had plenty of time with me."

"But you were my boyfriend then. Now, I want one-on-one time with you as my fiancé." Courtney smirked, tugging my lip between her teeth.

Her logic was sound, I decided.

I loved the idea of spending some one-on-one time with my fiancée.

32

Epilogue

ELOISE

THREE MONTHS LATER

Courtney Henderson was going to marry Joshua Madey. Joshua Madey, the lead singer of Carbon Cut, which was the most popular rock band right now.

Because of course she was.

I couldn't imagine anyone better for Courtney.

I watched the couple as they inched their way closer to the food at the end of the engagement party that I had organized for them. They looked like complete opposites, especially now that Josh was rocking his natural brown hair color. Courtney looked like a ray of sunshine with her honey blonde hair styled half up, half down. Complete with beach waves. Her champagne-colored dress complimented her light tan nicely. Josh wore a navy suit and white shirt, no tie, that brought out all the different colors of the tattoos that were visible on his neck and hands.

Josh was almost a head taller than Courtney at a shocking six feet four inches tall.

Almost one inch taller than Logan.

Ugh. Nope. Not thinking about that guy.

Courtney wasn't big on huge weddings, but she was big on checking all the usual boxes for the big day, to Kate's relief. Kate and I had been talking off and on as we organized upcoming wedding events, like tonight's engagement party, because she wanted to control how much media coverage they got.

While she agreed to let Courtney and Josh do small gatherings, Kate had them agree to let a photographer roam the rooftop party and take pictures for social media and news articles.

Tonight, we overlooked the beach on the rooftop of a swanky hotel in Dana Point, California. My dad played golf with the owner of the hotel, so it took little to no effort to reserve it for a celebrity's engagement party.

Even though, because of Josh's rockstar appearance, the owner probably would have preferred to host literally any other celebrity's engagement party.

Oh well.

Exposure was exposure.

Josh was a smiley and sweet guy, even covered in tattoos and piercings. He, like Courtney, had the ability to light up a room and get along with everyone he met.

Unlike Logan.

I shook my head and pinched my thigh under the hem of my own blush dress, scolding myself for letting myself think about that asshole again.

Because I was pretty confident that I hated myself, I glanced around the rooftop to see if I could locate him.

Ah, there he was.

Standing in a far corner with Beck and Susan, who were signing to each other animatedly, was Courtney's gym buddy. He was tall, had tan skin, curly brown hair that he had recently trimmed for tonight's party, and dark brown eyes that had the ability to peer into your soul.

Okay, maybe not.

That's just how it felt when he was glaring at you with nothing but pure judgment.

Something I had experienced firsthand.

It was the first time I had seen him dressed up, wearing light grey slacks that hugged his ass and thighs that he worked so hard for. He wore a white button up shirt with the sleeves rolled, no tie. Chest, forearm, and bicep muscles displayed in all their glory with how tight the fit was. I was pretty sure he was going to be one of Josh's groomsmen, which irritated the shit out of me.

Sure, they were both good friends with Logan, but he was also the *fucking worst.*

To this day, I literally had no idea why he despised me.

The first time I had seen him at the gym, after following Courtney in another desperate attempt to escape my mom's expectations by adamantly not going to her yoga class, I was perfectly pleasant.

Polite.

Friendly.

Everything I had been taught to be to ensure I didn't ruffle any feathers.

Logan's reaction? The body language of someone who wanted me to fuck right off.

So I did. I ran away in tears.

I was pretty sure Courtney had scolded him for it because we have had a few awkward attempts at socialization since then. It was clear that Logan was attempting the bare minimum to get on good terms with me, but I wasn't going to settle for half-assed politeness.

Nope.

Plus, we had the language barrier that made things significantly difficult.

Logan must have felt me staring at him, because he quickly turned his head towards me and locked his dark soulless eyes on mine. Even though I felt my face heat from embarrassment at being caught, I held his gaze for two extra seconds before I glanced away, a bored expression on my face.

Letting him know that he wasn't going to get to me.

Though, I failed. After a few awkward seconds of looking around the rooftop that was slowly clearing out, I glanced back at Logan to find his eyes on me still.

My heart jumped in my chest from the feel of his gaze on me, and I struggled to ignore it.

He mimicked me, holding my eyes for about two seconds before turning away with a bored expression. He sipped his stupid masculine looking drink with an orange peel in it, as he focused his attention back on the conversation happening between Beck and Susan. I felt irritation rising in me and went to take a sip of the champagne I was holding.

When nothing but glass touched my lips, I realized I had already drained it.

Whoops.

Not wanting to get tipsy and embarrass myself tonight, I decided to head to the bar to get a bottle of water. As I gestured to the bar tender, I glanced back towards the happy couple, taking in their pained expressions as they were stopped yet again by someone who wanted to share their congratulations.

Courtney and Josh both held small plates of food in their hands, untouched.

They were clearly desperate to eat something but couldn't because of the revolving door of guests that kept claiming their attention. Once the bartender gave me a bottle of water, I decided that I should play defense for them.

I took a couple of gulps of water then capped the bottle, turned around, and halted quickly before colliding with somebody.

Logan.

Ugh.

I had to tilt my head up to look him in the eye, and not focus on his scarring.

Eloise, Logan signed after setting his empty glass on the bar top. He used my name sign. Even though everyone else called me "Lo" most of the time, whenever Logan used my name sign, I pictured him using my full first name. It didn't make sense, it's just what my brain came up with.

"You," I replied, not using his name because he was annoying.

Logan's dark brows lowered, picking up on my vibes.

Are you having fun? Logan asked, mouthing his words dramatically and signing slowly for me. I blinked at him. I had been taking an online ASL course that actually kicked ass, and even though I was far from fluent like him and the others, I was way more capable than I was the first time he and I met —when he was irritated that I didn't understand ASL well enough to communicate with him perfectly.

When he basically told me to fuck off with one hard look on his stupid face.

I guess I should thank him, really, because he was one major domino to fall in my own deconstruction of my proper upbringing. It was okay if people didn't like me, and I couldn't change everyone's minds. It was almost freeing to learn, thanks to therapy, how much more comfortable I was with myself once I started to not need certain individuals' approval.

When it came to people like my parents, however, I still struggled. I battled internally whether or not I desperately needed their approval or attention, or if I was a functional adult on my own no matter what they thought of me.

Logan St. James, though? I couldn't give two fucks what he thought of me.

Anymore, anyway.

I was a work in progress.

"I'm having a blast," I spoke monotone, giving him no hope that I was enjoying his presence, "Until now."

Logan frowned a little.

Because burn.

I'm sorry, Logan signed and mouthed. I would have known that sign without the mouthing, but he still thought I had the ASL knowledge of the toddlers that I worked with.

"For what?" I asked, tucking the water bottle under my arm and crossing my hands.

Logan inhaled a deep, clearly irritated breath as he scrubbed a hand through his perfectly styled curls, making the button up shirt he was wearing fight for dear life to stay on his body without ripping at the seams.

"You know what," I held a hand up, halting him before he even had a chance, "It doesn't matter." I moved to step around him, but his rough calloused hand reached out and gripped my bicep.

The rage of a thousand feminists rose in my chest, making me turn to give Logan my most heated glare. He quickly let my arm go and took half a step back. He looked both annoyed and frightened, and if it wasn't for his inability to vocalize to keep me from running away, I would have said something about touching me without permission.

But Logan couldn't speak, so the only way for him to get someone's attention was to either touch them or wave his hands in their line of sight.

It does matter. Logan explained slowly with his lips and hands. I raised an eyebrow, disbelieving, *I am bad at first impressions.*

"And second," I replied, "And third. And fourth."

Logan shook his head, *No, I was only rude the first time we met.*

"You're kidding, right?"

The large man just blinked at me, clearly disbelieving what I said. I widened my eyes in shock as I straightened my spine and started jabbing at his chest with my finger.

"The time you were *oh so shocked* that I can hold a tune?" *Jab.* He retreated a step, "The time you mocked me for accidentally signing vagina?" *Jab.* He smirked at that memory, before retreating another step. He was backed up against an empty table now, unable to retreat more. "Or, I don't know, every fucking time you gave me dirty looks or glares because the sight of me seems to disgust you?" *Jab, jab, jab.*

Logan's large hand wrapped itself over mine, halting my assault in between his pecs.

I tugged on my hand, but his rough one held tight as he hit me with a frown of his own. In a blink, he used his grip on my hand to swap places with me. Now, I was trapped with a table at the back of my thighs, and his large frame looming in front of me.

What about that time you smashed pie all over me? Logan signed and mouthed, which I probably needed. He towered over me, the heat of his body seeping into mine as we glared at each other, *How about when you made fun of my genitals because of the vehicle I drive?* Another step towards me, making me grip the edges of the table as I craned my neck to hold eye contact, my pulse racing in my veins. *What about when you called me The Hound from Game of Thrones?*

I felt my throat dry up at that.

I did call him that.

Which, in retrospect, was super shitty thing to do.

The Hound was a well-known character on the TV series, and he had horrible burns that marred his face from when his brother had stuck his head in the hot coals of a fire. It's a messed up back story, but that was the vibe of literally every single character on the show.

The Hound was known for being the ugly, deformed brother.

Logan didn't deserve to be mocked for his looks. For his scars.

That was below the belt.

"I'm sorry," I gulped and glanced at his scars in reference, before meeting his eyes again. "You're right. That was a horrible thing for me to call you."

Logan stood in place, his eyes searching my face as he let my apology sink in.

What about the pie? He asked.

"Nah, I stand by that." Because I was petty.

His lips twitched, *the joke about my cock?* The only reason I knew that he used that word was because he finger-spelled it for me, assuming I didn't know the sign for penis. I did. Per Taylor's suggestion, I learned all the curse words and body parts, because I wasn't going to fuck up like I did on pie-mageddon.

"No, I stand by that one too." I shrugged, feeling heat fill my cheeks from Logan's nearness, and his use of the word "cock".

Logan pressed his lips in a hard line, then nodded once as he glanced all over my face. We just stood there, Logan towering over me, his chest slightly heaving as we sized each other up. I was immediately brought back to a memory from almost a year ago, of a moment that we shared in the bathroom of Josh's condo. After I had smashed pie all over him. It was embarrassing, and because I was feeling emotional at the time, I did my best to write off the experience. I actively tried not to think about it, how embarrassed I was for that awkward moment between Logan and me before I sprinted out of the bathroom.

I kept my lips closed like him, which made my heavy breaths in my nose that much more dramatic. My nostrils must have been flaring like a crazy person.

Which was the only explanation I had when Taylor quickly walked past us in their own slacks and button up shirt, saying, "Smash," at Logan and me as they made their way towards Courtney and Josh.

I peered around Logan's large frame just in time to see Taylor jog up to the two and wrap their arm around the shoulders of whatever guest was claiming the couple's attention, allowing them a few seconds to throw some bites of food into their mouths.

Ugh, that should have been me.

But I was deterred by Logan fucking St. James.

I frowned, and glanced back up at Logan just as he glanced back down at me.

"Look, we don't have to like each other," I spoke, tucking

my hair behind my ears and readjusting the water bottle still tucked under my arm.

I don't dislike you, Eloise, Logan signed, widening his eyes as if he was exhausted with the conversation. I rolled my eyes at him.

"I don't believe you, but it doesn't matter. I don't care. If you really do care, consider yourself on probation with me until I do believe you." I gave Logan a pointed look so that he would step out of my way, freeing me from my trapped position against a random empty table.

Quickly, so quickly that I wouldn't have believed it happened if I didn't witness it myself, I felt Logan's warm hand wrap itself around my fingers that weren't holding a water bottle. I halted my step, giving the guy a questioning look as he quickly lifted my hand up to his mouth so that he could press a firm kiss against my knuckles.

Air whooshed from my lungs at the contact.

Holy hell.

He had just kissed my hand.

Like a gentleman.

Like a Duke in some historical romance novel.

Like a guy who wasn't completely disgusted by my mere presence.

He gave me fleeting eye contact as he did it, before quickly dropping my hand and sauntering over back towards Beck and Susan, who were still signing actively in the same spot he had left them in.

What the hell was that?

Blushing, irritated, and confused, I shook my head once as

I watched his retreating form. Logan glanced over his shoulder once, nodding at me politely as he shoved his hands in the pockets of his slacks and turned back towards our friends.

My heart was racing in my chest.

What the hell do I do with that?

THE END

Eloise's story is coming 2024

Acknowledgements

First, thank *you* dear reader for taking the time and effort to consume this story. I am grateful for any sort of attention my writing receives, and I wouldn't be confident enough to share these stories with anyone if it wasn't for the love and hype I have received from those who read my stories. Thank you. I am nothing and no one without you.

I would also like to thank my beta readers. My beta readers for this story (specifically, Candi, Maverick, Yara, Jessie & Jo) were so incredibly helpful and taught me so much about writing and storytelling. You all provided the perfect amount of criticism and feedback, balanced with hype and love, and positive vibes. I appreciated every word you shared, and it truly helped me make Courtney & Josh's story so much better.

Next, my sensitivity readers. I know that it's tricky writing stories about characters with conditions that I have only witnessed with a view from the outside looking in, but having deaf and hard of hearing sensitivity readers proof my stories to ensure that my characters are written authentically and respectfully brings me so much peace of mind. I have learned a lot from you all as well, thank you for being patient with me and educating me when I needed to be. I hope that readers can relate to or find comfort in these characters. I only wish I could have encapsulated every single person's experience with hearing loss.

Also, my husband and partner, Clayton. Thank you. You have been so patient and encouraging with this journey of mine (even when I printed 200+ pages to proof this story, even though you hate printers and printing and anything that isn't in digital format lol). Thank you for being proud of me and telling our neighbors about my books, even when I die of mortification because I don't know how to handle the fact that our neighbors will read a spicy scene that I wrote.

To Shady-Jadey and G-Spot Johnson, and my other close friends who have encouraged me to take this journey since day one, before you even had the opportunity to read a single word I wrote, thank you. Your friendship is so special and important to me. I'm so glad we became as close as we are.

My child, Madeline, for being the most patient toddler in the world when your mom hyper-fixates on writing and lets the iPad be the parent for a couple of hours. You're a real homie.

To Kelly, for being the most supportive mother-in-law in the world and for proofing my stories repeatedly, even though our reading preferences are a little different, and you would probably prefer it if I wrote my books with fewer curse words and more closed doors. I appreciate you cringing through my manuscripts for me time and time again.

Thank you to Nicky, for being the nicest editor. Your additional fun comments on your feedback bring me joy. I'm so glad the internet connected me to you.

To Ashley, for being a friend I can send any random smattering of writing at the most random times of the day. I am so glad we were roommates during that first semester of college.

Andrea Andersen is an author living with her little family in Southern California. Using her maladaptive daydreaming to her advantage, she likes to write love stories filled with kisses, laughter, and happily ever afters. When she isn't writing, she can be found rewatching her favorite TV shows or taking too many naps.

Other books by this author:
WHAT IT MEANS TO BE WHOLE

Socials:
Tiktok: @andreaandersenauthor
Instagram: @andreaandersenauthor

www.ingramcontent.com/pod-product-compliance
Lightning Source LLC
Chambersburg PA
CBHW070556300726
48975CB00006B/1609